Rutherford Park

a novel

The
SNOW
GLOBE

JUDITH
KINGHORN

AUTHOR OF
THE LAST SUMMER

PRAISE FOR THE NOVELS
OF JUDITH KINGHORN

The Snow Globe

"**Both** a gripping tale of family secrets and a comedy of manners, Kinghorn's novel paints a vivid portrait of love and its perplexing complications. Set against the backdrop of Europe in the years following the Great War, *The Snow Globe* is a fascinating journey back in time. Historical fiction fans will not want to miss this gem!"
—Renée Rosen, author of *What the Lady Wants*

"**An** absolutely delicious book. . . . The period is beautifully observed, and we are expertly drawn into a suspenseful blend of tangled relationships and shocking discoveries. Daisy's coming of age in the 'brave new world' of postwar England had me holding my breath. Elegant and evocative to the last word."
—Elizabeth Cooke, author of *Rutherford Park* and
The Wild Dark Flowers

"Mysteri   ngs to
life a los   f how
we chan   ating
layers a   to be
missed."

                         ting of
                       Death

"Kingho   il pur-
suits, an   horn's
manipul   l's romantic b   ye for
authenti   *oklist*

. . .

"Kinghorn's prose is lovely, lavishly describing both the characters and the setting, which leaves the reader with a strong sense of time and place. The characters themselves are engaging and well developed. Fans of Kinghorn's remarkable debut novel, *The Last Summer*, will surely be pleased with this second effort. For readers yet to discover Kinghorn's novels, this book is sure to create a whole new legion of fans." —Historical Novel Society

"[A] beautifully written and tangled tale of love, loss, and longtime friendships. Kinghorn plays on the emotions stirred up by memories and how we each perceive the past. The lyrical prose and hints of mystery, betrayal, blackmail, jealousy, and regret make for a touching, thought-provoking, and compelling read. Kinghorn evokes the years before the war as she skillfully envelops the reader in her imaginative, tragic tale." —*Romantic Times* (4½ stars)

"Exquisite . . . a sensual and visual feast of a story, and a powerful follow-up to last year's enthralling debut, *The Last Summer* . . . a mesmerizing book of finely wrought words. The evocative tale of an elderly woman for whom the past is both a comfort and a tyranny, a place that holds unutterably beautiful memories and painful events that torment and haunt. . . . Thoughtful, delicately crafted, and imaginative, *The Memory of Lost Senses* is a page-turning, atmospheric mystery story but with a powerful, all-consuming love affair burning deep at its core to direct the action . . . and steal our hearts." —*Lancashire Evening Post* (UK)

"A witty, clever, and compelling tale, with a beautiful love story at its heart. I loved it." —Jane Harris, author of *The Observations* and *Gillespie and I*

The Last Summer

"Well-drawn characters combined with flawless writing make Kinghorn's debut a triumph. This story kept me up for many nights in a row, and I couldn't turn the pages fast enough. Un-put-downable and relentlessly intriguing, this is a tale for the ages. I expect it's not the last we'll hear from this talented storyteller; at least, I hope not!" —*Dish Magazine*

Other Titles by Judith Kinghorn

The Last Summer
The Memory of Lost Senses

The
SNOW
GLOBE

JUDITH KINGHORN

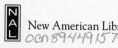
New American Library
OCN 894491574

New American Library
Published by the Penguin Group
Penguin Group (USA) LLC, 375 Hudson Street,
New York, New York 10014

USA | Canada | UK | Ireland | Australia | New Zealand | India | South Africa | China
penguin.com
A Penguin Random House Company

First published by New American Library,
a division of Penguin Group (USA) LLC

First Printing, March 2015

 REGISTERED TRADEMARK—MARCA REGISTRADA

LIBRARY OF CONGRESS CATALOGING-IN-PUBLICATION DATA:

Kinghorn, Judith.
    The snow globe / Judith Kinghorn.
    p.   cm.
    ISBN 978-0-451-47209-0 (softcover)
    1. Young women—England—Fiction.   2. Families—England—History—20th century—Fiction.
I. Title.
    PR6111.I59S66   2015
    823'.92—dc23   2014036483

Printed in the United States of America
10   9   8   7   6   5   4   3   2   1

Set in Goudy Old Style MT
Designed by Alissa Theodor

For my mother, Elizabeth

Birds do it, bees do it, even educated fleas do it.

—Cole Porter

The
SNOW
GLOBE

PART ONE

December 1926

Chapter One

When Eden Hall was first built, the local newspaper received a number of letters about its electric lights. They were dangerous, too bright, and had no place in the country, people wrote. *These Londoners* should stay in the city if they wanted that sort of thing.

A quarter of a century later, and two weeks before Christmas, Eden Hall was once again in the newspaper. This time not because of its size or bright lights, or in fact because of anything to do with *it*, but because eighteen-year-old Daisy Forbes had joined the nationwide manhunt for missing writer Agatha Christie and had volunteered her family home as a meeting point for those searching the surrounding hills and valley known as the Devil's Punchbowl.

"Volunteers wishing to assist the Police in the search are invited to meet at Eden Hall this Saturday, December 11th, at 9 o'clock . . . Refreshments and facilities will be available," the paper stated at the end of its front-page bulletin, titled THE MYSTERY OF MRS. CHRISTIE.

By nine o'clock on Saturday morning more than 150 people had converged on Eden Hall, and more kept coming. They stood about in the dank December gloom, clutching Mabel Forbes's Crown Derby and Wedgwood china as Daisy and Mrs. Jessop, the cook, refilled cups from the large tea urn.

For seven days, ever since Mrs. Christie's Morris Cowley motorcar had been found abandoned at a nearby lake with an expired driving license in it, the nation had been gripped, and like the airplanes scouring the countryside, conjecture buzzed in the icy air: Had Mrs. Christie been kidnapped? Had she been murdered? Was her husband in some way involved?

When the local police constable climbed onto the old mounting block with a megaphone, a hush descended and heads turned. The policeman spoke in a solemn voice; it was a grave and serious situation, he said. He pointed to the map pinned to the coachhouse doors, asking everyone to note the areas marked with red ribbon and requesting that they organize themselves into groups of four or five. No one, he advised, should walk through the valley of Devil's Punchbowl alone.

Daisy listened as grisly questions were tossed through the mist at PC Trotton; murmurings and then louder debates broke out in huddles. A man had been seen behaving suspiciously down at the crossroads two days earlier. Yes, a few had seen him. No, he wasn't from these parts. An outsider. But was he a murderer, too? Was the man lurking in the fog-shrouded heathland waiting to strike again? For some minutes PC Trotton struggled to regain control of the assembled crowd; then he remembered his megaphone and re-

minded everyone in a newly stern voice that, as yet, no crime had
been committed.

It was almost ten o'clock when Stephen Jessop strolled across
the gritted courtyard to Daisy. The last group—with knapsacks,
binoculars and sticks—had already disappeared through the five-
barred gate into the woods, accompanied by Trotton and two of his
colleagues.

"Thanks for waiting . . . Sorry I'm late," said Stephen, rubbing
his hands together, then cupping them over his mouth.

"We're meant to be in groups of four or five, Stephen, not two."

"Ah, but that's probably for those who don't know the terrain.
And we do."

"No, it's for reasons of safety, Trotton said."

Stephen smiled. "Well, you're perfectly safe with me."

Daisy shook her head and began to walk. "Why are you so late?"
she asked.

"I slept in."

"I can't believe you slept in when all *this* is happening. I've barely
had any sleep and been awake since half past five."

"Yes, well . . . you are a little obsessed."

"Obsessed? I'm concerned—like everyone else. Apart from you,
it would seem."

"I've told you what I think. It's a publicity stunt. Has to be."

"I don't think the government would be quite so involved if it
were just a publicity stunt, Stephen. I read that Sir Arthur Conan
Doyle's very worried now, too. He's given a spirit medium one of
Mrs. Christie's gloves so that she can use it to try to find her," she

added, turning to him as she walked through the oak gate into the woods. Overhead, the now-familiar burring of a small airplane circling distracted her, and she paused to look up. "Yes, all very queer," she said. She lowered her gaze, met his eyes. "What? Why are you smiling?"

"No reason," he said, and they walked on beneath the evergreens.

Three years older than Daisy, Stephen had lived at Eden Hall since the summer of 1909, when the Jessops adopted him. The then four-year-old orphan had come down from London on a train accompanied by a cousin of Mrs. Jessop, and though Daisy had no memory of that momentous day, she had heard how very shy Stephen had been and how very happy Mrs. Jessop had been to meet her new son.

For all intents and purposes a general servant, Stephen had been officially employed at Eden Hall since he'd finished school at fourteen. More recently, after the scandal of the previous year, when Howard Forbes's chauffeur had put a young kitchen maid in *the family way* and Howard had sent them both packing, Stephen had been called on to step in. He had never driven a motorcar, but Howard had told him that it was easy enough and that he could spend an hour or two practicing on the driveway. And so up and down and up and down Stephen and the Rolls went, clanking and grinding, juddering and stalling, as Daisy and her sisters looked on. The girls had anticipated—almost hoped for—a repeat of Aunt Dosia's performance of earlier that year, when she'd decided to have a go in Howard's old Austin Twenty and had—at some speed— driven the vehicle straight off the driveway through the Japanese garden and into the lily pond. But no such drama occurred, and now Stephen was *Jessop* and lived above the garages in the coachman's flat.

He was, Daisy often thought, the nearest thing she had to a brother—an elder brother—because he'd always been exactly how she imagined one to be: protective, informative, knowledgeable and sometimes teasing.

Halfway down into the valley, standing on the ridge by the old wooden bridge, Daisy lifted her father's binoculars from their leather case. The mist was clearing, the low winter sun breaking through the vaporous cloud, picking up flecks of color in the otherwise drab and scrawny heathland. Far below, she could see clusters of people moving in and out of the shadows on the tree-lined pathways.

"Everyone seems to be heading in the same direction . . . toward Thursley," she said. "Trotton specifically said we had to spread ourselves out, not follow each other," she added, putting away the binoculars and turning to Stephen, who was rolling a cigarette. "I don't know how you can do that at a time like this." She jumped down from the embankment. "Don't you realize? This is *international* news."

Stephen said nothing. He tilted his head, lifted his lighter to the cigarette.

"You're so annoying," she said, watching him. "If poor Mrs. Christie is found, it'll be no thanks to you."

Beneath his cap his dark hair looked greasy and uncombed. He obviously hadn't had time to shave or to wash, she thought. He wore the dark green scarf she had given him last Christmas, knotted at the front of his pale neck and tucked into his sweater, his jacket collar pulled up high around it. He shivered and then stamped his feet as he sucked on his cigarette. "Come on, then," he said, walking on. "Who's dallying now?" he called back, jogging off beneath the pine trees.

By the time Daisy caught up with him they were at the very bottom of the valley, where the stream was wider and gushed in a torrent over rocks and boulders swept down from the hills over millennia. He sat upon a tree stump and made a point of looking at his wristwatch.

"Yes, very funny," she said, not looking at him, walking slowly toward him. "There may have been a murder committed and you're treating it as though . . . as though it's all some sort of game."

"I don't believe we're going to find Mrs. Christie—or any clues to her disappearance—around here, that's all. Her car was left at Newlands Corner, Daisy. That's some miles away."

"Then why bother to come along? You were the one who first suggested we look here."

He stood up, took off his cap. His hair *was* dirty. He looked a state.

"Were you perchance at the Coach and Horses last night?" she asked, kicking at the soft earth with her boot.

He took a moment to reply. He said, "Yes, I was. And I'm sorry for being late, and for being . . . flippant."

She nodded.

"Will you forgive me?"

She turned to him, blinked and shrugged her shoulders. "I always do, don't I?"

"Yes, you do," he said, newly contrite, unsmiling, staring back at her. "Always."

"It's important for a Theosophist to give back and to forgive," she said, walking on.

Stephen smiled. "Remind me again what it's all about."

"It's about the reciprocal effects the universe and humanity have on each other . . . the connectness of the external world and inner experience," she said, stopping to pick up a tiny piece of bark and looking at it closely. "To acquire wisdom one has to examine nature in its smallest detail . . . Like this," she said, stretching out her hand.

He took the bark, stared at it for a moment or two, then looked back at her. "What wisdom is there to be gleaned from this?"

"That's for you to find out."

He put it inside his jacket pocket and they walked on beneath the pines, then out into the beautiful wild expanse, following the old packhorse tracks of smugglers, sandy pathways through tall gorse and dark holly, juniper and thorn. Daisy spoke at length about what she had read of the case in the preceding days' newspapers, pausing every once in a while to summarize her conclusions or pose a question to herself or simply to stare out across the wilderness and say, "Hmm, I wonder . . ."

It was shortly after midday when they sat down on the wall under the stunted tree by the deserted cottage some three miles from Eden Hall. Daisy lifted two hard-boiled eggs from the canvas fishing-tackle bag she had worn strapped across her, as well as a bottle of Mrs. Jessop's homemade ginger beer.

"So very peculiar," she said for the umpteenth time. "No sign of a struggle . . . no ransom . . . no body . . . no witnesses," she went on. "And yet, I can't help but feel the answer's right in front of us all."

Stephen said nothing.

Other than a child's shoe—which, for some reason, Daisy had picked up and put into her bag—and, here and there, the remains of campfires and discarded bottles, they had found nothing. They had passed some of the other searchers, heading back in the direction of Eden Hall and shaking their heads, and walked through a small gypsy encampment where a grubby-faced boy had raised his hands to his ears and stuck his tongue out at them.

"Perhaps she's taken a turn, like Noonie," Stephen said, using the family's nickname for Daisy's grandmother, Mabel Forbes's mother. "Perhaps she's suffering from amnesia."

Daisy turned to him. "But Mrs. Christie's not old. She's younger than my mother."

"Just a thought . . . and I hope for your sake it's not what I think it is. Otherwise, she's made a bit of a laughingstock of us all."

Daisy shook her head. She passed him the brown bottle. *"This,"* she said, "is no publicity stunt, Stephen, I can assure you. It's gone beyond anything like that."

They sat in silence for a while, peeling hard-boiled eggs, flicking small pieces of shell onto the sandy earth around them.

"You're not still thinking of emigrating, are you?" Daisy asked.

It was an idea Stephen had only recently mentioned to her. He'd told her that he'd seen advertisements offering help with one's passage to New Zealand, as well as help with finance to set up a farm.

"I'm not sure," he said. "What do you think?"

"I told you, I think it's an awful idea," she said quickly. "Think how sad your mother would be."

"And you?"

"Yes, and me . . . I'd hate it if you weren't here."

"Because?"

"Because," she said, smiling back at him, "who would there be to annoy me?"

"I'm sure you'd find someone."

High above, two birds fought with each other, ducking and diving, moving in circles, squawking loudly in the otherwise silent valley.

"I think it's an awful idea," Daisy said again. "To leave your home and go off to the other side of the world."

Stephen turned to her. "But it's not my home. It's *your* home, and my parents' home, I suppose. I don't really know where I fit in here."

"I thought you were happy, thought you loved this place."

He nodded. "I do, I do, but . . . well, it's hard to explain and probably impossible for you to understand."

"Try me," she said, reaching over and taking the bottle from his hand.

He sighed, pulled out his packet of tobacco and cigarette papers. "It's complicated," he said. "But I imagine I might feel differently if I'd known my real parents."

"Ah, I see," said Daisy, as though it all made perfect sense to her now.

"It's not that I'm unhappy," he said, glancing up at her.

"What is it, then?" she asked, watching his fingers roll the tobacco.

He shrugged. "Just the not knowing, I suppose."

"I've told you before, you should ask your mother."

Stephen shook his head. "I can't. She's never raised the subject with me, and I don't want to upset her, don't want her to think I need something more, or that she's not been a good mother to me, because she has and I love her dearly," he added, lighting his cigarette. "I love both my parents."

"Then you can't leave them. I know it would break your mother's heart if you sailed off to another continent. She'd never see you again. You'd never see her."

"Perhaps . . . perhaps," he said, nodding, pondering, looking downward. "But I can't stay here. Not if I want to do something with my life," he added, looking up at Daisy.

By the time they set off back in the direction of Eden Hall, Daisy had forgotten about Mrs. Christie's disappearance. The only disappearance she could think of was Stephen's: suggested, impending and hanging in the damp, pine-scented air between them. But it was impossible for her to imagine the world—her world—without him in it.

To Daisy, Stephen Jessop belonged more to that place than she and her sisters, or even her mother and father. He knew every pathway, each copse and dell. Together, they had pioneered the woodland, fields and valleys around them. Together, they had named every plant and tree. He had been the one to teach her which mushrooms were poisonous and which were not, and about didicoys and travelers, and the legends of the Devil's Punchbowl. He'd risked his life climbing up trees, crawling along branches, just to bring down a nest or eggs to show her; been the one who'd taken her to see the fox cubs and watch the badger set at dusk, the one who'd made her a slingshot and shown her how to use it, and the one who'd given her three marbles, a jar of tadpoles and a hawk-moth caterpillar for her tenth birthday.

And Stephen knew everyone, too, even those passing through, like the tramp who had once marched up and down at the crossroads with a stick on his shoulder, sometimes shouting up at the sky. Another casualty of the war, Stephen had explained.

"He thinks his name's Fletch, but he can't remember much else."

"You mean he doesn't know where he lives?" Daisy had asked.

"Where he *lived*," Stephen had corrected her. "No, he can't recall where he's from, or where he was before the war, but he thinks it may have begun with a B. Of course, he thinks he's still in the army, on duty, which is why he marches up and down like that. He's keeping watch."

"But he might have a family somewhere . . . looking for him."

"Or more likely presuming him dead."

Daisy had suggested that perhaps Captain Clark could help Fletch, but Stephen had said he didn't think so, that Captain Clark, too, was "damaged."

Captain Clark lived in the same lodgings as old Mrs. Reed, the former cook at Eden Hall, and was another who walked in that soldierly way, following a line, lifting his feet a little too high, his arms straight down by his sides. Daisy had seen plenty of war veterans, particularly up in town, where they slept on park benches and sat about on the pavement or in wheelchairs outside tube stations, selling matches or begging. And even those with limbs—without any obvious physical injury—were easy enough to spot because of that walk . . . or the strange haunted look in their eyes . . . or the tics.

It had been the previous winter, when food was disappearing from the larder and Nancy, the housekeeper, had told Mabel and Mabel had told Daisy and Daisy knew that it was Stephen—taking it for Fletch, because she had been the one to suggest it—that Captain Clark shot himself. He had gone in to lunch as usual, then gone for his constitutional up on the hill and put a bullet in his head. Mrs. Jessop had said it was sad but at least he had no family and hadn't done it in poor Mrs. Reed's earshot (which, and regardless of the pun, struck Daisy as a stupid remark because everyone knew Mrs. Reed was quite deaf). It had been in the newspaper, and there had been an inquest, which told them what they all knew anyway: that it had been suicide resulting from "unsound mind." Shortly after that, Fletch had disappeared.

Long before Fletch, during the war, Stephen had attended lessons in the schoolroom with Daisy and a few other local children. And he had been included in every birthday party, each nursery tea: teas with the ruddy-faced, tartan-clad cousins from Scotland, and teas with the silent children recently moved to the area whom Daisy's mother had taken a shine to. "New friends!" Mabel would say, clapping her hands together. Those had been the worst teas: tense affairs with spilled drinks and red faces and curious, resentful stares.

And then there were the pea-flicking, bread-throwing children from London.

They weren't all orphans, Stephen had explained; some of them had parents, but they were too poor to look after them. These children had continued to come each summer during the war, and for a few years after it, sleeping in the night nursery—turned into a dormitory—at the top of the house, a different group each year. *They* were anything but silent. They came through windows rather than use doors and slid down the banisters rather than use the stairs. They loved fighting and swearing and climbing—walls, trees, drainpipes and the greenhouse roof, until two of them fell through. They all had nits, and rivulets of green running from their noses to their mouths, wiped onto their sleeves. Almost all of them smoked, and they liked to start fires and give people frights, and they were always hungry. "Bleedin' starvin'," they said, each day, at every time of day.

Everyone's nerves were frayed to tatters by the time *they* left. But Stephen had been the go-between, able to understand them as well as he did Daisy and her sisters.

Even now, Daisy often thought of Janet Greenwell, whose head had been shaved and whose sad little legs were paler and thinner than any Daisy had ever seen. And she remembered the crippled boy, Neville, a caliper on his leg and such thick lenses in his spectacles that they made his eyes appear small. "Crippled Chinky," the others had called him, shouted after him as he limped off up the brick pathway of the walled garden.

Only once had Daisy summoned the courage to confront them,

only once had she shouted back at them that they were cruel bullies and then gone after Neville, whom she'd found slumped next to the rabbit hutch, his stiff leg stretched out in front of him, like a war veteran—but without any medals for bravery.

"They don't mean to be vile; they're just ignorant," she'd said, sitting down next to him on the grass, longing to wrap her arms round him. He'd not said anything, had quietly wept, wiping his nose on his gray shirtsleeve, staring through his thick spectacles at his useless leg.

The day before Neville left, Daisy gave him the book she had won at the flower show for her vegetable animal (a horse, made from potato, carrots and peas, with ribbons of cucumber peel for its mane and tail, had earned her second prize and a "highly commended" badge from the judges). She had thought long and hard about which book to give him but plumped for *A Shropshire Lad* mainly because of that word, *lad*. Inside, she wrote, "Dear Neville, I hope I'll see you again and that you'll come back here one day without the others. Yours, Daisy M. Forbes." When she told Stephen, he'd shaken her hand and told her that she was the kindest person he knew.

Always, after these children had gone, Eden Hall returned to its usual quiet and calm. It was a place of order and routine and of bells—to announce breakfast or lessons or lunch; the dressing bell, the dinner bell, each day had been punctuated by that sound. Months, seasons and years had passed and the bell still sounded. For Daisy, little had changed. But the thought of Eden Hall without Stephen, the idea of his not being there, of never seeing him again . . .

No, Stephen couldn't emigrate, Daisy thought, watching him

walk on ahead of her, pulling back gorse and holly and brambles as they made their way through thickets and knee-high heather. She would speak to her father, she decided; wait until he was home for Christmas, find the right time and speak to him about all of this then. After all, he'd been the one to sort the legalities of Stephen's adoption, and he might even be able to offer Stephen a job at the factory . . . Either way, she concluded, her father would know what to do. He always did.

Chapter Two

Situated in a quiet enclave of the Surrey Hills known as Little Switzerland, Eden Hall was one of a number of newer mansions hidden from sight. Tall hedges, trees and banks of rhododendrons screened it from traffic passing along the road to its south, but its gated entrance and long curving driveway hinted at what lay beyond.

In autumn and winter, the house and its gardens were often lost, engulfed by the swirling mists and low cloud. But in early spring, when the mists cleared and before the trees were covered with leaves, a few of the upper rooms at Eden Hall commanded spectacular views across three counties: Surrey, to the north and east; Sussex, to the south; and Hampshire, to the west.

Howard Forbes claimed that, on a clear day, beyond the distant northerly ridge known as the Hog's Back, one could even make out the dome of St. Paul's—though more often than not, the only visible sign of the capital was the dense smog belched up from the city's multitudinous chimneys and factories. But somewhere on that murky horizon stood a street named Clanricarde Gardens and the Forbes family's London home: a stucco-fronted town house Howard had inherited at twenty-two years of age.

Eden Hall was different. For Howard, it represented his own achievements, the culmination of and testament to his hard work: his dream, his vision, built with the proceeds from his thriving business, Forbes and Sons. The company, passed down through three generations, manufactured white lead, oil paint and varnish at its large factory at Forbes's Wharf in Ratcliff, Middlesex. Its products included special anticorrosive paints and antioxidation compositions for ships, as well as their famous patented white zinc paint, which was claimed not to stain or discolor.

At the dawn of the new century, shortly before his marriage and as a thirtieth birthday present to himself, Howard had purchased his acreage in Surrey, which included an old farm. Later, standing on the lofty site clutching the hand of his eighteen-year-old bride, Mabel, and with an emerging local architect named Edwin Lutyens, Howard Forbes had looked out over the far-reaching views and explained his vision to Mr. Lutyens: a substantial country house with *impressive lines, tall chimneys and immense gabled rooftops.* He had stipulated windows, lots of them—round ones, square ones, large and small—and doors a giant could walk through. He wanted something future generations could be proud of.

Howard got what he wanted: a grand country house in the medieval vernacular style, and with its double-height entrance hall, sweeping staircase and oak paneling, double-height drawing room and oriel windows, the place was every bit as impressive as Howard

Forbes's vision. And yet there was some humbleness about the place, too, Howard thought, for Mr. Lutyens had used only locally sourced timber, stone and bricks and had retained a few of the old barns and cottages from the original farm.

Despite its appearance, inside, Eden Hall was modern—twentieth-century modern: It had electricity, central heating and two bathrooms, with running hot water, flushing lavatories and William De Morgan ceramic tiles. But it had been Mabel who'd been responsible for the interior decor, for the Morris & Co. bedroom wallpapers and curtains and for the velvets and silks and hand-printed linens. She had chosen every paint color and textile, each item of furniture. And having put her own stamp on the place, and with a natural preference for country living anyhow, Mabel decided early on to make Eden Hall the family's primary residence.

Mabel had grown up in the country; it was what she knew, where she felt happiest and most comfortable. Howard, she said—and thought—would be able to divide his time between London and Eden Hall, and while he was working, she would throw herself into creating that home, a country idyll: a place her husband could escape to from the stresses and strains of the city, a place where their children could grow up with space and fresh air in abundance. She would, she'd conceded, visit London—particularly during the season, and particularly if they had daughters. They had both laughed at this.

Howard and Mabel had been fully committed to having a large family, and Howard—like any normal man, he'd said—wanted sons and needed them to carry on the business he had taken over from his father. But of the eight babies Mabel had conceived and the four she had carried to full term, only the three girls survived. Howard's longed-for son and heir, born prematurely during the war and named Theo, after Howard's father, had clung to life for only seven weeks.

But Howard and Mabel's plans had been fulfilled, in part. For while Howard spent his weekdays in the city, Mabel had remained with her daughters at Eden Hall, establishing a home—that country idyll they had both longed for—managing the house and gardens and staff and attending to her charity work. And when Iris, their eldest daughter, moved out, Mabel's mother moved in. Now newly married Lily also lived in London and only Daisy remained at home.

Like the interior of the house, the gardens at Eden Hall were a testament to Mabel. For a quarter of a century she had helped seed, sow and water; watched and waited. And, like Mabel, Eden Hall and its gardens had matured. The house's honey-hued stone had mellowed to a silvery gray and its garden's once inadequate shrubs had taken on more voluptuous shapes. The landscape overflowed with rhododendrons and hardy shrubbery, softened by the billowing herbaceous borders and broad, sweeping south lawns, where a gritted terrace stood guard like a moat between man and nature. And the Japanese garden, with its drooping wisteria, azaleas, bamboo and acers, its pond with water lilies, miniature stone bridge and stone lanterns, was Mabel's pride and joy, and only just coming into its own, she claimed.

The main driveway wound a circuitous route through the scenic western gardens, where the rhododendrons loomed largest and a few ancient trees remained, before emerging in front of the south-facing house with its vast oriel windows and broad front door. The driveway then continued through an archway to the courtyard, cottages, coach house and garages, and, eventually, became the back driveway, or tradesman's entrance, and ran down the eastern side of Howard Forbes's estate to the road.

To the north of the house, brick pathways led to the tennis court, the orchard and the pink-walled kitchen gardens and green-houses. Beyond this, the land fell away steeply to woodland, where bridle paths and tracks zigzagged beneath the lofty pine trees into the valley known as the Devil's Punchbowl.

Shortly after the house was completed, the National Trust had acquired this land, and it had become a popular place for walkers and ramblers, particularly in the summer months, when Howard had from time to time found campers behind the northern shrub-bery, or short-trousered foreigners ambling across his striped lawns. However, invariably polite, he had sometimes taken these tourists on a guided tour of his property and offered them a glass of sherry at the end of it.

More than any trespassers, the ever-increasing number of local property developers irked both Howard and Mabel. The new houses being built on the nearby site of the recently demolished mansion the Laurels, now to be known as Laurel Close, made them both privately wonder if Eden Hall, too, would one day be demolished. Would theirs and Mr. Lutyens's vision—their painstaking planning over windows and aspects and views—be reduced to rubble and dust, only to reemerge in the shape of a dozen poorly built houses, sold off at exorbitant prices and collectively known as Edenhall Close? It seemed to be the way things were going. What had once been secluded and peaceful, sought after for its natural beauty and charm, was changing.

"The world won't be content until it has motored here, there and everywhere—honking its horn, widening every road and putting up electricity cables and streetlights," Howard had recently said to his wife. Mabel had thought better than to remind him that he was a horn honker himself, or that they had added to the cables and lighting in that part of the world.

Howard had been like this a lot recently: agitated and complaining. Fearful. It was his age, Mabel thought; he felt out of step with the times. Modern times. And though she sometimes felt this way also, she was quietly determined not to fall too far behind. But it was tricky, a balancing act, she thought, to set an example for her daughters, to hand on wisdom and age gracefully, while wanting— still feeling the need—to live and have new experiences.

"New experiences!" Dosia, her sister-in-law, had declared to her the last time they had seen each other in London. "That's what you need, Mabe. What we all need."

Mabel had created an idyll, an orderly idyll, where the dressing bell sounded at six thirty and the dinner bell at seven twenty-five, but she was bored of bells and order. She was bored of Eden Hall. She had had no new experiences for a quarter of a century, and what she longed for, privately longed for more than anything else, was a lover.

Chapter Three

Ten days before Christmas, Mrs. Christie was found, alive and well and staying at a hydropathic hotel in Harrogate, where—Iris told Daisy—she had been registered under another name: that of her husband's mistress.

"What an almighty lark," Iris said on the telephone. "And all to teach that wretched husband of hers a lesson."

"Do you honestly think she planned it all?" asked Daisy.

"Of course!" shrieked Iris. "And what a brilliant wheeze."

"Really? I read that it's cost the country a fortune *and* been the biggest manhunt in history."

"Hmm, well, the bill should certainly be dispatched to Colonel Christie," Iris said and snorted. She seemed to find it all amusing, like everything else.

"Poor Dodo," Iris went on, "I know you've been awfully caught up in the whole thing—Mummy said—but it has been frightfully entertaining . . . We should all be writing to Mrs. Christie to thank her for keeping us so riveted."

Daisy shook her head. She felt for Mrs. Christie—because of her marriage problems, and hoped they wouldn't interfere with her ability to write—but she also felt cheated. For if what Iris said was true, if Mrs. Christie had staged the whole thing simply to teach her husband a lesson, the whole country had been nothing more than pawns in her own domestic squabble. Stephen was right. Either way, it seemed as though the writer's disappearance had been some sort of publicity stunt . . . and what publicity she had garnered.

"Are you excited about Christmas, Dodo? Have you unpacked your snow globe yet?" Iris asked.

Daisy rolled her eyes. "I am eighteen, you know. I've grown out of all that."

Iris laughed. "Oh, darling, we *all* know what you're like."

"Have you been out dancing much?" Daisy asked.

Dancing: It was Iris's obsession. And everybody was doing it, she said, even the Prince of Wales, whose dancing she raved about—"Such fabulous rhythm and so extraordinarily light on his feet!"—and with whom she had danced on more than one occasion at the Embassy in Old Bond Street. It was Iris's favorite club and only a short walk from her second favorite, the Grafton Galleries. These places and others seemed to be like second homes to Iris, and Daisy had heard enough about them to know them all, vicariously.

"Almost every night . . . London's simply *devastating*," drawled Iris.

Devastating: It was Iris's favorite word. She used it to describe almost everything, or everything she had a passion for, but it had to be said in a particular way, and in a much deeper tone of voice. And it wasn't just people or places that were devastating to Iris; even a hat could be "simply devastating."

"And when are you coming down?"

"I'm not sure . . . maybe Christmas Eve."

"I rather think you're expected to be here before then."

"Really? Oh, well, maybe I'll cadge a ride back with Howard, if I can bear it."

Iris was always so mean about their father, and for absolutely no reason. "You can always get the train," Daisy suggested.

Iris laughed again. "Have to dash now. Bye, darling," she said, and the line went dead.

When Daisy walked into the hallway, her mother was standing in front of the Christmas tree with a clipboard and pen. Scattered around the tree and across the floor were the tattered boxes and crates Daisy had helped Mr. Blundell bring down from the attics.

"We really do need to get the thing decorated," said Mabel.

The *thing*? It was a tree. A magnificent Christmas tree, thought Daisy, staring up at it.

"The electric lights will only be a problem if your father gets involved," Mabel went on. "He has an uncanny knack of breaking the wretched things."

More *things*. What was wrong with her? They were beautiful lights. Prettier than any others Daisy had seen. "Blundy said he'd help me decorate the *thing* tomorrow morning."

Her mother slid her a look. "It could've been done by now, Daisy. If you spent less time wandering about dreaming, less time chatting on the telephone—which, may I remind you, is very costly and *not* what it's designed for—you would achieve more . . . And please don't roll your eyes like that," she added.

"Sorry."

"We must make sure the tree's decorated and the lights are up *and* working before your father arrives home," Mabel said. Then she turned and marched off down the passageway toward her boudoir.

Maybe she was cross with Howard, Daisy mused, watching her mother disappear into a doorway. He had not been home in more than two weeks. But it was a busy time for him. He had had various dinners and functions to attend up in London and had long ago stopped asking Mabel to accompany him, because, as everyone knew, she didn't enjoy those sorts of events and preferred to be at Eden Hall. And yet, though Mabel claimed to love the place—and ran it like a sergeant major, Daisy thought—she no longer seemed to enjoy it in the way she once had. She spoke about it as though it was a job, and a job she had grown weary of. She was like a Henry James heroine, one of those formidable women whose sense of duty left them unable to breathe properly.

When Daisy stepped outside, the sky was translucent. A fiery sun shone through the black trees and danced on the moth-colored stone. She found Stephen shutting up the greenhouse, a solitary figure in the peaceful shadows of the walled garden, where hen coops and a long-vacated rabbit hutch stood in a far corner. There, too, were the little house and wire-covered run once inhabited by Sherlock, Daisy's tortoise, who'd failed to wake from his hibernation the previous spring and whose grave lay on the other side of the wall, next to that of a goat named Charlie.

"You were right," said Daisy, walking up the brick pathway

toward Stephen. "It seems it was all just some massive publicity stunt." She had decided it would be indiscreet to share Mrs. Christie's personal problems with him.

"What was?"

"Mrs. Christie . . . her disappearance."

"Oh, that."

He was unusually quiet, and she followed him back to the yard and watched him as he began to stack logs on a wheelbarrow.

"What do you think of my coat?" she asked, referring to the long fur coat her grandmother had given her, and suddenly desperate for him to look up at her.

"Noonie's?" he asked, glancing at her only very briefly.

"Not anymore. She's given it to me."

"It suits you," he said, without any smile.

"So what are you doing tonight? Do you want to come and play some cards? Listen to the wireless? You know my grandmother's just bought another—so she can have one in her room, next to her bed, and the new one in the drawing room."

He stretched his arms up into the air, interlinked his fingers and brought them down on his cap. "I don't think so, Daisy . . . not tonight."

The lights in house were being switched on, illuminating the gritted courtyard, pulling them out of the shadows. Mr. Blundell, the butler, was on his rounds.

"It's getting cold. You should go inside," said Stephen, staring at her.

"I don't want to. Not yet. I want to stay here and talk to you . . . I feel as though you're angry with me and I don't know why. Is it about the whole Mrs. Christie thing?" she asked. "Because if it is, or was, I'm sorry I was so pigheaded and dragged you into it all. And I'm actually rather cross myself—with *her*."

Stephen laughed. He pulled off his cap and ran a hand through his hair. "I'm not angry with you. I'm never angry with you. You know that. But I do get . . ."

"Yes?"

"Frustrated, I suppose."

"By me?"

"Yes," he said quickly, tilting his head to one side, narrowing his eyes.

"I see," she said, though she didn't and couldn't. "Well, I can only apologize . . . because I really don't mean to be."

"I know this," he said.

It was inevitable that their friendship had changed, Daisy thought, watching him as he continued to stack logs on the barrow, from those days when he'd been eager to see her, turning up at the house most evenings to see what she was doing and spend time with her. It was inevitable, she supposed, that he'd prefer to spend his evenings at a public house. It was what young men like Stephen did, her mother had told her. But Daisy missed his company. Missed their friendship.

"Are you going to the pub?" Daisy asked, adopting his terminology.

"Not sure. Might be," he said, without looking up.

Daisy often wondered what went on there—apart from drinking. She'd have liked to be asked, be invited, *and* be allowed to go. The only time she had been to the local public house was last Boxing

Day, when the hunt had met there and she and Iris had stood about with their parents holding glasses of punch, then watched the horses and hounds set off in search of some poor fox. She had told Iris then that she thought it all very uncivilized and that she'd not go again. But she'd meant to the hunt, not to the place.

"Well, if you change your mind . . . ," she said.

Then Mr. Blundell opened the back door and asked Stephen if the logs were ready, and Daisy turned and went inside.

She walked down the passageway to the kitchen, said hello to Mrs. Jessop and to Nancy and Hilda, and went up to her room. She threw off her coat, lay down on her bed and thought once more about Mrs. Christie and what, exactly, had driven her to stage her own disappearance. In truth, Daisy still couldn't believe it had been a publicity stunt. It seemed so drastic, so desperate. It had been a cry for help, Daisy thought, sitting up. And no different from all those times she had run away to the summerhouse; for she had, she suddenly realized, staged a few disappearances herself.

That evening, the dressing bell sounded at six thirty, the dinner bell at seven twenty-five, but there were only Daisy and her mother at dinner, seated at one end of the long dining table.

"Noonie's not feeling too grand, is having a tray taken up," said Mabel, shaking out her white linen napkin. "But I quite like it like this," she added, smiling. "It's rather cozy, isn't it?"

"Yes, rather cozy," said Daisy.

Mabel peered at the bowl of watery green liquid in front of her, then sniffed it. "Cabbage?"

Daisy shrugged. "Greenery."

"Holly!" said Mabel. "Holly soup? What an idea," she added, giggling at her own joke as she picked up her spoon.

She was in a better mood, Daisy thought. Perhaps Howard had telephoned, or, and more likely, her new best friend, Reggie.

"They'll all be upon us next week," her mother continued. "But quite a few less than I'd thought . . . I had a letter from Rivinia today. Unfortunately, she took a tumble out hunting last week and has broken her wrist, poor dear. She's quite devastated not to be able to get south . . . She so *loathes* being stuck in that drafty pile and having to wear tartan for Hogmanay," Mabel went on, referring to her cousin who fled the Scottish borders each New Year in favor of the bright lights of the south. "And one of dear Dixie's reindeers has taken ill, so we shan't be seeing her, either," Mabel added, referring to another cousin, an animal lover extraordinaire for whom Christmas was a year-round festival.

"What about Aunt Dosia's friend Harriett? Is she coming to stay again? She was so much fun last year—with all her mad outfits and her dancing—and she promised she'd be back," said Daisy.

"No, apparently Hattie has a boyfriend."

"A boyfriend?"

Mabel nodded. "A divorced chap in the Foreign Office. Simon Something-or-other. And, according to Dosia, rather lovely—despite an unusually penetrating manner."

"And Sophie and Noel?" Daisy asked.

"Saint Moritz. Again," said Mabel, fluttering her eyes. "Though I do hope they don't put dear little Freddie and Jessie on that toboggan run again. Not after last year."

"The Cresta Run," said Daisy. "Is that why you were tense earlier? Because certain people aren't going to be here?"

Mabel laughed. "I wasn't tense. And to be honest, I'm rather relieved not to have quite so many to stay this year. There'll be more than enough with all of us and Dosia . . . and Reggie, of course."

"Of course . . . And where is he tonight?" Daisy asked. "I thought he might be dining with us again."

"He had some military dinner to go to."

Reggie—*Major* Reginald Ellison—was a widower and lived at High Pines: a Gothic-style mansion situated a little way down the road to the west of Eden Hall. He'd served out in India for more than two decades, returning to England and early retirement only the previous year. Major Ellison had no children and lived at his "pile"—as he called it—with a young couple he'd brought with him from India who acted as housekeeper and gardener and whatever else he needed. The initial appearance of these two had caused quite a stir in Little Switzerland, particularly the day they boarded the omnibus and sat opposite Mrs. Jessop in *nothing more than sheets*. But later, Mr. and Mrs. Singh—she, in her exotically colored saris; he, in his silk *pancha* with shirt, jacket and tie—had become a common enough sight about the locality.

It had been Howard who had established the friendship, quickly inviting the major over to Eden Hall, eager to hear about far-flung parts of the empire. But with Howard up in London each and every week, it had been Mabel who'd developed and cemented the friendship with Major Ellison. He often came to dinner or called in for morning coffee or afternoon tea or for an early evening aperitif after walking his dog on the common. And he had been the most wonderful help to Mabel with the wedding arrangements at the end of last summer, when Lily married Miles: on hand to direct the men putting up the marquee, the deliveries of tables and chairs and crockery; driving Mabel hither and thither, always there to offer calm reassurance. He had taught both Iris and Daisy to drive, sitting with them as they took turns and had a go about the lanes of Little Switzerland. And thus, Major Ellison had become Reggie.

When Lily had had a row with Miles, shortly after returning from their honeymoon in Scotland, and had sent Mabel a telegram to say that she was leaving Miles and would be arriving on the 4:20, it had been Reggie who had gone to collect her; Reggie who had sat with her, talked to her, wiped away her tears and then driven her back to the station in time for the 7:42. When Daisy and Mabel returned from what Mabel described as a "completely pointless and totally exasperating" visit to a dressmaker at Farnham, it was Reggie who'd sat and listened to Daisy as she explained why she did not want another pretty floral summer dress; Reggie who had then gently conveyed this to Mabel. And when Noonie took a turn late one night in November and was found out on the front driveway in her nightgown (on her way to see someone called Samuel, she'd said), Reggie had immediately driven over and been the one—the only one—who was able to get her back indoors.

"It must be strange for Reggie," said Daisy, "to be back in England after so many years in India, to be cold and shivering again."

"I think he's used to it now," Mabel replied.

"But why are they all coming back?"

"Coming back?"

"Yes, from the colonies . . . that new family, the ones who've only just moved into Westfield House and were in rubber—or was it tea?"

"Their name is Chapman. And it was tea, in Malaya."

"So the Chapmans from Malaya, the Pritchards from Ceylon and the Williamsons and Reggie from India. Everyone who's moved here recently seems to have come back from somewhere exotic."

Mabel shook her head. "I'm not altogether sure why," she said. "The world's changing, and I suppose when change is afoot one returns home . . . to stability."

"Like losing one's nerve?"

"Yes," said Mabel. "I suppose it is a bit like losing one's nerve. Change is hard . . . to adapt to new circumstances, new ways, particularly when one is older or has a family to consider."

"I don't intend to get old," said Daisy, as Nancy appeared and lifted away their plates of barely touched rissoles. She saw the housekeeper shake her head. As the baize door swung shut, she leaned toward her mother and asked, "How old do you suppose Nancy is?"

"She's two years younger than me. She's coming up to forty."

"And she was never married?"

"She was engaged. He was killed in the war."

Daisy nodded. The war still hung over them all, young and old. Like an ever-present but reticent guest, it stood alone, lingering in a shadowy corner. And how could it not? For so many, it seemed, had been robbed of husbands, children, a future. And yet it was hard to imagine Nancy *engaged*, with a man, with a family that weren't the Forbeses, a family of her own. "She looks older than forty," said Daisy.

"Her hair turned gray prematurely—and very quickly. She aged; she changed."

"How sad," said Daisy, trying to imagine.

"His name was John Bradley. He was a farmer. Nancy hardly ever mentions his name now, but she always used to say he was one in a million. And he was, literally; he was one of the one million men killed at the Battle of the Somme . . . She still has her trousseau," Mabel went on in a whisper, staring at the candle. "An old pine blanket box up in her room, with her unworn wedding dress, her mother's veil and the ivory silk nightgown I bought for her—for her wedding night."

"And never worn."

"No, never worn, never worn on a wedding night . . . John would have inherited the farm by now; she'd have had her own home, own family. I don't suppose she'll ever be able to forgive Germany or Kaiser Wilhelm."

When Nancy reappeared with Mabel's coffee, Daisy and her mother both sat up and smiled brightly. And as the baize door swung shut once more, Mabel said, "Oh, and I've invited Benedict Gifford to join us again this year. The poor man has no one, and I know you enjoyed his company last Christmas and in the summer."

"Oh yes," said Daisy. She'd forgotten all about Ben. "I don't think Iris rates him," she said after a moment or two. "She called him obsequious."

"Iris *can* be rather cruel," Mabel said, shaking her head. She took a sip from her coffee cup. "You know, I've always felt—had an inkling—that you might marry someone older," she said. "Not Ben Gifford," she quickly added, "but someone older."

"Like you and Daddy?"

"Yes . . . yes, sort of like that."

To have a marriage like her parents', marry a man not dissimilar to her father—principled, honest and kind—was Daisy's dream.

Chapter Four

It was five days before Christmas and Mrs. Christie's story had slipped from front-page news to a small insert on page eleven, offering her fans an update on her well-being. Now the newspapers were predicting a white Christmas, and Mrs. Jessop was being difficult.

Mabel had gone to the kitchen with a conciliatory approach, an open mind—she hoped. But when Mrs. Jessop stared back at her across the kitchen table, her arms folded, Mabel quickly realized they had reached an impasse.

"Really . . . I think Lang is an English name," said Mabel again.

Mrs. Jessop said nothing.

Ever suspicious of foreigners—or anyone new to the area; *outsiders*, she called them—Mrs. Jessop had said her piece and vowed that she could not buy any meat from the new butcher. She had told Mabel in no uncertain terms that she would prefer to take the number 18 to Farnham than "experiment" with a man she had no knowledge of, and who had—if she could be plain, and after all, that's what she was, a plain-speaking, plain cook—what she believed could be the trace of a German accent.

"There is no need, no need whatsoever for you to take the bus to Farnham, Mrs. Jessop," Mabel went on, knowing that reason was hopeless. She had gone there to plead one last time, but the woman was intransigent. "We don't have an account at any butchers at Farnham, and I'm not sure they'll make deliveries this far," Mabel added.

Mrs. Jessop blinked.

"Well, if you feel you must . . ."

The antipathy toward Germany ran deep in some and was understandable, Mabel reminded herself as she left the kitchen. But the suspicion of foreigners that had begun during the war had left a lingering xenophobia. People still spoke about spies and about the likelihood of another war, particularly Mrs. Jessop and Nancy, whose imaginations seemed to know no bounds, Mabel thought, breathing in deeply as she walked toward the hallway.

There was the familiar aroma of lavender and logs; the scent of a house filled with flowers each summer and fires each winter; the smell of candles and dogs, and mud and the country; the fading sweet scent of fruit, and the warm, earthy smells of old leather and beeswax: the lingering fragrance of a quarter of a century.

The tree was newly festooned with baubles and illuminated by fruit-shaped frosted-glass lights: pale violet pears and yellow apples. Mesmerized for a moment, Mabel remembered other Christmases, before the war, before people had gone and everything changed, when the children had been small and the place filled with chaos and laughter—and her mouth curved up at one side.

Clambering on all fours—pretending to be a lion, a wolf, a wildly roaring but forgiving beast that only he and his children understood—Howard had chased his squealing girls around the tree and up the stairs for bath time and then, later, carrying Daisy in his arms, brought them back down, sweet smelling and pink.

The grandfather clock in the hallway struck five.

"I've unpacked my snow globe," said Daisy, standing in the drawing room doorway clutching it in her hand. "I'm listening to Beethoven," she added, turning away, humming.

Mabel followed her. She watched Daisy place the glass orb on a table by the oriel window, next to the Victorian taxidermy diorama. Mabel hated the stuffed birds, encased in glass, their tiny feet pinned, their lifeless eyes staring out. She wished her mother had sent the thing to the auction house with the others, but Noonie had made a gift of it to Mabel, along with various ornaments and china and once fashionable objets d'art: the term Noonie used for anything of no apparent use or beauty, but perhaps of some value.

When Noonie moved in to Eden Hall, she had brought with her the accumulation of a lifetime, albeit distilled, and the relics and heirlooms of other lifetimes before hers. The room, Mabel thought now, resembled an aging, overdressed woman no longer confident of her style, or of any one style. And yet there remained— here and there—the trace of some former discernment, a singular mind. But silks once vibrant were now sun bleached; velvets once sumptuous, worn and faded. The room was choked with too much of everything, and even Mabel's cherished Meissen porcelain and Viennese glass were quite lost in the sea of clutter.

As the ormolu clock on the mantelshelf belatedly chimed five, Mabel noticed car headlights on the driveway.

"Someone's here . . . looks like a station taxi," said Daisy.

But no one was due to arrive, not yet. "Possibly a delivery," Mabel suggested, turning to Mr. Blundell as he crossed over the hallway in answer to the bell. She heard the distant sound of the Dutch clock on the wall in the kitchen, the cuckoo clock down the passageway, and made a mental note to speak to Blundell about the clocks not keeping time. Then she heard the voice: "Hello, Blundy, how are you? Isn't it bloody freezing?"

Dosia.

"Surprise?" repeated Dosia seconds later. "But I sent you a telegram to say I was coming earlier."

"Oh yes, there was a telegram . . . I forgot to tell you," said Daisy, turning to the hallway table.

Mabel took the telegram from Daisy's hand: PLANS CHANGED STOP ARRIVING TODAY STOP ON THE FOUR TWENTY STOP.

The telegram had arrived that afternoon while Mabel was out delivering cards and had lain on the table, disappearing beneath a pile of yet more cards.

"I can't believe it's happened again," said Mabel, throwing down the telegram and putting her head in her hands. The last time Dosia had visited there'd been a similar mix-up with train times and no one had been at the station to meet her.

"You really should have telephoned," Mabel went on, helping her sister-in-law out of her moth-eaten fur and forgetting for a moment that Dosia had yet to have a telephone installed at her London flat, or rather, that Dosia refused to have a telephone installed at her London flat on grounds of its being a "completely unnecessary expense."

"Now, where's the rest of your luggage, dear?" Mabel asked.

"That's it."

Dosia pointed down to an unusually small suitcase, similar to one Daisy had once used for her doll's clothes.

"That's it?"

"You know me, Mabe. I'm not a fusspot when it comes to fashion. And I thought this should see me through," Dosia added, running her large hands over her tweed-clad hips.

It was her usual garb, that tweed skirt—always slightly askew at the hem, a familiar brown sweater, woolen stockings and laced leather brogues. As ever, there was no trace of makeup on Dosia's aging yet still innocent face, and her baby-fine hair, which she claimed to have had "done" especially for Christmas, stood up on end when she removed her battered cloche hat.

"Rather sweet, isn't it?" said Dosia, swiveling the felt hat on her hand. "I got it at the Save the Children jumble sale. Sixpence! Can you imagine? Daylight robbery, really, but naughty old Beatrice has made a bed of my other," she said, referring to one of her numerous cats.

Christened Theodosia Hermione Evangeline Forbes, Dosia was Howard's only surviving sibling. Howard and Dosia's two brothers had been killed in the war, along with Dosia's fiancé, Hugh. Like her brother, Dosia was tall and broad shouldered and had a long stride. Unlike her brother, she was what Mabel deemed a free spirit and had, in her youth, been arrested a number of times for chaining herself to railings and throwing bricks through shop windows in support of Votes for Women.

It was still queer to think of Dosia in jail . . . A criminal? It was a ridiculous notion, Mabel thought, smiling and nodding to Blundell as he lifted the tiny and quite obviously weightless case. "The usual room, thank you, Mr. Blundell," said Mabel.

As Dosia fell into an armchair in the drawing room, Mabel noticed the thick plumes of dust rise. She would need to speak to Nancy again about Hilda. And as Dosia went on to explain that her train had been delayed due to "some poor wretch" throwing herself onto the line at Woking, Hilda herself appeared with a tray of tea and her usual surly expression.

"Always happens this time of year," said Hilda, bending over, slopping milk into cups. "My ma says it's 'cause folk can't face being stuck with their families at Christmastime. Makes 'em go a bit loopy."

"Yes, thank you, Hilda," said Mabel.

By the time the dressing bell sounded, Dosia had dispensed with her brogues and was stretched out on the sofa, her large feet—encased in darned stockings—resting on the padded footstool. The bell was ignored, and at Noonie's request, *Time for a Tune* was put on the wireless. When the dinner bell sounded, the four women headed for the dining room, where a branch of mistletoe hung above the door from a blue velvet ribbon.

"Daisy," said Dosia, taking her niece's arm and looking upward. "Are you perchance hoping to be kissed this Christmas?"

Daisy shrugged. "Perhaps."

"Ah, first kisses," murmured Noonie. "I still remember mine . . . with Samuel. I was *so* in love with him."

Mabel's mother, Daphne, owed her original nickname to Iris, who when she had first begun to speak had called her grandmother "Neenie." But it had been Daisy who had changed this to Noonie.

A small woman, like Mabel and Daisy, Noonie ate very little and was painfully thin. She had had her only child, Mabel, late in life and had been a widow for almost two decades. But she had not wept at her husband's funeral and, though she'd observed a short mourning period and worn the requisite black, she had not missed him, Mabel knew. For most of their marriage, Mabel's parents—Daphne and Gerard Taylor—had led separate lives, and while Daphne had remained in the country, with Mabel, in a house not far from where Eden Hall would one day emerge, Gerard had resided in the city. Sometime after his death, after the reading of his will, in which a Mrs. Monica Sutton and two children were left a property in London and a considerable amount of money, Daphne had burned every photograph she could find of her husband. She had then dispatched every other reminder of him among various charities and a local auction house and used some of the money he'd bequeathed her to demolish his vast orangery.

Now in her mid- to late seventies (no one knew her exact age and, it seemed, neither did she), Noonie still took pride in her appearance, wearing her white hair piled up in a bun and favoring dresses over the new and more modern separates, but with hems never more than an inch or two above the ankle. And though the changing times and fashions fascinated her, she openly admitted that she could no longer imagine the future and preferred to revisit the past, specifically that time before Gerard.

"Are you still a communist, dear?" Noonie asked Dosia toward the end of dinner, which had consisted of oxtail soup, followed by pheasant, red cabbage, leeks and beetroot in a white sauce.

"I was never a communist, Noonie. But I am and will always be a socialist."

"Ah yes," said Noonie, nodding. "I always muddle those two. Of course, I'm not a political woman myself. Well, we weren't brought up to be so in my day. But that's all changed . . . like everything else," she said, scraping the crystal bowl of vanilla cream. "And I forget now who the man is . . . the one in charge," she added.

"The prime minister, Mr. Baldwin," offered Mabel.

Conversations flowed simultaneously.

"So have you met anyone . . . anyone special?" Dosia asked, leaning forward, staring at Daisy.

"Mr. Baldwing!" declared Noonie.

Daisy shook her head. "I haven't been anywhere to meet anyone."

"Not Baldwing, Mother: *Bald-win*. Mr. Stanley Baldwin."

"But what about you-know-who?" whispered Dosia.

"Baldwin?" repeated Noonie.

Daisy smiled. "No, I've told you—it's not like *that*."

"What is it like?"

"A big mustache . . . Yes, I can picture it now. He does have a mustache, doesn't he, Mabel?"

"I'm not sure. It's hard to describe," said Daisy.

"No, you're thinking of Mr. MacDonald, Mother."

"But he does have something about him, doesn't he?" said Dosia.
Then conversations merged.

"*Mr. MacDonald?*" said Noonie, turning to Dosia.

Daisy laughed.

"Yes," said Dosia. "It must be that big mustache of his," she added, winking at Daisy.

After dinner, the women returned to the drawing room, where Dosia played some of Iris's records on the gramophone and danced with Daisy while Mabel and her mother looked on. But when Mabel got up and began to dance too, her mother swiftly followed. It was only when Blundy came into the room to check on the fire that Mabel realized how loud the music was, how ridiculous they might look to him—Dosia doing some strange ballet-type dance and leaping about the room, Daisy following suit, Noonie with her long dress hitched up and in a world of her own—and she quickly sat down.

Later, in her boudoir, after the other women had gone to bed, Mabel was relieved to find a note from Mrs. Jessop, in her usual telegraphic style: "MISTER LANG. SAYS. NO MORE VENISON TILL NEW YEARS. HAVE ORDERED PEASANT AND GINEY FOWL. INSTED."

Hallelujah! Mabel thought, another small obstacle overcome. It was so very tricky with domestic staff these days, but no one wanted the unenviable task of having to replace them—particularly not a cook. They were without doubt the hardest to find. Like gold dust, she thought, kissing Mrs. Jessop's handwritten note.

Mabel glanced to her list, now satisfyingly awash with small check marks. Only one detail—a person—remained unconfirmed, and the question mark next to the name bothered her more than it should have. She had yet to receive a reply to the letter she'd penned so carefully, then stamped and taken to the post office herself. She smiled. They would come, she thought; they'd simply not be able to stay away. And Mabel picked up her fountain pen, crossed out the question mark and placed a large check mark next to the name.

Chapter Five

Two days before Christmas, shortly before the dressing bell sounded, and as snow began to fall, Howard Forbes's silver Rolls-Royce drew to a halt outside the oak front door. Minutes later, a black taxi pulled up behind it and his elder daughters, Iris and Lily, stepped out.

That evening, dinner as usual was served promptly, and almost exactly an hour and fifteen minutes later the family rose from the table and repaired to the drawing room. As the clock on the mantelpiece struck nine, Daisy and her father stood hand in hand at the oriel window watching snowflakes fall. Behind them, the murmured voices of Daisy's mother and grandmother, her sisters and aunt, mingled with the sound of Debussy emanating from the wireless.

"Magical . . . ," said Daisy.

"Like you," her father whispered.

Once described as Olympian, Howard Forbes towered over his

youngest daughter, for Daisy had taken after her mother in physical appearance, inheriting Mabel's heart-shaped face, pale skin and gray-green eyes, and the very same five-foot-two-inch frame. Howard, on the other hand, had bequeathed his dark looks and height to his two elder daughters.

"We should make a wish," said Daisy. "You used to tell me that if I made enough of them, one or two would undoubtedly come true. Wishes made gazing up at stars and over rainbows and birthday candles and lost teeth. Wishes made throwing your precious pennies into streams and fountains, and wishes made over my snow globe at Christmas. Do you remember?" she asked, glancing at the globe on the table beside them.

Inside the glass orb were tiny pine trees, a replica of Eden Hall in miniature and hand-painted gold stars—each one studded with a tiny diamond at its center. A present to Daisy from her father when she was no more than five years old, the snow globe was brought out each year and placed in the same spot, its limited appearance making it a veritable treasure of Christmas. And Daisy continued to be mesmerized by it. She imagined them all—herself and her family—inside the miniature house: tiny people with giant souls and infinite love in their hearts, safe and warm beneath the glass, beneath those diamonds and gold stars.

But tonight there were no diamonds in the sky. No silver moon, no gold or guiding star was visible. It was simply that the universe was black and the earth was white, Daisy thought, staring out through the window once more. Yet there was an unexpected alchemy to this, to the tiny white crystals dancing out of the darkness toward them and the light and the softly crackling "Clair de Lune."

"Yes, a lot of wishes," Howard conceded languidly. "And have any of them come true?"

"I can't tell you that," she said, smiling.

When the telephone rang, neither one of them turned.

"I'll get it!" Iris called out. "Hello . . . Yes, it's me . . . Hello, darling!"

"You used to tell me them *all*," Howard continued. "You used to tell me as soon as you'd made a wish what it was you'd wished for. You could never keep a secret."

"No, not from you."

"And can you now?"

"Keep your secrets or my own?"

"Your own, of course. I wouldn't dream of burdening you with mine."

Daisy laughed.

"No, darling, absolutely not," Iris's voice went on. "I'm stuck down here for the *whole* time."

"The great shame of it—which I suppose is a secret in itself—is that I have no secrets . . . and yet, I'm rather longing for some," said Daisy.

Now her father laughed. "You shouldn't. Secrets are invariably things one's ashamed of, whether about oneself or another."

In the dim light the contours of his face were sculptural and gray, and his smile fell away a little too quickly. His silver hair was swept back from his brow and the line of his mouth—thinner, slightly downturned at the corners now—lent him a more severe look than Daisy was used to or wished to see. It struck her then, and for the very first time, that there was something more than mild frustration locked in his features: the trace of some private unhappiness or perhaps loneliness. And as Daisy gripped the smooth flesh in his hand a little tighter, she heard Iris again: "Like being sedated, darling . . . Quite . . . Of course . . . You, too. Good-bye, darling."

Daisy looked over at the large mirror hanging above the fireplace, saw Iris sashay across the room and up to it, pucker her painted lips and blow a kiss back at her.

"You must think of something to wish for," said Daisy, turning her attention back to her father. "And concentrate. That's what you used to tell me."

He'd been the one who had taught Daisy to dream, and it was one of the reasons she loved him, loved him above and beyond all others, and yet he had been absent for so much of her life. For a moment she saw her younger self waiting once more upon the wall by the gated entrance, waving furiously, then climbing down and running across the grass toward the car so the two of them could walk that last stretch together, hand in hand. Those moments when she had had to cram it all in, tell him everything before the others: . . . *and Lily said . . . and Iris told me . . . and it's simply not fair, is it?*

Her father had always taken time to listen to her, nodding at the latest great travesty of justice, the catastrophic events of that day or week, and the inhumanity of the treatment meted out to her by her two elder siblings, from time to time gasping or shaking his head in disbelief. And yet he had not lied to her and did not pander to her tears, but sensitively, tenderly and seemingly with great thought and care he used the word *we: We must be reasonable . . . we need to set an example . . . we must try to understand . . . we must not reduce ourselves to that level.* It was, had always been, *we.* In his capacity as judge, jury or ombudsman, his words—*my last words on this*—were a true and lawful verdict, to be upheld and obeyed, and then, sometimes, repeated back: *Well, Daddy says . . .*

To Daisy, her father remained invincible, unsinkable, like a mighty ocean liner barely swayed by the unpredictable and truculent currents in which Daisy increasingly found herself—or imagined herself to be. His manners, morals and virtues were unquestionable. He seemed to know all that there was to know. She could, she often thought, tell him anything, because he understood and because she believed in him and believed him.

"Have you done it? Have you made your wish?" she asked.

"Yes."

"Well, don't tell me."

"I wasn't going to."

"Good."

"Have you made yours?"

"No. I'm about to now . . ."

Daisy closed her eyes tight and kept them closed for some minutes, concentrating on the word *happy*: happy home, happy family, happy father. Then, "Done!" she said, opening her eyes and turning to him. But he said nothing and continued staring out through the window, his expression impassive, his gaze fixed beyond the blackness, beyond the confines of that house and even its land.

"You don't seem particularly cheerful tonight. Is anything the matter?" she asked.

Her father sighed and smiled and cast his eyes downward. "I'm a little tired, that's all. And I rather need a drink, but there doesn't appear to be any soda water—or any ice."

"Mother gave Blundy the night off. He's gone with Hilda to the concert at the village hall." She paused for a moment, then, quieter, she said, "Not right now, not tonight, but at some stage I need to talk to you about Stephen."

"Stephen?" he said, turning to her.

"Yes, I need to talk to you about his life . . . his future. I think it's important, and I'm concerned, very concerned."

Howard smiled wearily. He raised his hand to her brow and pushed back a wisp of hair. "My angel . . . always so concerned about everyone," he said. "We shall sit down first thing tomorrow and talk about Stephen."

"In private?"

"In private."

Daisy wrapped her arms around his waist. "I love you," she whispered. She stood on the very tips of her toes to kiss his cheek. "I'll fetch you some soda water and ice," she said, then stepped away from him into the brightness of the room.

She lifted the silver ice bucket from the drinks trolley, placed it on her head and attempted to walk like Iris across the Turkey carpet toward the door, hands on hips. Inevitably it toppled. Luckily she caught it. Her grandmother gasped, shook her head. "Such high jinks . . . There'll be an accident yet."

She crossed over the hallway swinging the empty bucket like a child crossing sands to the sea, and took a short cut through the dining room, where candles still flickered among strewn linen napkins. She paused at the baize door, smiling at the hushed voices of Mrs. Jessop and Nancy on the other side. And then she pushed gently, very gently . . .

"Don't look at me like that. It's the truth."

Daisy leaned closer.

"I'm telling you, *he is*. He's back with that fancy woman of his," continued Nancy. "Mrs. What's Her Name, the actress."

"Mrs. Vincent," offered Mrs. Jessop.

"That's her. Margot Vincent. It's where your Stephen drives him every Sunday night . . . Well, an actress; it's only to be expected, I suppose. It's poor Madam I feel sorry for, turning a blind eye all these years while he gallivants about up there, leading a double life."

"Mr. Forbes may not be a saint, Nancy, but he's not all bad . . . I know that much."

"Well, I'm not so sure. Not anymore."

"He's done many good deeds," Mrs. Jessop muttered.

"Oh, I know you said he was good to that poor bastard child, but—"

"Don't use that word," Mrs. Jessop interrupted. "I happen to know the child's very loved."

The sound of a chair scraping the kitchen's stone floor made Daisy step back from the door. The universe rocked; the room slid sideways. And as random images spiraled toward her like the snowflakes she had a minute ago been watching, there was a strange juddering vibration—inside her chest, her throat, her head: like a motor over-revving and stuck in acceleration—because there had been no warning, no warnings of any bend ahead. Enlightenment had come with the same impact as a car traveling at great speed hitting a wall.

Dazed, she turned and walked back to the hallway and sat down on the bench by the tree. Somewhere in the distance she could hear music intermingled with laughter and shrill-sounding voices. Somewhere in the distance she could hear *him*: as smooth as velvet, innately charming and in control. And somewhere in the distance she heard herself whisper, *Daddy*.

When Daisy finally rose to her feet she was still trembling. And though her heart continued to pound, that initial downward dash had become an ever-slowing reeling sensation. But a new weight rooted her, making her feet reluctant, her limbs heavy. And so, slowly, very slowly, empty-handed, her arms hanging down by her sides, she moved toward the open doorway, the music, the voices, and crossed over the threshold. She cast her eyes about the room, over the silk brocades, tapestries and tasseled velvets, over the crowded mahogany and walnut surfaces glinting with silver and china and glass; and the snow globe, with its miniature house and pine trees and diamonds in the sky. All ornamentation, she thought: all of it a lie, shielding him—her father.

And there he was, Howard Forbes, a dinner-suited arm resting upon the black marble mantel, empty glass in one hand, cigar in the other.

"No ice?"

He didn't deserve a response. She couldn't offer him one. She stared back at that familiar smile: one craved a moment ago, craved every moment ago. She wanted to speak, wanted simply to say, *Oh, Daddy, tell me it isn't true . . . please tell me . . .* Then her mother spoke: "Is everything all right, dear? You look as though you've seen a ghost."

Daisy did not look at her mother, could not look at her mother. And she couldn't offer up any words in case they were the wrong ones. Words were now muddled, and *fancy woman* and *bastard* had built a monster.

And then the monster spoke: "Dodo? Whatever's the matter? It's Christmas—remember? The season to be jolly . . . peace and goodwill and all that, hmm? Come here . . ."

He put down his glass and moved toward her—cigar in mouth, arms outstretched. What happened next would become blurred with the passage of time, for some. And certainly Lily wasn't to know and had always teased Daisy in that way, calling her "Daddy's girl." But right at that moment those two words were obscene to Daisy, an insult every bit as revolting as the man who was about to put his arms around her.

When Daisy raised her arm, it was a swift, instinctive move. She gave no thought to the burning cigar, which caught and scorched the side of her hand before flying in an arc across the room and landing in her grandmother's lap, causing the old woman to screech and jump from her chair—knocking over the heavily laden butler's tray and colliding with Dosia, clutching a decanter of sherry. Daisy did not hear her own words, shouted—some might say screamed—at her father: "Don't touch me!"

In the commotion that followed, amidst the cacophony of three yapping dogs and Debussy, still, and louder and more dramatic than ever, Lily burst into tears: because scenes did not happen at Eden Hall, and because it was Christmas, and because—Daisy supposed—Lily didn't and couldn't understand. Then, after the mess of broken glass and spilled drinks had been cleared, after Mabel had asked someone to please turn off the wireless, after Noonie had been pacified with "just a small sherry, please," after Lily had called Daisy a "stupid little fool" and after Iris had told Lily, "Oh, do shut up; you know nothing anyway," Howard quietly excused himself and went to his study, leaving the six women to ponder *their* hysteria.

Chapter Six

At first, no one spoke. Iris sighed and fluttered her made-up eyes heavenward. Lily stretched out the fingers on her left hand, pouting sulkily at her diamond engagement and wedding rings. Noonie sniffed, took a sip of her sherry and turned to the empty chair next to her as though about to speak, but then stopped. And Dosia sat with her eyes closed, quietly humming "Hark! The Herald Angels Sing."

"Leave it," said Mabel—unusually curt, unusually loud—when the telephone rang and Iris leaped to her feet. "Please, leave it, dear," she said again, quieter.

Iris sat down.

Mabel's mouth twitched. It was Christmas, she reminded herself. *Christmas.* These things happened. There was no point in screaming, becoming hysterical—too many of her sex had succumbed to that, and where had it got them? She quickly glanced at

Dosia. It had—in a way—got them the vote, given them a voice. But the term *hysterical*—so derogatory, and so often used by men, so often used by her own father—had made Mabel confused about that other word, *passion*.

Mabel looked over at Daisy, gazing once more into the snow globe on the table next to her, daydreaming again. But what on earth had made her attack her father like that? So out of character . . . She glanced again at Dosia, whose eyes remained tightly closed; then she turned to her mother, who stared back at her and shook her head: *No*.

No. Noonie was right. It must be left alone. Despite her forgetfulness, her mother still had moments of clarity.

Mabel cleared her throat. "Mrs. Jessop tells me there might be as much as five inches of snowfall tonight." It was a start. She had to keep going. "Yes, she says we're in for a very cold spell . . . and even worse to come in the New Year." She smiled up at the ceiling: "But a white Christmas will certainly be very pretty . . ."

"It always used to be so," said Noonie, eager to take the baton and run with the conversation. "Do you remember when you were young, Mabel? There was *always* snow at Christmas."

Mabel tried out a little sound of amusement. It was not the time to disagree with her mother. "Oh yes, always." She ran her hands simultaneously over the upholstered arms on either side of her chair. It was a struggle, but they had to get back to where they had been, somehow. She looked to her mother for reinforcement.

"Of course, in my day," Noonie began, a little croaky but nonetheless committed; and Mabel smiled, the warmth of relief flooding her tense body, grateful to her mother for another well-worn anecdote, removing them further from what would in years to come be referred to as the Cigar Incident.

Daisy's outburst, her irrational behavior, had been a momentary lapse, Mabel concluded, smoothing out a crease in her crepe jersey dress. *Sometimes we'd* all *like to scream,* she thought. Even she. Oh yes, even she. Though she had long ago learned how to scream in silence, or how to stuff a handkerchief into her mouth. And if she had not, where would she be now?

But flightiness and sudden rages were, Mabel had read, common traits among modern young women who were given to thinking too much. And Daisy was quite modern . . . Not as modern as Iris, perhaps, but modern enough. And Daisy appeared to think a little too much. She was without doubt the most enigmatic of Mabel's three daughters, and she would need a certain type of man to cope with such a passion for pondering. Was Ben Gifford the one? Mabel doubted it, and it would be over Howard's dead body—or so Howard had said at the end of Ben's unfortunate and overly long stay with them last summer. But there was plenty enough time for Daisy. It was Iris Mabel was concerned about. Iris: There was a conundrum. But before Mabel could contemplate this further, the telephone rang out once more. Iris immediately looked to her mother, who nodded. And they all remained silent as Iris took another call.

"The *Embassy?* . . . *Tonight?* . . ."

"Ah, sounds like an emergency at the embassy," whispered Noonie. "Is she very involved there, Mabel?"

"It's a club, Mother . . . a nightclub."

"No, 'fraid not . . . 'Fraid so . . . Yes, tricky . . . I *wish* . . . And you, darling . . . Good-bye."

Iris sat back down and glanced to her mother: "Awfully sorry. About the telephone, I mean."

"You must tell the people at the embassy to send you a telegram in future," said Noonie. "The telephone line needs to be kept clear for emergencies. Isn't that right, Mabel?"

"Oh my, I almost forgot to tell you all," said Lily, coming to. "I've decided to go with lilac for our guest bedroom. It goes with the fabric I've chosen and I've always adored that color. Miles says—"

"If you don't mind, I think I'll go to bed now," said Daisy, interrupting her sister and standing up. "I'm sorry about earlier. It was . . . completely irrational. I don't know what came over me," she added.

"Emotions are far better out than in," said Dosia. "I'm a fervent believer in free expression . . . And I don't in the least blame you for wanting to slap my brother. I've longed to for years. In fact, there are very few men I've met that I have *not* wished to slap," she added, winking at Daisy.

Everyone laughed, including Mabel, who beckoned Daisy over to where she was sitting and then took hold of her daughter's hand. "Let's say no more about it. But perhaps it would be nice if you went and bid your father good night. I think he'd like that."

It was close to midnight and Mabel had been at her desk for some time when her husband opened the door of her lamplit boudoir. It was a small, cluttered room with lace-draped French doors leading out onto the garden, situated on the eastern side of the house, next to the morning room and opposite Howard's study and the billiard room.

Mabel stared back at her husband's bewildered face. "I've told you, Howard, I have absolutely no idea. I rather think *you* should know what you did to upset her, not me. Did she come and say good night to you? I asked her to."

Howard shook his head.

"Well, you must have done or said *something*."

He appeared to be genuinely mystified. He looked tired and, Mabel noted, rather hurt.

"We had been chatting . . . about nothing in particular as I recall, wishes and secrets . . . the usual sort of Daisy stuff . . . ," he began hesitantly, remembering. "Then she went off to fetch me some ice. I thought she was taking a while, and then . . . when she returned, well, you saw."

"Perhaps it was that. Perhaps it was the fact that you sent her off for ice," Mabel suggested with a shrug of her shoulders. "You know how she disapproves of people drinking." She cast her eyes to the clock on the wall and then to her paper-strewn desk. It was much too late for any inquisition. "You of all people should know by now how emotional—dare I say *passionate*—we women can sometimes be."

"And what do you mean by that?"

"My dear, think of your own mother . . . your sister, your daughters . . ." Mabel went on, taking care not to include herself in the lineup. "I'm quite sure it'll all be forgotten in the morning . . . and she'll explain, apologize. And if not, well, you must ask her directly why she behaved toward you in that way."

Howard nodded. He bent down, kissed his wife's forehead. Mabel watched the door close; she listened to the sound of his footsteps fade. "Good night, Howard," she whispered. Then she closed her eyes, inhaled deeply and reminded herself not to dwell on him or on the past. It was Christmas, another family Christmas, and they had to get through it. *She* had to get through it. And this year she had a special surprise for Howard.

She smiled and returned to her lists.

Benedict Gifford was to be collected from the 12:26—along with Lily's husband, Miles; which would make them nine for luncheon . . . and dinner—or eleven, if Patricia and Bernard Knight made it through the snow. Then she remembered: Reggie. "Ten . . . or twelve," she said aloud, relieved.

Aside from meal plans, numbers and menus, there was on Mabel's small desk a list of Christmas presents—those wrapped marked with a capital W, the initials of the recipient next to each item. There was a list of rooms allocated to guests with dates in and dates out and notes on specific needs—such as Miles's desire for coffee instead of tea to be brought in to him at eight, and her mother's need for a chamber pot (to be emptied each morning). There was a "Laundry" book, a "Mending" book and a "Dressmakers & Tailors" book, a ledger for staff wages and another for general household expenditure. There were invoices, paid and unpaid and pending; and invitations, and RSVPs, and postcards and letters—from friends, from family and from charities dependent on her support.

This was Mabel's life, or had been, once. Because many of those books and habits—though Mabel hung on to them, perhaps in denial, or in longing for what had been and waiting for its return—were, in truth, redundant and quite unnecessary. The number of servants at Eden Hall had late one summer and in a matter of weeks dropped from fourteen to seven, then to five. Of the seven men from Eden Hall who'd gone off to fight, two had survived, but only one had returned there to work. And regular houseguests—those vibrantly colored Saturday-to-Monday creatures who had spilled out of cars and into the house, filling it with noise and laughter—were, too, a thing of the past. The war had silenced the party, and now it was simply too costly to live like that.

When Mabel finally rose from her desk, she turned off the lamp, paused by the window and pulled back the curtains. Snow continued to fall, blanketing the contours beyond in ever-thickening white, creating newly fat shapes of the topiary and specimen trees. From where she stood, Mabel could see the light of Daisy's room, burning so brightly that even through the veil of falling snow it appeared for a moment as though the window were open. Briefly, Mabel wondered what her youngest daughter was doing. Hopefully collected, hopefully composed, she thought, moving away.

Climbing the stairs, Mabel ticked off and added to the list in her head: rooms and beds still to be aired . . . clean towels and new cakes of soap to be put out . . . At the top of the stairs she paused and thought for a moment of looking in on Daisy. But it was late and she was weary, and she simply could not cope with any more histrionics. Furthermore, it was, she knew, only the very beginning of a potentially hazardous week. As she passed her husband's bedroom door she could hear the low rumbling from inside, picture him lying on his back, mouth open. He hadn't always been like that, she thought, and a glimmer of a younger Howard fought to break through in her memory. She pushed it away. There was no point in remembering, not now. It had been too long, much too long. Excluding the cursory kisses of their weekly hellos and good-byes, and the others reserved for special occasions and birthdays, Howard had not touched her in years, and she tried to remember how long, exactly, it had been.

Hanging her dress away, closing the wardrobe door, Mabel sought to recall the last time. She stretched up her arms, pulled on her nightgown, feeling the silken fabric fall over her naked body like gossamer in a spring breeze, and slowly moved to the bathroom. She raised her eyes to the face in the mirror: the dark curls now silvering at the temples; eyes once bright now dull; the lines around those eyes and the other lines—running from either side of her nose to her mouth, her chin. Time, not Howard, had taken her and made her *his*, she thought. She pressed the two tiny slivers of soap together in her hands, turned on the taps and washed away the threat of tears. Then she picked up the rough towel and held it to her face.

"Six years," she said finally, turning back the voluminous eider-down. *Six years*, she thought, climbing beneath the cold linen and pulling up layers of blankets. She stretched out an arm, pushed a switch and turned onto her side, rubbing her feet against the warm hot-water bottle at the end of the bed, wrapping her arms around herself, remembering.

Howard, once so dashing, so attentive and in love with her, had all but vanished from her life. Now she and her husband were more like business partners, running a home, a family; making the day-to-day—or rather, week-to-week—decisions about that place. He came; he went. Inevitably weary. But he had not always been like this, she thought, her heart lurching once again.

At first, she had blamed her husband's neglect on the war. Not that Howard had gone to the front, thank God. He had escaped that horror because he and his business were deemed necessary, and because he'd been too old anyway, even then. No, she had blamed the war simply because *it* was blamed for everything: from a general collective malaise to each individual shift in attitude. *It's because of the war* had been said by so many and for so long that Mabel came to believe it was also in some way responsible for the state of her marriage; that the profound anxiety of those long dark years had eked away Howard's love for her.

She could, she thought now, have allowed him some sort of re-prieve, perhaps, then. But their estrangement had continued. *And all this time, all these years . . . untouched . . .* smiling at late arrivals, smiling at early departures, smiling at telegrams to say DELAYED; smiling back at the children, alone. All the time hoping, hoping that this year—this month, this week, this night—he might come to her, reach out to her and love her once more. Through six springs, six summers, six autumns and winters, she had waited . . . Or had she? *Five*, she corrected herself, smiling and closing her eyes.

Downstairs in the kitchen, Mrs. Jessop was also counting: "Half a dozen guinea fowl, four brace of pheasant . . . makes eight . . . three rabbit, four pigeon, two goose, one turkey, one ham."

She would get Mr. Jessop to pluck a few of the birds and skin the rabbits first thing, make a fricassee . . . get Hilda on to the ice cream for the peach melba while she made the meat loaf and pastry for the pies: two ham and egg and two pigeon. But four pigeons wouldn't do, wouldn't be enough . . . She'd have to send Stephen out with his gun again. But no, Stephen would be needed to clear the driveways and then for chauffeuring from the station. And she couldn't ask Mr. Jessop, because that was what had set him off the last time: the sound of the gun or the feel of it in his hands—she could never be sure which it had been.

Mrs. Jessop's husband didn't say much. In fact, he had barely spoken since returning from the war. And though at first, it had been queer to be with someone so silent, Mrs. Jessop was long used to it now, and long in the habit of improvising during their one-sided conversations, answering any questions she (and others) posed to him *for* him. And he was a very agreeable sort. And he adored Stephen, and Stephen was ever so good with him, so patient and gentle and caring.

Mrs. Jessop had long since hung up her apron and sat next to the range, still warm, in a wheel-back chair. Beside her hung a variety of long-handled copper pans and ladles and skimmers and large spoons—slotted and wooden. A toasting fork and two flat-irons stood on a rack in front of the range, along with the old bellows she still liked to use, and hanging below the knife box were the old snuffers and scissors for candles.

These hard objects were a queer source of comfort to Mrs. Jessop, and she liked to look at them. They hadn't changed, and they reminded her of her childhood, that time when she'd worked in the fields, harvesting and haymaking from dawn till dusk with her grandfather and grandmother, her parents and siblings. At seven years old she'd been driving small birds from the turnip seeds; scattering off rooks from the peas; waving about a stick tied with a white handkerchief; working from six in the morning until nine at night.

Mrs. Jessop liked to remember. She liked to sit there at that time of night, when she didn't have to share the kitchen with anyone else, when the only sounds were those reassuring creaks and clanks and shudders of pipes or floorboards, or the drip of a tap, and now the intermittent whirring of the new refrigerator in the scullery. Not that she was at all sure of that, mind you. In fact, she had only just sat back down from checking on it, staring at it from the safe distance of the scullery doorway, when it had started its strange juddering again and given her a fright. Well, they'd managed for enough years without one, and the use of electricity to keep food cold didn't make much sense to her; an unnecessary expense, in her opinion. But folk seemed caught up with newfangled gadgets these days, and they were advertised all over the place, even in *True Love Stories. Fair enough,* she had said to Mr. Jessop, *if you have that much money to burn,* and he had agreed with her, had nodded—in that way he always did.

Hopefully no one would ever suggest replacing the range, she thought, glancing to its blackened facade. Three sturdy doors—two eyes and a nose—looked back at her beseechingly, like a familiar old face threatened with extinction. It would be over *her* dead body. Nobody in their right mind would cook with electricity. She certainly would not. And yet, it seemed to her as though the world wouldn't stop until it had changed *everything.* And for no need. More money than sense, she sometimes thought, because you could buy almost anything these days, even ice cream. She preferred her own, using the old wooden ice cream maker, where you put the chopped ice into the outer bowl and the cream, sugar and other ingredients in the inner bowl and then turned the handle, slowly, over and over, until the cream was gelled—the way she had been taught all those years ago.

Mrs. Jessop's thoughts continued to drift. Plagued by nostalgia, she more than hankered for the past. It was to her like the iridescent tip of a dragonfly's wing hovering in the long, sultry summer of her memory. She wished with all of her heart to be back in that place, to feel the warmth of the sun on the back of her young neck once more, to catch a glimpse of *him* once more.

"Michael," she whispered.

One of the reasons she liked to be alone in the kitchen at this time of night was so she could think about him and sometimes say his name out loud. Everybody liked to do their thinking in private; it was the only way to think properly, and certainly the only time she could. If she had been at the cottage with her husband, well, she couldn't have thought about Michael, because it would have been disloyal . . . and he might see her smile or something and wonder what she was thinking about, and then she'd have to tell him because she didn't believe in lying and it would very likely set him off on one of his turns, and she didn't want that. No, it was always better to think about Michael in private.

Whenever Mrs. Jessop thought of that time, and of Michael, it was impossible for her not to remember her cousin Nellie and Mr. Forbes. She cast her eyes over the table—already laid for breakfast, over the assortment of eggcups and teacups and plates, the image in front of her transforming itself to a smaller table, a basement kitchen and Mr. Forbes holding the tiny infant in his arms. He was ever so good with babies, destined to have a few, at least. Destined to be a father, she thought. No, he was not a saint, but he was a good man at heart.

"All in the past," Mrs. Jessop murmured.

But the past almost always came calling at this time of night, and in the roll call of lost names Mrs. Jessop was tempted always to remember the others, those who had once been with her at Eden Hall. She began to go through the names in her head and then stopped. She didn't want to get maudlin; it was Christmas, and they were in a better place now anyway. But it was hard not to think of them at this time of year, and hard not to see and hear them, too: the ghosts of the kitchen and servants' hall. And yet so much had changed, so many had gone, that that time often seemed like a dream to Mrs. Jessop. As though she had imagined it all. As though she'd imagined him, Michael.

She smiled, closed her eyes . . .

The sun had been high in the sky, the grass long and filled with buttercups and poppies. She could hear the stream, the sound of bees, nothing more. Nothing more. He said, "This is perfect." He said, "You're perfect." He said, "Remember this always."

She had not imagined him: She had known great passion once.

The clock on the wall chimed the half hour. The house was silent; *everyone asleep,* she thought, easing herself to her feet. The pain in her hip was always worse at night, and she had been sitting in that chair for far too long. The pipes let out another shiver, swiftly followed by a loud judder. She hoped they wouldn't freeze and burst again. She straightened herself with a grimace, cast her eyes about the room, then tilted her head, listening for a sound from the scullery. But the machine, too, seemed to have at last gone to sleep, and so she turned off the electric light and headed down the passageway to the back door, reminding herself in whispers about tasks for the morning.

It was still snowing when Mrs. Jessop stepped into the yard with her flashlight, and as she pulled her shawl up over her head she saw the light in the window of the coachman's flat. She smiled. She was lucky to have them both, she thought: one, asleep no doubt but alive; the other, wide awake and up to who knew what. *It is what it is and that's that,* she said to herself, closing the door of her cottage.

"Dear Daisy," Stephen wrote, and then paused. He still wasn't sure how to put into words what he wanted to say, and the nips of malt whiskey, which had set him off wanting to write the thing in the first place, now blurred the words on the page as well as his thinking. He heard the clank of a door down in the yard and lit another cigarette.

He wondered where she was, what she was doing at that moment. Asleep, he imagined: fast asleep and dreaming . . . Maybe dreaming of him, he thought, allowing himself an indulgence that curved the corners of his mouth up into a weary smile. Oh, to feature in one of her dreams. That alone would be enough. Yes, that would be enough to keep him going for . . . for a whole year, at least. And how could he expect anything more?

He glanced down at the name and bit hard on his lip. It was a ridiculous notion, he thought, wobbling again, but he had to tell her, had to ask her. Taking liberties, his mother would call it. But she was old-fashioned and locked in the past, and times had changed—hadn't they?

He crumpled the paper in his fist, closed one eye and took aim at the grate: *If I hit it, she's mine.* It was his ninth hit—out of thirteen. Not bad, he thought, but not good enough.

"Dear Daisy," he began again.

Down a darkened passageway, behind another firmly closed door, Daisy sat at her desk with her journal. She wore the long beaver-fur coat her grandmother had given her, her flannel striped pajamas and thick woolen socks. Despite the freezing temperatures outside, the curtain was pulled back and a mullioned window stood open. Snow had settled on the outer stone ledge, and powdery flakes danced into the room, where the embers in the grate still glowed orange. From time to time Daisy lifted her head, absently following a tiny crystal's whirling descent, tapping her pencil on her lips.

Daisy's room was one of the smaller rooms at Eden Hall, was in fact the smallest bedroom, and had been hers for more than twelve years, from when the war started and she'd been moved down from the night nursery on the top floor. The mahogany desk contained two lockable drawers, one of which was where Daisy kept her journal, along with a few irreplaceable treasures: various pebbles, some marbles, a dried-out hawk-moth caterpillar in an old cigar box, a broken slingshot and some poems scrawled on scraps of torn pages in a slanting hand. Inside the other drawer were less valuable items: buttons and ribbons, postcards, items of jewelry and the hand-me-down Elizabeth Arden rouges and lipsticks Iris had given her.

On top of a chest of drawers was the china phrenology head from Aunt Dosia, which showed every part of the brain and its corresponding function, such as AGREEABLENESS and SPECULATION. Next to it, a bookcase containing every book Daisy had ever read and her old collection of scrapbooks—with transfers and cuttings pasted in crooked—butted up against a line of cupboards, the front panels of which were covered in the same paper as the walls, a gray and pink trellis pattern. A variety of pencil sketches and watercolors—some faded, many poorly framed, of petals, leaves and stems, fungi and butterflies—adorned the walls, along with a signed photograph of Rudolph Valentino.

Having gone to bed early, having had time to think *and* down a drink (gin, purloined from the larder while Mrs. Jessop was in the servants' hall), Daisy now had no doubt—none whatsoever—that what she had overheard was true. Her father, Howard, had a mistress. He was nothing more than a philanderer, a rich philanderer. "Nouveau riche philandering hypocrite," she wrote in her journal, underlining the last word twice. He was in all likelihood a sex maniac, and probably no different from that man she'd recently read about who had kept three separate families and countless women in various parts of north London. And that poor child, she thought, shaking her head, remembering Nancy's words; somewhere, she had another sister or brother.

It was her own fault, she decided, that she felt such shock, such pain. She had romanticized her father, endowed him with qualities he had never in fact possessed. He was less than ordinary, because ordinary implied a modicum of decency, which Howard clearly lacked.

She would speak to Stephen first thing in the morning, she decided. She needed to hear from him where, exactly, he drove her father each and every Sunday evening. But why had Stephen *not* told her? "Sworn to secrecy?" she wondered out loud. And yet did a promise to her father override and mean more to Stephen than *their* friendship? If it were true—she shook her head; she knew it was true—Stephen had been colluding with her father, colluding in her father's double life.

She held her nose, took another swig from the bottle and lit another of Iris's Turkish cigarettes, then sat back in her chair, placed her feet upon the desk and tried to focus her thoughts.

Yes, she'd get an address from Stephen. "But what can one do— even with an address?" There was no way she could get up to London, and what would she say in a letter? What she wanted to do and what she *could* do were two different things. What she wanted to do was go up to London and confront Mrs. Margot Vincent; what she wanted to do was march into her father's bedroom right now, cigarette in hand, and shout, *Fucking wanker,* like those boys who came to stay during the war. But what good would that do? And if her mother knew all of this anyway, *if* she had been turning a blind eye, hadn't she also been protecting him? And wasn't she then also culpable?

It was all too confusing. Unbelievable. She needed to think . . .

And why did women *not* think? Why did they allow themselves to be . . . to be used in that way? After all, it was about to be 1927! And how could women ever claim equality if they allowed themselves to be used like that? Enslaved to men, pandering to them, protecting them. What the world needed were more women like her aunt Dosia. She didn't care what any man thought, what *anyone* thought.

A new possibility occurred to Daisy: Mabel *and* Margot Vincent were both being used by her father. One to run his home and look after his family, the other to . . . No, she could not bear to think about what her father and the actress got up to. She shook her head—he was over fifty! And she imagined Mrs. Vincent must be equally ancient.

Daisy lifted her feet from the desk and picked up her pencil. She glanced at the cigarette in her hand. It had gone out again. There was a definite art to this smoking lark. She leaned forward, tossed the thing out of the open window, then nipped her nose, took another swig, shivered and wrote: "I have tonight taken up drinking and smoking and tomorrow I shall cut off my hair."

She paused again, sniffing the air. It was a queer, unpleasant smell, acrid, almost like burning, she mused. Seconds later, after she had flicked the lit cigarette end from the fur of her coat, stumbled, picked up the phrenology head and seen the crack—a hairline fracture running through JUDGMENT—her passion finally broke. And she sat down on the floor and wept.

Daisy did not hear the door open. She saw Iris's vermilion toenails cross the carpet in front of her, heard the window close. She felt the china head as it was lifted from her hands. Then she heard herself through her tears: "He's a liar, Iris . . . He's a bloody liar."

"Yes, darling, I know."

Chapter Seven

Exhausted from her private revolution of the night before, feeling like death and as white as the newly fallen snow, Daisy rose and dressed quickly. Still shivering, she pulled back the curtains, took in the alabaster landscape beyond the iced pane of glass, then laced up her leather boots, pulled on her fur coat and her hat and went down to the kitchen. She waited a moment before pushing on the door; waited to check that the conversation had moved on from the previous evening.

It was safe. Mrs. Jessop was speaking about God. There was always a lot of talk of God and goodliness and acceptance of one's lot at Christmas, and Mrs. Jessop always spoke about Him in a different voice, with a carefully considered pronunciation, as though He might be listening. A telephone voice, Daisy thought, not that Mrs. Jessop used the telephone, and quite possibly never had.

"It's what's wrong with the country," Mrs. Jessop was saying, huddled by the range and still wrapped in her shawl. She stared into a large gurgling pan, her face engulfed in steam, her forehead already damp. The kitchen as usual smelled of boiled cabbage and beeswax and carbolic soap. "If I was prime minister," she went on, "I'd have it top of the agenda. Oh yes, I'd make church compulsory . . . make God compulsory."

"You can't make Him compulsory. That would be like . . ." Nancy took a moment. "Like communism. Anyway, I blame the war," she said. "When you think of all that praying . . . and for what?"

"But it's not just about this life, is it? No. Blessed are the poor, for theirs is the kingdom of heaven, Nancy."

"Oh, morning, miss," said Nancy, looking up from the silver cutlery spread out on the table in front of her and noticing Daisy. "Off out into the snow, are we?"

"Yes, thought I'd take a stroll."

Nancy stared at her: "Hmm. You do look like you could do with some fresh air."

"Is Stephen in the coach house?"

"No, clearing the driveway. Been at it with Mr. Blundell since gone seven," Nancy replied.

Mrs. Jessop turned to Daisy, and it was then—under the cook's narrowed gaze—that Daisy realized she felt different, newly exposed in front of them, as though their knowledge of her father's immorality somehow tainted her, too; as though they judged her by him. She moved quickly toward the door to the passageway. Mrs. Jessop called after her, "Mind how you go; it's ever so slippy out there."

The passageway at the back of the house had a herringbone-pattern red tiled floor and unpainted stone walls. A row of round windows overlooked the yard on one side, and on the other was a line of small, cell-like rooms, each with a stone floor and barred window: the scullery, with the new refrigerator (Mrs. Jessop had refused to have it in the kitchen—on grounds of safety, she'd said) and large game sink; the larder, with its slate benches and well-stocked shelves; and the butler's pantry, flower room, boot room and parcel room. At the very end of the passageway—next to the door, the tradesmen's entrance—was the locked gun room, as well as the storerooms for coal and logs.

Hilda was already busy in the flower room, wrestling with freshly cut holly and evergreen foliage. Old Jessop stood in the boot room in his apron and hat, his back to the open door, a variety of shoes and boots lined up on the bench in front of him. As Daisy walked on she heard him ask himself, "Now, is that there black or is that there brown?" It was unusual to hear the man speak.

Beneath the bars, the panes in the half-glazed door were opaque with ice, and Daisy paused for a moment to examine the intricate pattern of crystals; like a microscopic universe of burst stars, she thought, scratching at the glass. When she stepped outside, all was still and eerily quiet. The pale sky billowed, heavy with unspent snow, and long spears of ice hung from the drainpipes and gutters and from the shriveled ivy that clung to the walls of the coach house. Daisy walked on, following the newly dug gritted pathway through the snow, across the courtyard and out to the driveway. The only sound to puncture the silence was the occasional soft whoosh as snow slid from a gable or fell through the branches of trees.

When she spotted the men toward the end of the driveway, Daisy began to march more purposefully, and as she neared them she called out to Stephen. He looked up and stood for a moment leaning on his shovel—staring back at her—before propping it on his shoulder and walking toward her. Daisy took a deep breath and pinched her cheeks.

Stephen raised his cap, nodded. "Daisy . . ."

"I was hoping I'd find you . . . I need to speak with you." She moved nearer. "I need to know about Margot Vincent."

Stephen looked away, closed his eyes.

"I can't believe you knew and never told me. I can't believe you kept this from me."

He put down the shovel, anchoring it upright in a drift of snow, and then looked back at her. "I couldn't tell you," he said, shaking his head. "I couldn't."

"Where does she live? I want an address."

"London, Flood Street, number sixty-six." He pushed back his cap, placed his hands over his face. "Your father will be mortified."

"No, he mustn't know. I don't want him to know that I know. You must promise me that you won't say a word."

Stephen nodded.

"Promise?"

"I promise."

"Is she married?" Daisy asked. There were lots of women, Daisy knew, who prefixed their name with *Mrs.* who weren't actually married.

"Widowed, but only recently."

"Children?"

"One. A son. His name is Valentine."

"*Valentine?* What sort of name is that?"

"The sort of name an actress gives her son."

"Have you met him?"

"Yes."

"What's he like?"

"Nice . . . I think you'd quite like him."

"How long has it been going on?"

"I'm . . . I'm not sure."

"How long?" she asked again.

"Quite a while, I think . . . but—"

"Does she have big bosoms?"

"Daisy . . ."

"I hate her."

They stood in silence for a moment, neither one prepared to look at the other. Then Daisy said again, "I can't believe you never told me . . . that you've kept something so important, so huge about me, my life, from me."

"I'm sorry."

She stared back at him, into his eyes—suddenly wretched and guilty and tired. She shrugged her shoulders. "And I thought we were friends," she said, and then she turned and walked away.

Veering off the gritted pathway, trudging through the snow, Daisy felt unusually hot beneath the layers of wool and weight of fur. Her head pounded, her limbs felt heavy and her mouth had a bitter, metallic taste to it. When she arrived back at the house, Nancy poured her a cup of tea and offered her some toast, but the smells in the kitchen made her more nauseous than ever. And later, as she sat beneath the oriel window in the drawing room, with her paints and paper, a jar of water and a fine sable-hair brush, Daisy felt no better.

The light, which was always good in that room, so good Daisy had often thought it would be perfect as an artist's studio, was brighter than ever this morning. The gold leaf-patterned wallpaper and faded bronze- and copper-colored velvets and silks shone with an iridescence that reminded her of a sun-drenched autumn morning. That short time, usually in November, she thought, when trees clung on to their burnished leaves, dazzling the eye before they fell.

Daisy was still undecided on her life's vocation, whether to become a painter or a writer, and now it seemed not to matter. It was the stuff of dreams, she thought: a fantasy as childish as the notion of heaven . . . or a true love . . . or a faithful husband.

She turned to the snow globe on the table next to her. Even now, if she stared into it long enough, she imagined she could see them: still Lilliputian but cold and shivering, desperate to break free but trapped behind the minuscule windows of a minuscule house, in a minuscule snowbound world. If she smashed it, broke the glass, she could perhaps set them free, set herself free. Because Eden Hall was a prison—albeit a luxurious prison—and she had only ever escaped once.

It had been three years before, after she had pleaded with her father to allow her to go to a coeducational boarding school not far away. "*Bedales?*" he'd repeated. "It's not even a proper school, is it?" Daisy had been there for only two terms when she mentioned the Sunbathing Society and her parents agreed that an education in nude sunbathing was not what they were paying for.

Recently, she had appealed to her father again, telling him that she'd heard of the perfect course for her at the South Kensington School of Art. But once again he had not been forthcoming. Artists, he said, were invariably penniless, troubled souls who squandered what little money they made on gin and cigarettes. Did she really want *that sort* of life? At the time she had laughed, ruffled his silvering hair and told him that he was becoming an old curmudgeon.

"You're talented, I know . . . but seriously, Dodo, painting? It's hardly a profession . . . and you do not need a profession. Your future husband will surely arrive one day with that."

"Iris has a job."

He smiled. "Iris's little shop is a hobby, my dear. She sells dresses to her friends. And anyway, Iris isn't you."

"I could get a job," she said sulkily. "And then I could fund myself, be independent. I'm sure I could find something . . . Perhaps in an art gallery or a bookshop . . ."

Her father laughed. "My dear girl, it's out of the question."

"But why?" she persevered. "Why is it out of the question? It's not as though I'm suggesting I want to run away and join the circus or become an actress . . . and I'd be able to look after you," she went on, "live with you during the week in London . . . we'd be able to go out for dinner, to the theater . . . It must get so lonely for you being stuck up in town all week on your own."

Howard ran his hands over his hair. "Well, that's another thing. I may sell the house in London."

"Sell it?"

"Yes . . . it's . . . not needed," he said, glancing up at her. "As Iris prefers to live elsewhere, rent a flat, and I have my club . . . it's become rather superfluous. Though I'd prefer it if you didn't mention this to the others, at least not yet."

"Of course."

The house in London probably was superfluous, a luxury, Daisy concluded. Lots of families they knew had disposed of one of their homes of late. It was, as Noonie said, the way things were going. And her father must get lonely stuck up there all week on his own. It was no wonder to her that he'd prefer to spend his weeknights at his club, where there'd be company, other men like him. It had already struck her as rather selfish of Iris to insist on having her own flat when there was a perfectly good home she could have lived in with poor Howard. But her father and elder sister hadn't seen eye to eye for years and so it was probably best that they did not live together.

"I shall be sad to see the place go," she said, for want of anything better and feeling a wave of sympathy for her father. "But I could live with Iris . . . She has a spare room."

He shook his head.

"But I'm eighteen—nearly nineteen," she pleaded, "and you said—you said that when I was eighteen you'd think about it; you said you'd think about me going to London."

"Daisy, Daisy, Daisy. You're eighteen, yes, but you're still too young to go off and live on your own."

"But I wouldn't be on my own," she said eagerly. "I'd be living with Iris."

She had gone on once more about the awfulness of her life, how terribly unfair it all was, how he couldn't possibly begin to imagine what it was like; how men got to do all the exciting things, got to go to all the best places, were able to do exactly as they pleased. Her father had muttered, grunted, not said anything discernible. Would he please think about it? she'd asked. Yes, he'd conceded, he would give it some thought; but there could be no promises.

That had been almost three months ago and nothing more on the matter had been said by either one of them since. Now she understood Iris's reluctance to live with their father, and his to have her—Daisy—come and live with him. How he must have panicked when Iris had announced—because that was what she had done; she never asked for permission—that she was going to live in London, and furthermore, that she was going to rent a flat in Chelsea and set up a business nearby.

How easy it was to make sense of *everything* once one was in possession of the facts, Daisy thought now. She dipped the fine sable tip of her paintbrush into the verdurous color on the palette and glanced up at the branch of holly lying on the polished surface next to her, propped up against the snow globe. But her head continued to pound, and when her mother appeared in the drawing room doorway, Daisy gave up and put down her paintbrush.

"Jessop's gone to fetch Benedict and Miles, but I fear for him on those snowy roads . . . and the trains are bound to be running late," said Mabel.

She came and stood next to Daisy by the window, her hands clasped tightly in front of her, and Daisy—watching her, taking in all of her—thought, how can he not love her? How can he be so cruel?

Mabel raised her eyes, watching snowflakes descend once more. "Tiresome, really," she said, thinking aloud. "I shall have to tell

Mrs. Jessop to delay luncheon until one thirty . . . though she won't be happy, and your father so hates meals to be late."

"Well, he's not the bloody king!"

Mabel shot her a look.

"Sorry."

Mabel moved over to the table, picked up the branch of holly and stared at it for a moment. Then she pulled an embroidered handkerchief from her sleeve, wiped it over the table's polished surface and left the room, taking Daisy's holly with her.

It was almost two o'clock by the time the newly swelled family assembled in the dining room and sat down to Mrs. Jessop's rabbit fricassee with dumplings as hard as the ice outside. Looking down the long linen-covered table—newly festooned with arrangements of berried holly, eucalyptus and ivy, each one as evenly spaced as the three candelabra—Mabel apologized for the *unavoidable delay*. Howard sighed, pushing the hardened lumps to one side of his plate. And Noonie said, "Oh, I forgot to tell you, Mabel. I've decided to stop eating meat . . . because of my *teeth*," she added in a loud whisper, and offering her daughter a clenched smile, she revealed her new false teeth.

Miles, as usual, monopolized the conversation, his booming voice louder than ever as he went on and on about his work at the bank and interest rates and the likelihood of a promotion: January, he thought. How Lily put up with him Daisy did not know, but Lily had always wanted to marry a banker, as though they had unlimited access to the vaults. Their wedding present from Howard had been a three-bedroom house in Putney, from which Miles could easily commute by train into the city. Lily's life was made up of tennis and bridge, shopping, afternoon calls and at homes, emulating—albeit on a different scale—something of her mother's and grandmother's lives. She simply lacked the imagination for anything else, Daisy thought.

They would have a typically suburban life, Iris had said, and she'd predicted that Miles would probably one day keep a mistress in some shabby part of town. "It's the sort of thing bankers do," she'd added.

"Are you still a socialist, Dosia?" asked Miles now.

She must get so bored of that question, Daisy thought. But before Dosia could reply, Howard intervened. "Miles . . . please. No politics at luncheon."

There then followed some discussion about Daisy's pallor, initiated by Mabel, who said, "You really are awfully pale, dear . . . are you still feeling under the weather?"

"No, I am not feeling *under the weather*," Daisy replied, unintentionally sharp—and glancing over at Ben Gifford.

"She's certainly taken on the hue of the weather," Iris suggested.

"Or the hue of the Christmas tree," added Lily, smiling at Miles.

"Green!" said Noonie. "The girl's quite green, Mabel."

"Fresh air's what's needed," declared Dosia, standing up to reach over and fork Howard's dumplings. "Young girls these days don't get enough of it. Of course, I've always slept with my window wide open, even in winter, and have never had a problem with my cycle."

"Does Dosia keep a bicycle in her bedroom at London?" Noonie quietly asked Mabel.

Daisy tried to smile. She pushed her food about—arranging and rearranging it in different locations on the patterned Crown Derby, lifting only the tiniest of morsels to her mouth. It was the smell, she thought, that made her feel so nauseous. But her head continued to pound, and in truth, she felt worse than ever.

When pudding arrived, a hitherto silent Howard raised a hand and declined peach melba, but Noonie took his *and* hers, saying, "Peaches! I could live for all eternity on tinned peaches!" Howard then pushed back his chair and rose to his feet, muttering something toward the window about heartburn, and excused himself. After that, everyone seemed to slump in collective relief.

Daisy glanced up at Ben, sitting directly opposite her, between Lily and Iris, but her profound disappointment in her father seemed to have eked into everything and everyone around her. Benedict Gifford was less than she'd been expecting. He was not at all as she remembered him. He was older, a good deal older, and his hair was thinning and not dark after all. He did not look at her, had barely said a word to her since his arrival, and when he did speak she was surprised by his voice: tremulous and slightly high-pitched. But Daisy, too, had been unusually quiet, mainly due to the nausea—which swept over her at regular intervals, and through which she had been on the point of excusing herself and running to the cloakroom; but also because she had decided not to speak unless she had to when her father was in the same room.

It had stopped snowing and Lily suggested a walk through the grounds after lunch, which everyone agreed would be rather lovely. They could take the old toboggan from the coach house, Miles said, and head over to the Devil's Punchbowl. Then Nancy came in with the tray of coffee and a telegram for Mabel.

When Daisy heard the name, she at first wondered if she was simply more ill than she'd realized, maybe even delirious. But then her mother said it again. Coincidence surely, Daisy thought, smiling and feeling her face flush. Mabel remained turned toward Nancy, giving an update on the numbers for dinner.

"Do apologize to Mrs. Jessop, but I've only just received confirmation," said Mabel, and Nancy—with an odd sort of smile, Daisy noted—left the room.

"Confirmation?" repeated Daisy.

"Yes, only just had it confirmed. Mrs. Vincent and her son, Valentine, will be joining us for Christmas."

Daisy glanced over to Iris, who seemed oblivious and was talking to Dosia; she looked to Lily, who was busy making eyes at Miles, and then to Noonie, as she slithered a last peach into her mouth. Daisy felt sick. She felt hot. She stammered, "But . . . but . . . *who* is this Mrs. Vincent? And why is she coming here?"

"Daisy! Really. Where are your manners?"

"I think I need to speak with you, Mother. In private."

Chapter Eight

Mabel sat down at her desk, seemingly unperturbed but momentarily distracted by the ever-increasing paperwork and scrawled lists in front of her. "Gracious, so much to do," she said with a sigh. Then she turned to Daisy, standing in stupefied silence. "And so?"

"Well . . . it's just that . . . I think you need to know . . ."

"Yes?"

"Know a few things."

Mabel blinked and shrugged. "A few things . . ."

"I'm not entirely sure about Mrs. Vincent."

"Not sure? What on earth do you mean?"

Daisy began to pace about the room and then stopped. Her head spun. She said, "We don't know her."

"*You* don't know her, perhaps, but Mrs. Vincent happens to be an old friend of your father's."

"Do you know her?"

"Yes, of course I do. Not as well as Daddy, but I've met her on a number of occasions. She's an actress, a rather fine actress. And she's also a widow and has only her son, Valentine. So I decided to invite her for Christmas."

"*You* invited her?"

Mabel smiled as she nodded.

Like a lamb to the slaughter, Daisy thought, as another wave of nausea rose through her. "Oh, Mummy . . . But Margot is . . ."

"Ah, so you have heard of her. She is rather famous, and I do believe you *have* met her, when you were quite small—after your father and I took you to see her on the London stage in—"

"You mean he's known her all these years?"

"Yes, since long before he met me."

"I don't want her to come . . . And I don't think you know what you're doing."

"Please don't be silly, Daisy. I know what I'm doing. Your father's been working very hard and this is a little surprise for him," said Mabel, glancing away. "It's always lovely to see old friends."

A little surprise for him, Daisy mused, *a little surprise . . .* She felt hot, she felt sick and for a moment she thought she might faint. She grabbed hold of the mantelshelf. "When is she arriving?"

"In an hour or so, and I expect—"

"An hour!"

Mabel stood up. She stepped toward Daisy and placed her hand on Daisy's brow. "Oh my, but you're feverish."

"I'm not feverish, Mother. I'm simply a little . . ."

Daisy heard Mabel say something about sitting down, but as the lights began to flicker, her mother's words were sucked out of the room, and then everything went black.

It must have been a little while later, because Daisy had that sense of being more removed than she should have been from what came before. She could hear the voices. Her father was saying it looked nasty and her mother said it probably wasn't as bad as it looked and that Nancy would tidy it up. But how could Nancy be expected to tidy up the snow?

When Daisy opened her eyes, she was lying on her back on the tartan chaise longue in Mabel's boudoir. Howard was seated on the cane chair next to her, leaning over her, stroking her brow. She pushed his hand away.

"Dodo," he said, "what's all this about, hmm? Your mother tells me that you don't want anyone coming to stay . . . but it's Christmas, your favorite time of year, and we always have people to stay at Christmas."

Iris and Lily stood next to Mabel: Lily watching intently with her arms folded, Iris smiling kindly and Mabel frowning.

Daisy heard Lily whisper, "I really think you should send for the doctor . . . what with last night and then this."

Bloody Lily. She'd call out the doctor to attend to a midge bite.

Daisy tried to sit up. "No, I don't want any doctor. I don't need a doctor. I'm fine," she said.

Mabel immediately moved closer. "Do lie down, dear. You've had a rather nasty fall."

That's when Daisy felt the pain and lifted her hand to her head. Her hairline and forehead were wet, sticky, and when she looked at her fingers they were coated red.

"You fainted," Howard said, watching her. "And as you fell you caught your head on the corner of your mother's desk."

At that moment Nancy appeared clutching a bottle of iodine and a roll of white cotton. Howard stood back while Nancy bathed Daisy's head, Nancy all the time looking back at Daisy and cooing, "Poor love . . . poor little lamb . . ."

"Will it need stitches?" Howard asked, hovering.

"No, I don't think so," Nancy replied. Then, to Daisy, she said, "But I'm afraid you won't be able to wash your hair for a few days. Not until that cut you've given yourself is all better, but I think I've got most of the blood out."

"No, I don't need a bandage . . ."

"Oh, but you do. Best keep it clean and protected."

"But for how long?"

"Only a few days."

"Only a few *days*! It's Christmas . . . I can't possibly go about with a bandage on at Christmas. I'll look like an idiot—and in front of everyone . . . in front of . . ."

Daisy didn't and couldn't finish the sentence. And it wasn't the thought of wearing a bandage that made her dissolve into tears, though she knew it would seem like that to those present; it was that everything was spoiled and gone wrong. And as she tried to turn away, covering her face with her hands, it was her father who was suddenly back at her side, saying, "Dodo, please don't cry."

Daisy turned to him. "This is all *your* fault . . . all of it!"

It was then that Nancy left the room, followed by Iris and then Lily. Howard rose to his feet with a heavy sigh, and Mabel said,

"She's had a fall, Howard, bumped her head. She doesn't mean it. I know."

The two of them then carried on a whispered conversation just as though Daisy were not there: "What about sending for Dr. Milton? Just to be on the safe side? . . ." "No, Howard, there's no need. She'll be fine. I'll stay here with her; you go . . ." "Are you sure? . . ." "Yes, quite sure. Nancy will serve tea in the drawing room. Keep everyone amused and I'll be along in a little while . . ." "I'll bring you a cup of tea . . ." "No, there's no need. I'll be along presently, Howard. Please, just go . . ."

Howard left the room, and Mabel—after telling Daisy to "have a nap, darling. You'll feel so much better after a little snooze"— moved over to her desk and began to rustle papers.

Daisy turned onto her side and watched her mother: the busy back, the tiny frame—organizing their lives, all of them. Where would they be without her? It was an unimaginable, dark thought, and Daisy pushed it away and glanced about the room. Lamplit, small and cluttered, it had a womblike feel and always had had to her. Mabel's sanctuary, her boudoir, was the place she could almost always be found. How many times had Daisy run in from the garden and raced down the passageway, sliding in her stocking feet along the polished parquet floor to announce some great injustice or drama; to tell tales or to be given a kiss to make everything better? And she could tell tales now, but how could Mabel make everything better?

"Mummy . . ."

"Yes, darling?"

Daisy stared at the shape of her mother: *Turning a blind eye for years* . . .

"Oh, nothing."

Mabel and Howard collided in the passageway.

"I've just seen a taxi on the driveway. We're not expecting anyone, are we?" Howard asked.

"Yes, actually we are. It's a little surprise I've organized for you, dear."

Howard feigned a grimace and took hold of his wife's hand. "You're too good to me, Mabel, really, you are."

They walked together toward the main hallway, where the Christmas tree stood resplendent. The door to the outer lobby stood open and a car engine rumbled beyond. Mabel could hear the gramophone in the drawing room and Dosia and Noonie becoming heated over cards. She could hear the distant clanking of pans from the kitchen, and she fixed her smile.

Blundy appeared first, carrying a large hatbox, a portmanteau and a dark red leather jewelry case under his arm. Mabel watched her husband. She saw his eyes narrow as he stared at the jewelry case, saw his smile fall away. She took a deep breath and stepped forward. "Margot! How lovely to see you again. It's been too long . . ." Then she turned to her husband: "Surprise!"

"Surprise!" echoed the woman, smiling at Howard and waving her hands in the air.

Chapter Nine

When Daisy awoke, it was dark outside and her mother had gone. She lifted her hand to her still aching, newly bandaged head, then slowly rose to her feet and walked over to the wall-mounted mirror. In the dim light her face was exactly the same, apart from a shadow beneath her right eye. The white cotton bandanna lent her a look she would have welcomed years before, when she had pleaded with her nanny to bandage any small cut or bruise: to appear wounded and brave. Now she *was* wounded, and yet her real wound was not visible. How many seemingly healthy, perfect and whole people walked about with invisible gaping wounds? she wondered, moving away from the mirror and opening the door.

The thing to do was stay calm, she thought, walking down the long passageway. To control one's feelings—anger, rage, irritation. To be more like Mabel: smile . . . turn a blind eye . . . turn the other cheek as the Bible said, and for Mabel's sake more than anything else. But how dare that trumped-up floozy push her way into *their* house at Christmas! Daisy stopped: Mabel had invited her.

Daisy could hear the voices, ever louder as she tiptoed across the hallway toward the bright light of the room. She paused outside the open doorway. Ahead of her, the three spaniels—Pippa, Ruby and Boy—lay sprawled out on the rug in front of the fire, snoring loudly amidst the chatter and chink of teacups. She moved her eye to the crack in the door: She could see Iris on the other side of the room by the gramophone, looking through records with Dosia and shimmying again, and love-struck Lily and Miles sitting in the window, and Howard, loitering in the middle of the room with Ben. She crouched down to see beneath the arrangement of winter foliage obscuring her view on the other side of the door, only to glimpse the skirted bottom half of three female figures seated together on the large sofa, two of which she knew belonged to her mother and Noonie. Quietly, carefully, she pushed the Chippendale chair along the polished floor nearer to the door, slipped off her shoes, climbed up onto its leather padded seat and moved her eye back to the crack . . .

"See anything interesting?"

Daisy jumped—almost but not quite losing her footing.

"Steady," the voice whispered.

She turned. His dark hair was slicked back and he bore a striking resemblance to a young Valentino: *Every inch a Valentine,* she thought. He smiled up at her. "I'm Valentine."

"Yes, I know who you are."

She took hold of his hand, soft and warm, and stepped down from the chair. "I was actually trying to get a cobweb," she said, glancing downward, putting on her shoes.

"Nasty things."

She could detect amusement in his voice, and as she turned to push the chair back into place, he said, "Allow me."

"I'm Daisy . . . Daisy Forbes."

"Yes, I thought so," he said, turning back to her and glancing to her bandaged head.

"I had a fall earlier."

"And very nearly another just now."

"If it's all the same with you, I'd rather you didn't mention any of this . . . to anyone."

"Wouldn't dream of it. Forgotten already. Are you going to go in?"

She nodded, and he stepped aside to let her enter the room.

Noonie cried out, "Ah, and here she is, our wounded little soldier!"

Mabel quickly rose to her feet and rushed over. "Oh, darling, are you feeling quite better?"

Daisy nodded. As she did so, Valentine Vincent walked into the room—past her—and joined the others by the window. Then Mabel said, "Margot, here's my poor Daisy, who had such a horrid fall earlier."

A woman in mauve rose from the sofa. "Dear Daisy . . ." She put down her teacup and came over to where Daisy stood with her mother. "I was so very sorry to hear about your accident. A moment of distraction, loss of concentration and, oh my goodness, what can happen."

In the same way that her son was every inch his name, Mrs. Vincent was, to Daisy, every inch the actress. And there were many

inches of her. Tall, large boned and voluptuous—and with unfash-
ionably large breasts, Daisy noted—she possessed a voice that was
at once sure and deep, commanding and tremulous. Her face was
made up, powdered and rouged, and her golden hair was piled up in
that Edwardian way.

The actress turned to Mabel. "I myself had the most *horrendous*
fall last winter at His Majesty's."

For a moment Daisy thought she meant the palace and had a
flash of Mrs. Vincent tumbling headfirst down a gilt staircase.

"My ankle gave way and I simply crashed down the theater steps
and landed in a heap! Luckily nothing was broken. But my poor
ankle has never been the same."

Her eyes smiled as she spoke and her fingers moved in slow ges-
ticulation as though describing a ballet—not a random fall, Daisy
thought.

Mrs. Vincent turned to Daisy, glancing once more to her bandaged head, smiling and frowning at the same time, empathizing,
Daisy thought. "Alas, old bones don't heal the way *gorgeous* young
ones do," she said.

She appeared to Daisy to be acutely conscious of every nuance
and inflection, each pause and intake of breath; overly sincere in
the way people a little in love with themselves were; possessed more
by herself than by anyone else. Each and every utterance—from her
own lips or someone else's—evoked a little smile, as though she
knew and understood it *all*. Everything.

Mrs. Vincent turned. "Valentine, dear heart . . . Val, do come
and say hello to poor Daisy. She's had the most *frightful* day."

He moved easily across the room. He wore a dark blue velvet

jacket, white shirt and dark paisley-patterned cravat. "A pleasure to meet you," he said, extending his hand for a second time.

Maybe it was the fire—they *were* standing directly in front of it—or maybe it was the effects of her fall or the awful situation they were all in now or the one in the hallway minutes earlier—but Daisy suddenly felt a tremendous heat and felt her face flush.

"My God, you look like a veteran from the war, darling," Iris called over.

"I fell," Daisy said again, as matter-of-factly as she could muster, reaching up to the lopsided bandage once more.

As Mabel and Margot sat down, Howard came over to where Daisy and Valentine stood, closely followed by Ben, who tutted and grimaced and then said, "Poor old you"—more to the fireplace, it seemed, than to Daisy.

Iris was playing more of her new dance music on the gramophone, and when it suddenly became quite loud Howard called out, "Do turn that racket down. I can't hear myself think!" He was tense, Daisy could tell. And she wondered how it felt for him right at that moment, with his wife and mistress in the same room, all his lies and deceit safely under one roof, at Christmas.

He moved closer to her. "I thought you wanted to talk to me? Something about Stephen, you said . . ."

Daisy shook her head. "It doesn't matter."

"You said it was important."

"It's not . . . Not now."

She moved away from him, toward Valentine Vincent. "So, Mr. Vincent . . . What do you do with your life?" she asked.

"Val, please," he quickly replied, then, more hesitant, repeated,

"What do I do with my life . . . ?" He smiled, glanced downward. "Well, I'd like to say I'm a writer."

"A writer? Then say it. Why not?"

"Why not, indeed. I must learn to. But until I find a publisher for my novel . . . well, I'm never sure of laying claim to that title."

"Quite right, too," said Howard, moving nearer. "After all, a doctor can't treat patients and call himself a doctor until he has qualified . . . Stands to reason a writer shouldn't call himself a writer until he's been properly published."

"Properly?" Valentine repeated.

"Yes, a proper publisher and not one of those shabby outfits that takes money to print up any Tom, Dick or Harry's nine-hundred-page memoirs about . . . about pig farming in Yorkshire—or whatever!"

Daisy saw Ben nod emphatically. "I disagree," she said without looking at her father. "If Valentine"—Val still seemed a little overfamiliar to her mind—"wishes to call himself a writer, which is precisely what he does and how he employs his time, then he should say it and be able to say it without anyone asking for . . . qualifications. We wouldn't ask a painter how many pictures he had sold in order to establish how worthy he was to call himself that, would we? A writer you are, Mr. Vincent, and, I'm sure, a very good one at that. Don't listen to my father . . . he's a philistine," she added in a whisper loud enough for Howard to hear.

Valentine smiled at her. Howard feigned a laugh. And then Ben laughed too. But for some reason, and Daisy could not fathom why, Ben Gifford seemed different. He stood clutching his cup and saucer, smiling downward at the rug. He appeared gauche and awkward and indifferent to her, and all of it—all of *him*—was beginning to irritate her. Looking at the two men standing next to each other, Daisy noticed only Ben's age and Valentine's youth, the mediocrity of one and the charisma of the other. He must be at least thirty, she thought, glancing again at Ben. And suddenly it seemed as though there might yet be some noble purpose to Mrs. Vincent's emergence in her life.

Like her, the woman had aged, Mabel thought, staring back at Margot and smiling. Her hair, softly tinted, still golden, was graying at her temples, and she was more lined than Mabel remembered, particularly around the mouth, which Mabel now studied as Margot spoke. She was happy for Margot to talk. Happy to sit back and watch and listen. And Margot liked to talk and clearly enjoyed the sound of her voice.

The actress sat bolt upright on the sofa next to Mabel, holding her cup and saucer on her lap. She was corseted, Mabel could tell, and the mauve ensemble with buttoned breast—her stiffness and lines—brought to mind an upholstered button-back chair. Rather like the one standing directly opposite them, thought Mabel, glancing to it.

"Do you think Howard's pleased I'm here?" Margot whispered, leaning closer to Mabel.

"I'm sure he's delighted."

"I do hope so. When you wrote to me saying you wanted it to be a surprise for him, well, I did wonder . . . You see, I'm not sure he likes surprises."

"Doesn't he?" asked Mabel, widening her eyes.

Margot laughed. "Well, of course, I wouldn't really know, but I somehow imagine he doesn't." Her smile fell away. She lifted a hand to her hair, barely touching it, gently smoothing it, and looked over to where Howard stood with Daisy and the others. "I only ask because he's barely spoken to me . . . and I'm not altogether sure he was quite so pleased to see me when I first arrived," she added, her voice trailing off.

"Oh, I think he was. It was just . . . as you say, a surprise. "

The actress reached over and gripped Mabel's hand. "You're too sweet . . . And really, it's just heavenly to see you again, dear, dear Mabel. How long do you suppose it's been?"

"Six years," Mabel replied, perhaps a little too quickly, she thought.

Margot gasped. "Six years . . . Heavens, it feels like six months to me. And you know you haven't changed? No, not one bit. You must tell me your secret, Mabel."

A number of things came to Mabel's mind. She could have said, *Fresh air and life in the country*, she could have said, *Elizabeth Arden*, or she could have said, *Not being touched by a man in six years*.

Mabel said, "We've all aged, Margot. It's inevitable, I'm afraid."

Margot's eyes fluttered. "Isn't it too depressing? And so different for men."

Mabel shook her head. "They age, too."

"But not in the same way, dear. It's all so much easier for them."

Mabel was aware of Howard watching them, and as Margot went on, talking Mabel through her own exhausting beauty routine and offering to show her a cream she'd recently bought at vast expense at Harrods, Mabel kept her smile firmly in place and made sure she appeared as though she were hanging on to Margot's every syllable.

Throughout dinner, Daisy surreptitiously studied Margot and her father. Mabel had seated the woman on Howard's right, Daisy on his left. Thus, Daisy was forced to speak to him, to them, to make conversation or reply, at least, to their inane questions: How was her head? (Howard.) "Fine." Was she excited about Christmas? (Margot, as though she were a child.) "Not particularly."

She didn't mean to be rude, but she felt angry and uncomfortable. And she felt embarrassed and awkward each time Nancy or one of the servants appeared. What must they make of it all? And yet her mother, sitting at the other end of the table with Reggie by her side, seemed fine, quite happy.

"I must say, I absolutely adore your snow globe, Daisy," said Margot. "Where did it come from?"

Daisy wanted to say *From your lover, the man sitting between us, and you can have it, for all I care*. Instead, she said, "Yes, it's beautiful, isn't it? It was a present from my father."

Howard smiled, and Daisy realized it was the first time she'd seen him smile in a while.

"Daisy used to think it had magical powers," said Howard, looking at Daisy and not Margot. "She used to think that if you made wishes over it at Christmas they were bound to come true."

"How charming . . . And did they? Did any of them come true?"

Margot asked, picking up her wineglass and blinking eagerly at Daisy.

"No. None of them came true," Daisy replied, watching her father's smile fall away. "But I've only recently realized this."

"Oh, dear," said Margot, her voice filled with disappointment. "But one must never give up . . . Perhaps you should make another wish this Christmas . . . In fact, we all should. We should *all* make a wish over your snow globe, a wish for 1927, and then write them down and seal them in a box," she added excitedly. "Then, this time next year, we can see whose wish came true . . . Now, wouldn't that be fun?"

Daisy shook her head. "I'm sorry. I don't believe in any of that anymore," she said. And then she pushed back her chair and excused herself.

It was like being trapped in a nightmare, a badly written play where every line spoken was irksome and false, Daisy thought, wandering about the drawing room alone. But every single thing felt irksome to her now, from the cluttered surfaces within that room to the feel of her clothes against her skin. And as the other women filed into the room for their coffee and petits fours, she wasn't sure if she could stand much more. So when Ben Gifford appeared in the doorway and asked Mabel if he might be permitted to have a word with Daisy, Daisy smiled with relief.

"Thank you for rescuing me," she whispered, closing the door behind her.

"Rescuing you?"

"I'm finding it all rather difficult—with Margot and everything."

He stared back at her blankly. But when he said, "Can we go somewhere private to talk?" Daisy wondered if he knew, knew everything and more, and was about to divulge some new horror to her.

Benedict Gifford had only recently been promoted to general manager of Forbes and Sons. He had served in the war. Unlike his two elder brothers, uncle and cousin, he had survived two years in the trenches, only to return to lose his widowed mother to the Spanish flu epidemic. Shortly after this he had begun working for Howard.

It had been during the nightmare of the general strike earlier that year that Howard, encouraged by Ben, had gone down to the wharf with Daisy, donned an overall and operated a crane. That was when Ben had proved himself to Howard, Daisy thought, for her father had relied on him to negotiate with the unions.

Ben had visited Eden Hall a number of times and had ended up staying for more than a week in the summer when he'd taken ill with food poisoning—though Mabel had claimed it couldn't possibly be, had insisted it was something he'd brought down with him from London. As he recovered, Daisy and he had gone for walks about the grounds, and she had taken to reading the newspaper to him. The day she'd read about the actor Rudolph Valentino's sudden death, she had wept openly in front of him. They had been sitting together on the bench by the pond in the Japanese garden and he had put his arm around her and said, "I'll be your Valentino." And Daisy had been sad to see him go, *her* Valentino.

She had received a lengthy letter from him after his return to London, in which he had complimented her on her "uncommon kindness in a world increasingly short of it." He had mentioned "the sometime loneliness of bachelorhood," saying that to be welcomed into a family such as hers, even for a few short days, was a privilege. It was all very formal, and he signed himself off using his full name. She hadn't replied, but she had thought of him. There was something old-fashioned and very decent about him; he was not dissimilar to her father, she had thought.

"What is it?" Daisy asked, closing the door of Mabel's boudoir.

"Please don't look quite so worried . . . I simply want to talk to you, that's all."

Daisy sat down in the chair by Mabel's desk. Ben stood alongside her, in front of the fire, staring down at the assortment of cards and framed photographs on the mantelshelf.

"But you wanted to talk to me *in private* . . ."

"Yes," he said, turning to her. "Yes, I did. I do. But first of all, I need to ask you something. I need to know if there's . . . anyone special in your life . . . A young man?"

Daisy shook her head.

"Good. I was a little worried about *our* Mr. Vincent."

"Valentine? . . . Why?"

"He's been staring at you rather a lot . . . But that's not the point. The point is I don't trust him, and I don't particularly like him. I wanted to warn you not to be too . . . charmed. You see, I've met plenty like him." He paused and smiled. "The sorts who claim to be artists and go about in secondhand clothes and ladies' silk scarves . . . contriving to look poor *and* cultured. I'm afraid our Mr. Vincent's just another bone-idle Chelsea dilettante."

"You sound a bit sour."

Ben shook his head. "Not sour, just honest."

"Well, I don't really know him; I've barely exchanged a word with him. And I very much doubt I'll ever see him again after this Christmas."

Ben turned away from her and glanced along the line of framed photographs once more. "And what about that chap who lives here—the one who sometimes drives your father?" he asked.

"Stephen. What about him?"

"You told me, told me last time I was here that you and he were close."

"We are—or rather, we were. But it's changed . . . it's different now."

She saw him nod. "I'm sorry. You must wonder why I'm asking you such questions . . . You see, your father had words with me last summer, and then again recently, before I came down here. He told me—warned me—that you were too young for any serious attachments."

"I'm nearly *nineteen*," she said.

"I know, I know . . . And, you see, well, I have to come clean, have to tell you that I *have* become rather attached, and I dared to hope you might feel the same way," he added, glancing to her.

Daisy smiled.

"That's a relief," he said. "I know this might seem a little sudden—unexpected—but I've thought about you a great deal since I was last here. I'm very much aware that you're still quite young—that I'm a good few years older than you, and that I must be patient, and may have to wait for you to . . . to better understand your feelings, and the nature of love and all that."

"Love?"

"Yes, it's not an emotion that comes easily, not to men like me anyway, but I think I may have fallen in love with you."

It wasn't quite the declaration Daisy had so often imagined. She would have preferred less hesitancy, more fervor. The way Rudolph Valentino declared his heart when he appeared in her room and explained how it had in fact been the lack of her in his life that had contributed to his passing. But standing in the soft light of Mabel's boudoir on the eve of Christmas Eve, knowing that the world beyond was white and thick with snow, knowing that those within the house were marooned, Daisy thought it all seemed quite romantic.

"Of course, I shall have to speak with your father," Ben said now, turning to her.

"Oh, really, why?"

He smiled. "Because, dear Daisy . . . I wish to marry you."

Was this a proposal? He hadn't gone down on bended knee, hadn't actually *asked* her. And right at that moment she could think of nothing to say. Her mind went blank. Ben stared at her. Then, as he began to lower himself, she said, "No!" And she rose to her feet. "No, I'd rather you didn't speak to my father—not now, not yet. You see, he has a lot on his mind just at the minute . . . and, well, what with it being Christmas and me being only eighteen, I think it would be better if you waited. It's all been rather hectic here," she added, trying to laugh. "Yes, there's been quite a lot going on . . ."

Ben straightened himself. He was no longer smiling.

"I'm very flattered . . . honored," said Daisy. "It's just the timing . . ."

He took her hand, lifted it to his mouth. "That's fine. I'm prepared to wait." And then he pressed his lips to her skin.

Chapter Ten

Howard sighed and paused by the window. "Completely out of character . . . *quite* out of character and most inconvenient," he said, his leather brogues squeaking as he turned and paced back across the floor in his tweeds, an unlit cigar clenched between his fingers.

It was Christmas Eve and Mabel had vanished.

"Oh, for goodness' sake. Does it really matter if lunch is a minute or two late? So much fuss about nothing," said Iris, flicking at the pages of a magazine. "Only in Little *Engerland*," she muttered, referring to their particular enclave of Surrey, her name for Little Switzerland.

Howard turned by the door and marched back to the window.

"I think Iris is right," said Margot (*Margot* to them all now), and then, in a reassuring, soothing tone, she added, "Sometimes we women do need a little time to ourselves."

Iris glanced at Daisy and rolled her eyes.

"Maybe they've gone tobogganing," Daisy said. "Reggie's quite lively, you know . . . quite a bit younger than you."

It was the first time Daisy had addressed her father without any anger in her voice since the Cigar Incident. She had dispensed with her bandage; the cut in her hairline was healing and had scabbed. And the shadow beneath her right eye—which the previous night she had anticipated to be bruising—had also subsided.

She saw her father tug at his pocket watch. It was almost half past one.

"That's it. I shall have to go and look for her myself," he said, turning—striding and purposeful, tossing his unsmoked cigar into the fire as he passed. "Ridiculous," he muttered as he left the room.

Margot rose quickly to her feet. "I shall go with him," she whispered, wrinkling her nose in apology.

Perhaps her mother had run away, like Agatha Christie, Daisy thought. Perhaps she'd already checked in to a hydropathic hotel as Mrs. Margot Vincent . . .

Daisy lay back in her chair. She looked over at Iris. "I hope Mummy hasn't run away . . . like Mrs. Christie, I mean."

Iris laughed. "She went off with Reggie in his car at about twelve. He has those chain things—you know, the ones for snow?"

"You knew! You knew and you never let on."

"Yes, I knew. She said they'd only be an hour or so . . . And anyway, Father's bloody obsession with mealtimes is ridiculous."

They sat in silence for a moment or two; then Daisy said, "Iris, do you hate him?"

Iris licked a finger, flicked a page of the magazine. "Not hate, exactly . . . more dislike."

"And Margot?"

"Why should I hate her? Latest squeeze, dear. Here today, gone tomorrow . . . back another day."

"Mummy said she's been around for years, that she and Daddy were once sweethearts . . ."

"Yes, she's probably the one he goes back to. A sort of filler-in, you know."

"Filler-in?"

"When there's nobody else, between the others."

"Does he have others?"

Iris shrugged. "One imagines so."

"I see . . . And does Lily know?"

"Haven't the foggiest," said Iris, putting down the magazine and yawning. "Although . . ." She paused. "I rather think she must . . . But you know her; she'll never comment on anything much, other than which one of her friends is in the *Tatler* or what she's read in the *Daily Mail*. And what does any of this matter to her? She has her own home, own life now."

"But what about Mummy? Do you think she knows?"

Iris tapped the end of her cigarette on its enamel case and pushed it into her cigarette holder. "She must know. You said she'd invited her."

Daisy nodded. "That's what she told me. But I think she did it simply because Margot and Daddy are old friends and she thought it would be nice for him."

"*Daisy*," said Iris, elongating the name and shaking her head. She flicked the silver lighter and lit her cigarette. "But I suppose that's marriage for you," she said with a voice full of smoke. "And that's men for you, darling. You need to learn."

"But they're not all the same. They're not all like Daddy."

Iris snorted and rose to her feet. "Really? And of course, you would know."

"You're so cynical, Iris . . . so anti-men."

"And with good reason. Look at your father." She glanced over at Daisy. "What a fine example he is."

"He's *your* father, too. And anyway, he's not *all* men."

"No, he's not—thank God." She walked over to the window. The ledge outside was thick with snow. She said, "I rather think you need to get away from here . . ." She turned to Daisy. "You should come and live with me . . . come and live with me up in town. We'd have a wizard time, you know? I'd take you to Marcel and get your hair cut; get you into some fabulous new clothes, make you up and make you beautiful. And we'd be able to go dancing—go dancing every night. God, I adore dancing." She began humming a tune and shimmying, that way she did. "Or I suppose you could marry," she said, "use that as your ticket out of here. Not that it would be a ticket to freedom, mind you . . . but I suppose you could get divorced if you didn't like it, or him, or whatever."

"Iris!"

"What?"

"One does not get married to become *divorced!*"

After that, Daisy didn't want to tell Iris about Ben's declaration of the previous evening—though she would have done normally, would have told Iris before anyone else. But nothing was normal anymore. And to mention Ben's proposal now—after what Iris had told her, and after everything she'd just said—seemed discordant and badly timed. And that's what she thought of the proposal: badly timed. It was the reason she had asked Ben to wait. *Wait until things calm down,* she had thought; *wait until things are back to normal.*

But what was or had been normal was all a lie, according to Iris. And if it was all a lie and her world had been built on lies, how was she to know what was true and real, or what she felt? But what would happen if she didn't say yes? There might never be another proposal of marriage. It might be the only one. She had recently read a novel where a woman had refused a marriage proposal in her youth, never to receive another, realizing too late that the man who had asked her had been *the one.*

She glanced over at Iris, who was still humming, still shimmying. Iris's movement and tune were reassuring. Iris was always reassuring.

Daisy went and stood with her sister by the window. Outside, Howard slid and staggered about in the snow, looking lost and pathetic; and they could hear him: "Mabel! Mabel!"

"Do you think he has any other children?"

"It's quite possible, I suppose," said Iris.

"I told you what Nancy said, about another child."

"Well, then, you know, don't you?"

Daisy nodded.

Iris sighed. "Someone needs to go and tell Mrs. Jessop that lunch will be delayed," she said. "And I'd rather it wasn't me."

Mrs. Jessop had left Hilda to keep an eye on things so that she could step into the larder to have a moment and a sit-down. She kept a stool there for that very purpose and knew full well that Nancy used it too. She'd been having a little daydream about her retirement, thinking of that place by the sea. Somewhere near Brighton . . . A new bungalow, perhaps, with fitted carpets and a modern bathroom. She could already picture it: the trimmed privet hedge and white painted gate, the south-facing bay window with its broad sea view.

She'd have a three-piece suite, one in dark green velvet like Madam's, a nice dinner service—Wedgwood or Crown Derby, she thought—and a good bed with a proper horsehair mattress and a headboard. And she'd have navy blue curtains with long tasseled silk fringes in the front room, the one with the big bay, and a Turkey rug and her mother's whatnot with all of her Royal Doulton ladies on it. It would be nice to have them all out, be able to display them all properly, she thought. She had only a few out in the cottage, and they were not her favorites. Her favorites remained wrapped in tissue paper inside their boxes, though she sometimes liked to get them out to look at and imagine, particularly Annabella with her large hat and swirling pink dress and basket of flowers. She liked to imagine herself as Annabella . . . carrying her basket of flowers, holding on to her hat as she walked across the windswept field, toward him . . . Michael.

The only person she had ever shown her ladies was Nancy—

because Nancy liked things like that and could appreciate them. Nancy had been surprised, as Mrs. Jessop knew she would be, said they must be worth a fortune, as Mrs. Jessop knew they were. Nancy had said that they were the most beautiful figurines she had ever seen. And it was no surprise to Mrs. Jessop that, after she'd shown Nancy all seventeen of them, and after she'd asked which was her particular favorite, Nancy hadn't had to think long before saying, "Oh, well, I think it has to be Annabella."

Poor Nancy, Mrs. Jessop thought now. It hadn't been easy for her losing John . . . losing a future. But Nancy had coped, got on with it; they all had. They'd had no choice. Luckily for her, she had a husband and a son. She had a family.

Mrs. Jessop didn't listen to gossip, particularly not where Mr. Forbes was concerned. Speculation had always poured in the kitchen, and it stood to reason with someone like him, successful and handsome. Powerful. And of course women *would* throw themselves at him . . . and what was he expected to do? He was a man, after all: only flesh and blood. And actresses? Well, it's what they were known for.

Nancy, who had seen Mrs. Vincent close up, spoken to her, unpacked and put away her clothes—"A lot of large items of silk lingerie," she'd reported to Mrs. Jessop the previous evening—reckoned the actress wasn't really Mr. Forbes's type at all. She had told Mrs. Jessop that the woman was big, *too* large, and nothing like Mrs. Forbes.

"So you don't think there's anything in it?" Mrs. Jessop had asked Nancy in a whisper.

"I'm not saying that . . . I mean, there must be, mustn't there?

No smoke without fire. But I can't fathom it. Really, I can't. And who invited her? That's what I'd like to know."

"Well, he must've done. Mrs. Forbes certainly wouldn't have . . ."

"And Mr. Forbes is hardly likely to invite his fancy woman down here for Christmas, now, is he?"

Mrs. Jessop had shaken her head. None of it made any sense. But then marriage—all marriages, including her own—remained something of a mystery. And she knew that neither she nor Nancy, despite all their reading, were experts in the field of romance.

"Maybe that's how it works," she'd suggested, not quite knowing what she meant.

Nancy had stared at her, wide-eyed. "How *what* works?"

"Marriage."

Mrs. Jessop closed her eyes for a moment. She had long ago realized the impermanence of earthly relationships, but from time to time the realization of her life came to her with sudden new pain. She would be fifty-three on her next birthday, and she would, she thought, still like to share something of herself with someone. To be held and loved once more.

"I knew I'd find you here," said Nancy, opening the larder door. "No, don't rush. Mrs. Forbes has apparently been delayed . . . though no one seems to know *where*," Nancy added.

Barely a mile away from Eden Hall, sitting in a car by the gateway to a cemetery, snow falling on the windscreen, the engine running to keep them warm, Reggie Ellison handed Mabel a small gift-wrapped box.

"A very small token of my . . . ," he said, without finishing the sentence.

Mabel unwrapped the package slowly, lifted the lid, then looked up at him and smiled. "Oh my, they're beautiful, Reggie. Thank you."

The only man to have ever given Mabel jewelry was her husband, and though she wasn't sure what significance the gift held, she knew she had to accept it, and graciously.

Minutes earlier, Mabel had placed the wreath upon the snow-covered grave and then stood silently in contemplation and prayer. She had not cried.

Reggie had been the one to persuade her to visit, had told her that she must and had promised to drive her there. It hadn't been easy. It was the first time she had visited in more than six years.

"I wish I'd been here for you then," said Reggie.

Mabel shook her head. "That time's all a blur to me now," she said. "I was so utterly lost . . . How could I grieve for a son I'd known and loved for weeks when so many were grieving for sons they'd known and loved for years, decades? I couldn't . . . I didn't. And Howard was in London . . . and I had the girls to think of . . . I cried in private, of course, and I slept a lot," she said, turning to him, trying to smile. "I think I slept through an entire year . . . Yes, it was a queer sort of twilight existence, and if it hadn't been for the girls . . . well, I think I'd have run away."

Mabel had never spoken about that time before, not to Howard, not to anyone. Her hands trembled as she spoke, as she fiddled with the tissue paper wrappings of her gift. And when Reggie placed his hand upon hers and stared back at her with tears in his own eyes, it seemed to her as though he understood her in a way Howard did not, never had and perhaps never would.

"Do you still want to run away?" Reggie asked.

Mabel nodded. "Sometimes."

"Then perhaps you should . . . Perhaps you should run away, for a little while, at least. I think it'd be very good for you."

Chapter Eleven

Christmas Eve luncheon was a strange affair to Daisy's mind. Howard remained almost completely silent, staring down the long table with mournful brown eyes at his wife. Like one of the spaniels, Daisy thought. Mabel, on the other hand, appeared brighter, breezier and unusually effervescent. She appeared to find everything amusing. Even when Ben knocked over the gravy boat, soaking the white linen in glutinous brown liquid, she simply smiled and shrugged her shoulders.

Margot barely spoke. She sat next to Howard—looking quite beautiful, Daisy thought—pushing about her food with not exactly a frown but a sort of pouted, concentrated mouth. Reggie, sitting on Mabel's right, was the one in command, or so it seemed to Daisy. The one to ring the bell and explain "the sinking of HMS *Gravy*"; the one to pour the wine—Mabel first; the one to ask Nancy to serve coffee in the drawing room. But then he was a *major*, Daisy reminded herself, used to organizing and planning, logistics and locations.

When Reggie rose to his feet, rubbing his hands together and suddenly saying, "Right . . . last one to the drawing room's a nincompoop!"—and everyone, bar Howard, Margot and Noonie, jumped up and raced from the room, pushing and shoving through the doorway, careering across the hallway, then arguing about who was the last to have entered the room—Daisy thought once again how much fun Reggie was, and how unlike her father. She saw her mother fall breathless into an armchair, carefree and laughing, saw Reggie's tender gaze. And in that moment Daisy felt such gratitude toward him. He had made Mabel laugh. In spite of the bizarre and cruel situation, he had made her mother laugh. There was hope.

Charades—in which Dosia excelled—were followed by tea, which was followed by the usual quiet period leading up to the dressing bell, when people yawned and sighed and conversations were desultory, meandering, leading nowhere.

Noonie sat next to the wireless with the *Radio Times* on her lap, asleep, joining Dosia and the three slumbering dogs in a soft guttural chorus. Mabel fiddled on with threads and scissors and her embroidery, from time to time looking up to smile—at anyone, or at Reggie. Howard hid behind a newspaper, rustling it as he cleared his throat and turned a page—with a surreptitious glance across the room at Mabel, or at Reggie. Margot flicked through the pages of *Country Life* magazine, from time to time lifting her gaze toward Howard, and Ben sat alone at the far end of the room playing patience on the baize-topped card table.

The young—as Mabel referred to her children and their friends collectively—sat dotted about in a variety of chairs, fashions and poses: Lily and Miles sat huddled over their wedding album, whispering and giggling; Iris—having been banned by Howard from playing any music—sat quietly, for once, lost in her novel; and Valentine Vincent, who also held a book, watched Daisy playing with a strand of her hair and staring into the snow globe.

As usual, there were to be carols around the tree at seven. This was a long-standing tradition at Eden Hall, and the whole household—including the servants and whoever happened to be staying—was expected to be there, on time *and* in full voice.

Once, before the war, the hallway had been flooded, jam-packed and crowded with black-and-white starched uniforms, ostrich feathers, diamonds and pearls. And though this Christmas Eve tradition had survived and Mabel continued to invite their neighbors—and their servants, too; those they still had—it wasn't the same.

People seemed to have lost their enthusiasm, Mabel thought, for Christmas, for celebration. Each year fewer and fewer people showed up, and where once their guests would have come with an army of servants trailing in after them, now you'd be lucky to get a single maid in uniform. Last year, Patricia Knight's housekeeper had come in a cardigan over a housecoat and a woolen hat—which she had kept on her head for the entire duration. And Dosia hadn't been much better: appearing in the hallway in the same creased tweed skirt and sweater she'd worn all day, her usual laced brogues (leaving a trail of dried mud wherever she went, Mabel remembered) and her hair all this way and that. But it was important, Howard said—and Mabel tended to agree—to keep up these traditions and customs, to dress properly and set an example. And so they continued

with their carols and, afterward, mince pies and sherry before Howard said a few words and the family lined up to shake hands with
their diminished staff and diminished guests and wish them all a
"Happy Christmas."

Tonight, Reggie was to return to High Pines—in order to dress
for dinner—and then come back to Eden Hall with the Singhs. He
was keen for them to be included in all things, to embrace England
and English culture. When Reggie stood up and said that he would
be back in an hour or so, Mabel said, "Bring an overnight bag. It's
silly—and dangerous, as much as anything else—you traipsing back
and forth in this weather. You're spending the day here tomorrow,
so please—bring your overnight bag and I'll ask Nancy to air a bed
for you . . . and of course the Singhs are very welcome to stay too,
if they wish."

Reggie smiled, but before he could speak, Howard put down his
newspaper and rose to his feet, saying, "Really, dear, I'm quite sure
Reggie would far rather sleep in his own bed. It's hardly an epic
journey for him, not as though he's driving to London," he added,
laughing, looking about the room.

Mabel ignored her husband. "Seriously, Reg, if you'd like to stay
over, you're most welcome—more than welcome. And it'll simply
mean you're here for tomorrow."

"Yes! Do stay, Reggie," Iris called across the room.

"Well, you're all very kind . . . but I'd hate to put you to any
trouble, Mabel."

Howard moved swiftly. "Not at all, dear boy. You know you're
always welcome, but I completely understand—always better to
wake up in one's own bed, eh?"

Mabel didn't look at Howard. She smiled back at Reggie and said quietly, "It's absolutely no trouble; we have more than enough room . . . and I'll be much happier knowing you're here, that we're all present and correct for Christmas."

There then passed a moment—a long moment—when no one spoke, and other than the sound of snoring, everything went quieter than before. Howard stared at Mabel, who stared at Reggie, who sighed. "Well, if you're quite sure, Mabel . . . thank you, that'd be marvelous. Yes, really. Marvelous."

And that was that. Reggie went off to drive the short distance home, get changed for dinner and return—with or without the Singhs but *with* his overnight bag. *The young* one by one left the room, and Margot excused herself, saying, oh my, was that the time and that she, too, must freshen up and dress for dinner. Howard stood fixed. Mabel fiddled, snipping at threads with her scissors.

"Very nice of you and all that to invite the major, but don't you think you have enough?"

"Enough?" Mabel repeated without looking up.

"We do have quite a full house. And . . . well, I'm not sure about him. Not sure at all."

Mabel smiled. "You're beginning to sound like Daisy."

"Really? I thought she liked him."

Mabel looked up. "Oh yes, she does. She likes him very much."

"Look here, Mabel," Howard began, and then the dressing bell sounded.

"Righto," he said, after a moment or two. "I suppose I'd better go up and change."

"Yes, you do that," said Mabel, snip-snip-snipping once more, almost holding her breath.

As the door closed, she put down her scissors and looked up. The sudden realization that there had been some sort of shift, that it was no longer she watching Howard but he watching her, that she had the power to crush him, to not only ruin his Christmas but also possibly ruin his life, made her gasp, and as she did so she felt a sharp sting and glanced down to see that she had pierced her thumb with her needle.

Daisy lay on her bed with Iris, sharing a cigarette. She couldn't decide which dress to wear: the navy blue silk with cream lace collar, or the new green velveteen—a Christmas present from her mother . . . though she had intended on keeping that for tomorrow.

"Depends," said Iris. "Whose eye do you want to catch?"

Daisy giggled and dug her elbow into her sister. "Really!"

"Seriously, you have three of them to choose from. You need to decide which one."

"Three?"

Iris handed the cigarette back to Daisy, then sat forward and turned to her younger sister. "You know, the name Dodo suits you far better than Daisy."

"Mm, really?"

"Yes, because it's what you are. A complete and utter dodo!"

Daisy smiled. "So . . . three?"

Iris raised her hand: "Mr. Gifford," she said, pulling down her index finger. "Stee-phen . . . ," she said, elongating the syllables and pulling down her middle finger. Daisy closed her eyes. "And now . . . now the rather delicious Valentine Vincent," Iris said, pulling down another finger.

Daisy tried to blow a smoke ring. "Well, let's be honest. Stephen doesn't really count, does he?" she asked, glancing to Iris.

Iris shrugged. "Can do—if you want him to . . ."

Stephen. He was one of the very few people—apart from Iris (and her father, up until hours ago)—whom she felt able to talk to openly and about almost anything. She quite loved him, she thought, but not in *that* way. "And even if I was madly in love with him," she said, thinking aloud, "nothing could ever come of it."

"Oh, darling, don't be so old-fashioned. Times have changed— and *are* changing." Iris paused, took the cigarette from Daisy's hand. "Look at Susan Knight. She didn't take any notice of convention— class, whatever you want to call it. She married for *love*."

"But Susan's parents more or less disowned her. They've only just started speaking again—after three years!"

"So? They're speaking, they got over it and Susan—clever woman—is now married to the man she wanted to marry and not to that dreadful mustachioed lawyer from *the suburbs* that her parents wanted her to marry. Do you remember him? God, he was ghastly! She may not have the lifestyle she could have had, but she's happy—and *free*. And the two go together: You can't be happy unless you are free, and you can't be free until you're truly happy— which means being true to yourself first and foremost." She paused again. "If I met and fell in love with someone now—no matter who they were and no matter what anyone said—I'd give myself to them . . . and I'd be with them, whatever it took."

"I thought you didn't believe in marriage."

Iris laughed. "I didn't say I'd *marry* them!"

"You mean you'd live in sin?"

"I mean I'd live *in love*, darling. I couldn't give a hoot what convention says, really! Who wants to be conventional?" She shuddered. "And anyway, most of our so-called conventions were invented by men—men like Howard—as a form of control, of course."

At that moment Daisy, who had been trying for some time, blew a smoke ring that rose into the air in a perfect circle. "Look at that—I did it!"

Iris smiled, then continued: "No, to remain free, to be truly free, I believe one must live outside of conventions. I have no desire to be shackled as Mrs. Anyone, and as I don't intend to have children, there's little point in my marrying."

Daisy didn't say anything. She was confused. Iris seemed to believe in love—but a particular kind of love, one that required no commitment. But if she didn't wish to marry, to have a family of her own, what sort of life was she planning for herself? Even *with* a flat in London, even with her shop and all those clothes and all that dancing, was spinsterhood *really* freedom? And what would happen, what would she do when she was too old to dance or sell clothes? Sit about in her trousers and read novels for the rest of her life? No old ladies wore trousers; she'd *have to* go back to dresses then. And as for having lovers, which Daisy presumed was what her sister had meant when she had said that she'd "give herself," it seemed a little casual . . . and cheap. Surely she was worth more than that?

Daisy wanted to ask Iris about the sex side of things, how that would work, how she would be able to *not* have children—a baby— if she had a lover. Iris appeared not to have thought this through properly, and it concerned Daisy, because living in sin was one thing, but a baby out of wedlock was quite another. She pictured a rotund Iris trundling down the road toward Birch Grove, the nearby home for unmarried mothers, her small suitcase in one hand, her cigarette holder and a Turkish blend in the other.

"I don't believe in sex outside of marriage," said Daisy, staring straight ahead, toward the window. "It's not fair on the children."

Iris turned to her. "What *are* you on about now?"

Daisy looked back at her sister, wide-eyed. "The *children*, Iris, the babies . . . the babies born from sex outside of marriage who then have to be put into homes . . . And don't laugh! It's wrong to start making babies when you're not married and can't give them a proper home."

Iris had not laughed, but she had put her hand to her mouth to cover her smile. "Oh, darling," she said, still smiling, unable not to, and taking hold of Daisy's hand. "I forget, I forget that there's still so much you don't know."

Daisy got up off the bed. Iris could be so patronizing sometimes. She went over to the window, opened it and threw out the ciga- rette. It was dark outside, but the tall lamps lining the driveway and along the front terrace were already lit, ready for their guests and further illuminating the unusually bright snow-covered garden. A hard frost had formed over the top of the snow, making it spar- kle like diamonds under the lights. Christmas Eve: It all looked magical, Daisy thought, only half listening to Iris, who was saying something about them having to have a little chat if she came up to live with her in London.

"Oh, really," said Daisy absently. "About what?"

"Something called a Dutch cap, darling. You need to know."

"Dutch what?" said Daisy.

"Contraception. How to avoid getting pregnant . . . There's a fabulous woman called Dr. Stopes who's set up clinics to teach women like you—like us," she quickly added, "how to avoid all of that."

"Oh yes," said Daisy, "I think I may have read about her in *Modern Woman*."

"I say, does Mummy know you read that magazine? I'm not sure she'd approve."

Daisy turned to her sister. "Mummy buys it for me."

"Gulp," said Iris. "Things have certainly moved on *here*.

"So, Valentine Vincent . . . ," Iris began again after a moment. "What do you make of him? I rather think he has potential."

Daisy sat down on the chair by her desk. "I'm not sure," she said.

"Why not sure? He's quite a dish . . ."

"A, he has a rather silly name, and B, he's Daddy's tart's son."

"She's not a tart," Iris responded quickly.

"Yes, she is. She's having an affair with a married man . . . She's a tart."

Iris climbed off the bed. She was wearing her dark gray wide-legged trousers—the ones their mother had gasped at—with a green silk shirt and striped tie. She wore a bandanna around her dark hair, cut and shingled by someone *terrifically expensive* called

Marcel at Harrods, and bright pink lipstick and matching nails. She looked completely marvelous to Daisy: so modern and defiant, and so very London, Daisy thought.

Lily claimed Iris dressed that way simply to annoy Howard, who abhorred women in trousers, and perhaps it was true, because when Iris had appeared in her trousers, shirt *and* tie at breakfast that day Howard had simply stared at the tie with a very thin mouth, in a sort of silent apoplectic rage. The tie, Daisy thought, had been a step too far for him, and a wonderfully brave step on the part of Iris, who had no time for nonchalance. She despised passivity, adored intensity in all things and had once told Daisy that she intended to have a full and reckless life. She seemed to have no concern for danger or, sometimes, for others.

"The thing with you," Iris said now, "is that you want everything to be neat and tidy. The goodies and the baddies, black and white . . . and it simply doesn't work that way, darling. There are gray areas. There are things you don't yet understand."

"Like what?"

"Like marriage."

"What do you mean?

"Well, you probably still think married people love each other."

"And don't they?"

Iris shook her head. "Most of them simply pretend."

"But they must like each other, surely. In order to get married in the first place."

"No, not necessarily."

"They must at least admire and respect each other . . ."

Iris laughed. "I don't think so."

"And our parents?"

"Hmm, potentially finished. It could end in divorce."

Divorce. The universe rocked once more. Daisy's life flashed before her: She saw herself in a short dress and lipstick handing out bowls of soup to a queue of middle-aged women, including her mother; she saw Howard, unshaven and begging on the streets; she saw Eden Hall with a leaning, cobweb-covered FOR SALE sign at the bottom of the driveway. Divorce? It meant only one thing: ruination. Nothing would be the same.

Iris was still speaking, saying something about *it* no longer having quite the same stigma it once had, that *it* was becoming more accepted and had even become quite fashionable in America, or so she'd heard.

Daisy steadied herself. Divorce. She hadn't thought of it. The only person she knew—had heard of—who was divorced was the woman who'd recently moved into a cottage near the crossroads. She didn't even have a name, was simply referred to as the Divorcée. Like a fairground attraction, the Fat Lady in the tent on the promenade at Southsea or the Man with Twelve Toes, the woman was a novelty: both fascinating and to be pitied.

"Don't look so shell-shocked," said Iris. "I was being a little flippant. But it's good to be prepared."

"Nothing is certain," Daisy said shakily.

"Of course. And it's up to Mabel, really, and depends on what she wants to do."

"Do?"

"Yes, whether she wants to continue here—with her life as it is. It was different when we were young, but we're all grown up, and you'll leave soon enough; she must know that. She'll be here on her own. I imagine she's pondering on it all and considering her future."

"What do you think . . . What do you think she'll decide?"

"I really don't know. And that's the truth, darling. But you need to open your eyes. It's time for you to grow up, to know and accept that . . . well, that nothing is perfect. Nothing is black and white. Everything is gray . . . Undecided," she added, smiling tenderly now at Daisy.

Yes, time to grow up, decisions to be made, Daisy thought; a whole life to be forged, new people to be met . . . Suddenly, it all seemed impossibly exhausting. Iris stared back at her, reached out and took hold of her hand. "Don't frown so, dear. It'll give you lines," she said. "But do try not to be quite so judgmental. And don't damn women just because men use them. We're all at their mercy one way or another; we're all of us tarts when it comes to our fortune with men. And as for Margot," she went on, quieter, glancing away, "well, she's hardly a tart, and we don't really know her, what she's like, or why she and Howard are—"

"Fucking?" interrupted Daisy.

Iris gasped, then laughed. "You are naughty," she said. She released Daisy's hand and moved toward the door. "We'd better get a move on."

"The bell hasn't gone yet, has it?"

"It went ages ago."

"But what about Ben? You haven't said . . . Do you rate him?"

"As a *gofer*, yes; as your future husband"—Iris shrugged her shoulders—"not really. But it all depends on what you want, Dodo. See, *gray*! It's all gray."

"I want to be in love."

"Ha, you can't make *that* happen just like that," she said, snapping her fingers. "Or if you do, I can guarantee it'll be a disaster."

"But he's a decent enough sort, isn't he? . . . Ben, I mean."

"Go with the blue," Iris said, and left the room.

Mabel had decided on silver-gray crepe de chine and pearls. Not the Cartier pearl and diamond choker Howard had presented her with on the occasion of their twentieth wedding anniversary, but the Tahitian black pearls Reggie had presented to her earlier that day.

Now, standing in front of the long mirror in her dressing room, with Nancy—once *her* maid, now her housekeeper—looking on, she allowed herself to smile back at her reflection. She reached up to the strands of pearls Nancy had fastened at her neck and then fussed over and arranged about her bosom.

"They are rather lovely, aren't they?" said Mabel, feeling the perfect imperfection of the pearls beneath her fingers.

"Oh yes, and I have to say, ma'am, I don't think I've ever seen you looking lovelier."

Nancy was being kind, Mabel thought, because years ago she had surely been lovelier. And she wished for a moment that Reg had known her *then*, in that time of youthful loveliness, so that he had a memory of it, of her. Instead, Howard had all the memories, and they were quite wasted on him. And yet it pleased her and made her feel better about herself as she was now that Reg held her in such high esteem, that he listened to her, clearly valued her opinions and looked at her with such . . . What was it? she wondered. A sort of intensity that made her feel as though she were naked in front of him, completely and utterly exposed; as though he could see into her mind and read her thoughts.

She had forgotten this, was relearning it now and in so doing realized that she had known it before, many years ago. The closer she and Reg became, the more vulnerable she felt in his presence, and it was the intensity of his attention, his determined, resolutely steady focus—undiluted by the distractions of spouse or family— that seemed to draw her in and seemed increasingly hypnotic. She wondered if others were able to see it, too. Not that Reg would or could necessarily mesmerize *them*, but that they would somehow be able to see his effect upon *her*.

It had been like that today. She could not recall the last time she had felt so at ease in another's presence. Any silences in their conversation had simply been a blissful pause in which to languish. On the way to the cemetery they had talked about Daisy, in the main, her behavior of late. Reg said that she was simply growing up, that she had reached that place of— What did he call it? Disenchantment? Disillusionment? Something like that. "She's watching us all, figuring us and everything else out," he said. And then he'd told her that Daisy was the one most like *her* and that he had no doubt at all that she would "get there."

Later, back at the house, at lunch and afterward, Mabel had felt the thrill of a new intimacy between them, and each time she'd caught his eye she had felt her heart palpitate. The thought of seeing him again this evening, and in minutes, made her heart do a little flip.

"Your cuff, ma'am?" Nancy said, interrupting her thoughts and holding out the diamonds, the ones Howard had given her two years ago, on her fortieth birthday.

Mabel stared at the diamond cuff and then at the dazzling array glinting from the open jewelry case. Howard had always been very generous. Each year and for so many years, he had presented her with expensive jewels, when the only thing she'd wanted was a little of his time, the reassurance of his love and affection. Instead, as she and their marriage withered, she had been given tokens, costly tokens, things Howard liked to see her wearing, so that he could admire them, feel proud of them—*his* gifts to her. And she had capitulated. She had worn his diamonds, his pearls, his rubies and sapphires, and then felt grateful when he admired them.

"No. I think not. Only these tonight," Mabel said, lifting her fingers once more to the black pearls. And she watched Nancy carefully place the cuff back on the tray and close the case.

Nancy had been with her at Eden Hall from the start. She had seen it all: each announcement and celebration, each and every loss or gain. She had been the one to pick Mabel up from the blood-soaked bathroom floor one windswept stormy night, tenderly bathing her, wiping away her tears, drying her and then helping her into her bed, saying, "There'll be another, ma'am. There'll be another." She had been the one to move Howard's personal possessions from their bedroom to his dressing room and explain to him what the doctor had said, that there could be no more babies for Mabel.

For all of these reasons and more, Mabel trusted Nancy, and right at that moment she'd have liked to be able to confide in her and tell her of her plans, but there was a line one never crossed with servants. And so instead Mabel moved over to the jewelry case, opened it, pondered for only a moment, and then—stretching out her hand—she said, "This is a Christmas present, and a thank-you, Nancy . . . for everything."

Mabel knew the rubies were worth enough for Nancy to be able to buy herself a house, a small house perhaps, but something of her own.

Chapter Twelve

There was a bad smell in the hallway. One of the dogs had made a mess by the tree, and Howard, already agitated about the lights—two of which had gone off—and unable to wait for Blundy, had taken it upon himself and was bent over, in white tie and tails, with the dustpan and brush from the drawing room fireplace.

Daisy held her hand over her nose. She had ignored Iris's advice and wore her new dark green velveteen dress. The dress fit her well enough, but her red petticoat hung down beneath the hem and her bun—despite her wrestling with brushes and hairpins—was lop-sided and insecure, and she could feel it slowly unraveling, slipping down her neck each time she turned her head. Thus, glancing about the hallway—trying not to turn her head—she saw Margot, with Lily and Miles, *again*; Reggie with the Singhs, both looking shy, their eyes cast downward; and the Knights and a number of other neighbors. She caught Valentine Vincent's eye and quickly removed her hand from her nose and smiled back at him. He was distractingly handsome, she thought, glancing between him and Ben and realizing Benedict Gifford could never compete in looks.

As Nancy, Mr. and Mrs. Jessop and the others began to emerge from the passageway, whispering, all of them looking in the direction of their famous houseguest, followed by Howard, back from the yard and smiling tightly now, a hush fell and heads turned as Mabel descended the staircase. Reggie put down his glass, swiftly moved over and took Mabel's arm. And as song sheets were passed about, everyone arranged themselves in a semicircle round the tree, where Howard was once again busying himself with the electric lights, switching them off and on and on and off and looking back at Blundy for the thumbs-up that *all* were now working. This went on for some time, and people began to sigh and shuffle, not least Noonie, who loudly pointed out that people had come for carols, *not* a light show.

Eventually, after another of the lights popped and the whole lot went out, carols were begun and sung, with Old Jessop's baritone leading the mass in "Away in a Manger." There then followed "Silent Night," "Hark! The Herald Angels Sing," "The Holly and the Ivy," and "O Little Town of Bethlehem." But it was during the penultimate verse of the final carol—"Ding Dong Merrily on High"— that Daisy noticed Stephen, his eyes almost closed, his body swaying perilously close to the unilluminated tree. He appeared to be rotating: going round and round in circles without moving his feet, while all the time mouthing words. Daisy glanced over at Mrs. Jessop, who, like her husband, appeared lost in the moment, oblivious to anything other than the rapture of the verse.

When the singing ceased, the glasses of champagne and sherry and the tiny mince pies laid out on silver trays were passed round the hallway by Mabel and Iris and Lily. Daisy, too, should have been on duty. That's the way it was done at Eden Hall on Christmas Eve: The family—that is, Mabel and the girls—waited on their servants and guests. But as this was happening, as Howard stepped up onto the staircase, chimed on his glass with a spoon and then began to speak, Daisy had already moved over to Stephen Jessop.

She tugged on his sleeve: "Stephen . . . ," she hissed. He seemed to be asleep on his feet. She pulled once again at his arm and he opened his eyes.

"Amen!" he said—in a voice loud enough to make Howard pause his address and look over, along with everyone else.

As Howard cleared his throat and continued, "And so I'd like to extend my thanks to all of you who work here at Eden Hall . . . ," Daisy led Stephen into the passageway.

"Are you ill?" she asked, staring at him as he blinked—once, twice, three times. "My God, you're owled . . . aren't you? Oh, Stephen, what *are* we going to do with you . . . ? You can't go back in there like this." She glanced down the passageway. The only thing for it was to get him back to the coachman's flat. And so she took his hand in hers and led him toward the kitchen, and on.

Mabel stood clutching a plate of mince pies, and she smiled and nodded as Howard extended his thanks to her. But he seemed reluctant to stop.

"Next year, my wife and I will celebrate twenty-five years of marriage . . ." Howard paused long enough to allow the few claps to subside. "A silver wedding anniversary is—I think we'd all agree— a great cause for celebration, and a time of gratitude and perhaps reflection . . ." He paused again, and Mabel so wished he'd stop there. "So twenty-five years . . . ," he rumbled on, "a quarter of a century and three wonderful daughters later, I'd like to ask my wife to come up here and join me . . ."

Howard beckoned to Mabel, and Mabel handed the plate to Nancy, then moved through the huddle, smiling, nervous, wondering what was to come.

Howard took her hand as she stepped up to him; he kissed it, and then, staring back at her, he continued. "Tonight, I'd simply like to take the opportunity to say thank you to my dear wife," he went on in an uxorious fashion, "for not only providing me and our beloved children with an extraordinarily happy home, but for making Eden Hall such a wonderful place for us all."

There were a few shouts of "Hear! Hear!"

Then Howard said, "Ladies and gentleman, please join me in raising your glasses to my wife, to Mrs. Forbes."

"To Mrs. Forbes!" everyone echoed, glasses held aloft.

Daisy opened the door, ran her hand over the rough plaster wall and flicked a switch. A naked bulb threw a murky glow over the steep staircase. The small lobby smelled of mold and damp and Jeyes Fluid. She took Stephen's hand, pulled him inside and kicked the door shut behind him.

"Daisy," he said, standing against the wall, staring back at her, "I'm fine. I know what I'm doing."

"I don't think so."

"And I know so."

He reached out, pulled her nearer. There was a new intensity about him—in his face, his eyes, his whole demeanor—that both excited and frightened her, and made her heart beat faster. And as he lifted a finger to her face, tracing its lines, following each contour—across her brow, her eyes, down her nose to her lips, her chin, her neck; his touch as delicate as the brush of a butterfly's wing, as warm as the summer evening sun—she felt herself begin to fall, fall once again into a deep, dark place, an unfathomable rippling vortex.

Then he took hold of her hand and led her slowly up the stairs.

Because of the carols, the dinner bell had not rung that evening. But when Mr. Blundell struck the small gong in the hallway at precisely eight thirty, where the family and their guests stood about the tree clutching their glasses, Mabel noticed Daisy's absence and asked Lily to fetch her down from her room.

"Kindly ask Mrs. Jessop to give us five minutes," said Mabel to Blundell. It was Christmas Eve; there was no rush.

"She's not in her room," said Lily, minutes later, descending the stairs.

"She's probably just stepped out for some air . . . I'm quite sure she'll be back at any minute," said Iris.

"Some *air*? It's freezing out there," said Mabel.

As Iris and Howard went off to check other rooms, Lily turned to Mabel: "Oh my, what if she's had another one of her turns? We all know what she's like, and she *has* been acting queerer than usual . . . She may very well have amnesia—after that fall she had. I've read that it can sometimes be delayed . . . She may be out there, wandering about and lost in the snow."

"These sorts of things *always* happen at Christmas, don't you find?" said Noonie, turning to face Margot's ruffled lace bosom. "People disappearing . . . murders . . . suicides . . ."

"Mother!"

Iris reappeared in the hallway. "She's not anywhere downstairs."

"Well, if she chooses to miss Christmas Eve dinner, that's her own fault," said Mabel, beckoning people toward the dining room door. But as they began to move, Howard appeared on the staircase. "She's not in the house," he said, loud and solemn. "I'm going to look for her."

Everyone stopped and stared as Howard moved swiftly across the hallway to the outer lobby and reached for his coat. Suddenly, there seemed to be the vague hint of something more sinister in their midst.

"I hope she hasn't been kidnapped," murmured Noonie.

Then Reggie called after Howard, "I'll come with you, old chap."

Within seconds the other men stepped forward, as though it were a call-up for another war, and Reggie was in his element, directing them hither and thither.

Mabel smiled at Margot. "Always a drama with Daisy," she said, rolling her eyes heavenward. Then she took a deep breath, turned and headed for the kitchen to inform Mrs. Jessop that dinner would need to be delayed.

Stephen released Daisy's hand at the top of the stairs and stood aside to let her enter.

The room was sparsely furnished, lit by a single lamp. The paint on the walls had bubbled and was peeling off the plaster. Daisy wasn't sure what to do or say. She had never been in this place before, never been in this situation before, with him or with anyone else. She turned to him. He stood next to a bookcase, his head slightly bent, staring back at her, biting his lip. A new sensation swept through her, and she took a step backward, away from him.

"I need to talk to you," he said, and then gestured to a chair by the unlit fire.

She sat down in the old armchair, one she vaguely recognized from a time before. "Is it about Mrs. Vincent?" she asked, glancing about the room. "Because if it is, I'm not sure I want to hear."

"No, it's not about Mrs. Vincent," Stephen replied.

He moved over to her, sat down on the rug at her feet, crossed his legs and looked up at her.

She watched his eyes move down her body to her legs, her feet, felt his touch again, tracing the front of her stocking, her ankle, and then the warmth of his hand encircling it.

"Not about Mrs. Vincent . . . ," she said.

He raised his eyes to hers. "No, it's about you . . . you and me."

"You and me," she repeated.

He smiled. She felt his grip on her ankle tighten.

"I love you, Daisy. I've loved you for as long as I can remember, and I know I'll love you till the day I die."

At first, Daisy thought she might be dreaming, and she pinched the flesh on the back of her hand, once, twice, three times . . . She wasn't dreaming. And she was pleased she was sitting down, because she was trembling, shaking and shivering—and not from any coldness. She wanted to say, "I love you . . . I love you, too." But the words wouldn't come.

"And I want you to come with me . . . to New Zealand," Stephen was saying now, and she realized he'd been talking for some time. "I know it's the other side of the world," he went on, "but just imagine it, imagine the possibilities . . ."

Daisy stared back at him: the tousled thick hair and dark eyes, the curve of his beautiful mouth and long jaw. She loved him, how—in what way—she still wasn't sure, but she couldn't go with him to New Zealand. How could she? Her father would go mad. Literally. It would kill him. She pictured herself high up on the deck of a ship, waving down to her parents and Iris on a quayside through a blizzard of streamers: her mother sobbing, Iris blowing kisses and Howard waving his fist. Then she took herself out of the equation and placed Stephen on the deck, waving down to her as the ship sounded its horn and moved slowly away . . .

And as her silence continued, as they sat staring at each other, his smile faded. He tilted his head to one side, breathed in deeply, then looked away and shut his eyes.

"I had to tell you," he said. "And I'm afraid it required some Dutch courage."

Chapter Thirteen

"But did you not realize?" Mabel demanded. "Did you not think?"

"No. I'm sorry, I just lost track of the time."

"Really, Daisy, how *can* you forget the time—and then stand about the yard in the freezing cold—for almost an hour . . ." Mabel reached out and grabbed hold of Daisy's hands. "But your hands are warm."

"Well, I wasn't out there the *whole* time. I moved about, kept coming inside," Daisy went on, aware of both Iris's and Lily's scrutiny. "I just felt sick"—she shrugged—"and thought it best to keep out of the way."

"You'll have pneumonia next, my girl," said Noonie, unusually stern faced. "I hope you're wearing a vest."

Mabel glanced at the ormolu clock on the mantelpiece. She raised a hand to her head. Almost nine o'clock. They had never eaten this late before, certainly not on Christmas Eve. Now *all* of the men were missing. And it was entirely Howard's fault, she thought. Such an overreaction to Daisy's absence, and no doubt brought on by guilt, she mused, heading back to the kitchen.

It was shortly after half past nine by the time everyone—or almost everyone, because Miles had failed to reappear—had been rounded up and herded into the dining room by an unusually shrill-sounding Mabel. The meal, she knew, had quite literally gone to pot, and Mrs. Jessop, who normally emerged from the kitchen on Christmas Eve to receive the family's thanks, refused to come through to the dining room.

And who could blame her? Mabel thought. The hors d'oeuvres were as shriveled as Howard's expression; the roast beef had dried out and was cold; and the Yorkshire puddings—which Mrs. Jessop prided herself on—were like old plaster, or so Noonie commented, somewhat gleefully.

The other result of the long delay to dinner was that everyone had had far too much champagne. For Blundy had taken it upon himself to go round and round the drawing room with the linen-wrapped bottle, topping up the ladies' glasses as though it were a drinking competition at the Olympics, Mabel thought now, woozily. She had tried to catch his eye, tried so many times to offer him a sign, saying, *No more, please. Thank you!* And it wasn't *the young* Mabel was concerned about; it was her mother, who, more loquacious than ever, had found it difficult to maneuver herself through each doorway: a problem, Mabel realized, if one is walking sideways.

Now her mother found every utterance hilarious and was *still* clutching a glass. Mabel tried to catch Howard's eye, tried to signal to him, nodding in the direction of Noonie. But Howard simply stared blankly back at her. And Daisy, the culprit and cause of the delay, appeared unusually subdued and pensive. Mabel heard Iris say, "Penny for your thoughts?" and saw Daisy smile back at Iris and shake her head.

Later, as Howard and Dosia helped Noonie up the stairs, Miles finally appeared in the hallway.

"Well . . . you see, I knew Daisy was back," he began, sheepish under Lily's scrutiny, "because I bumped into Stephen Jessop . . . and we somehow ended up at the Coach and Horses."

"*Stephen?*" Daisy repeated.

"Yes, Stephen," said Miles, nodding once too often for Mabel's liking. "And as the feller's going off to New Zealand . . ."

"Who's going to New Zealand?" asked Howard, descending the stairs.

"New Zealand?" repeated Mabel.

"Who's going to New Zealand?" said Howard again.

"I've always rather fancied going to New Zealand," said Dosia.

But Miles was now whispering to Lily, who stood with her arms folded, her head turned away.

"Right. Well, I rather think Miles should have something to eat," said Mabel. "I presume you haven't dined, Miles?"

He shook his head. "I'm terribly sorry about all of this, Mabel."

Howard turned toward the drawing room, shaking his head, muttering to himself about no one telling him anything anymore, and Mabel led her son-in-law off toward the kitchen, reminding herself wearily, silently, that the provision of meals was one of the primary roles of a mother, even a mother-in-law.

In the drawing room, Iris played Paul Whiteman on the gramophone, and she and Margot Vincent seemed like new best friends, Daisy thought as she sat down. The two women sat together beneath the oriel window, smiling at each other, moving their heads and hands in some private blissful rhapsody to Irving Berlin's "What'll I Do." Lily had disappeared upstairs to her room, sulking about Miles, and Dosia had gone to talk with her.

After so much disruption, the struggle to get everyone together, Mabel had insisted that the men take their port in the drawing room. They sat at the far end of the room in a smoky huddle round the card table with their glasses and cigars. Daisy sat with her back to them, their cigar smoke, like the music, drifting over her as she thought of Stephen's words, which were from time to time—whenever the music quieted and ebbed away—interrupted by politics.

"Self-government!" her father bellowed. "Mr. Baldwin should pay heed to Winston," he added loudly, not anticipating a cessation in the loud crackle of Mr. Whiteman's orchestra.

"I'm afraid your empire has had its day, old chap," said Reggie, and Daisy detected the trace of a smile in his voice. "You simply can't halt progress—nor should we . . ."

When Dosia reappeared, she sat down next to Daisy on the sofa. "Everything all right with you?" she asked, patting Daisy's hand.

Daisy smiled and nodded. Of anyone, of everyone, she'd have liked to talk to Dosia, to tell her what had happened with Stephen and ask her advice. But it was impossible to do so then and there, and she'd have had to shout it all out above the din anyway, which would certainly not be the thing to do.

The music picked up again, and over it, through it, muddled in with love and New Zealand, was Howard: "Astounded! . . . willful destruction . . . communism . . . end of us." Someone laughed: Reggie, Daisy thought. And she heard Ben saying something about people predicting the empire's end for as long as he could remember but he couldn't see it happening in his lifetime, and Reggie used the word *certain* and said whether any of them liked it or not *it* would happen. Then Iris and Margot began to sing: "Blue days, all of them gone, nothing but blues skies from now on . . ."

At the other side of the house, a tight-lipped Mrs. Jessop slammed a Crown Derby plate down on the pine table.

"Just a few slices, please," said Mabel, meekly.

The large knife in Mrs. Jessop's hand seemed to move through the air toward the lump of cold meat in a decidedly haphazard fashion, to Mabel's mind—producing terror. Miles looked on vacuously from the table.

"We're all frightfully sorry about this, Mrs. Jessop," Mabel said. "I know it's terribly late to be . . . And after dinner was . . ."

Mrs. Jessop stopped and turned to the clock on the wall, knife in hand. She said nothing, simply stood staring at it for a few seconds, then turned and began slicing the meat.

"Well, if everything's quite under control . . . ," Mabel said, without finishing the sentence and without waiting for any answer, and she left the kitchen.

She walked back along the passageway and sat down on the bench in the shadows by the unlit tree. She could hear Margot singing, "Blue days, all of them gone, nothing but blue skies from now on . . ." Sadness swept through Mabel. She felt her head begin to shake, felt a tear escape and roll down her cheek.

It was a while later when Daisy heard the men emerge from the billiard room and Ben ask her father if all the women had retired and Howard say, "Well, yes, of course," and quite sharply, as though it were an impertinence to be asked such a question. Now the house was unusually silent, the room empty but for the two of them, and she, locked in a trance, a sort of stupor, was lost in Stephen's words.

Stephen Jessop loved her. He loved her. The universe had taken something away—her romantic, idealized notion of her father—and then given something back. Unexpectedly, she had crossed a threshold, she thought, grappling with reason for a moment: She had left her childhood and moved to a new plane, which required a new understanding. One in which from the ashes of disappointment rose hope, freedom, new vistas and the possibility of independence. To run away with Stephen, to travel to the other side of the world with him, was surely the stuff of romantic fiction. And yet it was real. It was possible. And before this day she had not known. Because Stephen's love was different from her mother's, father's and siblings', and different, too, from the measured affection Ben Gifford called *love*.

This love knew no boundaries or borders; this love planned and moved forward, crossed oceans and went back in time. This love remembered. This love—too intimate to be affection—was as luminescent as the embers glowing in front of her and as unfathomable as the shapes within the dimly lit room.

When, eventually, Valentine spoke, his voice was soft and mellow, more than a whisper but not quite whole. He said, "This is my favorite time of day." It was not a question, invited no reply. And so they continued their silence for a little while longer, until he rose to his feet, walked over and offered Daisy a cigarette. He sat down, nearer to her now, and staring upward he said, "You know, I don't blame you for disliking my mother or me."

She felt newly magnanimous, cocooned in love. "I don't dislike you—or your mother," she said.

"But I wouldn't blame you—if you did."

"It's . . . a difficult situation, but part of life, I suppose. And you and I are innocent, not party to . . ." She couldn't think of the words at that moment and left the sentence.

"I understand you and Benedict Gifford are sort of engaged," he said after a while.

Daisy smiled again. "No, we're not sort of engaged . . . *or* engaged."

There were footsteps in the hallway and Blundy appeared in the doorway. "Ah, I do apologize. I thought everyone had retired for the night, miss."

"Not quite, not yet, Mr. Blundell," Daisy replied.

The man nodded and closed the door.

"You're quite different from other girls of your class."

"I'm not entirely sure what you mean by *my class*. My father's in trade—as his father was before him. We're hardly aristocracy. We're paint makers, traders who've done well; that's all. And isn't England filled with traders and market-stall holders?"

Val didn't look at her, but he smiled. And the *not* looking and the smile intrigued her.

"What about you? I know nothing . . . other than you write . . . and that your mother is an actress and happens to be my father's mistress."

She saw him wince, then close his eyes. "I'm sorry," she said, and then she rose to her feet and walked over to the table, where the snow globe sat next to the large glass-domed taxidermy diorama.

"I was looking at that earlier . . . it's rather beautiful," he said.

"The birds?"

"No, the globe."

"I used to think that, too. I used to think it was magical."

"And now you don't?" he asked, moving toward her.

"No, I don't . . . I don't trust it."

She picked it up, gently shook it. And as she watched the tiny snowflakes fall upon the tiny Eden Hall, she felt his breath on the side of her face as he asked, "And why do you no longer trust it?"

"Because it's an illusion."

As she placed the globe back down on the table she felt something graze her cheek and turned. He didn't flinch, didn't speak. He didn't smile and neither did she. Her heart did not pound; the earth did not give way. And when he placed his mouth over hers, she closed her eyes and imagined Stephen.

The landlord rang the bell again: "Last orders, *per-leeze!*"

Stephen raised his head and glanced around the pub. There

were still a few: the couple sitting beneath glinting horse brasses in
the snug by the fire, holding hands; and others up at the bar. He
smiled at the old bearded chap seated near him, then looked back
at the girl, her elbows propped on the wooden counter in front of
him: a strawberry blond blur, all eyes and red lips.

"I'll be finishing soon," she said. "So don't you go rushing off
anywhere."

She stood up, ran her hands over her waist, her hips. "There's
plenty of sloe gin and baccy at my house," she said, moving away,
winking at him.

He tried to smile. He'd forgotten her name.

"I'm sorry . . . I didn't intend to do that," Val said, stepping away
from Daisy. "Forgive me."

They walked through to the hallway and stood in awkward silence at the foot of the stairs. He bowed his head, "Good night,
Daisy," he said, and he waited as she went up first.

But there was no way she was going to be able to sleep. She felt
the same as she did after she'd had that revolting tarlike coffee the
last time she'd been in London and she and her mother had met Iris:
her heart beating quickly, her mind veering off in every direction.

Inside her room, Daisy paced in circles. She'd been kissed. She'd
been kissed at last, but not by the one she had wanted to kiss her.
The one she wanted to kiss her said he loved her but seemed reluctant to kiss her. The one she didn't want to kiss said he might love
her and that he wanted to marry her. And the one she *had* kissed
considered it a mistake.

Moving in circles, round and round, Daisy's thoughts returned to one person: his face, his look of despondence when she'd realized the time and jumped up. She had never said, *I love you . . . I love you, too.*

She stopped, closed her eyes: She had not given him anything. She'd simply said, "I'm sorry, I have to go." That was all.

She glanced at the clock by her bed, then picked up her coat.

"It's Tabitha," she said again.

She had linked her arm through Stephen's, and all he felt was its weight.

"Just look at them stars," she said, halting abruptly on the snow-covered road and lowering the beam of her torch. "There'll be no more snow tonight."

Stephen was no longer sure of exactly where they were, or of where they were headed, and at that moment he didn't care.

"I've always quite fancied you, you know," Tabitha began again as they gingerly moved on. "Yes, I quite like the silent types, me . . . Still waters run deep, my mother says . . . It's a film, you know? . . . Came out in the war, I think . . . Some of those old ones are ever so good . . . I love the pictures, me . . . The Regal get good films now, you know . . . Yes, all the new ones . . . Laurel and Hardy, Charlie Chaplin and that other funny one, the one who falls over all the time," she said, beginning to giggle at the mere thought of the nameless man. "We could go there, you and me . . . Saturday matinee . . . I love the Saturday matinees, me . . . They have Mrs. Peabody on the piano then; she's ever so good . . ."

On and on and on, Stephen thought. Tabitha was certainly *not* a silent type, and yet the incessant flow of her words was strangely comforting to him.

"So what do you say? Shall we?"

"Yes . . . why not," he said.

As she gripped his arm tighter, he briefly wondered what he'd just agreed to, but it didn't matter: He'd be gone from there soon enough. Probably never see the girl again. He felt a vague twinge of guilt. He said, "But I can't make any promises, not at the moment."

"Well," she said, "I hadn't expected any promises, Stephen Jessop . . . at least, not yet."

The next thing Stephen knew he was on his back with a giggling Tabitha sprawled half on top of him. And he was laughing too. Laughing up at the night sky and the hopelessness of his situation: because right at that moment it was funny, all of it. That he had asked Daisy Forbes to consider running away with him to New Zealand, that he'd told her he loved her, that he'd thought— imagined—she'd agree: It was so funny that for a while Stephen could barely breathe. When he did finally stop laughing, he heard Tabitha say his name in a new voice. Then she took his hand and pulled it inside her coat, her blouse, and onto her breast.

The flesh was soft and warm, and a million stars shone overhead. "Daisy," he whispered.

The door was unlocked, the light in the lobby still on, and Daisy moved quickly up the stairs.

"Stephen . . ."

She crossed over the sitting room, knocked and then opened another door. A wrought-iron bed with a knot of blankets, two impoverished pillows and a pair of discarded long johns lying upon it took up most of the room. A small chest of drawers leaned at an angle next to it, butting up against the low window. There was no wardrobe, no space for a wardrobe or for anything else, but pinned on the wall above the bed—slightly torn, frayed along its edges and creased from folds—was a map of the world, a third of it shaded pink.

She moved over to the chest. Scattered on its surface were a few pennies, a packet of cigarette papers and a pamphlet titled *Discover New Zealand*. She picked up the pamphlet, casting her eyes over the color picture on the front: a man and a woman walking arm in arm toward green mountains. Then she saw the piece of paper and her name, "Dear Daisy . . ."

The writing was slanted, difficult to read and dated two days before, the fateful day she'd learned of her father's infidelity.

Dear Daisy,

I have loved you for so long I can't begin to remember. And I pretty much reckon that I know you better than most and that I love you more than anyone—because I love ALL of you, every-thing about you. The way you speak and say my name, the way you raise one side of your perfect mouth when you smile and then look downward. I love your dimple, the tiny mole on your cheek beneath your left eye, those tiny fine hairs that curl along your high brow and that one strand you pull at and wind round your finger. And your fingers, every one of them, and each thumb, and the way you blow your hair away from the side of your mouth before you speak, and the way you walk—with your shoulders sometimes hunched up around your ears, deep in thought. And the way you stare at things, even a dried-up leaf, examining it as though it's one of the Seven Wonders of the World. I love that you come to me and ask me stuff, and then come back and ask me again. I love that you talk to yourself and the mad old clothes you wear, that old fur coat you wander about in, and all those hats, and your bare feet in summer, your bare feet in summer walking on grass . . . And the shape of you, sound of you, color of you

Her hands shook; her eyes burned. She put down the letter, placed the pamphlet over it. Then she turned, ran back through the room and down the narrow staircase.

Chapter Fourteen

It was an exquisite morning, Daisy thought as she waited for the others to assemble outside. The temperature had risen overnight and a white mist hung over the hill, splintered by thin yellow shafts from the pale sun. The air was filled with the susurration of melting snow, the drip-drip sound from branches and icicles.

"Miles can *walk*," announced Lily, scowling as she emerged from the house with her husband trailing after her.

"Well, I'm certainly not walking in these shoes," said Iris, following them both out, a dead fox hanging from her shoulder, and, for once, wearing a dress.

"I'll walk with Miles," Daisy offered quickly.

"I'd prefer to walk, too," said Valentine.

Daisy smiled. She and Valentine had exchanged a polite "Good morning" and "Happy Christmas" with each other at breakfast, but no more than that.

"I'm in the doghouse," said Miles, as the three of them set off down the driveway. "I'll be treading on eggshells all bloody day . . . and that's just how my damned head feels."

Valentine laughed. "Forget about the dog's house; it's a hair from the animal that you need."

Daisy linked her arm through her brother-in-law's. "How was Stephen—when you saw him last night?" she asked.

"Same state as me . . . or worse."

"Did he seem . . . upset, unhappy?"

Miles shook his head. "He was quiet. But he's always quiet, isn't he?" he asked, turning to her.

"And what did he say to you about going to New Zealand?" she asked.

"I can't remember . . . just that that's where he thinks his future lies. Seems to think he'll be better off there than here."

But as they headed through the gateway, onto the wet road, Miles said, "Ah yes, it's all to do with some girl or other."

"Isn't it always?" said Valentine.

The three had almost reached the church by the time Reggie's car passed by, with Mabel in the front and Noonie, Dosia and Lily seated in the back. It was closely followed by Howard's, with Stephen at the wheel, Howard up front, and Margot, Iris and Ben in the back.

"Poor Gifford," said Miles, shaking his head as the car disappeared round the corner. "Must be bloody awful being told what to do the whole time . . . to be owned by Howard."

"We all are to some extent, Miles," said Daisy. "Or have you forgotten that he paid for your house?"

Church was filled with more than the usual fur stoles and homburg and trilby hats, and more than the usual pious faces. The Forbes family and their guests filled two pews reserved for them at the front. And though Daisy sang or mouthed the words to some of the carols, and said each *amen* on cue, she was distracted. It had ever been thus. Going to church had always made her think on herself, and some of her best and most vivid dreams had happened under the damp and stained plaster of that lofty ceiling.

She was aware of the person likely as not sitting at the back of the church and had turned, looking over the sea of hats and plumes, to find him. But she had not seen him. Staring ahead, facing the altar, she pictured the slanting hand once more, wishing she could recall all of the words, the exact words. She imagined Stephen, sitting at his table, writing them . . . But had he been drunk then, too? The hand had been *very* slanting . . . Doubt whispered in her ear, replacing the word *love* with *lust*. It was a word she knew went with *drunk*. She closed her eyes: She would have to think all of this through, would need to write everything down and ponder some more.

Through most of the service Daisy studied Valentine Vincent, in the pew immediately in front of her. She noted the way he remained bolt upright when the rest of them knelt in prayer, the fact that he was the only one not to go up to take Holy Communion; the way he tilted his head to one side so that the dark hair resting on the collar of his camel-hair overcoat rose to reveal the pale skin on the back of his neck; the way he followed the service, carefully turning flimsy pages, and, from time to time, the sound of his voice as he joined in with the singing . . . The only man who had kissed her.

But why had Stephen not kissed her? He'd been about to, she thought; when they'd stood together in his tiny lobby and he'd pulled her to him, hadn't he been about to kiss her then? But there had been so many moments when they'd been only a whisper away. And she could remember them all, going right back to the time he'd sucked the wasp sting from her wrist: standing in the greenhouse, his eyes locked with her own tearful ones, his mouth pressed to her skin. When she'd told him a few days later that she had been stung again—and this time on the other wrist, he'd examined her arm closely, running his fingers over and around her flesh, and then looked up at her and smiled. There was no sting, he said.

That was the problem with Stephen, Daisy thought, lifting her eyes back to the stained ceiling: He was simply too honest; *too* good.

Sitting toward the back of the church, Mrs. Jessop looked down and ran a gloved hand over her new navy blue coat. "Pure wool with cashmere," she'd said to Nancy earlier that morning, twirling about the kitchen. It had been her Christmas present to herself, bought at Elphicks department store in Farnham with some of her savings and all of her Christmas money from Mr. and Mrs. Forbes.

Her husband had smiled and said, "Very nice," in the usual way. But she knew she'd given herself something better than nice. She had given herself something promised to her years before, when she'd stood outside a shop window on Oxford Street, with Michael.

"I'll treat you to a new coat this winter," he'd said. "Which one do you fancy?"

She hadn't been sure. They were all so expensive.

"What about that navy blue one?" he'd said, pointing. "Pure wool with cashmere, it says."

She'd laughed, told him he could buy something like that for her after they were married, after they'd saved up enough for a deposit on that cottage and were settled.

He'd pulled her to him, and in broad daylight—on that sun-drenched busy street—he'd kissed her.

"You're having it," he'd said, smiling back at her. "You're having pure wool with cashmere. I'm not having my wife go about cold and shivering next winter."

Pure wool with cashmere, Mrs. Jessop thought, raising her eyes, smiling up at the brown stained ceiling.

Mabel had waited inside the church doorway for Howard, had held on to his arm as they walked down the aisle, each of them smiling and nodding at acquaintances and neighbors. Now Howard sat pressed up against her side. The pew *was* a little crowded, but each time she shuffled to make space for him, he seemed to move along too.

During the vicar's sermon, Mabel remembered her excursion of the previous day. She thought of her son outside in the churchyard, beneath the snow and frozen earth, and she closed her eyes: *Dear angels, keep my boy warm, wrap him in your love and glorious light and keep him safe for me . . . always and forever. Amen.*

If he'd lived, Mabel thought, opening her eyes, my life would be different. And she tried for a moment to picture a ten-year-old Theo, dark haired like his father, still in short trousers, all gangly legs and missing teeth. She would never have let Howard send him away to school; she'd have kept him with her, had him sitting there alongside her now, holding his hand, smiling back at him as he shuffled and whispered through the service. A boy, she thought, still just a boy.

When Howard placed his hand upon Mabel's, resting in her lap, she almost jumped. But she waited a minute before pulling them away. How could he know? How could he ever know or understand?

Mabel stared at the gray velvet cloche hat in the pew in front of her. She heard the vicar say something about the sanctity of marriage and heard Howard sigh. She watched dust motes dancing in a shaft of luminous light and saw the years ahead unfurling like a long carpet; saw herself alone at Eden Hall, silver hair bent over a tapestry, wrinkled hands fiddling shakily with threads, and she and Howard returning to that church, week after week, year after year, as Theo slept on, ignored, forgotten, unspoken.

"No."

Howard leaned toward her. "Hmm?"

She shook her head, fixed her gaze on the large floral arrangement at the foot of the pulpit. Could she do it? Could she really leave Eden Hall? There was her mother to consider, and Daisy. Though Daisy was less of a concern: She could go and live in London with Iris. An image of Daisy staggering out of some nightclub doorway flashed in Mabel's mind, and she shuddered and closed her eyes for a moment. *But if I don't do it now, I never will,* she thought. *I have to do it. It's not as though I'm asking for a divorce . . .*

And as though hearing her thoughts, the vicar's voice boomed the word *divorce,* and Mabel jumped again

Less than an hour later, when everyone was back at the house, standing in the sunlit drawing room with a glass of sherry, Stephen and the vicar helped Howard through the front door. Margot, in her gray velvet and silver fox stole, followed, carrying Howard's gloves, hat and cane. He had slipped by the war memorial outside the churchyard gate.

"Bloody stupid!" Howard said, limping, grimacing and shaking his head. "Bloody stupid."

Mabel directed the men to the drawing room, where they helped Howard to the large sofa. "Shall I send for Dr. Milton?" she asked.

Howard shook his head. "No, there's no need. I'll sit with it up for a while . . . I'm quite sure it'll be fine in an hour or so," he said, looking back at her beseechingly.

As people stood about offering sympathy by way of explanations—"So easily done"; "Could have happened to any one of us"—Nancy appeared with a bucket filled with snow and ice, and Mabel ushered the vicar, now holding a glass of sherry too, and her guests back into the hallway, closing the door and saying, "I think we'll let Howard have some privacy." She was in many ways still a Victorian and had no desire to see naked feet—particularly Howard's naked feet—in her drawing room before luncheon.

"How did it happen?" she asked Margot.

"I'm not sure . . . but I imagine it was his weak ankle."

"Oh yes," said Mabel, "his weak ankle. You'll have to watch that."

Chapter Fifteen

Mrs. Forbes had been to the kitchen. There was no alternative. Christmas lunch would have to be delayed, she'd said, in order that Mr. Forbes's ankle could be dealt with and the swelling given time to subside. "I know, I know," she'd said as Mrs. Jessop dropped a wooden spoon onto the bench and raised her hands in the air.

"It's most unfortunate and I can't apologize to you enough, Mrs. Jessop, but these things happen. And I absolutely insist that you all dine first. The family can wait."

It didn't seem right to Mrs. Jessop: Never in all her years had the servants eaten their Christmas dinner before the family. But as she said to Nancy, who was she to cast *spersions*.

When Mrs. Jessop finally untied and removed her apron, she waved it about her hot, flushed face and then sat down next to Nancy. Mr. Blundell said grace: "For what we are about to receive may the Lord make us truly thankful. Amen." Then he raised his glass, "To the cook," he said. "To Mrs. Jessop."

"Well, tuck in, everyone, and a happy Christmas to us all," she said, trying to smile.

There were eight of them seated at the table, including their guest, Mr. Blundell's friend, Mr. Brown—the butler from Beacon House, whose family had gone to a place called Saint Morrits for the duration. He was an odd combination: a sweaty little man, sulky in the face and a bit of a show-off, too, Mrs. Jessop thought, which seemed wrong for someone in his position—even if his family were in the Alps. He seemed only to want to talk about that place, which the family had taken him to, once—and to imagine and then announce what the family were likely to be doing at any given moment. Each time he'd gone silent, whenever Mrs. Jessop had asked him—because he'd been hovering about the kitchen for that long, watching her—if he was quite all right, he had simply shrugged his shoulders. Not once had he asked if he could help, even when Hilda—more slack-jawed than ever—dropped the jug of bread sauce on the stone floor. It wasn't her fault, Hilda said; she had been distracted. And it was a fair comment.

"Glue-vine?" Hilda had repeated, on her hands and knees, mopping up the spilled sauce.

"Yes, it's a local drink," said Mr. Brown.

It sounded quite disgusting to Mrs. Jessop.

The man had then said how magnificent the *shallies* were "when seen twinkling across the mountainside at night." Mrs. Jessop presumed they were some sort of nocturnal animal with eyes like a cat or a fox: A wild shalley perhaps? And Hilda must've thought the same.

"So you don't see them during the day?" Hilda asked.

Mr. Brown had laughed. "Why, yes, of course," he'd said. "Many of them are huge, as big as this house."

The man was clearly a fantasist, Mrs. Jessop thought, either that or on some queer medication. Then, more sympathetically, she wondered if Mr. Brown was in fact a war veteran like her husband.

The table, the long one from the kitchen, had been moved back into the servants' hall—where it used to be when there'd been more of them and they had taken their meals there and not in the kitchen. Nancy and Hilda had decorated the room with paper streamers and tinsel and bits of holly. And everyone looked ever so smart in their civvies, Mrs. Jessop thought: Smart as carrots, they were. And the table, with a proper linen cloth on it, very nice. Yes, ever so nice, she thought with a sigh, finally picking up her knife and fork.

Mrs. Jessop liked Christmas Day. She liked being there at the big house, cooking. Well, it was the best day of the year for any cook, and she'd rather be cooking there than in her own pokey kitchen. And his lordship was always very generous at Christmas, always made sure they got a few bob extra in their packet—as well as the wine, which she now sipped; then she nodded across the table to her husband.

Poor Old Jessop, she thought, watching him. But he enjoyed his food. And, like her, he enjoyed the occasional tipple. He enjoyed the simple things now, and had done so for many a year.

He'd only just been appointed head gardener when she first

came to Eden Hall. They'd married the following year. He'd been older than she'd anticipated a husband to be, and quieter and less passionate—a good deal less passionate. But by that time she'd known all about the repercussions of passion, and settled on him for his kindness and honesty and reliability. And, after all, she'd been no spring chicken herself.

It was the year after their marriage that Stephen had arrived and, a few years later, the war. She hadn't realized, none of them had, that it was the beginning of an end, or that it would go on for so long, or that afterward, even those who came back, who'd been spared, would be so . . . different.

Three years in the trenches had knocked it out of her husband. And it had taken her a while to realize that, to understand. Because he'd never spoken of it—of any of it—and even early on, when he first came back and had nightmares and night sweats—which still happened from time to time—and the shakes, tremors and head-aches, well, it was enough for her to know that the things he didn't speak of lived on, with him, and with them. In her mind, in her memory, the war was a thick, dark mist that had descended and engulfed them so that they'd all been lost. When they finally emerged, nothing was the same. There was *before* the war and *after* the war. That was all.

The Isaac Jessop who had gone off to war had never come back. But sometimes, when he smiled or stared back at her with those watery blue eyes—eyes forever damaged by mustard gas and fire and a vision of hell—she caught a glimpse and was reminded. But there were still those private moments, moments when she wished her husband could be more like one of the heroes in the True

Romances that Nancy passed on to her to read: the ones who told their women what was what and where they were headed (usually to London, and in a fine carriage). She liked to read them in bed with her cocoa as her husband slept beside her, and then compare notes with Nancy over their elevenses: whether the hero had been right to shield his young ward from the truth about her errant mother, or errant father, or her spent or unspent inheritance, and whether they'd have lived happily ever after. She liked to continue the story, speculate on what would and could have happened after The End. She always imagined lots of kiddies and long and blissfully happy lives, but Nancy usually foresaw obstacles: the evil brother or cousin in the West Indies or one of the colonies—or the one killed in the war not being dead at all—returning to England to claim Something or Other Towers or whatever the place was called.

Mrs. Jessop wished her husband had a bit of an imagination, and she wished he still had opinions, too, because it got ever so lonely having opinions on your own. But he seemed to have left all of that *over there*. All that talk of what they'd do, the places they'd see, what would happen in their lives, had come to an abrupt halt in 1914. They had still not been to Brighton, and now she doubted they ever would.

But it is what it is and that's that, she thought now, watching him in his yellow paper hat and three-piece suit, with his pa's old watch chain hanging across his waistcoat.

In truth, it had been an emotional few days, what with it being Christmas and after so many late meals, and then seeing That Woman at the carols last night, and again at church this morning.

And thinking of poor Madam and all she had had to put up with, and with That Woman and all her swank in Madam's house and as bold as brass sitting at Madam's table on Christmas Day, eating Madam's turkey and goose, and pulling Madam's crackers. Well, it was wrong, plain and simple wrong. And she felt guilty. She felt like a traitor, as though she had been inadvertently colluding with the enemy, or worse, she thought with a shudder, as though she were a German.

Thinking of all of this—That Woman, the Germans and the war—had quite put Mrs. Jessop off her food. For her, the meal was spoiled. She pushed her sprouts to the side of her plate, put down her knife and fork. And then, glancing about the table, she wondered if any of the others felt the same. It would never have happened in Mrs. Reed's day, she thought, none of it. *She* would have done something. And she would never have allowed for any sulkiness or bragging in *her* kitchen, either.

She had been at Eden Hall for almost two years when Mrs. Reed, the former cook, who everyone knew was really Miss Reed, retired and went to live in lodgings situated between Birch Grove, the home for unmarried mothers, and the Golden Hind Tea Rooms. These three buildings were right beside the bus stop, which was very handy for Mrs. Reed, and also handy for the women with straining coat buttons and small suitcases that Mrs. Jessop had often seen on her day off from her usual table by the window at the Golden Hind. Months later, she had sometimes seen and recognized one or another of these women again, more streamlined but still clutching a small suitcase. And as she'd watched them at the bus stop she had pondered the tragedy of it all. To have to travel to foreign parts, wait to give birth, then give away a baby and catch a bus home.

One day, watching one she vividly remembered from the time before, because she looked ever so young, Mrs. Jessop had found herself quite overcome, had had to wipe away a tear and fight the urge to get up and go out across the wet road to . . . She wasn't sure what, maybe offer the girl comfort. And it was made worse because the girl seemed to look right back at her. Mrs. Jessop had raised her hand above the arrangement of plastic carnations, had tried to smile; then the bus came, and as it stood there belching smoke into the drizzle, Mrs. Jessop hoped with a burning passion that when it moved on the girl would still be there, and if she was— if she was still standing there—she would go out to her and offer her something more than either of them knew at that moment. But the bus departed, and the girl with it. And Mrs. Jessop still thought of her, like Michael.

"Not like you to have no appetite," she said, glancing at her son's pale face. He had been a loving son, dutiful, kind and ever patient with her husband, and she hoped with all her heart that his recent restlessness wouldn't take him too far from her.

Stephen felt rotten. He couldn't remember what time he'd gone to bed, but his alarm had gone off far too bloody soon; that was for sure. It had been a struggle to get himself up and get the car round the front in time. And no sooner had he got back from church and put his head on the pillow than Nancy was at the door, telling him he had to get back down there because Mr. Forbes had had a fall.

Now his head pounded and he kept having flashbacks of himself and Tabitha Farley, the barmaid from the Coach and Horses. And though he could remember only some of what had happened the previous night, he had a pretty good idea, and an idea where his missing jacket might be.

"Eat up! You won't get anything like this in New Zealand, you know," said Hilda.

"New Zealand?" Nancy repeated. "That's in Australia, isn't it? Are you thinking about emigrating, Stephen?"

"Just an idle dream, Nancy."

"Well, I'd thank you to keep your dreams closer to home. What's wrong with round here?" his mother asked.

"They don't have Christmas in Australia," said Hilda through a mouthful of food.

"Don't they? Do you hear that, Stephen? They don't even have Christmas in Australia," his mother repeated.

"Oh, but they do," said Mr. Brown. "It's just that in the Southern Hemisphere it happens to be in the summer."

"In the summer? Well, that's plain wrong," said Nancy. "Christmas is meant to be in December . . . it's our Lord's birthday and you can't go and change that willy-nilly and as you please."

"Ah, but you see," Mr. Brown began, putting down his knife and fork and adjusting his paper hat—which kept slipping down his balding head to his bony nose, "the summer is in December down there." And as the conversation sank to a new level of confusion, Stephen rested his head in his hands and closed his eyes. He had neither the inclination nor the energy to join in this particular debate.

New Zealand. Would he ever get there? Not if he kept going back to the Coach and Horses, he wouldn't. Not with Tabitha Farley always finishing when he was and asking him to walk her home and putting his hand down the front of her blouse. Not with all that going on. And Daisy . . . Daisy Forbes?

"Elbows off the table, Stephen!"

He opened his eyes, sat up in his chair and tried to smile back at Hilda. Feeling more lugubrious than ever, he was, he thought, an idiot—a complete idiot—to even for a single beer-soaked minute entertain the thought that someone like Daisy would ever in a million years go with someone like him: a servant, a drunk and another one who couldn't keep his flies done up.

Chapter Sixteen

There was a choice of turkey or goose, roasted potatoes, endless vegetables and accompaniments, sauces and gravy, all followed by a flickering blue-flamed pudding, carried in by Mrs. Jessop—looking quite different in a navy blue jersey dress and red paper hat. Mabel served the plum pudding, handing the bowls down the table, and seconds later Daisy called out, "It's me! I have it!" She lifted the sixpence from the soggy mess in her bowl and held it up for everyone to see. A polite hush descended.

"Now, are you going to make a wish—or do you still not believe in them?" asked Margot, smiling.

But as Daisy closed her eyes she heard Margot whisper to Mabel, "You know, I always longed for a daughter . . . and now I'm to have one. For Valentine is engaged to be married, and his fiancée, Aurelia, is the sweetest, kindest creature that *ever* lived."

Daisy opened her eyes.

"How wonderful," said Mabel. She tilted her head toward Valentine. "Many congratulations to you, my dear."

Val smiled. He glanced from Daisy to his mother, then back to Daisy.

"They haven't set a date, as it hasn't been officially announced yet, but we're thinking of late summer, perhaps September," Margot went on. "I think it's the perfect month for a wedding."

"I like June. We were married in June," said Lily, turning and smiling at a contrite Miles.

"Mabel and Howard were married in September," said Iris, staring over the table at Margot. "They celebrate twenty-five years of wedded bliss next year."

Margot smiled. "Yes, I know. I was there . . . Seems like yesterday."

"Oh, I say, is there to be a party?" asked Dosia, turning to her brother.

Howard smiled at Mabel. "I rather think there should be . . ."

Mabel said nothing.

"In the meantime," Howard continued, "I believe a toast is in order . . ." But as he tried to rise to his feet, he grimaced with obvious pain and quickly sat back down. "Forgive me, please, for not standing . . . but a toast is a toast all the same. To Valentine and Aurelia."

"To Valentine and Aurelia!"

Valentine forced a smile, said a quiet thank-you, then picked up his spoon and stared down at his pudding. And as Mabel and Margot went on discussing weddings, Daisy offered, "Aurelia's a very pretty name . . ."

Valentine didn't look at Daisy. He frowned slightly, tilted his head to one side, but said nothing.

Then Margot, overhearing Daisy's comment, said, "Isn't it just? And it *so* suits her. Some people are born to have a certain name, and she was born to be Aurelia. It means *golden* . . . and she is," she added, wide-eyed and smiling. "She's truly a golden girl!"

"She certainly is," agreed Howard.

"You've met her?" asked Iris.

Howard stammered. "Well . . . er, yes, I believe so . . . think I may have done . . ."

"Surely you'd remember whether or not you had met Valentine's *golden girl?*" said Iris. "Anyone would remember meeting an Aurelia, I think."

Howard stared at Mabel.

"Yes, I believe you did meet her, once," said Margot. "It was when I played Judith Bliss at the Criterion. *Hay Fever* is such a marvelously funny play . . . Have you seen it, Mabel? Oh, but you must—it's one of my favorites, but then dear Noel is my absolute favorite playwright and such a *darling* man."

At that moment Valentine pushed back his chair, turned to Mabel and said if she didn't mind he rather needed to take some air.

"Of course, my dear," said Mabel.

Minutes later, as they all rose to their feet, Daisy saw him through the dining room window, walking away from the house across snow-covered lawns, his collar pulled up, his head down, his hand moving to and from his face as he smoked. It struck her then, at that moment, that he didn't seem altogether happy, and she assumed it was guilt—because of last night: kissing her when he was in fact betrothed to another. She half thought of going after him, but what could she say? She had no experience of *engaged* men—of any men at all, come to that. But they all seemed rather confused and tortured to her.

It meant nothing, she thought, watching the camel-hair coat disappear into the woodland. *My first kiss meant nothing, to either one of us.*

After lunch, everyone sat about in the hallway inhaling eucalyptus and pine and damp dog as Howard reached down, read out tags and handed over the festooned packages. There were the usual bath salts and soap, mittens and handkerchiefs, calendars and books and new cloth- or leather-bound diaries marked *1927.* Daisy had already taken a look and rummaged. Had felt anything marked with the message "To Daisy." She knew it was there, knew it was coming, but Howard left it until last.

"To our darling Dodo, Happy Christmas from Mummy and Daddy," he said without looking at the tag and walking toward Daisy with the large wrapped box. He placed it at Daisy's feet, kissed her forehead. "Happy Christmas, darling."

It was a Remington typewriter, the one she'd asked for, in a dark gray mottled leather case and with large round buttons no finger could miss. She turned to her mother: "Thank you . . . thank you so much."

"You really should be thanking your father. I had no part in it."

Daisy looked at her father, who remained a few feet in front of her, staring back at her and smiling. "Thank you, Howard," she said. He could never again be *Daddy.*

"Yes, I see what you mean . . . ," said Stephen, taking a cigarette from the proffered packet. "To be honest, I'm in a bit of a similar situation myself."

The two of them were sitting in the armchairs on either side of the fire in the sitting room of Stephen's flat. They had bumped into each other out in the yard, where Stephen had been chopping a few more logs, to save his father doing it, and Valentine had been—well, loitering about, Stephen thought.

They had met many times before, and it was nice, Stephen thought now, to be able to return a bit of hospitality, because Val had always been good to him. Anytime he'd sat outside in the motor—reading the newspaper, waiting for his nibs—Val had emerged on the doorstep, invited him in, taken him to the basement kitchen and offered him a cuppa. Nice chap, he'd thought. Of course, they didn't have a lot in common—other than a mutual distrust of Benedict Gifford, who had always talked down to Stephen. But during the course of the preceding year he and Val had become friendly and had talked about this and that: the weather, the floods, the strike, cricket. They had never really talked much about girls, women, though Stephen had mentioned Daisy, how many times he wasn't altogether sure. But now that Val had shared something of his own intimate affairs, Stephen had felt it not unwrong and maybe even sympathetic to mention his own dilemma.

"Bit like you," Stephen said, "in love with one, probably—most definitely—the wrong one, and stuck on a track with a bit of a fast one."

"But you're not engaged to be married?" asked Val.

"No, thank God, I'm not. Not to her anyway, not to the fast one . . . but I wish I was to the other."

Neither one of them used any names. This—to both—kept the conversation entirely aboveboard and confidential. Val had simply said that while he was engaged to one girl—someone his mother had introduced him to and liked, someone he'd thought he loved—he'd recently fallen for another. And quite out of the blue, quite unexpectedly. But it had thrown him, made him question everything.

"And I've suddenly realized how little I know about her—my fiancée. How little we know about each other. You see, we haven't known each other very long."

Stephen explained that his situation was different: he was in love with someone he'd known for years. When Val said to Stephen, "So what's the problem?" Stephen wasn't sure what to say, how to explain. Then he said, "Class . . . background, that sort of thing."

Val stared at him, narrowing eyes for a moment. "It's not Daisy . . . not Daisy Forbes, is it? Because I know you liked her. I remember you talking about her quite often, and telling me . . ."

Stephen sucked hard on his cigarette. He wondered, thought for a minute about coming clean, telling Val the truth, but then he decided it was probably best to follow Val's example and keep names out of it. "No, not Daisy," he replied.

"So . . . what's she like?" said Val, leaning forward, stubbing out his cigarette. "Pretty?" he asked, glancing up.

Stephen nodded, his lips sealed. He wanted to describe her, was desperate to describe her, because after watching her for the best part of ten years, he knew it was something he could do, and do very well. He knew that he could describe her in such extraordinary detail it would reveal her identity. *Daisy* . . . how that name quickened his heart.

"And the other, Miss Fast Track?"

Stephen laughed. He looked away for a moment, remembering the previous night. "That's a sorry tale," he said.

"Why's that?"

Stephen shook his head. "She has this way . . . when I'm a bit owled, of getting me to . . . you know, walk her home and so on."

"And so on?"

"Yes, *and so on.*"

"And does the other one know—the one you're in love with?"

Stephen shuddered. "No, she does not, thank God. But it's got to stop, got to," he said, refreshing their glasses with the malt whiskey Howard had given him. "I don't even want to . . . but when I've had a few, when she . . . you know, asks me to walk her home, and then . . ." He looked up at Val, and Val nodded.

"Hard when it's on offer, eh?"

They sat for a while in silence, their eyes fixed on the small fire. Then Stephen sat back and said, "So what about you and this young miss, the one you've fallen for? What's she like?"

Val stared back at Stephen with a strange smile.

"Well?" said Stephen, smiling back at him.

Val took a sip of his whiskey. "You know what? I'm going to tell you . . . but you must keep it in confidence, yes?"

Stephen nodded. "Of course."

"It's Daisy."

Stephen barely heard what came after, but when Valentine said, "And then I kissed her," Stephen's glass of malt whiskey slipped from his fingers to the floor.

Chapter Seventeen

It was a fine day with a clear sky and soft breeze, and Stephen had been up early. For lack of anything better to do—or rather, for something to do, to distract him—he'd decided to wash the Rolls. But even as he worked, a sequence of images flooded his mind. And one in particular took him back, to a midsummer evening some three years before.

He had been in the greenhouse with his father, potting up geraniums for Mrs. Forbes, watching the man's shaky hands as he carefully tended the plants, listening as his father intermittently hummed some half-forgotten tune that had surfaced in his memory. Stephen had loved those moments, when there had been just the two of them, working in warm security, in virtual silence; his father from time to time glancing up to smile in sheer, undiluted pleasure at the sight of a tiny bud or newly opened petal. Simple stuff.

But this night, as his father went off to fetch more compost,

Daisy had appeared in the doorway. And that image of her standing in the doorway of the greenhouse was seared in his memory. She had been wearing a pale blue cotton dress and a broad-brimmed straw hat, and the westerly light, still bright and golden, had shone through the thin fabric of her dress, revealing the shape of her legs. She had stood there for some time, picking at the peeling paint and saying something about something not being fair.

"They're all against me," she'd said, and then screamed.

He'd moved quickly, seen the sting and not thought for a second of what was needed: had simply lifted her wrist to his mouth. A few days later, when he was painting the garage doors, she had come up to him—quite calmly—telling him that she thought she had been stung again, this time on the other wrist. But there had been no sting, none that he could find. He could have pretended, could have put her skin to his mouth again, and he'd wanted to. But somehow it seemed wrong. And he could not lie: not to her. She was—had always been—worth more than that.

Later, he had wondered whether she had been playing with him, whether she had known all along that there was no sting. This in itself had fascinated him, excited him and given him endless hours of pleasure—imagining the machinations of her desire and intent; but, ultimately, it seemed too much to hope. And yet there had been other times when she had sought him out—to ask him the name of something or to help her find a particular leaf or plant or nest, to draw or paint. And though he loved that she came to him, loved that he could help her and cherished the times, as he always had, when they were together and alone, he wondered if his love—so undiluted and luminous—was as obvious to her as it was to him.

And so for a while, in order to counteract this, to somehow dim and diminish and cloud it, he had adopted a more dismissive approach. Had been studiedly offhand with her and avoided any eye contact, because that was the worst, when she looked at him— directly at him—and he looked back at her. He knew then that he was lost and that she would surely see. But this indifferent approach hadn't lasted very long, simply because he found it so difficult to be like that with her, and because to *not* look at her was one of the hardest things he'd ever done and had meant he'd made up for it by staring when he thought she wasn't looking and had then been caught out, which was possibly worse, and more embarrassing.

Once, when they were younger, there had been an easy and uninhibited camaraderie between them, with no consciousness of any division in their station, what they should or should not do, how they should or should not be, what they could or could not say. They had been friends, equal in everything other than their age and sex, and sometimes—because he was older—their knowledge. But as the years passed, as they'd grown older, this had changed— on his part, at least. Daisy the girl became Daisy the woman, and there was nothing Stephen could do to stop the love he'd first felt— when he'd wished she had been *his* sister. Sisterly love turned to something altogether different, and by the time Stephen carved their initials on the trunk of the great beech by the gate to the woods he was already dreaming of his future with her.

When Stephen glanced up and saw her, walking across the courtyard toward him, he put down the chamois leather and quickly ran his hand over his hair. He'd dreamed of her, woken up thinking of her, walked out hoping for her. This day was no different from any other.

"I imagine you had a bit of a sore head yesterday," Daisy said, smiling.

"Just a bit."

"I wanted to—"

"I hear you and Valentine have become quite friendly," he said quickly, interrupting her. And immediately he wanted to kick himself. He'd promised himself he wouldn't mention it, wouldn't say anything at all. He'd spent half the night telling himself that Vincent's kiss had been stolen rather than given, and then lain awake at dawn torturing himself again with the image of them together. How long had their kiss lasted? Had Daisy enjoyed it? Was she in love with him?

"What do you mean?" Daisy asked.

He couldn't hold back. "He told me, Daisy," he said, louder and more dramatic than he intended, and sounding like a jealous lover—even to his own ears. "Valentine told me what happened between you," he added, quieter.

"Oh, that," said Daisy, turning away from him. "It was nothing. Anyway, he's engaged to be married."

"Which makes it all the more wrong."

"I agree. It was a mistake . . . a huge mistake. And really, I never wanted to kiss him."

"So why did you?" he asked, unable to stop himself.

"I'm not sure . . . Are you jealous?"

"No, but I was concerned. You've only just met the man," he added, trying to laugh.

"Concerned? Your own behavior that same night was hardly exemplary. You were drunk, Stephen."

"Yes, and I want to apologize. I know I made a fool of myself . . . It's not something I'm very proud of."

Her hair was loose, pushed behind her ears and hanging down beyond her elbows. She wore her long fur coat and a dark green woolen beret pulled so far down her head that it almost covered her eyes, which were shielded by a pair of sunglasses—belonging to Iris, he presumed. She kicked nonchalantly at the gritted yard, her hands pushed deep into her pockets. Then she looked up, stepped toward him and blew a strand of hair from her mouth.

"Really, why do you think you made a fool of yourself?" she asked.

She was smiling again now, and he couldn't help but smile too. On one side of her mouth—the side that curved up, because she had that lopsided way of smiling and always had had—there was a dimple; a tiny crescent of a dimple that had been there as long as he'd known that smile. When she turned away—still smiling—she removed the sunglasses, lifted her head and squinted up at the sun. He took in her profile with an all too familiar yearning: the line of her chin, pale skin of her neck. What it must be to hold her, to hold her and kiss her, he thought.

She turned to him, stepped nearer. "Well . . . ?"

He was in his overalls, hadn't yet combed his hair or shaved and looked a sight, he knew. He said, "*Well* . . . ," staring back at her, "I hope I didn't make you feel uncomfortable or anything."

"Stephen, of every man I know—and granted, I don't know too

many—you're the least likely to . . ." She paused. "You're the one I most trust."

He wanted to say then, *Oh, Daisy Forbes, I Bloody Love You. I Love You So Much.* But instead they stood smiling at each other, for what seemed to him like a blissful eternity. Eventually he said, "That makes me happy. And I hope it'll always be the case."

She looked away, embarrassed, he thought, and began kicking at the ground once more. "The other night," she said tentatively, "when you talked about going to New Zealand . . ." She turned and glanced at him sideways with a new coyness. "Do you remember what you said?"

He nodded.

"Did you mean it?"

"I told you, I think I made a bit of a fool of myself."

She shook her head. "No. Don't say that. I know you were . . . tight, and it sort of makes sense, but I need you to tell me the truth . . . I need you to tell me if you meant what you said."

"Every word and more."

She stared back at him and nodded. Then, with a newly serious expression, she said, "I need to tell *you* something. The thing is, Stephen," and he closed his eyes for a second or two, relishing the sound of his name on her lips, "I came back to your flat to tell you that . . . well, you see . . ." She paused. And he waited. But as he waited, as he stood waiting for words he was famished for, something began to flicker in his peripheral vision, and as it gathered substance and grew more solid and dark, he became aware that whatever it was, was moving at quite a pace from the back driveway toward them. *Don't look . . . Finish the sentence . . . Tell me.*

"Stephen!"

It was Daisy who turned away first; he simply followed her gaze. But the sound of his name on another's lips shattered the intimacy, stopped Daisy in her tracks and threw his heart like a small stone from a cliff. It was gone. The sentence could never be recovered. He knew it the second he turned his head and saw Tabitha Farley carrying what very much looked like his missing suit jacket.

"You forgot this the other night," Tabitha said, moving rapidly toward Stephen and eyeing Daisy with a tight smile and a tart, "Morning."

"Daisy Forbes—Tabitha Farley; Tabitha Farley—Daisy Forbes," he said, introducing them plainly, then closing his eyes. Of all the moments for Tabitha Farley to appear. Tabitha Bloody Farley who had never in her life set foot on Eden Hall soil . . .

"Ah yes," he said, regaining control and opening his eyes. "I was wondering where I'd left that." He glanced to Daisy, who looked back at him, eyebrows raised, intrigued. "I was going to head over to the pub to see if it was there, in fact . . ."

But as soon as he'd said this he wished he had not, because Tabitha then began: "No, you silly, you didn't leave it at the pub; you left it at mine! And I don't know for the life of me how you walked home in the freezing cold in the middle of the night without it, but I said, I'll make sure it gets back to him and, well, what with it being Christmas Day yesterday, I said, well, I won't take it up there today because he'll probably be busy and he won't need it anyway if he's indoors, and everyone's always indoors at Christmas . . . but I knew you'd be wondering and I wanted to make sure you got it, so here it is," she ended breathlessly, passing him the creased garment. She then moved alongside him, linked her arm through his and stared back at Daisy, who said something about it being a glorious morning and then turned and walked away.

He watched her go, watched her go as if she was leaving his life forever, and Tabitha must have sensed something, because she said, "Oh, did I just interrupt something? I almost feel like I have."

And he wanted to say, *Yes, you have, you've interrupted my life's dream.*

Mabel stood at the window looking up at the pale sky. Reg had already gone, had left after breakfast to set off for Dorking, where he was to spend Boxing Day with his late wife's sister and family. He could of course have returned home the previous evening, but she had managed to persuade him to stay another night. "Why?" she had said. "Why go back there when you don't need to, when you can go directly to Irene's from here?"

She glanced at the envelope, propped up on her desk and addressed simply to "Mabel." It was silly, really, how she felt about a note, and nothing more than a simple thank-you, but it was from him to her, and even the sight of her name in his hand made her feel quite giddy.

Their good-bye had been brief. He had said, "It's been perfect. Thank you." That was all. When he had held her hand, then lifted it to his mouth, she had smiled: His mustache always tickled her. Then he had handed her the note. Now, standing at the window in her boudoir with the door closed, she imagined him arriving in that place, Dorking.

She was pleased that he wasn't returning to High Pines yet. She had never told him, never said anything to him about the place, but it felt to her like a mausoleum; was always so cold and empty: too big for one person. She hated to think of him there alone. And, if she were honest, she didn't care for all his Indian furniture and artifacts. They simply didn't fit into a house in Surrey, she thought, becoming distracted. Was that Daisy—crossing over the lawn in that ridiculous old coat? She shook her head, moved away from the window and sat down at her desk.

Jessop would need to bring the car round for midday if the Vincents were to catch the 12:35 . . . if there was a 12:35, for no one seemed sure of the train timetable. And if there was no train, well, Jessop would simply have to drive them back to London.

It had been a surprise, the announcement of their departure a day early, not that she minded. In fact, she would, she thought, be a little relieved to see them go. Margot had said it was because of Val, that he had decided he needed to get back to work, which seemed queer to Mabel, because he didn't *really* work, as such; he wrote, which he could surely easily do there. And as Howard had said earlier, when he'd come to speak with her about their train, it wasn't as though he had any deadline or publisher waiting.

"Perhaps it's not him," Mabel had suggested. "Perhaps it's Margot who wants to leave . . ."

Howard had laughed and said, "Well, whichever one of them it is, I couldn't give a damn, to be honest." But honesty, she knew, was not Howard's strong suit, and she detected some irritation or even anger in his voice. She wondered if her husband and Margot had perhaps had some sort of falling-out, because there had, as Reg had pointed out, been a certain frostiness between her husband and his *dear friend* over the last couple of days.

Howard had never quizzed Mabel, never asked her why she had invited Margot. He knew. Mabel smiled. She had long since stopped hating Margot Vincent. In fact, she'd been surprised to discover that she quite liked the woman who had been in her husband's life, been his confidante, for so many years. Without a confession from Howard, she'd never know for sure when his affair with Margot had begun, but of one thing she was certain: It was over; their relationship was platonic.

One of the reasons she had invited Margot for Christmas was so that she could see the woman again and watch her with Howard. She had seen for herself that there was no frisson, that while Margot was very possibly in love with—or in need of—Howard, he was . . .

Mabel sat up in her chair. Could it be? Was it possible that Howard was in love with *her*? The thought made her laugh out loud, and she shook her head. The timing was indeed curious. And yet it no longer mattered, any of it, because she had made her decision. And though the thought of leaving Eden Hall was still shocking— what would Howard say? how would they cope without her?—she now longed to escape, to escape from it *all*.

She glanced down at the scrawled lists scattered over her desk. Then, one by one, she picked up each piece of paper, tore it in two and dropped the pieces into the wastepaper basket by her side.

⤫

The snow-covered lawns were punctured by what seemed to Daisy to be thousands of footprints—birds, foxes, cats, dogs, deer and humans, which crisscrossed and zigzagged and led off in every direction. The thaw continued in the incessant dripping from every shrub and tree and had turned the once powdery snow to a watery slush underfoot. It would all be gone by tomorrow or the next day, she thought, sensing an end and raising her hand to her brow to squint up at the magnificent redwood against the pale winter sky.

She crossed over the driveway, trying to find and follow the pathway to the Japanese garden, treading carefully, feeling for the steps through her rubber boots. Here, there were minimal footprints. The white crystals she had watched falling from the oriel window with her father only four nights before remained almost undisturbed. But the ice on the pond had melted away to a small circle, and the old bench, which had looked for a day or two like a sumptuous white sofa from her bedroom window, offered only a thin icy cushion now. She ran a gloved hand along the slats, pushing off the snow to reveal the silvery lichen-covered wood, and then sat down—pushing her hands deeper into the torn pockets of her ancient coat.

The large bamboo bush had collapsed from the middle under the weight of the snow, and all was pale and silver and green. She watched a robin fly down to the edge of the pond, begin stabbing at the glacial water with its beak, its tiny head glancing up and around in jerky movements.

Tabitha? It was a cat's name, surely? But that girl wasn't worth thinking about: a waste of her time and energy. And so was Stephen. He was no different from her father and had just proved himself so. And Valentine Vincent was no better either, she thought, and really rather rude—because he had barely spoken a word to her since they'd kissed. A new wave of indignation rose in her. She smoothed down the fur pile of her coat. "I should have slapped his face," she whispered. At least *he* would be leaving shortly . . . he and his mother. And good riddance to them both.

Benedict Gifford was the only honest one among them. After all, he had declared his intentions, behaved like a gentleman and never taken advantage of her *or* toyed with her emotions. He had not written words that were quite clearly lies, he did not have a fiancée, nor did he leave his clothing lying about in women's houses. He was, in a word, decent.

"Very decent," she said. And the robin flew off.

Stephen Jessop, on the other hand . . . No. She did not want to think about him. Would not let herself think about him. But the fact that he had gone back to that place, the Coach and Horses, and then . . . then somehow ended up at that girl's house where goodness only knows what had happened, but where he'd certainly been comfortable enough, warm enough to dispense with his clothing, and after telling her, telling *her* only hours before—"only hours before!"—that he loved her, had always loved her, and that he wanted to take her off to . . .

"New Zealand!"

A liar. That's what he was, another bloody liar. But why had he said those things—and what did he think she would do, throw herself at him? Thank God Tabitha Whoever She Was had appeared. And thank God she hadn't said what she was about to say. She gasped and shook her head.

And that note, she thought, raising her eyes to the sky once more. *I need to forget it.* Because Tabitha had, in that two-second look, with her arm linked through his and staring back at Daisy, told Daisy all she needed to know: Stephen and Tabitha were lovers.

"Oh, Daisy, what a silly little fool you are . . ."

The tear, which escaped from beneath her sunglasses and rolled down her cheek, surprised her, until she decided that she had in fact chosen to cry, because it was part of a great catharsis that would only make her stronger and make it easier to start afresh. And that's what she needed to think of and look to: new horizons and new people, so many new people to meet, she thought, wiping away more tears and trying to smile.

She could hear the familiar rumbling of a car engine in the distance and knew it must be Stephen warming it up, ready to transport the Vincents to the station. "He'll probably marry her, go to New Zealand with her, and I will never see or speak to him again," she whispered.

Iris was right: She needed to get away from there. She was, she realized, bored by the stalemate of her life, the relentless disappointment and unending expectation of something more than nothing. She was uninspired by everything and everyone around her, because she had watched and waited for too long. Was this all there was? she thought, glancing around her. Was *this* to be her life? At that moment she longed for every single thing to be different; a yearning so great, so powerful, so all consuming, that it no longer mattered whose feelings might be hurt.

She rose to her feet, resolute, and returned to the house by way of the ragged rhododendrons and hidden pathways of the northern shrubbery, and then via the yard. The car had gone, the garage doors were closed, the place deserted. She glanced up to the dust-covered windows of Stephen's flat and wondered if Tabitha was there, inside, waiting for him to return from the station, and if his "Dear Daisy" letter to her was still by his bed. As she opened the back door and threw off her gumboots, another thought occurred: Perhaps Stephen had written to Tabitha also. Perhaps he was in the habit of writing to women; perhaps that was his seduction technique. She walked down the narrow passageway pulling off her heavy coat and hat, shaking out her hair, the sting of jealousy slowly giving way to the reignited prickle of indignation. She paused by a round window, staring out momentarily at the yard. Yes, with or without her father's permission, she would go and live in London with Iris.

And she saw herself in wide-legged trousers on a velvet carpet beneath a glass porch; she saw herself with vermilion-painted lips and matching fingernails clutching a long cigarette holder and talking animatedly to people eager for her opinion. She'd reinvent herself. Have her hair cut, undoubtedly. Take up cocktails and dancing, definitely. People would be astounded by her energy, describe her as a whirlwind, an inspiration . . . She'd call everyone *darling*, blow kisses indiscriminately and laugh at things that weren't funny. She'd have lovers, probably be married more than once . . . *and* cited in divorce actions. And one day, eventually, she'd pen a shocking memoir, in which she'd talk about her life and the men she had known and *not* loved.

But first there were a few things she had to do.

Nancy and Hilda were having their elevenses, huddled over a magazine on the table—which they quickly closed and turned over when Daisy walked into the kitchen.

"Is Mrs. Jessop about?" Daisy asked, glancing upward and rolling her eyes sideways—in the way Iris sometimes did—already adopting her new demeanor.

"She's gone to the kitchen garden with Mr. Jessop, but I'm sure she'll be back soon," said Nancy. "Is there something I can help you with?"

"No, not really," she replied. "I just met Tabitha . . ."

"Tabitha Farley?" Nancy asked.

Daisy looked back at her. "I'm not sure—not sure *which* Tabitha."

"You'd know if it was her," said Hilda, wiping shortbread crumbs from her lips.

"She's a friend of Stephen's," Daisy said, after a moment.

"She's that, all right, and plenty more be—"

"She works at the Coach and Horses," interrupted Nancy, rising to her feet. "That's how he knows her," she added, gathering up plates and cups.

Daisy nodded. "Oh, so are they . . . courting?"

Hilda sniggered and Nancy shot her a look.

"I'm not sure . . . Perhaps," said Nancy, "but I don't think it's anything serious . . . just a dalliance."

Daisy smiled and then nodded again. "Ah yes, a dalliance, of course," she said, and laughed. It was another one of those things she'd normally have asked Iris about: what the parameters of a *dalliance* were, what was involved. But what did it matter? If Stephen wanted to dally with a Tabitha, that was fine by her. She glanced up at the clock on the wall. There was no time to waste: She needed to find her mother.

Mabel, as usual, was in her boudoir. But this morning she appeared to be having some sort of clear-out: tearing up paper, ripping pages from notebooks and dropping them into the overflowing basket by her side. Daisy stood for a minute, watching, listening to her mother's humming; then she took a deep breath and stepped forward, into the room. "I've decided to go to London to live with Iris," she said.

Mabel didn't say anything. She glanced up, smiled and nodded.

"I'm leaving. I'm going to find a job, be independent . . ."

Still Mabel said nothing and continued to tear up sheets of paper.

"I'm *leaving* here," Daisy declared, with slightly more fervor. "I'm leaving Eden Hall."

"Yes, I hear you," said Mabel, calmly, quietly, not at all as Daisy had been expecting.

"And you have nothing to say?"

Mabel stopped. She rose from her desk and moved toward the French doors. "I don't think there's very much *to* say. It sounds to me as though you've made up your mind."

"Yes, I have . . . I'm suffocating in this place. I can't breathe. There's nothing and no one for me here—apart from you," she quickly added. "And all I seem to do is wait . . . wait for something to happen, to change," she went on, moving nearer to her mother.

"But I need you to support me in this . . . and I need you to tell Howard."

The two women stood side by side, staring out over the frozen gardens.

"In that case, we need to support each other," said Mabel. "Because I'm leaving, too."

Mabel joined Howard on the front doorstep. She kissed Margot on the cheek—powdered, rouged and reeking of Lily of the Valley—then she watched the woman step inside the car and saw Jessop place the rug over her lap. And as the vehicle slowly pulled away, with Margot's gloved hand raised to them, Mabel felt her husband slip his arm around her waist.

"Well, there they go," he said as the car honked its horn and disappeared beyond the tall shrubbery.

He turned to Mabel, but before he could say anything more, she said, "We need to talk, Howard. I have something to tell you."

Minutes later, Mabel closed the door of her boudoir and instructed her husband to sit down.

He sat down.

"I've decided to go away," she began and then paused. "I've been here for twenty-five years, and . . . well, I feel the need for a change."

Howard grimaced. He raised a hand to his chest, and for a moment Mabel wondered if he might be having another attack of heartburn. But she would not be put off. Not now.

"I'm going away with your sister on a tour of the continent," she continued. "I'll be leaving here next week . . . to stay in London with Dosia, where we'll sort our itinerary and do some shopping; then we'll be leaving." She saw her husband close his eyes. "Howard?"

He stared back at her, blinked a few times.

"Are you all right?" she asked.

"I'm not sure. Did you just say something about going away?"

Mabel tilted her head to one side. "Don't pretend you didn't hear me . . . Yes, I'm going away. I'm leaving here, leaving you . . . for a while, anyway."

"When did you decide this?"

"Oh, only recently."

"But I wanted to talk to you. I need to tell you—"

"No," she interrupted. "I don't wish to talk, not now. We can talk when I return."

"And when will that be?" he asked.

"I'm not sure . . . late spring, early summer, perhaps."

Howard leaned forward and placed his head in his hands. "Summer . . ."

Mabel sat down. "Dosia says we need at least four or five months if we're to do the thing properly . . . see everywhere. She says Italy alone will take far more than a month."

"It'll be costly."

"I'm funding the entire expedition myself, with the money my father left me. I've done my sums."

"And what about Reggie?" he asked, glancing up her. "Is *he* going with you?"

Mabel glanced away and affected a shrug. "He might join us at some stage . . . He thought perhaps the Riviera in late May."

Howard lowered his head again. "And Daisy?" he asked. "She's really far too young to be left alone here."

"It's all sorted. She's going to live in London with Iris."

"I see. But what about this place—and your mother, what about Noonie?"

"I've spoken with her. She's all for it . . . insists she'll be fine, and anyway, *you* will be here."

He looked up at her: "I will be here?"

"Yes. I'm afraid you'll have to be here, to look after my mother and to manage the place . . . just as I have these past twenty-five years."

Standing on the little wooden bridge, halfway down into the valley known as the Devil's Punchbowl, Daisy thought for a moment about dropping the globe into the swollen, fast-flowing stream, allowing the torrent to perhaps carry it off down the hillside. But there was every chance it would simply sink and rest there, and then she'd very possibly return to fish it out.

It was a symbolic act, she knew. But after everything that had happened during the preceding days, after discovering the truth about her father and about Stephen, it seemed a fitting gesture: not only an action to commemorate her liberation and Mabel's, but an action to liberate every Christmas ahead and forget every one that had come before.

In the distance she heard a car horn, and she moved away from the bridge and clambered along the snowy embankment, the globe clutched in her hand.

She stepped forward onto the ridge, where the hillside fell away in a precipitous drop. The sky was pale and low. Nothing stirred. The damp stillness hung like an unspent deluge above her head, waiting. Far below, a clump of pine trees almost as small as those inside the globe in her hand seemed to beckon and a new unsettling energy swept through her. She raised her hand, took it back over her shoulder.

She threw it high, watching its trajectory as it revolved through the air in a perfect arc and then fell, disappearing into the snow.

It was gone. Life had changed. It was time to move on.

Chapter Eighteen

Over the next few days a strange calm descended over Eden Hall. But beneath an atmosphere of resignation, of quiet acceptance, was the nervous energy of departure.

Outside, intermittent rain washed away the graying snow, leaving dirty peaks along the sides of forgotten pathways. Inside, Christmas was abandoned as trunks were brought down from the attics. Mabel began a new list, titled "Packing"; she pulled out sun-bleached florals and faded stripes and held them up to herself in front of her dressing mirror. She rummaged in old hatboxes, trying on straw hats, fiddling with bent brims and ribbons and silk flowers. She had not been overseas since her honeymoon, when she and Howard had spent a few days in Paris followed by a week on the French Riviera, where—Mabel was quite certain—Iris had been conceived.

And as Mabel packed bags—not to take away with her, but for jumble sales, she decided—Daisy dismantled her room; Ben Gifford returned to London with Lily and Miles; and Dosia left for West Sussex, where she was to spend the New Year with friends. Iris floated about the place, made a number of hushed, monosyllabic telephone calls and practiced her dance moves in the otherwise empty drawing room. And Howard for the most part remained in his study.

For three days Daisy avoided Stephen Jessop. When she walked into the kitchen the evening after the Vincents left and saw him up a ladder, replacing a lightbulb and mildly chastising his mother for ruining her eyesight by working in such dimness, she swiftly turned and left the room. The following day, when Hilda came to the morning room, where Daisy sat alone reading, and said, "Excuse me, but Stephen would like to know if it's possible to have a word with you," she told Hilda to tell him that she was "too busy." And later that same day, when he called after her as she returned from a walk with Iris—and though Iris turned and waved to him—Daisy pointedly ignored him and marched on through the front door.

"Have you and Stephen had a falling-out?" Iris asked as they hung up their coats.

"No, not really. I just don't wish to speak to him at the moment."

"But you'll have to say good-bye to him . . . He'll be awfully upset if you don't."

The day before Old Year's Night, Howard and Mr. Blundell carried Daisy's trunk down the stairs, across the hallway and out to the car. Howard had been touched by Daisy's request that he rather than Stephen drive the girls to the station and had told her so with tears in his eyes.

"I'll see you both in a few days," said Mabel, kissing Daisy and then Iris.

"But when will *I* see you again?" Noonie asked Daisy.

"Don't worry, I'll be back soon enough . . . I'll come and visit you."

It was only when the car had disappeared and as Noonie stepped back into the house that Mabel saw Stephen, standing at the entrance to the courtyard.

"They've gone," he said, walking toward her.

"Yes, to London . . . Daisy's to live there, with Iris. I'm sure she's told you . . . I hope she said good-bye?"

He shook his head.

"Oh, Stephen, I do apologize . . . How very thoughtless of her."

"I need to speak with you, Mrs. Forbes."

Mabel was keen to get back to her packing and had promised Noonie that on Howard's return from the station she would get Stephen to drive them to Farnham, to the sale at Elphicks, and then for a knickerbocker glory at the new ice cream parlor. A distraction to cheer up her mother, Mabel thought. But something in Stephen's tone made her think her mother's treat might not happen, and as she led him into the house, toward Howard's study, she prayed that he was not about to resign.

"I understand," she said, after listening to him, because she did. Why would he want to stay there? There was little enough for him to do and would be even less once she had gone and Howard was there alone. "But it is rather sudden, and to leave immediately . . . well, it's not usual, Stephen."

"I don't expect you to give me anything other than what I'm due, Mrs. Forbes. And of course—if you wouldn't mind—a character."

Mabel stared back at him. He had grown up, and yet this day he looked no different from the anxious little boy who had arrived there one summer's afternoon as she sat in the garden holding Daisy in her arms.

"Does your mother know?" Mabel asked.

"No, not yet. But I'm about to go and explain."

Mabel nodded. "This is your home, Stephen. You must always remember that."

Mabel wrote more than she normally would and used all the right words and phrases: *honest . . . diligent . . . trustworthy . . . reliable . . . no hesitation . . .* and finally, *very sad to see him go.* She folded the paper, placed it in an envelope.

Then she reached for Howard's checkbook and pen. She pondered for a moment, then wrote out the check and handed it to Stephen, along with the character.

"But this is too much . . . far too much. I'm only owed—"

"No," said Mabel, interrupting him, "I want you to take it. Please, don't say any more."

He looked uncomfortable and sighed as he shifted in his seat.

"When are you leaving?" Mabel asked.

"Soon. As soon as I've packed my bag."

"But Howard . . . Mr. Forbes will want to say good-bye, want to express his thanks to you . . ."

"I know and I'm sorry, but I don't want to be persuaded to stay.

I'd be grateful—extremely grateful—if you'd extend my good wishes and thanks to him."

Mabel nodded again. "And where are you going?" she asked.

"I'm not sure. But I'll be in touch."

As Mabel stood up, Stephen rose swiftly to his feet and extended his hand. Mabel stared at the hand for a second or two; then she moved round the desk. And as she held him, she thought of her own son, Theo; she thought of all those boys who'd gone off and never come home; and she remembered the little boy who'd once slept on the floor of Daisy's room and had a nightmare.

It had been during the first months of the war, that very first winter, after the pipes at the Jessops' cottage had frozen and then burst, flooding the place. The house had been full of children, another nine orphans from London, and—once again—mainly boys. But Daisy had asked that Stephen be allowed to sleep in her room, and Stephen was different; he was gentle. When she'd heard the sobbing, Mabel had gone to the bedroom, found Stephen huddled in a corner, crying and shivering. She'd taken him down to the kitchen, made him some cocoa, then led him to the morning room, where a fire still burned and it was warm. He'd told her that he was worried about his father and had dreamed of him. "I don't want him to get hurt . . . I don't want him to get killed," he'd said, staring up at her with huge, solemn eyes. They had been sitting side by side on the small sofa, and she had wrapped her arm around him, pulled him closer and done her best to reassure him. When she'd eventually taken him back up to the makeshift bed, tucking him in, securing him, he'd reached for her hand and kissed it.

"Gone?" Howard repeated, an hour later. "I can't believe you let him go—just like that."

"What else could I have done?" Mabel asked. "He'd made up his mind; he was determined."

Howard sighed, shook his head. "I'd have liked to have seen him, talked to him . . . He's been here almost all his life," he added, looking up at Mabel.

"Yes. Which is no doubt why he wished to go. He's an intelligent young man . . . and you and I both know he's wasted here. There's not enough for him."

"I remember the night he was born," said Howard, wringing his hands. "I remember holding him in my arms and wondering . . . wondering how life would be for him."

The love Mabel felt for her husband at that moment was sudden, unexpected and complex. She said, "I know how much you care about him, but you have to let him go."

"Let you *all* go?"

Mabel nodded. "Yes . . . but if you love us, we'll be back."

Mrs. Jessop had gone to the larder to cry in private about Stephen and to read the note he had given her, again. She hadn't expected to find Nancy there, arranging the tins and packets and potted meats like there was no tomorrow—and with tears streaming down her face, too.

"Is it John?" Mrs. Jessop asked, closing the door, biting back her own tears and wrapping her arms around Nancy's slender shoulders. She knew Nancy often took refuge there, to remember him.

"They're all leaving . . . all of them. And it's that bloody woman's fault," said Nancy, slamming the jar of Bovril down next to the tin of cocoa.

Mrs. Jessop slipped the folded note inside her pocket and blew her nose. She wasn't used to hearing Nancy swear, and she had forgotten about That Woman. But surely Mrs. Vincent couldn't be blamed for Stephen's departure. "There, there," she said. "They'll all be back, you know?"

"And what about us—what are we expected to do?"

"Carry on as usual?" suggested Mrs. Jessop.

"Like during the war?" said Nancy, looking angry now. "That's what it feels like, doesn't it? Everyone going . . . and us left here, as usual . . . and with what?" she asked, waving about the tin plate of pigs' trotters that Mrs. Jessop had cooked earlier especially for Mr. Forbes.

Mrs. Jessop sat down on the stool. She said, "What choice do we have? What choice do we have?" And then she leaned her forehead against the cool slate shelf and began to weep.

"I'm sorry," said Nancy, putting down the plate and taking hold of the older woman. "I wasn't thinking about your Stephen . . . And you're right, they'll all be back soon enough and so will he. Because you're his mother, just like his own mother, and he loves you as such . . . yes, he does, he loves you as such."

Mrs. Jessop pulled away. She stared back at Nancy with swimming eyes: "Do you think so? Do you really think so?"

"I know it. He's told me so countless times . . ."

Mrs. Jessop reached into her pocket.

"What's this?" Nancy asked, taking the folded paper from the woman's outstretched hand. Mrs. Jessop nodded at the note. Nancy unfolded it and read: "Dearest Mother, please don't fret about me, but try to understand my need to find my own way. I have no intention of abandoning you, but rather, wish to do something for myself—and hopefully, one day, make you proud of the boy you took in, and have loved and cared for all these years. Please explain to Father. I love you both and will be in touch soon. Yours, Stephen."

Nancy smiled at Mrs. Jessop. "Ah, well, that's all right, isn't it? And you see, he does love you."

"Yes, but I don't know where he's gone, Nance . . . he wouldn't tell me. Said he'd be in touch once he's sorted . . . Once he's *sorted*? What does that mean? I'm just hoping and praying it doesn't mean ruddy New Zealand . . . Whatever will I do . . . ? Whatever will I do if he ends up there?"

"You could always follow him, go there," said Nancy. "Maybe that's what he means . . . Maybe he means to send for you once he's sorted."

"But what about Old Jessop?"

Nancy shrugged. "Husbands don't seem to feature in travel plans these days."

Mrs. Jessop shook her head. "I couldn't leave him. I'd have to take him with me."

It was a while before the two women emerged from the small room, by which time they had rearranged the larder shelves *and* planned the decor and layout of Mrs. Jessop's bungalow in New Zealand.

"Did you manage to finish *A Love Like No Other?*" Nancy asked as they walked back into the kitchen.

"Oh yes, I finished it last night. And what I wanted to ask you was . . ." And as Mrs. Jessop went on, the two women put on their aprons, picked up their knives and began to peel the newly dug potatoes lying by the sink.

Stephen stood on the train platform with his suitcase by his feet. The character, a letter of reference from Mrs. Forbes, along with the check from her—a very generous check, which Stephen would add to his savings—were safely tucked in the inside pocket of his jacket.

Earlier, standing at the crossroads waiting for the bus to take him to the station, Stephen had seen the car heading back to the house, Mr. Forbes at the wheel, and he'd stepped away from the roadside and hidden behind a tree. He didn't want to be seen, didn't want the vehicle to stop and Mr. Forbes to get out and talk to him, try to persuade him to stay. And perhaps it was wrong, he thought, not to say good-bye and extend some thanks to the person who'd employed him for all of his life, who'd played a role in his adoption, in bringing him to that place. But he had lost respect for the man who'd embroiled him in his deceit and caused Daisy so much pain; a man who, as far as Stephen was concerned, had everything, and pissed on it.

This was the beginning of a new life, one away from Eden Hall, away from the woman who had been his mother for longer than not, away from the war-damaged man he loved and had called

Father, and away from every reminder of Daisy. His twenty-one years could be measured in those three people, he thought; and perhaps his auntie Nellie, though he hadn't seen much of her of late.

His mother—whenever Stephen thought of her, he couldn't help but smile—had been understandably upset, but she'd known it was coming, his departure. And he would not return there, to her, he decided then and there, until he had bought her something luxurious and expensive, and perhaps even a little decadent, he mused, smiling a little more and raising his eyebrows. And how could he not love her? She was, and would forever more be, his *mother*. And his father . . . Whenever Stephen contemplated his father, his heart ached. It ached for the pain he would never be able to erase, for the words his father would never be able to speak, and for the horror that gentle soul had witnessed. And yet, damaged, silent, without prejudice or judgment, Old Jessop had been better than many a father.

And Daisy?

Daisy . . . Stephen raised his eyes to the milky white sky. What was the alternative? he thought, steadying himself, reinforcing his resolve. To stay on there, idle, counting the days until her next visit, looking on from the sidelines as she became engaged to another, married another; to be the one to drive her and her new husband from the church? There was no alternative.

There could never be another Daisy, but there would, he hoped, be another love. And as the train slowly approached the platform, he reached down and picked up his suitcase.

PART TWO

Summer 1927

Chapter Nineteen

No slanting hand addressed a Miss Daisy Forbes. No letter arrived from New Zealand. But there had been postcards from Paris, from Lyon, from Koblenz; from Switzerland and Italy; and then, in May, one from the Lake District, where Ben Gifford was on a walking holiday. "I look forward to our rendezvous on June 24th," it ended.

Daisy hid the card. Ben Gifford—and, more specifically, his yet-to-be-answered proposal of marriage—was not something she wished to discuss with Iris. She would make her own decision; she *would* be her own person, as her mother had told her to be when she'd left for the continent.

The week before he'd gone on holiday, Ben had taken Daisy to a tea dance at the Savoy. They'd twirled about the floor in a few old-fashioned waltzes and then attempted a tango. It was a world away from the sort of dancing that went on in the clubs Daisy had been to with Iris.

"Two years ago, George Gershwin gave the British premier of his 'Rhapsody in Blue' right here in this room," Ben had said, signaling to the waiter as they sat down.

"Were you there—here?"

"Yes, as a guest of your father's."

It had been the first time they had seen each other since Christmas, when, on his departure from Eden Hall, he had told Daisy he would give her time to settle in London, time to think about *their* future. As they took tea, he asked Daisy how she had been filling her time: had she been to any galleries or exhibitions or to the theater? Daisy smiled as she watched others glide sedately across the floor. She shook her head. "I've been too busy."

"Not with Iris, I hope . . . I don't mean to be disrespectful to your sister," he said, smoothing the sides of his newly grown mustache with a finger, "but I'm afraid I don't approve of her lifestyle, *or* her friends. You see, I know all about *that* set," he went on, unsmiling, staring at Daisy. "I've read about them in the newspaper. I'm afraid it's all drinking and drugs and nude cabarets, from what I can make out . . . Have you . . . have you been to any of those sorts of *dos* with her?"

"No," Daisy said quickly. "Not to anything like that. But I have been out dancing with her once or twice."

"To nightclubs?"

"Yes."

"I see," he said, and sighed. He crossed and uncrossed his legs, then turned his chair and moved it nearer to the table, covered with starched white linen and glinting silver. "I'd rather you didn't go to nightclubs, Daisy," he said, peering at the tall stand piled high with scones and tiny cakes and sandwiches.

"I don't . . . not anymore. I've given them up."

"Good. I don't want you being corrupted by your sister. And these parties . . . Well, I may as well tell you, the police know what goes on at them; they know all the addresses, the names of every-one involved . . . They have a list, and I have no doubt more arrests will be made in time," he said, pushing a cake into his mouth.

He had gone on for some twenty minutes or more about what he had *heard*. How the police had raided some of London's most fashionable addresses and found people half-naked, drunk, drugged and dancing, sometimes in the most compromising circumstances. He mentioned names, including that of Valentine Vincent. These parties, he said, started at midnight and went on until four or five in the morning.

Daisy did not tell him that it was actually six or seven, some-times later. Just as she did not tell him about Iris's new tattoo—the small butterfly that now graced her ankle. And she thought better than to tell him about Iris's cocaine tonic wine, her pick-me-up in a bottle at the flat. But she did tell him that Iris no longer went to *those* sorts of parties, because that's what Iris had told her. She had told Daisy that there were too many seedy characters, and old men and tarts, and people who'd got rich quick during the war. And the debauchery Ben spoke of was not entirely an accurate description of what Daisy had seen. She had witnessed peo-ple throwing away caution and having a good time, and there were risqué cabarets, and certainly alcohol and dancing, and perhaps there were even drugs—secreted away in dark corners; she suspected as much.

"I only have your best interests at heart, you know," Ben said. "After all, I want to marry you," he added in a whisper.

Daisy smiled. It was true: he did have only her welfare and best interests at heart; she knew this. But when he said, "I think we need to set a date," Daisy's hand began to shake and she put down her teacup.

"Don't worry, I don't mean for any wedding," he added, and feigned a little laugh. "But I think we need to set a date for when you'll give me an answer. A chap can't be expected to wait forever, you know."

"But you said you were happy to wait."

"And I have been. As I've said to you before, I'm quite content to have a longer engagement, but I think it only fair that you give me your answer soon." He reached to his inside pocket. "I thought perhaps June twenty-fourth," he said, taking out a small diary and flicking pages. "That'll be six months to the day since I first asked you . . . Ah yes, it's a Friday, so I shall be reasonably free," he added, pulling out a pencil from the side of the diary and scribbling something down. "I think six months is a long enough time to wait for a simple yes or no, don't you?" he asked, without raising his eyes.

It was all rather businesslike, Daisy had thought at the time, but that was Ben: practical, pragmatic, older and perhaps wiser. And by comparison to most others she had met, he was also reassuringly sane, and safe, for Daisy's life in London had got off to a dizzying start. The year had begun in a riotous blur of revelry, and the city, initially, had seemed frighteningly fast. But it hadn't been the traffic or the noise; it had been the frantic energy of people hell-bent on having a good time; determined to be seen *and* heard. And fast, because time moved quickly. Days were untethered, nights adrift, and there were no bells for mealtimes. The rule book in London had been thrown away, or perhaps thrown on the floor to dance upon, because dancing was *the thing.* Dancing until you could dance no longer, or until the band stopped playing and the sun came up.

Iris had wasted no time in introducing Daisy to her world of cocktails and dancing and nightclubs. She had introduced Daisy to her many nocturnal friends, including Luigi, who presided over the Embassy; and Kate, who owned the Silver Slipper; and *Darling John-nie* at the Kit-Kat Club. To Iris, these people were like an extended family. Proprietors, doormen, barmen and clientele, Iris knew them all, and everyone knew her. But Iris's voracious appetite for nightlife had quickly taken its toll on Daisy.

It had been on the last day of January that Daisy and Iris had seen off their mother and Dosia at Waterloo station, and Mabel had commented that Daisy looked "rather lackluster," and Daisy had laughed and said, "The result of trying to keep up with Iris."

Mabel had taken Daisy aside. "Don't *try* . . . Don't emulate your sister," she'd whispered, holding on to Daisy's hand. "Be your own person. You wanted to be independent . . . This is your opportunity. I don't want you to fail because you think you have to be like Iris. Make your own decisions—about what is right and wrong, what is best for *you*."

It was perhaps predictable maternal advice, but Daisy knew those parting words were Mabel's gift to her, and as her mother held her, she'd been unable to stop the tears—and the fear. The fear that she might not see her mother again; the fear that came with the sudden realization that for the very first time in her life her mother would not be there for her; the fear that came with a vague new understanding of what it meant to be alone in the world.

As Mabel stepped onto the train, she'd looked back at Daisy: "Don't forget. Remember what I said."

Daisy and Iris had watched the train pull away, disappearing down the track, Dosia's arm hanging from a window, waving a large handkerchief. Iris had then lit two cigarettes and handed one to Daisy. "Thank God that's over," she'd said. "I absolutely loathe good-byes." It was only then that Daisy had noticed the two tiny streams of black flowing down each of Iris's rouged cheeks.

By March, Daisy had stopped emulating Iris's dancing feet and found her own: a steady pair of feet to carry her to and from her job at a local bookshop. Iris had been appalled. "A *bookshop*! But why— when you can work for me?" she'd asked.

"Because I want to be independent . . . and working for you *isn't* that."

When Daisy had gone on, reading from the letter from Mr. Laverty, the bookshop's owner— "nine to five . . . Oh, and with an hour for lunch, and Wednesday and Saturday afternoons off . . . and two pounds six shillings a week . . ."—Iris had lain down on the small sofa in the sitting room of their flat, feigning a turn.

"Don't tell me any more. Please, don't read any more," she'd said, her hand to her brow. "It seems to me you're quite determined to become a tragic heroine yourself."

Iris's dress shop was doing extremely well, and she had recently moved the business to larger premises in Knightsbridge in order to have bigger parties and be able to invite more people. Iris maintained that fashion, like art and music and dance, was part of the New Freedom, as she called it. Fashion, she said, was not simply an expression of a woman's personality but a reflection of an ever-changing modern world.

"It should never stand still; it's like a dance," she'd told Daisy.

Iris had originally intended for her shop to pioneer only new designers and new fashions, and not be confined by gender stereotypes. Her shop would, she had said, when it was still just an idea, not sell simply beautiful gowns, but three-piece pinstripe trouser suits for women, collared men's-style shirts in brilliant colors and vibrant silks, and knitwear, paste and faux-gem jewelry, trilby hats with large diamante brooches, top hats—in velvets and silk brocades.

Iris had taken much of her inspiration from Madame Chanel, whom she had been introduced to at a party and had recently met again, and whose designs she now showcased along with those of a new Italian designer named Elsa Schiaparelli. The shop—or boutique, as Iris preferred to call it now—was simply named "Iris." A social hubbub, open only at certain hours and on certain days, never before midday or at the start of the week, it was a place where everything stopped for tea, or—and more usually—champagne. Iris threw by-invitation-only parties almost every week, with jazz music and cocktails served by the prettiest of her friends in the very latest fashions. At the beginning of last season she'd thrown her first "catwalk" party. Photographs of the event—Iris in top hat and tails with dozens of strands of pearls about her neck—had appeared in the *Tatler* and *London Life*, and she had lately been featured on the cover of *The London Magazine*.

But for all of this, Daisy had no desire to be Iris. She had realized during the course of the past six months that they were very different people. That while Iris craved—and seemed to need—hordes of people, and noise and laughter, Daisy simply yearned for one person with whom she could share her life.

Chapter Twenty

Mabel and Dosia had been in Rome for more than three weeks. They had traveled there by train from Florence, where they had spent almost a month, and, before that, two weeks in Venice. One needed to linger in Italy, Dosia had said, and so they had, and this country, these cities—Venice, Florence and now Rome—were indeed the high point of their trip.

The sun was once again high in the sky when the two women strolled out from the Hotel D'Inghilterra. Turning onto the shaded Via Condotti, they headed past the now familiar shops and the Caffè Greco where they had earlier taken breakfast. Emerging into the sunlit Piazza Di Spagna, Mabel opened up her parasol and Dosia put on her new straw hat adorned with dark red silk cherries about its crown.

As usual, the piazza was bustling with tourists, guides and street sellers, and as the women weaved their way through the noise and chaos toward the Spanish Steps, children selling bunches of violets tugged at their dresses. The two women climbed the steps slowly, dawdling for a while at the top to look down on the scene, then walked on, past the Medici Palace, along the broken pavement and into the Pincio gardens.

They had visited the Colosseum, the Roman Forum, the Baths of Caracalla, the Circus Maximus and the Vatican during their first week; and visited seemingly endless churches and basilicas during their second; then, exhausted by ruins and antiquities, and with blistered feet, they had settled into doing nothing much at all. But they had taken to coming to this place each morning—and sometimes in the evenings, too—to look out across the city.

Sitting side by side on a bench beneath a tree, Mabel reached into her bag and pulled out a letter. "I forgot to tell you that I received this yesterday," she said, smiling. "It's from Reggie."

"Ah, the major . . . and how is he?"

"Very well," said Mabel, unfolding the page. "He says the weather in England has been foul, a very wet Easter and rather chilly spring . . . He also says Howard has remained at Eden Hall the whole time I've been gone."

"Aha, that's a promising sign," said Dosia. "Though I'm not at all surprised. I told you, told you even before we left, that I was quite certain it was all done and dusted with that woman." She shook her head and tutted. "Men. They're like little boys. You have to take away their toys to make them behave."

"I hope you don't mean that I'm a *toy*?"

Dosia nudged her and laughed. "Sort of, dear girl, sort of."

"Anyway, Reggie *is* going to join us at Monte Carlo . . ." Mabel paused and glanced at Dosia.

"Fine by me. When will he be arriving there?"

"At the end of next week, the day before us."

"And are you looking forward to seeing him again?" Dosia asked, looking sideways at her sister-in-law.

"Yes . . . yes, I suppose so."

"You don't sound terribly enthusiastic."

Mabel folded the letter and put it back inside her bag. "I'm not sure," she said. "I'm not sure now what I think about him. What I think about anything . . ."

"You don't need to think. That's what this trip was all about; it was about you not having to think about anything for once," Dosia declared, and then sighed. "Oh my," she said, stretching her sun-tanned bare legs out in front of her, "I'm going to miss this, miss you and me . . . and our adventure . . . miss Roma," she added, raising her arms to the vista ahead of them.

"Yes, so will I."

"And what about Giancarlo?" Dosia asked, referring to the Italian they had been introduced to during their first week and who had taken them out to dinner a number of times. "Will you miss him?"

Mabel laughed. "He's ten years younger than me!"

"So? He's keen. Very keen. If you really wanted to get even with Howard," Dosia said, straightening herself and adjusting her dress, which really was too short, Mabel thought, "he's surely a more appealing option than the dear old major. You'd be far better doing it with him."

"Dosia! I do not wish to get even—as you call it—with Howard, and . . . and . . . I'm not quite sure what you mean by *doing it*. No!" Mabel quickly added, beginning to laugh again and raising her hands. "Don't tell me. I don't want to know."

"I might tell him," said Dosia, after a moment.

"Tell who—what?"

"Tell Howard about you and Giancarlo."

"But there's nothing to tell."

"He doesn't need to know that, does he?"

Mabel smiled. She had not told Dosia everything, and certainly not about last night.

It had been after midnight when Dosia went up to her room, leaving Mabel and Giancarlo alone on the candlelit terrace with their nightcaps. Giancarlo had once again become amorous, grabbing hold of Mabel's hand and kissing it quite ardently—as though it were a face with lips and not a hand—and whispering, *Mia bella May-bella*. And the wine and the heat, the sound of his voice—the way he said her name—and his dark eyes glancing up at her had made Mabel feel as weak as a newborn lamb. And she let him go on, kissing the back of her hand, then her palm, then taking a finger into his mouth, running his tongue over its tip so that she shivered and felt her edges begin to blur and blend with the sultry night.

Unlike before, she did not say, "Giancarlo, I'm a married woman." Unlike before, she did not pull her hand away.

"Oh, Lordy," said Dosia now, jumping to her feet. "We're meant to be having lunch with Dolly Cartwright!"

Mrs. Cartwright—or Dolly, as she had become to them—was a widow and was traveling with a paid companion, an awkward and painfully shy young woman known only as Miss Hurst. Dolly had been at the D'Inghilterra for more than a month by the time Mabel and Dosia arrived there. She spoke a number of languages—seemingly fluently—and made it her business to know everyone at the hotel: staff, residents and diners. But she also knew a number of titled Italian and English expatriate residents in the city, and it had in fact been Dolly who'd introduced Mabel and Dosia to Giancarlo and who had taken them to various palazzo apartment musical soirees and cocktail parties.

When Dosia and Mabel arrived at the Piazza Navona, hot and breathless, Dolly was sitting at her usual table at her usual restaurant beneath a large parasol, with a carafe of wine in front of her.

"No Miss Hurst?" said Dosia, pulling her chair across the uneven flagstones.

"She's gone to the Vatican. Again. Thinking of converting, I've no doubt," Dolly added in a whisper. "It's confession, you see, that pulls them that way. Yes, redemption," she drawled.

Dosia glanced over at Mabel. Dolly had clearly had a glass of wine already.

"So what have you two been up to?" Dolly asked, refilling her own glass and theirs.

"Nothing much," said Mabel. "Sitting in the Pincio gardens."

"Ah," Dolly sighed. "I do adore that place. Particularly at sunset, when all of Rome turns pink and the starlings swoop and soar . . . The first time Clifford and I came here—on our honeymoon—we used to go there almost every evening. Rome was a different place in those days . . . And of course it wasn't that long after the risorgimento," she added, rolling the R.

Dolly went on to talk about that time, that trip, her tiny blue eyes fixed on the fountain ahead of her and filled with love and nostalgia. She and her late husband had been married for more than fifty years and had never spent longer than a few nights apart from each other, she said. "I could never have been one of those women who abandon their husbands in London to live in the country. I could never have done that. And it would have been the death of our marriage," she proclaimed, feigning a little laugh. "But it seems to be the fashion back at home—doesn't it?—to leave one's husband to toil and labor, while wives play tennis and throw bridge parties. It's no wonder divorce is on the up."

"But it's no excuse for infidelity," said Dosia, glancing at Mabel.

Dolly took a sip of her wine. "No, but it's a valid excuse for loneliness, which can of course *lead* to infidelity. People today seem to consider marriage a disposable thing, something one can throw away when it becomes a nuisance or difficult . . . but it's a lifelong commitment—till death us do part— and sometimes it requires sacrifice, compromise and *effort*," she said, becoming more impassioned. "And, like anything else where there has perhaps been some struggle or effort, the satisfaction, fulfillment and sense of accomplishment are richer, the love stronger. Oh yes. I loved Clifford more deeply and steadfastly at the end of his life than I did when we first met and fell in love. Love is indeed like wine," she said, picking up her glass once more. "It simply improves with age."

Later that day, after Dosia led Dolly back in the direction of the hotel, Mabel sat alone by the Pantheon, and staring up at the continental sky, she pondered Dolly Cartwright's words and remembered Howard's early protestations. For she had been the one to insist on being in the country; she had been the one who had decided to live away from her husband, at Eden Hall; and then, lonely, embittered by his absence, she had felt abandoned.

Howard was no good on his own and never had been; he craved company and adored female company, and for the best part of twenty-five years Mabel had known this. Feminine attention put him at ease, and he had always preferred the female sex to his own, claiming that he found women easier, more forgiving and funnier. He wasn't so much a ladies' man as a man who preferred ladies. But though he admired spirit and wit and intelligence, Mabel knew he liked women to be a little vulnerable as well, to wear pretty frocks and have pretty names, and to hanker for a man to take care of them. He was, quite simply, old-fashioned, and slightly lost in a world where maidens no longer wished to be rescued.

Dolly was right, Mabel thought as she dawdled her way back through the narrow streets: The world was becoming a more difficult place for men, men like Howard, encouraged from the start to have a voice, opinions, brought up to be decision makers, protectors and providers; men who assumed that all women wanted to be looked after; men who took it for granted that this was enough.

Mabel paused. The warm air was filled with the scents of lemon and basil, cardamom and bay, and horses and bodies, and sometimes, the noxious reek rising from the ancient sewers. Like all of life, she thought: a cocktail of sublime sweetness and grim reality. Moving on, emerging from the shadows into the brilliant sunshine of the Piazza Colonna, the sound of a woman's voice and "O Mio Babbino Caro" crackled from the open window of a trattoria and there was Miss Hurst, standing on the steps leading up to a church doorway, eating ice cream, with a swarthy-looking Italian man by her side. And as Mabel turned away and walked on, she smiled. Dolly Cartwright may have been right about many things, she concluded, but she had yet to fathom her Miss Hurst.

Pausing to look in familiar shopwindows, staring at souvenirs she had no desire to buy, Mabel thought of Howard. That afternoon, and more than ever before, she had felt her husband's absence, and yet in that absence was his presence, too. It was the queerest thing, but the longer she had been apart from him, the nearer she felt to him. Now she wished he were with her, wished he were waiting for her at the hotel so that she could take him to the Pincio hill to sit with her and watch the sun set over the Eternal City. She wanted to share this place with him, wanted him to see it, too.

When Mabel finally arrived back at the hotel, she found her room filled with red roses: dozens of them, scattered across every surface—in cups and glasses and vases. She looked about for a card, longing to see *his* name: a line, a message. Then the door opened and in came Dosia. "So look at this," she said, her eyes wide as she glanced about Mabel's heavily scented room. And then she handed Mabel the small card, signed "Giancarlo."

Chapter Twenty-one

Three days before she was due to meet Ben, Daisy reached her decision. She could not marry him; she was not in love with him. And she still wasn't sure if he loved her. It was his age, she decided, walking home from work. He had simply decided it was time for him to marry, to look for a wife, and because she'd been kind to him, because they'd developed something of a friendship last summer, he'd plumped for her. By the time Daisy reached the steps up to the front door of the building, she felt relieved, and she hoped Ben might be, too.

The flat in Sydney Street was spread over two floors, the first and second, and had three bedrooms, including the small box room Iris called the Archive Room and used to store clothes, a sitting room, dining room, kitchen and small bathroom—with an electric water heater that juddered loudly—on the half landing. It was a drafty place in winter, and the dusty windows—which made the world beyond appear fogbound even on the brightest day—rattled each time a bus passed by. But the furnishings had been added to by Mabel and accessorized by Iris, who had a passion for draping almost everything in vibrantly colored fringed silk shawls, and who preferred vases of ostrich and peacock feathers to fresh flowers.

Daisy closed the front door quietly so as not to disturb Mr. Beal, who lived on the ground floor and had complained more times than Daisy could remember about the "fucking slamming." He had once appeared at the door of their flat, red in the face, almost foaming at the mouth, incoherent with rage and waving his walking stick about. He frightened Daisy in the same way all those other angry war veterans frightened her. They had a right to be angry, she thought, but not with her, and surely not about the slamming of a door; after all, it was hardly going to kill anyone. At other times, Mr. Beal was sweetness and light. Even the morning after his stick-brandishing tirade, when Daisy had met him on the doorstep as she left for work and he was bringing in his bottle of milk, he had smiled back at her and said good morning, just as though he had no memory of their last encounter.

When Daisy walked into the kitchen, Mrs. Wintrip was as usual standing at the sink, peeling potatoes with a burned-out cigarette between her thin lips. Daisy had never seen Mrs. Wintrip without her hairnet, beneath which were a multitude of rusting bobby pins and small curlers. She wondered if Mrs. Wintrip ever took off the hairnet and dispensed with the curlers, whether she ever pulled out those clips and allowed her hair to be, just be. Because it seemed a waste of time otherwise. But she liked Mrs. Wintrip and loved hearing about George, her husband—or rather, ex-husband, because

though they still lived together they were in fact divorced, or so
Mrs. Wintrip claimed.

Mrs. Wintrip was long known to the family. A cousin of Mrs.
Jessop's, she had been employed by Howard years before and reem-
ployed by Mabel at the start of the year, when Daisy first moved to
London. She came to Sydney Street each day to clean, cook, mend
and do laundry. Like Mrs. Jessop, Nellie Wintrip had spent her life
in service; unlike Mrs. Jessop, she had never been a cook and said
herself, "I'll make no bones about it: I'm no cook." She had what
Mabel described as a "remarkable way with words" and was, it
seemed, devoted to the memory of a young Howard Forbes.

Today, like every other day when Daisy arrived back at the flat,
Mrs. Wintrip boiled the kettle and made them both a cup of tea.
She told Daisy she had made a lovely mutton stew for her supper
and then asked if Miss Iris would be dining in. Daisy said she wasn't
sure.

"She's a card, that sister of yours . . . blowing in, blowing out,
never having time to eat . . . and all that *dancing*," Mrs. Wintrip
said, shaking her head. "It'll all catch up with her, you mark my
words," she added, bending down to put the peelings into the
bucket under the sink. Her mustard-colored dress rose at the back
to reveal the frill of her long crimson bloomers. She wore a brown
woolen cardigan darned at the elbows in blue, and pink carpet slip-
pers. Her thick dark stockings pooled around her swollen ankles
and misshapen feet.

"If I was her mother," Mrs. Wintrip went on, "I'd make sure she
had a good meal inside of her before she went out for any dancing."
She turned to Daisy: "You know, my only regret in life—apart from

George—is not having had kiddies. Not that I blame George. And that wasn't why I divorced him. No, I divorced him because of his carrying on with that floozy Eileen Shannon at number twenty-six. Oh yes. I said, George, we're *divorced*. Just like that, I did. Then I handed him the paper—you know, the degree nisi or whatever, what Bob had done for me."

"Your lawyer?"

"My brother."

"He works in law?"

"No, he works on the buses, dear. Usually the 134."

"But how could Bob sort out your divorce?"

"Oh, he's good like that. Can turn his hand to anything."

"What did George do?"

"What could he do? It was served to him, fate a company. He couldn't believe it. Was in shock. Just sat and stared at the thing. I said, she can have you now; you can go and live with her and her budgerigar at number twenty-six."

"What did he say?"

"He said, that's your brother's signature. I said, yes, he's *the witness*, and that's *her* name there—next to *the adulteress*. Well, of course, once she could have him she didn't want him."

Mrs. Wintrip went silent for a while and stared into space; then she sighed and said, "It wasn't that long after Stephen was born."

"Stephen?"

"Yes, he was ever so bonnie and good as gold, too," she added, unusually wistful. "Such a cold winter it was, you couldn't get enough coal for love nor money, but of course there was always plenty of coal at Clanricarde Gardens. Mr. Forbes made sure—"

"Clanricarde? *Stephen* was at Clanricarde Gardens?"

"Yes, that's where he was born. Born early and delivered by me!" she added triumphantly. Then, realizing something, she put her hand over her mouth.

"Stephen was at my father's house," Daisy said again, staring back at Mrs. Wintrip, confused.

"Oh, now, dear, you'll have to forget I said that. That's not for you to know."

"Stephen was born at my father's house and you delivered him . . ."

Mrs. Wintrip nodded.

"But he wasn't your baby?"

Mrs. Wintrip shook her head. "I can't say any more . . . shouldn't have said."

"You can tell me . . . I'm an adult now, Mrs. Wintrip. I won't say a thing to anyone; I promise," said Daisy, genuflecting.

"I've said too much already."

"But he lived with you," Daisy persevered. "Stephen lived with you and George."

"No, not George! He was with *her*, Eileen. And your father would've boxed his ears if he'd known the full extent of that carry-on. But because I was married, respectable, see, it was decided I should have Stephen until . . ." She stopped, shook her head again.

"Until? What was it you were about to say?"

Mrs. Wintrip stared back at her, awkward, shuffling, more reticent than ever. "I can't say any more, dear. But everything turned out well in the end . . . Your father saw to that." She picked up a cloth and began rubbing vigorously at the bench. Then she turned on the tap and said, "By the way, I've darned your stockings and sewed that button back on your blouse. I hung it up in your wardrobe with your brown serge skirt."

Daisy nodded and murmured a thank-you. Then she rose to her feet and left the kitchen. The landing had shrunk and the sitting room looked different and swayed a little as Daisy sat down, then stood up, then sat down again.

Stephen had been born at Clanricarde Gardens. He was her father's son . . . Howard's illegitimate child. He had to be. It was the only way any of it made any sense . . . Stephen was the bastard child Howard had been so good to . . . The one she'd overheard Nancy and Mrs. Jessop speaking about.

"My brother," she whispered, standing up again. "Stephen," she gasped.

Daisy thought of them once more in the lobby of the coachman's flat, when he'd been so close to kissing her. *Thank God, thank God, thank God . . .*

She sat down again, leaned forward, rested her head between her knees and tried to breathe. Slowly, she felt her heart regulate its beat and sat up. She breathed in deeply and glanced about the room. She heard Iris's voice: *Just as well you weren't in love with him;* saw Stephen's face staring back at hers, his eyes on her lips: *No!*

She got up from the chair and paced in circles about the rug in front of the fire, trying to focus on its pattern, trying to imagine a huddle of women in some hot tent in a desert making it. It was better to keep moving.

When Mrs. Wintrip stuck her head round the door in Iris's old velveteen turban and said she'd be off now if that was all right, Daisy smiled and nodded. There was nothing else to say to the woman, not that night. Asking Mrs. Wintrip to confirm Stephen Jessop was her brother seemed as preposterous as it was pointless. And Daisy wasn't sure she could bear to hear the facts confirmed out loud. Even at her most loquacious, Nellie Wintrip was fiercely loyal to Howard. She had told Daisy umpteen times that Mr. *Forbes* was a good man, though the woman's respect and admiration were quite at odds with Daisy's tarnished view of him.

But who was Stephen's mother? And why was Mrs. Wintrip so full of admiration for Howard if he'd made some poor woman pregnant, then handed the child to *her* to look after? Surely he was no different from all those other "young rapscallions" Mrs. Wintrip had gone to such great lengths to warn her about? It didn't make any sense . . . unless Howard had paid Mrs. Wintrip, and paid her handsomely.

The front door slammed shut, the building shook and another thought occurred: Was Mrs. Wintrip lying when she said the baby was not hers, and was Stephen in fact hers . . . her son with Howard? It was a bizarre notion, one that beggared belief. But Nellie Wintrip had once been young . . .

Daisy tried desperately to fire her imagination, to picture Mrs. Wintrip without the hairnet, without the burned-out cigarette stuck to her thin lip, without the wrinkled stockings and swollen ankles. But it was impossible to conjure the younger version, and the thought of her father and Nellie Wintrip—together—was too much, even for her imagination.

Muddled in with all of this, overriding everything else, was the now sickening remembrance of that moment in the lobby last Christmas, that moment she and Stephen had come so close—so very close—to consummating something *illegal*.

Daisy wasn't sure what time it was or how long she had been sitting there, staring into space, when she felt the reverberation of the front door slam shut again, followed by the familiar sound of Iris bounding up the rickety stairs.

"You slammed the door," Daisy said as soon as Iris appeared in the room.

"Oh God, I forgot . . ."

"*Again.*"

Iris threw down her bag and hat.

"There's some stew on top of the stove—it might still be warm."

"*Stew?*" repeated Iris, shuddering. "And on a day like this . . . Anyway, I've no time to eat. Piggy and the gang are picking me up in an hour or so. We're going for cocktails at Tilda's, then on to the Embassy—and probably to the Grafton after that. Want to come? It'll be devastating."

She had been to Marcel, Daisy could tell. It was a wonder Iris could fit in a job, even a dress shop type of job, between hair appointments and manicures and dancing.

When the telephone rang, Iris immediately picked it up. She laughed. "Oui, c'est moi," she said, and then offered a succession of one-word replies: "Divine . . . Heavenly . . . Quite . . . Absolutely . . . Agreed . . . Eleven." She laughed again, said good-bye, put down the receiver and turned to Daisy. "So, what do you think?"

"About what?"

"Oh, really! Are you going to get out of your dowdy bookshop garb and come dancing? Sitting in here every night reading tragic novels is going to shrivel you up, darling."

"And not eating will shrivel you up—*darling!*"

"Ha. I don't need to eat. Seriously, I never get hungry."

Iris turned toward the door.

"I need to talk to you," Daisy said quickly.

Iris stopped.

"I've discovered something quite . . . shocking."

But it wasn't shocking to Iris. And after Daisy had finished recounting the conversation she'd had earlier with Mrs. Wintrip, Iris merely nodded and said, "You know, I had wondered . . . He does rather resemble a young Howard . . ."

"Is that all you have to say?"

Iris shrugged. "What more is there *to* say? I think you're right, and it seems the most likely answer. Stephen was born in his house, cared for by his servants. I can't quite see our father in the role of benefactor to fallen women, can you?"

Daisy shook her head. "No, but I'm going to find out where Stephen is and write to him," she said. "He has a right to know."

"What? You're going to send him a letter and announce to him that he's our brother? Then what? Tell Mummy? I said it *seems* the most likely answer, but we don't know and might very well never know—because I'd lay a hundred pounds Nellie Wintrip shan't tell you, and based on his track record, Howard's hardly likely to come clean . . . And what on earth do you hope to achieve? You'll be opening up a can of worms—for Mummy, for Stephen, for all of us. My advice—my sisterly advice to you—is to forget about it. It's history, done and dusted."

Daisy said nothing.

"Seriously, darling, let it go. Forget about it. Will you? Will you promise me that? Nothing good can come of it."

"I think he should know, that's all."

Iris shook her head. "Sometimes it's better, kinder, to leave sleeping dogs alone. And this is one of those times, Daisy."

They remained silent for a moment; then Iris said, "One thing you may have forgotten in all of this is that there was another son, and he died, and when he died"—she paused, took a deep breath— "I think some small part of our mother died with Theo."

Daisy turned. The name was like a scald, a burn, a jolt.

"Such teeny fingers," she had said, her arms outstretched, eager and smiling as Mabel placed him into her arms.

"Gently now, hold up his head . . ."

"Like this, Mummy? Am I doing it right?"

"Yes, Daisy, like that."

He smelled of Mummy, of lavender and roses, and his skin, so soft, so very soft, as she pressed her lips to it.

"It's why she and Howard are the way they are," Iris was saying. "Why they can't look each other in the eye . . . or love each other. She'll never forgive him for not having been there, at Theo's birth, and then at his . . ." Iris paused. "His passing. That's why I don't want children," she added. "I couldn't bear it, you see . . . to love something so much and then lose it. It would kill me . . . kill me."

Theo. Theo Forbes. He had died at a time when everyone else was losing their babies, their sons. But was that when everything had changed for Mabel, for Howard? Had their love been lost then, too? Daisy wondered. The news of baby Theo's death had been

delivered to Daisy by her nanny, over jelly and custard in the nursery tearoom.

"Little Theo has gone away with the angels . . . to heaven,"
Nanny had said, frowning and smiling at the same time. "Tonight
we shall say special prayers, and—"

Before Nanny had finished, Daisy had run from the room, into
the corridor, down the stairs, right at the bottom and along the
landing toward her mother. It was Nancy who stopped her, grabbed
hold of her outside her mother's bedroom door and then held her as
she sobbed.

"There was never any funeral, was there?" Daisy asked now.

Iris looked away. "There was, but you were considered too young
to attend."

After a few minutes, Iris said, "You can't tell anyone, Daisy . . .
not Stephen, not Mrs. Jessop and certainly not Mummy. Do you
understand?"

Daisy nodded. "Yes."

Iris left the room, disappearing across the landing and up the
stairs to change from one outfit into another and touch up her
makeup. She was, had become, painfully thin, and the thinner
she'd become the less she ate—and the more she went out dancing.

When a car screeched to a halt on the street outside—horn
honking as though it were Victory Day all over again—Daisy immediately thought of Mr. Beal and called up the stairs.

Iris's head appeared over the banister. "Oh God, but I'm not
ready . . . Can you go down and let them in? . . . And do take a look
at Piggy's new car," she called down. "He's just bought the most
divine Bugatti."

By the time Daisy reached the bottom of the stairs, the banging of a doorknocker had replaced the honking of a car horn. She flung open the door, and Paul Trotter—known to all as Piggy—smiled back at her.

"I say, look at you, what an absolute little fizzer you are."

Daisy closed the door carefully and led him down the narrow passageway, hoping and praying Mr. Beal wouldn't emerge from the shadows with a stick—or a gun—raging about *the fucking door*.

"So, staying in again, what?" Piggy bellowed as they ascended the stairs. "You really should come out, you know . . . I could teach you the black bottom . . . it's an absolutely ripping dance. Iris adores it."

He was on his own, he said, because he had stupidly decided to pick up Iris first. "Should've known to collect *her* last!" He wore a canary yellow waistcoat and gray wide-legged trousers, so wide that only the very tips of his navy blue suede shoes were visible. He said they were going to pick up Valentine and *O-reel-yah* next, but there was room in the motor if she wanted to come along, too, he added, standing with her in the small sitting room, glancing at her up and down.

Iris had developed a firm friendship with Valentine. They had, they'd discovered, a number of friends in common. And Iris and Daisy had been to dinner at Flood Street; they had seen Margot again, and playing a quite different role, as mother and hostess in her own home. And while Iris got on enormously well with Val, Daisy had become friends with Val's fiancée, Aurelia. Daisy liked Val too, but there remained some sort of unspoken stumbling block in their friendship; perhaps due to that silly kiss at Christmas, Daisy thought, or perhaps simply because he preferred Iris's company to hers. And really, Iris was much more his type. They had, apparently, what Iris called "chemistry," which made Daisy wonder if there was something more than friendship between them.

"Oh, I forgot to take a look at your new car," said Daisy, moving over to the window. It did look splendid, even from that angle.

"She's an absolute beast," said Piggy, moving alongside her, reeking of sandalwood and patchouli cologne.

"Yes, I can imagine," said Daisy, lying, because she couldn't at all imagine a car being female or a beast, only to regret it because Piggy then went on and on in an alien language about its engine and horsepower, how he had taken the thing "up to" this or that speed, in this or that place.

When Iris appeared in a black, sequined, tubular dress and matching sequined beret and asked, "Opinions, please? This or my red satin?" Daisy and Piggy—in perfect unison—yelled, *"This!"*

"Are you quite sure you don't want to come with us?" Iris asked, and Daisy detected some new tenderness in her voice.

"No, I've some reading I want to catch up on."

"Well, if you change your mind, get a taxi and come and join us. You know where we'll be."

"Tallyho and into the night!" said Piggy. And sure enough, minutes later, Daisy stood at the dusty window and watched *the beast* roar off into the summer twilight.

It was a twilight bleached of color. Curtains weren't yet drawn. Opposite, on the other side of the street, were squares of illuminated animation. Like silent films, random stories all running at once, Daisy thought, watching the shapes and moving figures at one window and then another. Below, the lamplighter was out with his pole, and a couple strolled arm in arm, laughing, then stopping to exchange a furtive kiss.

The room behind her was dark and silent, her thoughts now languid. She pictured Eden Hall, saw shafts of pink-yellow light streaming in through the oriel window onto her mother's velvet sofas and chairs, onto the glossy patinas of mahogany and walnut and onto the polished oak floor: pools of shimmering, unfathomable color. She saw her mother, head bent over a framed tapestry; Mrs. Jessop, hair parted in the middle, pulled back into that tight bun and escaping in brittle strands about her ears and damp forehead; and she pictured Stephen, standing in the garden—a watering can in one hand, cigarette in the other.

But it wasn't like that. Not anymore. Her mother wasn't there; Stephen had gone.

And I don't want him to be my brother . . .

She raised her eyes to the line of rooftops, ever darkening against the pale yellow sky, and lifted her hand to her newly shorn hair. "Never get your hair cut," he'd said. Then, out of nowhere, she caught a glimpse of her snow globe: lying among the purple heather, its glass intact and glinting in the late evening sun. Discarded, abandoned, like Eden Hall.

I shall remember this day forever, she thought, turning away from the window. She glanced at the clock on the mantelshelf. She didn't want to be there, thinking of dead brothers and new brothers and fathers who lied and how the older you got the more questions there were and how none of them ever seemed to have any answers.

Hours later, wearing one of Iris's most daringly short dresses, clutching a glass of champagne and lost in the music, the heaving mass of bodies and energy, Daisy tried to forget about Stephen and everything else. And when a man she'd never seen before pulled her to him, she let him take her face in his hands and kiss her.

Chapter Twenty two

After days of unsettled, ominous skies, the clouds had cleared and Chelsea's pavements glistened in the sunshine. Everyone smiled: the uniformed nannies with their cumbersome perambulators, the Chelsea pensioners sitting on the bench beneath the horse chestnut trees, the butcher standing in his sawdust-strewn doorway and everyone on the bus.

As Daisy rose from her seat and pulled on the cord, she saw Ben, standing in the shaded doorway of the department store in his pale blue shirt, dark tie and trilby hat, his hands in his pockets, his jacket folded over an arm. They had chosen to meet there, because it was easier—easier for him, because it was beside the tube station and meant he didn't have to take a bus to the other end of the King's Road.

"Like the hat," Ben said when he saw her, and then he asked her if she wanted to go to the restaurant inside the store or try somewhere else.

"I don't have very long," Daisy replied, "so it's probably best if we just go here."

The hat was new. Daisy had bought it only days before—and in that very same store. Eyeing herself in the millinery department's mirror, she had for a moment—a very fleeting moment—caught a glimpse of someone quite beautiful, with a heart-shaped face and large almond eyes of gray-green. The girl in the mirror had stared back at her, blinking through wisps of mouse-colored hair with a quizzical, slightly forlorn expression. She had a smallish nose, a pronounced cupid's bow to her top lip. She smiled back at Daisy, lifting one side of her mouth to reveal a crescent-shaped dimple on her cheek. Daisy wasn't sure what to make of her, but she rather liked her in that hat.

Inside the store, as they waited for the lift, Ben asked Daisy how she was, if she had sold many books that day. As the lift attendant pulled back the grille, he whispered, "I'm sorry if I was a bit sharp with you on the telephone last night."

He had been sharp, but she, too, was feeling guilty, about the nightclub, about that foolish, reckless kiss and also because she knew things at the wharf were bad. A fire earlier in the month had been devastating, according to Ben. Luckily it had happened at night, when only a few night-shift workers and night watchmen were there, and they had all escaped unharmed. But the stocks of highly flammable paints and varnishes and oils had turned the fire to an inferno that had razed the factory to the ground. This was bad enough, but then Ben had discovered that Forbes and Sons was underinsured, and that money to rebuild the factory would have to be found elsewhere, which would mean Howard's private money. The house in Clanricarde Gardens had just been sold, and Ben had presumed Howard would have the funds available . . .

"But he hasn't," Ben said.

They had taken their seats at a table for two in a corner, next to an aspidistra and an elderly couple loudly slurping from soup spoons.

"What do you mean—'he hasn't'?"

Ben sighed. He stared at the menu lying open on the table in front of him. "He claims that Mr. Lutyens got carried away when he built Eden Hall, told me that the feller must've thought he was made of money and that—"

"But what's all this got to do with Eden Hall?" Daisy interrupted. "The place was built over twenty-five years ago."

The waitress appeared again, taking a tiny pencil from behind her ear, licking it and then noting their order on her small notepad. "And to drink?" she asked without looking at either of them. "Two cups of tea, please," said Ben. The woman picked up the menus and moved away, and Ben continued.

"It seems your father had to borrow money against the property in London to pay for Eden Hall. Both properties were in fact mortgaged, but also," he said, pausing, looking at Daisy, "he claims he has a few other personal debts."

"Personal debts?"

Ben shrugged, shook his head. "I've no idea. He didn't elaborate.

But it's quite clear to me that he has no interest in the business anymore."

"I don't believe that. It's his inheritance; it's a family business."

Ben said nothing.

"So can the money for the factory not be found?"

Ben said he wasn't sure. He'd already had to lay off some of the workforce; the rest were waiting, or working as best they could from the makeshift building hastily erected, using machinery and equipment that had been salvaged or borrowed. And because they hadn't been able to fulfill their orders—had had to cancel them—they had lost many of their long-standing clients, who had gone elsewhere. This, added to the steady decline in the business anyway, meant that unless money could be found, unless cash flow improved—and fast—Ben would have to lay off more men.

"But what does my father say?"

"Not a lot. He seems to have lost his appetite for business—and, as you know, he rarely comes up to town now. Of course, it was— has been—a very successful business, particularly in your grandfather's day, and then during the war and afterward, when there were so many ships to replace. But I'm afraid it's all changed."

"And my mother is oblivious to all of this . . . ," Daisy mused aloud.

Mabel had yet to return home. She and Dosia had been away for five months and were now, according to Iris, somewhere on the French Riviera—with Reggie Ellison.

"But more importantly, I want to talk about us," said Ben. "We agreed you'd give me your answer today, and—"

"Yes," she said, quickly. "My answer is *yes*."

He laughed. "That's very definite. I was prepared for . . . well, some sort of negotiation."

Daisy smiled. "A lot's happened since we last met . . . I think I've grown up."

He reached over, took hold of her hand. "Thank you. You've made me very happy. I shall of course telephone your father later today, to formally ask for your hand and speak to him about dates."

"Dates?"

He laughed again. "For our wedding."

"But I thought we were going to have a long engagement, and until it's been properly announced—which can't be until my mother's returned home—we're not officially engaged, are we?" She saw his expression change and quickly added, "What I mean is, there's plenty of time for us to think about a wedding date. And I'm quite sure that's the least of your worries," she added in a whisper.

"Well, yes and no. I presumed you'd want a big wedding at Eden Hall—like Lily's—and that takes some planning, I'd imagine."

"To be honest, the last thing I want is a wedding like that. I'd hate it."

"Hate it? But why?"

Daisy shrugged. "Waste of money . . . particularly in view of what you've just told me. And anyway, I'd far rather have a quiet wedding—without any fuss or expense—perhaps here in London, at a registry office."

"A registry office? I don't suppose your father will buy that idea."

"It's not his to buy. It's not about what *he* wants. And anyway, it's all a year or two off; we agreed to that, I thought."

For a while they sat in silence. He did not look at her and appeared to be sulking, but later, outside the store, he smiled at her tenderly and told her again that she had made him very happy. Then he kissed her hand and turned away toward Sloane Square without a backward glance.

The air was warm, the sky cloudless, and rather than wait in the heat of the sun at the bus stop, Daisy decided to walk on. Women in floral dresses and white gloves stood chatting beneath sun-bleached awnings, cooks armed with large wicker baskets surveyed lined-up crates of fruit and vegetables, picking up this and that to squeeze and smell. The aroma outside the greengrocer's was heavenly and reminded Daisy of home, of the greenhouse in summer, heady with the scent of ripe tomatoes, of the kitchen garden, perfumed by raspberries and strawberries and herbs . . .

Daisy noted her reflection in the shopwindow and adjusted her hat. A fiancée, she thought, walking on, nodding and smiling at the other women she passed. She had to admit, already she felt quite different: one of them. She wondered what her father would say when Ben called him . . . What could he say? He would give his permission, she thought, but no doubt insist on a long engagement. She felt a vague pang, a distant echo of something almost forgotten, whenever she thought of her father. She missed him, missed what they'd once had.

But her father, Eden Hall and the events of last Christmas seemed a lifetime ago to her now, and though she felt guilty about not having been back to visit Noonie, Iris had: She had gone back at Easter to check on things (someone had to, they'd agreed) and said that Noonie was perfectly well and happy, if a little more forgetful.

"They have their own routine," Iris had said, referring to their father and grandmother. "Each Tuesday they have a day out together in the car, an excursion to the coast or whatever. Thursdays, he drives her into Farnham—you know how she loves the department store there—and they have lunch out. And Saturday afternoons, he takes her to the matinee at the Regal. It all seems to work terrifically well . . . makes one wonder if he shouldn't have married Noonie instead of Mabel," Iris added, laughing.

Daisy had wanted to ask about Stephen, if Iris had heard anything, but Iris being Iris, she hadn't needed to ask. "And no one has heard a squeak from Stephen," she'd said. "So selfish of him," she'd added.

Now Daisy wished she hadn't told Iris what Mrs. Wintrip had said. And she wished she hadn't told her about Ben, too. But it had been at the end of that very long night, after she'd kissed some stranger and been adrift, and it had been like throwing down an anchor. She'd needed to tell someone. "Ben wants to marry me," she'd declared in the back of the taxi. "And I think I'll say yes."

She couldn't recall now exactly what Iris had said, but she had gone on at some length about Daisy being too young, about her not understanding love. But how could she tell her elder sister that she *did* understand about love? And how could she ever tell anyone, "I think I might have been in love with my brother?"

When Daisy heard her name and looked up, she half expected to see him, Stephen, standing there on the pavement in front of her.

"Oh, hello, Val."

He kissed her cheek. "You were miles away," he said, smiling. "I thought you were ignoring me . . . A lot on your mind?"

"No, just thinking of a few things I have to do."

"Time for a quick cuppa?"

"I'm afraid not. I've just had lunch with Ben and am meant to be back by two."

He pushed back his shirtsleeve and glanced at his wrist. "You've still got ten minutes, and who's going to notice if you're a minute or two late? There's only you there, and I'm quite sure you haven't reduced poor old Mr. Laverty to spying on you."

They crossed over the road to a small teashop on the other side, and as he pushed open the door for her, he said, "Coming to Iris's soiree tomorrow?"

"No, but seeing as she has so many, missing one doesn't really matter, does it?"

Val laughed. "True," he said.

Recently, the "chemistry" between Iris and Val had made Daisy uncomfortable. And it made her angry with Iris, whose flirtatious behavior was often quite shocking. However, she was pleased that they were all friends now. Sometimes she even forgot that Margot had been her father's mistress. Iris had told her that there couldn't possibly be anything in it anymore, that to be a mistress one had to be either "servicing the man or one of his homes." And as Howard never came up to London, as he and Margot communicated only by the occasional telephone call or letter, Margot was, according to Iris, relegated to a category called *former mistress.* "She's been put out to pasture," Iris had said. And Aurelia had also said as much, the last time the two of them had met for tea, when she'd told Daisy that she was convinced that Howard and Margot's relationship was platonic and had been for some years.

"Margot told me the only thing your father ever speaks to her about is Mabel and his marriage. I think Margot loves him, loves him dearly, but I don't think it's a requited love. I believe your father loves only one woman . . . your mother."

"So, how is Mr. Gifford?" Val asked as they sat down at the marble-topped table by the window.

"Fine," said Daisy. "Very well." She knew Ben would be furious if she said anything about anything to *him*. And he'd be doubly furious if he knew she was sitting having tea with That Vincent Chap, as Ben called him, minutes after she'd told him that she had to get back to the shop.

"How is Aurelia?" she asked.

He sighed. "Oh, all right, I suppose . . ."

She wasn't sure what to say. She looked up at him: "She's not unwell, is she?"

"Oh no, she's quite well, I believe. The malady is mine."

He looked perfectly fine to her.

The waitress brought them their tea. He placed his arms on the table and leaned forward, toward her. She lowered her gaze to the steaming cup, blowing on it, wishing she had gone back to the shop and not come for a cup of tea that was too hot to be drunk in the few minutes she had left.

"So lunching with Mr. Gifford, eh?" he began again. "It's rather a long way for him to come for lunch . . . he must be frightfully keen."

Daisy said nothing.

"You're not going to go and get yourself hitched to him, are you?"

"If I was, I'm not sure I'd tell you."

He narrowed his eyes, tilted his head, watching her. "Don't do it. Don't end up with that buffoon."

"He's not a buffoon, and I happen to like him . . . more than like him," she added, feeling she should in view of the circumstances. "Anyway, you don't know him. He's a very decent sort . . . I could do a lot worse."

"A lot worse? Is that your criterion for suitors?"

"Why are you asking all this, Val? Forgive me, but it's really none of your business," she added with a smile.

"I'm asking because . . . because we're concerned."

"We?" she repeated. "I'm not interested in what you think, and I'd prefer my sister talk to me about her concerns and not go about gossiping with other people."

"Am I *other people*?" he asked, smiling. "Because I happen to know that Iris has only mentioned it to me. You see, dear Daisy, we're just a tad worried about your Mr. Gifford and his motives."

Daisy snatched up her bag. "I'm awfully sorry, but I really do need to get back."

"Daisy . . . I only say this because I don't want you to make a mistake—a mistake which could alter the course of your life."

She stared back at him. "Perhaps it's a question you should be asking yourself. Are you in love with Aurelia? Are you *really* in love with her, Val? Because you might be about to make a mistake which will alter the course of your life—and you only have a few weeks left to think about it."

"I know this," he said, frowning.

"I must go . . . Sorry about the tea."

"If I don't see you before, see you at the party," he said.

"The party?"

"Your parents' wedding anniversary celebration?"

She had forgotten about that. "Ah yes, see you then."

Iris had told Daisy, after her last visit home, that Howard's big project, sole project, was the silver wedding anniversary party he was planning for shortly after Mabel's return. All he wanted to speak about, ask Iris about, were menus and guest lists, to seek her advice on the precise wording of the invitation, which he'd drafted numerous times. But the party her father was planning struck Daisy as expensive hypocrisy, nothing more.

Later that day, when the nearby church clock chimed five and, seconds later, the cuckoo clock on the wall of the shop chimed, too, Daisy pulled down the blinds, picked up her hat and her bag and turned the sign on the door to CLOSED.

The sky had turned to a paler blue. Golden-edged clouds floated high above the old trees heavy with leaves, and the air was filled with their rich sweetness. But the sweetness of the air did not marry with her thoughts, and turning into Sydney Street, Daisy felt irked once more by Valentine's words.

How dare Val allude to other motives . . . Was he implying that Ben was marrying her for money? *Hardworking and honest*: Ben had always been described as such by Howard. And in view of Howard's finances—which neither Iris nor Val had any idea about—it was quite clearly not the case: risible, Daisy thought.

And she had said yes to Ben because . . . because she cared for him. Not in a passionate, all-consuming way; it wasn't like that. She cared for him in a considered and respectful way. The way one *should* love the person one intends to spend one's life with. She wasn't like Iris: She *did* want to get married, have a family, a home. And becoming engaged—belonging to someone outside that coterie of hedonism—felt like grabbing hold of a life raft. It meant she would survive; it meant she had a future. No, Ben Gifford could never be described as wild or passionate, but he was a good man, as good a man as she was ever likely to meet, Daisy thought, marching on.

Mabel, in an uncharacteristically candid moment, had once told Daisy that passion was all well and good, but to build a life with someone, there had to be something more sustainable than passion—because it gets spent very quickly. And in a way, Iris had backed this up when she'd said that she wouldn't marry because all marriages ended up utterly passionless. And look what had happened with Howard and his scattered passions. A man such as her father was not the sort of man one should marry; far better to marry a man who was honest and trustworthy. And as for money, the only things it had bought her mother were a philandering husband and a large house with a Japanese garden in which to sit on her own. Daisy would *not* make the same mistake as her mother, she thought, climbing the steps to the front door and pulling out her key.

Iris was sitting in her red silk kimono. She was on the telephone and already holding what looked like a pink gin in her hand. She blew Daisy a kiss and then ended the call and told Daisy that she'd let Mrs. Wintrip go early. "The woman does go on so . . . I'm utterly fagged!"

"But it's not like you to be here at this time of day. Are you not well?" Daisy asked.

"I think my age is catching up with me."

"You're twenty-four, Iris," said Daisy, sitting down opposite her sister.

"Oh, darling, please . . . don't remind me."

"Who was on the telephone?"

"Your father," Iris replied, as though he wasn't hers.

"And? . . . Is Mummy back yet?"

"No, but Stephen is . . . Well, not back, as such, because he never actually went away, not to New Zealand . . . Apparently, he's here in London and has been since"—she raised her hands—"whenever. He has a publishing contract for a book," she added, throwing a bare leg over the arm of her chair and reaching in the other direction for her cigarettes.

"*Stephen?* He's writing a book?"

"I know. Exactly what I said. Apparently, he's been writing about natural history for years. Charting falling leaves and seasons and birdsong, penning poetry and that sort of thing . . . Oh, but he also has a job," she went on, "ferrying rich tourists about the city in a Rolls, and a flat above some swanky garage showroom."

Daisy smiled. "Yes, that makes sense," she said. "He's always been clever with words, always had an eye, seen everything."

"Clever with words *and* everything else, I rather think."

"I wonder what his first book's about."

Iris flicked her lighter. "A guide to the highways and byways of the Surrey Hills!" she said dramatically and then laughed. "Apparently, he's been contracted to do quite a few. Not just motoring guides, but also walking guides . . . You know how some people like to walk? According to your father, he has the opportunity to write more, and not just in England . . . No doubt the battlefields of France"—she paused and feigned a yawn—"as if they haven't been done enough already."

"And Howard told you all of this?"

Iris nodded.

"But how does he know?"

Iris shrugged. "Mrs. J, I suppose."

"Did you say anything?" Daisy asked. "Did you mention anything to Howard about . . . about Stephen's birth?"

"No!" yelled Iris.

"I'm pleased for him," said Daisy after a moment or two. "I'm pleased he's here and doing something different."

"*Different?* Darling, everyone knows writing pays peanuts."

"Oh, and have you told Val this?"

Iris snorted and shook her head. "To be honest, I think Stephen would have been far better off going to New Zealand."

Iris was being disingenuous. And she was perhaps irked that someone called Stephen Jessop had beaten another called Valentine Vincent. Like the unexpected outsider, Stephen had come from nowhere and would have his name in print long before Val, who was still working on his novel, *Spotlight*.

"We must tell Val," said Daisy, trying not to smile and picking up a magazine lying on the shawl-covered sofa next to her. "After all, Stephen might be able to give him some advice."

Chapter Twenty-three

Aurelia was waiting outside the tube station, as arranged.

"Sorry I'm late," said Daisy. "Mr. Laverty always seems to forget I have Saturday afternoons off. What time are we meant to be there?"

"Soon!" said Aurelia, grabbing her arm. "But I think I know the way."

Aurelia had heard of the palm reader through a friend and had persuaded Daisy to come along, too, saying, "After all, we're both at the same place in our lives, and it'll be interesting . . . or, at the very least, a bit of fun."

A few years older than Daisy, Aurelia worked as a teacher at an infant school in Pimlico, and her and Daisy's mutual love of literature—their admiration for and interest in a number of new, emerging women writers—had drawn them to each other and cemented their friendship. It was a friendship in which Daisy, with few friends in London, had taken comfort.

"Her name is Mrs. Larkin," Aurelia said, her arm still linked through Daisy's as they approached a cottage standing on its own on the edge of Hampstead Heath. Two roads crossed in front of the small dwelling, where a post box and leaning signpost stood on a grassy triangle beneath an ancient chestnut tree. "We're a little late, but I'm sure it won't matter. The woman said in her note to me 'two o'clock or *thereabouts*.'"

A graying picket fence encircled the overgrown shrubbery, which screened the cottage's dusty windows from the road, and the garden gate hung open on broken hinges.

"Ready?" Aurelia asked as they stood in front of the door.

Daisy nodded. Aurelia knocked.

The woman was tiny, smaller than Daisy, and had a front tooth missing from her smile. She took them into a parlor crammed with furniture, where streamers of dust hung from the beams of the low ceiling and a parrot perched on a stand behind an old wingback chair. At first, Daisy thought the bird was stuffed, until it suddenly called out in a fine baritone English voice, "This is London calling . . . this is London calling . . ."

"Be quiet, Roger! Come in, girls. Take no notice of *him*."

The woman sat down in the wingback chair, and Daisy noticed now that her jet black hair was in fact a wig, which seemed to have slipped forward a little, and from which tufts of white hair sprung out over her ears. Her lobes were long, stretched by years and the weight of her heavy, dangling earrings. The room smelled of stale food and sour breath, and a tarnished silver vase containing a few dead chrysanthemums stood on the mantelpiece, where a clock ticked loudly.

Mrs. Larkin asked them about their journey and how long it had taken them, as though they had traveled a great distance. She had never been on a tube train in her life, she said, and would never travel anywhere beneath the earth or in the sky.

"And you found the place all right?" she asked.

"Yes, your directions were very good," said Aurelia. "As soon as we came to the crossroads and I saw the leaning signpost, I knew."

The leaning of the signpost was the result of a great storm some years before the war, Mrs. Larkin said, pushing her wig back in place.

The room was uncomfortably warm, the window next to Daisy sealed tightly shut, with a multitude of dead flies lying among withered tomatoes on its sill. Beyond the glass Daisy could see a thistle-strewn field, perhaps once a lawn, she thought, and beyond that, in the distance, the murky London skyline.

"Now, who's to go first?" the woman asked.

Aurelia insisted that Daisy go first. And so Aurelia and the woman swapped places, and the woman took hold of Daisy's hand, spreading the palm out with her rough thumbs.

"Hmm, interesting," Mrs. Larkin began. "Artistic, intelligent . . . home loving, nature loving and sensitive, too . . . you feel things deeply."

Daisy glanced to Aurelia, who smiled back at her.

"A long lifeline . . . very long . . . ," Mrs. Larkin continued, "but there're breaks—conflict—in the heart line, and possibly more than one marriage. There's great honesty, here . . . but also some recklessness and perhaps too much passion," she added, glancing up at Daisy and winking. "And I see stubbornness, much conviction. You'll need to watch that," she said. She turned Daisy's hand over, folding the fingers, curling and uncurling them. She saw two children, she said, definitely two, and maybe a third. She folded Daisy's hand once more. It was difficult to say about that third one.

"You will learn from your mistakes . . . and you *will* know great love."

The woman smiled up at Daisy. That seemed to be it. But it wasn't enough, not nearly enough.

"Mistakes? How can I know?"

Mrs. Larkin gazed down at the palm in her lap once more. She ran her finger over the soft flesh of Daisy's hand, then closed her eyes and breathed deeply. And with her eyes shut, the woman said, "An older man, a charlatan . . . you must beware of him; you must beware of the charlatan." She opened her eyes. "That is all."

Now it was Aurelia's turn, and Daisy and she swapped places.

Mrs. Larkin sighed as she took hold of Aurelia's hand, stretching open the palm, tilting her head from side to side, moving Aurelia's hand this way and that. But there were no breaks or "conflict" in Aurelia's heart line; it was long and unswerving, Mrs. Larkin said. She would have a long and happy marriage.

"Just the one?" Aurelia asked.

"Just the one."

There would be four children, and the fourth was not a *maybe*— like Daisy's third. And there was no mention of any mistakes, or having to learn from them, and no mention of any charlatan.

Aurelia's life was going to be a settled, happy affair by comparison to her own, Daisy thought as she listened.

After Daisy and Aurelia had paid the woman and left the cottage, they walked back to the tube, to head into town and to Fortnum & Mason for tea.

"Conflicts . . . ," said Daisy again as they entered the station.

"Four children . . ."

"Mistakes . . ."

"*Four* children."

"A charlatan!"

On board the train, they giggled about their excursion, the woman's wig and her parrot, and whether it had been worth the shilling.

"Conflicts," Daisy said again. "You know, I really don't like that word."

"But she also said passion . . ."

"And recklessness."

"And a great love . . ."

Daisy shook her head. "And more than one marriage. I don't want more than one marriage!"

"*Possibly* more than one marriage," Aurelia corrected her. "She said possibly."

"It must mean divorce . . ."

"You might be widowed."

"I don't want to be widowed either."

"But is Ben your great love, do you think? Or is it someone else . . . ?"

Daisy stared back at her. "I don't think so. No, it can't be him. Unless . . ."

"Unless?"

"Unless my feelings for him change, and grow into something more than they are now."

"Or unless the great love is to be your *second* husband."

"Oh God, Aurelia . . . I wish we hadn't gone to the woman now. My life is going to be all reckless passion and mistakes . . . mistakes I'm going to have to learn from. And yours, yours is going to be bound up with Val in an unswerving love . . ."

"And I wonder, who is the charlatan?" Aurelia asked.

"Oh, that's easy. That's my father."

"Hmm . . . I don't see you as reckless, not in any way. Iris maybe, but not you. Old Larkin got *that* wrong. In fact, I rather think she got it all wrong. And it doesn't really mean anything anyway, dear . . . It was just a bit of fun."

"You don't know that. It might all be true."

"I do know it."

Daisy turned to her. "How? How can you know?"

Aurelia took a deep breath. "Because I know I'm not going to marry Val," she said, and smiled.

They had reached Fortnum & Mason by the time Aurelia finished telling Daisy the story of her and Valentine, how they had first met—in a central London library; how flattered she had been by his attention, his kindness and manners; and how, caught up in a moment, she had said yes to him. She explained to Daisy that she'd known for some time that she did not love him, not the way she should, or could, and that she now suspected he was in love with Iris.

"But when are you going to tell him?" Daisy asked as they were led to a table in the tearoom.

"Soon. Probably when I next see him."

"But that'll be next weekend—at the party at Eden Hall," Daisy said as she sat down.

Aurelia shrugged. "Iris will be there to pick up the pieces . . . though I very much doubt there'll be any. Other than injured pride, perhaps, I think he'll feel rather relieved to have me off his hands."

Daisy leaned forward, took hold of Aurelia's hand. "I'm so sorry."

"Don't be sorry, please. Be happy for me. I could have made a huge mistake . . . and then I really would need your sympathy. As it is, I'm content to remain unmarried, quite content to be a spinster"—she feigned a little shudder—"for a while longer."

Daisy said nothing. She felt uncomfortable thinking about Iris and Valentine, whom she knew were out together that day.

And then, as though reading her thoughts, Aurelia said, "It's not Iris's fault. It could have been anyone. In fact, I'm rather grateful to your sister—for showing me the extent of Val's love for me and mine for him. She's done me a huge favor. Truly, she has."

"I need to tell you something," said Daisy. "And the only reason I haven't told you before now is because it meant nothing, absolutely nothing, and because I didn't want to hurt you . . ."

"Yes?"

"Last Christmas, when Valentine and his mother came to Eden Hall, when I found out about my father and Margot . . ."

"Yes . . . What is it, dear?"

"Valentine kissed me."

Aurelia laughed. "Oh, thank heavens for that. I thought you were about to tell me something awful."

"Doesn't it bother you?"

"No, but I imagine it would if I loved him. And to be honest, I don't blame him," she added, pressing her hand upon Daisy's.

Daisy was relieved. Unburdened, she felt her confession had deepened the friendship. She said, "Now we're like sisters, you and I. And we will have no secrets."

"If we are to have no secrets, then tell me, why are you marrying Ben Gifford?"

Daisy thought for a moment. She wanted to say *love, its possibilities*. She said, "We're not yet"—and then stumbled over the word *officially*, and having to say it again. "Engaged," she added.

"Officially or unofficially"—Aurelia giggled—"you agreed to marry him." She handed Daisy the menu. "Don't tell me you're in love with him, because I know you're not, and you admitted as much earlier. So what is it? I'm intrigued . . . I know Val and Iris think—"

"Oh, please don't repeat what they think. Can we leave them out of this?"

"Yes, all right, but tell me. You can tell me . . . Why did you say yes? Why did you agree to marry him if you don't love him?"

Daisy put down the menu. "Because," she said, and then paused. "He asked me. Oh, don't look at me like that. I know it sounds pathetic . . . but he's a decent man, and he claims he loves me. And he'd asked me so many times, Aurelia, I had to say yes, eventually . . . But I wish I hadn't."

"It's not too late . . . It's never too late."

The girls ordered their tea, scones and cake. "A Saturday afternoon treat," Aurelia said, rubbing her hands together. She giggled again about Mrs. Larkin's wig, winced at the remembrance of the malodorous reek of the cottage and then, watching Daisy's face, told her to dismiss everything they had been told. "We shall be mistresses of our own destiny," she said, raising her china teacup into the air.

But Daisy didn't feel mistress of her own destiny, and she felt weighted by all the things she hadn't told her friend or anyone else.

"What is it?" Aurelia asked. "There's something bothering you . . . I can tell."

Daisy nodded. "Yes, and I need to tell you . . . need to tell someone."

Aurelia stared back at her. "You're making me nervous."

And so once more Daisy revisited last Christmas, this time including Stephen's note and declaration of love. When Aurelia clapped her hands to her mouth, Daisy said, "But wait, there's more." She then told Aurelia what she had heard from Mrs. Wintrip, *and* what she had overheard in the kitchen the previous Christmas. When she'd finished, the girls sat in silence for a moment or two. Then Daisy said, "So there you have it. Stephen is in all likelihood my brother . . . and I think I might have been in love with him."

"Oh, Daisy," was all Aurelia could say.

Chapter Twenty-four

The station had been busy, crowded with tourists and day-trippers bound for the coast with excursion tickets, but Daisy's compartment was empty. As the train pulled out of Waterloo Station, snaking its way through the blurred, hot city and into the suburbs, she sat back in her seat, closed her eyes and allowed the cool air from the open window to sweep over her face.

She would have traveled first class had she been with Ben, and now she felt a little guilty. Because hadn't she purposefully dawdled her way to the South Kensington tube station knowing she might miss the train and miss him? But Ben made her feel guilty about so much. All he ever spoke about was money and the business and *his* woes. Only the day before, on the telephone, he had droned on about the price of houses, wondering aloud how they were to find the money for a deposit.

It wasn't that she didn't wish to see him, Daisy thought. It was simply that it was a beautiful day and she didn't want it to be spoiled. Not yet. And she *had* looked for him, had glanced about the station concourse before going to the ticket office. She had been expectant, had presumed she'd missed the train, but the guard had told her there was still time, so she had dashed to the platform and boarded the first carriage she saw marked SECOND CLASS.

She could have motored down to Eden Hall the following day—with Iris, Valentine and Aurelia—but this would *not* have pleased Ben. And he would have felt left out because he had not been invited to travel with them, though even if he had he would have refused, Daisy knew. Ben's likes and dislikes were increasingly confounding, and Valentine's remark to her in the teashop, about making a mistake, and Aurelia's words to her the previous Saturday—over tea at Fortnum & Mason—had only served to fuel her doubts.

"You must call it off," Aurelia had said to her before they'd parted. "You can't marry him, Daisy . . . You don't love him. And you don't need to be married. This is 1927, and you're an independent modern woman, leading your own life, making your own decisions."

"Yes," she had said, euphoric on the words of independence, on orange pekoe tea and cigarettes called Lucky, she would call it off. So they had made a pact: They would both call off their engagements at Daisy's parents' wedding anniversary celebration.

"We will be there for each other," Aurelia had said, "and if no one wishes to dance with us, well, we shall dance with each other."

But now Daisy was having second thoughts. For the notion of intentionally hurting someone, of puncturing Ben's hopes and dreams—he who had done nothing wrong—seemed cruel and heartless, destined to be punished, somewhere, at some stage. Yes, she had to call it off; it was a mistake, she knew. A knee-jerk decision made after learning about Stephen, but now was not the time, she thought, certainly not this particular weekend. She would leave it a week or two, wait until things were better for him at work, at least. This seemed sensible, kinder.

As the man-made shapes and hard angles of the city receded, Daisy smiled at the sight of fields, the undulating soft curves in countless shades of green and gold. It felt good to be going home, and right to be making this journey alone. And though she was excited at the prospect of seeing her mother again, the thought of seeing her father again was queer. Added to this, and making her stomach do strange things, was the notion of seeing Stephen. Would he be there? Had he been invited?

The station had been a nightmare, and Stephen's third-class carriage was hot and noisy. It reeked of stale sweat and urine, and though he'd been lucky enough to find a seat—one next to the window—he did not want to look out on the brightness of that day, to see the blur of summer and be reminded of so many others gone before. He leaned his head against the glass pane and closed his eyes. He had not been back to Eden Hall in six months, and the thought of seeing a newly engaged Daisy filled his heart with trepidation.

His journey away from that place, and her, had begun last Christmas, when he had traveled up to London and secured lodgings—a small room—in a dismal part of south London. There, he'd quickly realized that he couldn't leave a hemisphere without *her*. Knowing this—and rankled by his weakness—and in his best suit, only suit, starched white shirt and dark tie, and with hope in his heart, he had attended interviews. But the men at each of the employment bureaus had shaken their heads when Stephen mentioned the word *clerical*, and then shaken them again at the mention of *administrative*.

"No," he had said, he had no leavers certificate—no certificates at all, or any diplomas.

They had all mentioned jobs in service.

"A chauffeur, perhaps?" one had suggested. "After all, Mr. Jessop, that's nearer to where your experience lies . . . and I do think you'd be better—more successful—approaching a domestic service employment agency, don't you?"

It was not the best time, Stephen had been told, and more than once, to be looking for a career change, especially if one was as untrained and as *unskilled* as he.

One afternoon in late January, standing in the wintry sunshine outside Oxford Circus tube station, Stephen had scanned the "Situations Vacant" and job advertisements in the newspaper once again. He'd recognized the name immediately: It was the place Mr. Forbes had bought his last Rolls-Royce, a place Stephen knew and had in fact been to a few times. He'd headed straight there.

The position needed to be filled as soon as possible. That was fine, Stephen had said; he was available, and yes, he could start immediately: "Monday if needs be."

"Well, young man, you've worked for Howard Forbes, acted as his chauffeur, and that and your letter of reference from Mrs. Forbes is quite enough for me. I'll see you on Monday."

And that was it.

Stephen's new job was to drive rich American tourists about London, allowing them to see the sights of the English capital from the comfort of a Rolls-Royce motorcar. But there was also the possibility—it had been mentioned—that if he proved himself, in time he might be able to work in the new showroom, helping to sell the cars. "On commission!" the man had announced. And, apparently, that was where the money was.

It wasn't an office job, but it was a job, and it had prospects. And though it didn't pay much, not at first, the American tourists were renowned for their generous tips. But more important than any of this was the fact that the job came with accommodation: a small flat above the showroom next to the office. "Because we need someone to keep an eye on our beautiful new showroom at night," the man had said.

It was just a start, Stephen thought. Better things would come. And so they had.

It had been when he was called upon to chauffeur an American expatriate writer—known to all as Mr. H—about the capital that things had taken off. Mr. H liked the girls and nightclubs and liquor—as he called it. One evening, he invited Stephen to have a nightcap with him at his hotel and gave him a copy of his new novel, telling Stephen in no uncertain terms to read it and to tell him what he thought. And so Stephen had, and did.

It was through Mr. H that Stephen met a publisher who said they were looking for someone to help write a new series of motoring guides to the British Isles, and Stephen told them that he believed it was something he could do. That had been in early March. By late May Stephen had penned most of his guide to Surrey. He had been allowed use of one of the older cars and had driven down each Sunday, touring some familiar and some not-so-familiar country lanes; and he went to the British Library, studied ordinance survey maps, local history books and other guidebooks.

This had been Stephen's life for the last few months, but the previous Saturday he had taken the afternoon off to pay a long-overdue visit to his auntie Nellie. She had been delighted to see him standing on her doorstep, and there'd been the predictable *oh my, how you've grown*, as though he were still twelve years old and not twenty-two, and the usual teasing and stuff about girls: Was he courting? Was there anyone special?

He'd been half tempted to say, *Well, actually, yes, Nellie, there is, and you look after her*. But he didn't. He smiled—almost a little too bashfully—and said not. And then, with studied nonchalance, he'd asked how the Forbes girls were keeping. And just as though she'd been waiting years to tell him, it all came tumbling forth. The older one was a *card*, Nellie said; glamorous, to be sure—and generous, too, because hadn't she given her the very frock she was wearing *and* "these stockings!" she added, reaching to her knees. But *the little one* was her favorite.

Without thinking, he nodded and said her name: "Daisy."

"Yes, Daisy . . . little Daisy," Nellie repeated, "but far too young to be here in the city alone. . . . To be frank, I'm surprised her mother allowed it. I can't for one minute think Mr. Forbes was happy about the arrangement."

"No, I don't think he was. But she's quite a determined sort. I don't think she gave them much choice."

"Much choice! She's nineteen years old, not twenty-one, Stephen."

"Well, I suppose they reckoned on her being taken care of by her elder sister—and you, of course. And she's engaged. I hear tell she's engaged to be married . . . ," he added, needing more.

Nellie rolled her eyes and shuffled. "Engaged . . . that slip of a thing? And what does *engaged* mean anyways? One thing I do know," she said with emphasis, shaking her head, "is whoever's engaged to her doesn't love her enough. I'll be very interested to take a look at this feller she's got herself engaged to when I go down to Eden Hall next week," she added.

The invitation, a thick white card with black scrolled lettering, stood on the mantelpiece next to a small framed photograph of Nellie and her husband on their wedding day. Nellie had been quick to show Stephen the invitation. "See that . . . 'Mr. and Mrs. Howard Forbes request the pleasure of Mr. and Mrs. George Wintrip,'" she said, pointing to the inked name. "Of course, I shan't be bringing *him*," she went on. "He'll only show me up. But I'm going to have a few days down there with your mother. No point in traveling all that distance for just the one night . . . And perhaps you'll be able to show me about the place, the lovely gardens and countryside, eh?"

"I'm afraid I shan't," he said. "I'm going down for the party because my mother insists, but I'll be returning here to London the following day."

Nellie listened intently as Stephen told her about his guide-books. She clapped her hands together. "Well, I never! I've no doubt you're going to end up a millionaire!" she declared.

Stephen smiled. Nellie's idea of success, of wealth, was borne of too many days on her hands and knees in someone else's house, returning to an idle, penniless husband each night. He sat back in his chair and stretched out his legs. The place hadn't changed since his last visit, some eight years before, after the war, when he and his mother had visited. "Strange to be back here," he said. "To think I spent some of my first few years here . . . with you."

"Do you remember any of it?"

"Of course," he said, only half lying, because he could remember some though not all of that time.

"Happy days," said Nellie, glancing away, smiling.

Stephen sat forward. "Nellie," he said, tentatively, "when you first took me in, were you told anything about my parents?"

Nellie pushed her crossed fingers beneath her and shook her head. "No, dear . . . just that they had gone."

Later, Stephen walked the hot pavement from Nellie's house in Fulham to the King's Road. His aunt had told him the location and the name. A dark green awning just as his aunt had described hung over the shopwindow, and from the outside it was hard to see who—if anyone—was inside. He had pressed up his hands, peering in through the glass, and could see the dark wooden shelves and tables of books. When he'd entered, the bell above the door had chimed and his heart had chimed too, but the only person to appear was an elderly gentleman in an old-fashioned frock coat, who had asked, "Looking for anything in particular, sir?"

He had stood for twenty minutes or more, surveying shelves, casting surreptitious glances to the door at the back of the shop, from which the elderly gentleman had emerged. Finally, before leaving the shop, he had asked the man, "Is Miss Forbes in today?"

"No, not on Saturday afternoons," the man replied. "Can I pass on any message, a card?"

Stephen had a card, a business card, but he didn't leave it or any message. He walked south and stood on Battersea Bridge for some time, staring out across the river toward Chelsea.

The train had stopped. Daisy raised her eyes to the verdant meadows and pastures; to the cows ruminating in the corners of fields beneath leafy branches; to the distant cluster of tile-hung cottages and slate steeple. It was a landscape she recognized and knew. She lifted her finger to the glass, stroking the trees, the cream-colored cows, tracing a church steeple all the way up to the blue.

She closed her book, lifted her straw boater from the seat next to her, then opened her purse to check for her ticket and for the sixpence for the porter. She put on her white gloves, fastening the tiny pearl buttons at her wrists, and as she waited for the train to move on, she wondered again if Ben was on the train and how she would explain her failure to meet him.

It was a jolt he hadn't expected: an unscheduled stop. Work on the line, someone in his carriage said. Glancing away, turning to a world drenched green, Stephen saw only white winter, and her, as she had been the last time he had seen her, standing in her fur coat, kicking at the ground. *You're the one I most trust,* she says quietly. She looks up at him. Her eyes are shining, gray-green shot with flecks of copper and gold: like late summer trees, he thinks. She moves nearer, smiles and says his name: *Stephen . . .* He feels the rise and fall of his chest, hears his own intake of breath. *Did you mean it?*

Every word and more, he thought, as the train moved on.

Standing beneath the stone archway, Daisy heard her name and turned to see Ben, pink faced and crumpled. It took seconds—less than seconds—for her eyes to alight on Stephen walking from the platform behind Ben. In a brown trilby hat and dark suit—looking as dapper as any city commuter, and taller than most—he was impossible *not* to notice. And so surprised by the sight of him, there, like that, Daisy failed to hear Ben's immediate protestations.

When Stephen raised his eyes and saw her, his face erupted into that familiar smile she'd so missed, and forgetting Ben, forgetting everything, Daisy said his name and stepped forward.

Stephen took hold of her hand, and they stood for some moments staring at each other and smiling, unable not to.

"Not in New Zealand, then," she said.

"Ah, the errant chauffeur," muttered Ben, pulling out his handkerchief and wiping his wet brow with it.

"No, not in New Zealand," said Stephen, still smiling, still holding on to her hand.

Ben cleared his throat.

Daisy pulled away her hand. "You remember Stephen?" she said, stepping back, turning to Ben.

Ben threw Stephen a quick smile. "So how are we meant to get from here to Eden Hall?" he asked.

Daisy glanced about the cars parked in front of the station. "Well, seeing as my father doesn't appear to be here, we'll have to take a taxi."

Stephen picked up his small suitcase and a bag from a familiar London store. "See you both tomorrow," he said.

"But where are you going?" Daisy asked. "Aren't you coming home?"

"Yes . . . I was going to take the bus."

"Don't be silly; there's no need to."

Minutes later, Daisy sat between the two men as they headed out of town in the back of a taxi. She kept her eyes fixed ahead as she asked Stephen about his job. His answers were as perfunctory and polite as her questions, and his questions to her as polite and perfunctory again.

Every window of the taxi was open, the air flowing through it scented with the fragrance of the summer hedgerows, of honeysuckle and wild jasmine, warm pine and heather. As the taxi emerged from the sun-dappled lane at the crossroads, Stephen turned to Daisy. "No Fletch, eh? I wonder where he is now."

Daisy looked back at him and smiled. "Yes, I wonder."

Without his hat, she saw now that the pale winter pallor of last Christmas had changed to a sun-burnished glow, and that he had cut himself shaving. She noticed once more the line of his top lip, thinner than the bottom; that his nose was not straight—like

Ben's—and that, smiling back at her, one side of his mouth twitched, as though he wished to say something more.

"Fletch? Who's that?" Ben asked.

"Oh, just someone we used to know and see about here," Daisy replied, turning her head to the road ahead once more.

There was so much Ben didn't know. And how could she ever begin to tell him, to explain that history, her history, which Stephen knew because he had shared it. She glanced down at Stephen's hands—strong, masculine hands—resting on his lap, fiddling with the felt brim of his hat: tanned, like his face, and cleaner than they used to be, she thought. His right arm rested against hers, and the feel of it and warmth of him made her eyelids heavy, as though she were drugged, happily drugged and languishing in some vaguely recollected paradise.

"What's in the Liberty bag?" Daisy asked after a moment.

"A present for my mother . . . a silk scarf."

Daisy looked at him again. But his eyes were closed, his face turned to the open window.

"So, Jessop, will you be coming to the party?" Ben asked as they approached the entrance to Eden Hall.

"Afraid so," he replied.

Daisy smiled.

"And bringing anyone?" Ben asked.

Stephen said yes, he would be bringing along a guest. As Daisy turned to him, he went on to explain that his mother had taken it upon herself to invite Tabitha Farley as his partner. "Because your mother had kindly written *and partner* on my invitation, my mother seems to think it's compulsory," he added, staring back at Daisy.

Ben laughed loudly. "Compulsory!" he repeated. "I like that . . . Yes, I rather like that."

Then the gardens unfolded in a haze of blue-green: immense herbaceous borders framing manicured lawns, trimmed shrubs and hedges of box, and the large canvas marquee, where men were carrying in rolls of carpet and stacks of gold-painted chairs.

"It all looks splendid," said Ben.

Yes, Daisy thought, *it does.*

They drew to a halt outside the open front door. Stephen took Daisy's bag from the trunk of the taxi and placed it down on the step. He smiled at her. "Well, see you both tomorrow," he said again, and then disappeared under the archway into the courtyard and the back of the house.

Watching him go, Daisy had a sudden and intense yearning to call after him, to shout out his name and see him turn to her and smile.

"Damned queer feller," muttered Ben, walking on ahead of her through the open door.

"Why queer?" Daisy asked, picking up her bag.

Ben glanced back at her. "The chap never even congratulated us."

"Congratulated us?"

"On our engagement!"

"Oh, that," she said, following him inside and wondering if Stephen knew. But as soon as she saw Mabel, walking across the hallway toward her, she dropped her bag to the floor and fell into her mother's arms.

Chapter Twenty-five

The meal that evening included potted shrimps, a cheese soufflé and sole Véronique. Mrs. Jessop had obviously been honing her culinary skills in Mabel's absence, Daisy thought. But there were only five of them at dinner: Daisy, Ben, Howard, Mabel and Reggie. Everyone else would be arriving tomorrow, apart from Iris and Val, who had changed their plans yet again and might be arriving later that night, Mabel said. And Noonie was once again having tinned peaches and ice cream on a tray in her room. According to Mabel, this was what she lived on now.

But despite any worries about Noonie, Mabel had lost a worrisome look from her features. Home for only ten days and still glowing from her months on the continent, she had fewer lines in her face and she was prettier, younger and more relaxed than Daisy had ever known her. She smiled and laughed a great deal, had taken up smoking and appeared to have developed a new sense of joie de vivre, a tolerance of all things and people, encapsulated in a new and irreverent humor.

"England really is so ridiculously stuffy and uptight by comparison—and for absolutely no reason," she told Daisy. "There, you can be whoever you want to be, do whatever you want—and nobody bats an eyelid. You really must go, darling," she added. "You must experience it all."

Reggie, as attentive as ever, backed up each and every one of Mabel's observations and pronouncements and laughed on cue. But from time to time Daisy detected some trace of mild irritation from Mabel toward him and wondered if they'd had some sort of falling-out overseas.

And she, too, was irritated. Irritated by Ben's fawning behavior toward Howard. He seemed desperate for her father's attention, uninterested in anything anyone else said. Feigning laughter whenever Howard said anything vaguely amusing, nodding whenever her father spoke. Ben was so pale by comparison to Stephen, she thought, watching him; so pale in every way.

But the most changed of them all was Howard. Iris was right: There was less of him. But with his weight loss he'd also shed years. For most of the meal he simply sat back in his chair, smiling as he watched and listened to Mabel, as though she were a vision dropped down from heaven. And watching him watching her, Daisy felt something hovering in the ether between her father's quiet demeanor and her mother's exuberance: a meeting of eyes, a lingering stare, or mirrored smiles; like a private joke or some secret, new understanding.

"Half a cutlet . . . *half a cutlet!*" Mabel was saying now, shaking her head. "She said, 'Don't worry about supper for us; we can always stop off on the way and share a cutlet if we get ravenous . . .'" Mabel turned to Daisy: "Does Iris *ever* eat?"

"She's following a special diet. I can't remember what it is . . . but you're allowed to eat blancmange . . . and beetroot. Anything beginning with the letter B, I think."

"Well, she seems to have moved on to Cs," said Mabel, lifting her glass to her lips and smiling—quite coquettishly, Daisy thought—down the table at Howard.

That evening, dinner went on for longer than usual. The wine flowed, and between Mabel's reminiscences and laughter, and Daisy's observations of a new dynamic at play, her thoughts drifted back to Stephen. Yards away, minutes away. The sight of him at the station, the realization that they had traveled on the same train; sitting next to him in the taxi, his disregard for Ben—and perhaps even for her; his strangely sad demeanor—his hat, his face, his hands . . . everything about him had imprinted itself boldly on her mind. She had missed him, missed him more than she'd realized, and now she longed to be with him.

She wondered how and when she could escape from that room and go to find him, because, at the very least, she wanted to mend things between them, to reestablish their friendship. Whether or not he was her brother, he had always been her friend, her very best friend. And she saw him once more emerge from the station, the brim of his hat shading his face. She saw his hands, his smile, his eyes . . .

"You're very quiet, dear," her mother said, breaking in.

Daisy shrugged. "Just a little tired."

"Well, an early night—a good night's sleep—will do you no harm," said Reggie, nodding at Nancy to clear away their plates. "We all need to be on top form for your mother's party tomorrow."

"My father's party, too," Daisy quickly replied. "It's their wedding anniversary, Reggie."

Daisy glanced at Howard, who smiled back at her, and Reggie laughed. "Of course. I didn't mean to leave the old feller out, you know."

When Mabel finally rose to her feet and said that if everyone didn't mind she was going to go to her boudoir and check on a few things, Daisy took her cue. "And if no one minds, I think I'll take a breath of fresh air before I retire—*early*, Reggie," she added.

"I'll join you," said Ben, pushing out his chair.

"No, please. You stay here . . . have a glass of port. I'm sure you'd rather," she said, offering him her best smile.

"You sure?"

"Quite."

She swept through the kitchen—offering a quick hello to Mrs. Jessop—before moving down the red tile–floored passageway and slipping out of the open door into the courtyard. She glanced to the door of the coachman's flat and then headed on, in the direction of the kitchen gardens. She knew he'd be there. When she saw him, standing by the cold frame, a watering can in one hand, cigarette in the other, she stopped and smiled and then moved slowly toward him.

He had dispensed with his hat and his jacket and tie, and his shirtsleeves were rolled back. His dark hair was cropped short at the back, and a thick, long wave hung over his forehead. As she approached him, he turned, and the frown she caught only a momentary glimpse of was replaced by a languid smile as he raised his forearm to push back the dangling lock.

She moved alongside him and stood with him in silence for a moment.

"So . . . ," he said.

"So," she repeated.

"Tell me."

She smiled, reassured by their understanding and that undeniable frisson. And then she quickly reminded herself of the facts: the hideous possibility—likelihood, she corrected herself. *But if he is my brother, is my love—affection—for him any less valid?* she wondered. She glanced to him: a young Howard, Iris had said, but Daisy couldn't see it. They were both dark, but Stephen's jaw was longer, leaner, and his nose and the line of his mouth were quite different.

"Tell you what, exactly?" she said.

The sun was beginning its descent, pouring molten gold over the tops of the trees, bouncing off the panes of the greenhouse. She lifted her hand to her brow.

"Shall we start off with . . . how you are, whether you're happy and how you feel about your impending marriage?"

"We're not . . . not exactly, not properly engaged," she stumbled, lowering her hand, glancing down to the yellowing grass.

"Ah, not *properly* engaged? So what is it, then?"

"Well, it's an engagement, I suppose . . . a sort of engagement. But I hadn't realized people knew. No one's really meant to know, you see . . . not yet."

"You mean it's a secret?"

"No. It's not a secret," she said. "It's just that it isn't official yet. Only a few people know."

"I see."

"But that's not why I've come out here, not what I came to say."

He put down the watering can and turned to her. He reached out, touched her hair with his finger. "You had it cut," he said, staring back at her and tilting his head to one side.

"It was a birthday present from Iris. But I still have it all . . . in a bag back in London," she added.

Despite the fantasy—the image she'd sometimes had of herself with short hair and painted lips—Daisy had been stubborn, had steadfastly refused to follow fashion and have her hair bobbed. Iris had despaired, had told Daisy that no one other than old ladies and little girls had long hair now. "And as for those eyebrows . . . ," Iris had said, shaking her head, "we really must do something with them." Daisy hadn't a clue what she meant. Did people actually have their eyebrows trimmed too? "They simply must be *done*. They're quite mothlike, darling," Iris had said.

Iris had won in the end—with the hair, at least—and an appointment with Marcel had been her birthday treat to Daisy. "You're going to look *so* pretty, so fashionable and chic, darling," Iris had told her in the taxicab en route to Harrods.

Daisy had had her hair cut a few times before, each time by Nancy, each time in the kitchen at Eden Hall and each time by only a few inches. But when she was twelve years old, more than six inches had fallen onto the kitchen floor, with a tearful Mrs. Jessop gathering up each discarded lock and loudly blowing her nose. Later, after seeing herself in the mirror, Daisy had been banished to her room for what Mabel deemed a "ridiculous hysteria."

So, after Marcel, after she'd seen the lengths of her precious hair lying on the floor of the salon, it felt like the severance of something far greater to Daisy, and she'd cried again. Marcel had flicked his hand, said a few words in French that Daisy did not understand and then had someone gather up the hair and place it inside a paper bag. As Iris settled the bill and pacified Marcel with enough kisses to twitch his sulky pout into a smile, the bag was handed to Daisy. Now the severed hair lay in the drawer of her dressing table at Sydney Street.

"Well, that's good," Stephen said. "Perhaps you can give your bag of hair to your fiancé—as a wedding present."

"Don't be like that."

"Like what?"

"Like . . . this."

"*This?*"

She saw his eyes, curious, defensive, and longed for him to make a joke, to smile or laugh.

"This is how it is, isn't it?" he began again. "You and me and life . . . Me, standing here with a watering can and a fag; you, coming to tell me that it's all fine and that we're still friends. Isn't that what you came out here to tell me? That we're still friends? And that it'll all be fine and dandy after you're married?"

She looked away. Daylight was fading. The sun had sunk farther beneath the beeches and pines, casting dark shadows about the pink walls where the nectarines and peaches hung full and ripe. "Yes," she said. "I did."

"Well, you don't need to. We'll always be friends, you and me. We both know that. And no matter what happens, I'll always be here for you . . . or perhaps not here, but there—wherever *there* is. Anyway, you know what I mean," he added, sounding vaguely irritated.

"Yes. And that's exactly what I wanted to say to you."

He nodded, as though agreeing more with himself than with her. "As long as you're happy," he said.

"What about you? Are you happy?" she asked. Though he didn't seem it at that moment, it was only polite to ask, she thought. And she wanted to know. And she wanted him to be happy. As she waited for his response, as another silence descended over them, she realized that she wished for him to be happy more than she wished for her own happiness.

"I'm not sure what happiness is," he said at last, staring into the distance. "I reckon there are good moments and bad moments, that's all. And I experience both, just like everyone else."

"I think it's all to do with love," said Daisy without thinking.

"And marriage?" he asked quickly, turning to her.

"Yes," she said. "That as well."

He looked away and pulled a packet of cigarettes from his pocket.

"What about Tabitha?" she asked.

"What *about* Tabitha?" he repeated, lighting his cigarette.

"I just wondered . . . it seemed to be quite something last Christmas."

He sighed. "It wasn't how it looked."

Right at that moment she wished she could pull back; she wished she could speak to him about nothing and anything, but it was impossible. She couldn't. From somewhere deep within her came a shrill little laugh—one she'd never heard before—and then she heard herself say, "Yes, well, it did rather *look* like something, and the timing of your decision to . . . to spend the night with her was a little curious, Stephen."

She couldn't quite believe what she'd just said, and yet there seemed to be more, desperate and bubbling, that had to be said: "And let me just tell you this," she began again, "if you're going to go round telling girls you love them and inviting them off to . . . to foreign places, and then sleep with some of them, and write letters to the other ones, and then . . . then . . ." But it was all too much. It boiled over and out of her in a strangely gurgled scream.

After that, she had no alternative but to make a hasty exit. She marched off in the direction of the house, then swiftly turned toward the woods.

She paused for a moment, mortified by her outburst, clinging to the silky old wood of the gate; then she pulled it open and walked on. It was cooler, more tranquil there. The sun shone low through the branches, breaking up the shadows with iridescent jets of shimmering light, illuminating desultory cobwebs floating in the warm evening air. The path was soft underfoot, narrowed by the season, by the dust-covered nettles and ferns and the wildflowers, thick and abundant and undisturbed. The remains of fallen trees lay rotting in sinister shapes, their ragged bark peeling off them like ancient wallpaper, and the little wooden bridge was green with moss.

As Daisy stood on the bridge, she pictured other evenings, nights such as this, when she had been there with him, building a dam, searching the water for unusual pebbles and fossils, chattering on openly, uninhibitedly, about anything and everything. How uncomplicated life had once been, she thought, moving toward the ridge from where, months earlier, she had thrown her globe. Then the surrounding valley had been white and thick with snow, the stream gushing in an icy torrent; now purple heather once again covered the slopes and the water trickled slowly across the boulders and rocks. She looked down over the precipice. Was it still there, or had someone found it and carried it off? She heard the sound of a gun reverberate across the valley, and then she heard her name.

"I'm sorry," he said as he stepped up onto the ridge and stood alongside her.

"My snow globe is somewhere down there."

"Your snow globe . . . the one your father gave you?"

"I threw it from here. It landed near those trees," she said, pointing.

He didn't ask why, didn't ask anything more. He said, "Come, I'll walk you back."

They took a different path and for a while they walked in silence. It was so easy, she thought, to be with him and be silent. Ben would have accused her of being antisocial or sulking, but there was never any such accusation from Stephen. Not that night, not ever.

At the top of the hill where the track met the tarmacadam road was an old broomsquire's cottage. Daisy had visited it once before—years before—with him. At that time it had been inhabited by an old man called Jethro, whom Stephen had reckoned was close to one hundred years old. The place was still the same dirty pink and still had the same untidy thatched roof. A woman stood in the open doorway, smoking a pipe, holding a large baby on her hip. She smiled and nodded to Stephen as he moved toward her. Daisy remained on the track and waited while they spoke. She heard Stephen laugh, say, "No," heard him say her name and saw the woman peer over at her with renewed interest. He stroked the child's head as he spoke, then turned away and rejoined Daisy on the track.

"What did she say?"

"She asked if you were my sweetheart," he said, looking downward. "But I told her who you were and that you were engaged to be married. That was all."

"I suppose old Jethro's long since passed away."

"Yes, a good few years ago . . . That's his great-granddaughter, Rosie."

"You know everyone . . . you've always known everyone, which is surprising considering . . ."

"Considering I'm not from here—wasn't born here? Maybe that's why," he said, turning to her. "Maybe I've had to make more of an effort . . . or maybe I'm more interested. Anyway, your family don't exactly mix with the locals, do they?"

Daisy stopped. "Yes, we do. Most of my parents' friends live round here."

He smiled. "But how many of them were born here, work here, have lived here for generations? Rosie's family have been here for hundreds of years, not a couple of decades . . . and I don't suppose your parents or their friends have any idea who she is."

Daisy said nothing. It was true enough; her parents didn't and never had mixed with the local working people, those families who had lived off the land and eked out an existence over centuries. And she had been brought up with only a few vetted friends, children whose parents her mother knew and approved of. And yet Mabel had also been the one to have all of those children from London each summer and during the war.

"My parents are not prejudiced that way; they're not snobs, Stephen," she said.

"No, they're not," he said quickly, emphatically. "And I didn't mean that. What I meant was, there's . . . there's this divide, and everyone has their group, their place, and they never mix. And I'm stuck in the middle, or that's how I feel. I'm not sure which group I belong to, but I know I don't wish to belong to one—to the exclusion of the other . . . if that makes any sense."

"Yes. You're a little like Ben in that way. He said something similar to me recently."

"No, I'm nothing like Benedict Gifford."

When they reached the yard, he lowered his head and said good night in what seemed to her an overly courteous manner. The air had grown colder and her bare arms were goose pimpled. Bats swooped over the darkened courtyard. Unable yet to face Ben, unable yet to enter that realm and make small talk, she walked on, round the house, and took the path to the Japanese garden.

She sat down on the bench by the lily pond, listening to the evensong chorus of birds until the lingering twilight dissolved and black dusk descended like the final curtain on the day, and only a solitary owl called out, and her thoughts blurred, deeper and more elusive than ever.

The moon was not quite whole and had a slice missing from its top, like the moon on the night of the Victory party so many years before. That night, when she had pointed it out to Stephen, he had said it was like the men who had been in the war and returned home with parts of their heads missing.

"But the moon will be whole again . . . and so perhaps those men will be too. The doctors will be able to help them," she'd said, reassuring herself.

But Stephen had told her that the doctors could only help with the physical wounds and, even then, only the appearance of those wounds. "You can't make someone forget everything they've seen or done," he'd added.

"I don't believe in war," she'd said. "I'm a conchie."

She wasn't entirely sure what that meant, but she knew it was the term for someone opposed to the war, and what Iris claimed to be. But when he'd turned on her, told her that it was unpatriotic to be an objector, that only cowards took that stance, and that she should be ashamed of herself for saying such a thing—particularly then, that night—she'd cried. And not for herself or for his harsh words, but for the moon—with its missing top, and all those men with their missing tops who could never be mended.

For Daisy, the war—initially—had simply meant the departure of servants, and they had all waved them off with small flags and glad hearts. It had meant a relaxation in the timetable of lessons, a new bedroom and more unlikely playmates from London. Meals had been different, fires restricted. But from time to time she had caught a glimpse of the newspaper, the long numbers, the photographs and images of that place, the war. She had been to church and prayed hard, as hard as she could, for those *over there*, and she'd relied on and listened to Stephen for analysis and commentary, just as she did on everything else.

When Daisy emerged from her trance—because that was what it had seemed like to her, as though she had been lost in some state of disconnectedness—she was clearer. She remembered the last time she had sat in that place, shivering, cold, hot with jealousy and still trembling from the ripples of an anxious rapture, still trembling from a single meaningless kiss, still trembling from those furtive words of love; yearning for some distant freedom that would make sense of life. But freedom, she had discovered, was a lonely place. A rattling window out of which one viewed more windows and other people, strangers. Freedom was invisibility, she thought now.

She had lost track of the time and wasn't sure how long she had been sitting there when she heard the footsteps behind her.

"Waiting for someone in particular?" Ben asked, sitting down on the bench by her side.

"Just taking some air."

"Oh yes, air. You like taking air. I forgot."

She heard him sigh, but she could think of nothing to say.

"If you're still sulking about the station," he said, "about me not waiting for you, I'm sorry. I've said I'm sorry."

"I'm not sulking, Ben. And it was probably better that we traveled down separately."

He laughed, a strange, hollow laugh, one that lent the night a newly foreboding feel. "It's getting cold out here and you're going to get chilled. Let's go inside," he said.

"I don't want to, not yet."

"Well, I'm not leaving you out here on your own."

"Why?" she asked, turning to him. "What do you suppose might happen? That I'll be eaten by a badger?"

"Don't be facetious, my dear. It's not becoming in a woman. It's late and we should go and be sociable . . . It's only polite."

The *don't be facetious* annoyed her; the *my dear* even more. She closed her eyes and then rose to her feet. As they walked up the driveway, neared the bright light of the front door, he reached for her hand and cleared his throat. "Daisy, dearest, I wondered if later you might allow me to come to your room to . . . to say good night to you?"

It was a request she had been dreading.

Chapter Twenty-six

"You do look well," said Daisy. "You really do look years younger."

"Well, I suppose that's the result of five months on the continent—and a new hairdo. But you have a new look, too," Mabel replied, smiling back at her daughter's reflection in the dressing table mirror.

Daisy lifted her hand to her hair. "Yes, what do you think?"

"I told you earlier, I like it . . . but I can tell that you don't."

"No, it's not that; it's just that I sort of miss my old hair."

Mabel laughed. "Too late now."

Mabel's room had its own distinct atmosphere and style and was filled with huge and reputedly valuable pieces of furniture. Ever fragrant, soft and warm, it was to Daisy an oasis of calm, imbued with Mabel's soothing manner, her femininity reflected in its tones and textures. The large pink roses on the voluminous chintz curtains, the dressing table delicately shrouded in muslin, with its antique perfume bottles and silver-topped jars, its hairbrush, mirror and comb; the sumptuous bed, with its neatly piled pillows and lace-edged cushions. It was, had seemed always, the most sweet scented of havens.

Daisy sat down on the chair by Mabel's dressing table. She watched her mother as she brushed her hair. The new hairdo came from Rome. The dress she had worn that evening, purchased in Paris; the shawl, from Koblenz. Her nightdress, from a "divine little place" in the South of France; the small beaded handbag, lying on the table next to the bed, handmade in Venice. There would be a shipment of "trinkets," Mabel said, arriving sometime soon. "Some souvenirs, a few little things for the house and some presents for you and everyone else."

Mabel, usually somewhat frugal and never overly indulgent with herself, seemed to have been on a spending spree across Europe. She obviously had no idea about the state of Howard's finances.

"Did it cost much . . . your trip?" Daisy asked tentatively. Discussing money had always been frowned upon at Eden Hall, particularly where Mabel was concerned.

"I funded the entire expedition myself," said Mabel proudly. "With the money my father left to me. Well, it wasn't a lot, but it's paid for my little adventure. And it was something I wanted to do for myself, without any financial help from your father."

Just as well, Daisy thought.

"So tell me," Mabel said, putting down her hairbrush, picking up a pot of face cream and turning to Daisy, "how are *things* between you and Benedict?"

"I'm not sure."

Mabel's eyes widened. "Not sure? Not sure about what?"

Daisy picked up a comb and ran her fingernail along its teeth. "Not sure about any of it, I suppose . . . not sure about him."

Mabel put down her jar of cream and swiveled round. "I thought as much. I think you need to bring me up to date . . . Your father told me you were happy, very happy, he said."

"Yes, I think I was, at first, perhaps . . ."

Mabel sighed. "I did tell you; I told you when I wrote to you in March that I'd prefer you not to get yourself embroiled in any liaison until I returned. To be perfectly honest, Daisy, had I known what would happen, I would never have consented to your going to London. Never. I'm sure I don't need to remind you that I was instrumental in persuading your father."

"You said he put up no fight?"

"Please, don't interrupt me. It's not just the fact that you're too young to be married; it's that Benedict Gifford's so much older than you . . . and so very different. I really can't for the life of me think what the pair of you have in common."

"You were younger than me when you married Daddy—*and* he's thirteen years older than you." Daisy had no desire to defend Ben or her mistake, but she could not allow the hypocrisy to go uncommented.

Her mother stared at her. "We're not talking about Daddy and I here; what we're talking about is the rather frightful mess you've got yourself into during my absence. And anyway, things were very different then . . . I'm sorry, dear, but I simply don't understand what you were thinking, or why your father gave his consent, and really, I do wish you had at least waited until I was home, until you could talk to me about it."

"He's invested some money in the business—which, by the way, is in a bit of a mess, in case you didn't know." Daisy wasn't sure why she said this, but she thought Mabel ought to know.

Mabel affected a laugh. "My darling, you don't agree to marry a man simply because he's invested in your father's business," she said, shaking her head. She turned back to the rosewood mirror, rubbing cream into her face with renewed vigor. "I knew, knew when your father cabled me, knew the moment I read the words, that it was a mistake . . . and I blame *him*."

"No, don't! Don't blame Daddy, please . . . it's nothing to do with him. It's not his fault."

Mabel's head turned again. "Nothing to do with him? You've just said he took money from that man and then gave his permission. And now you're embroiled in an unsatisfactory engagement— one which will undoubtedly have to be called off. And that has ramifications on you, my dear. No girl wants to have had more than one engagement; otherwise, it looks sloppy and ill considered." She slammed down the jar. "I knew I couldn't go away, knew it would all go horribly wrong. *That man* is incapable of managing anything."

She had gone back to her old self and appeared to Daisy to be having a battle with her face now, wrestling with her cheeks and forehead and breathing much too rapidly.

"I thought . . . I thought he appeared better—changed—at dinner," said Daisy.

"Oh, he's probably still feeling sorry for himself, that I dared to go away and leave him here for six months. That's all."

This, Mabel knew, was untrue, but she was cross with her husband about what they both now referred to as the Gifford Situation. In truth, she had been shocked by Howard's appearance and manner when she returned. She had been expecting someone decidedly older than the rather handsome, lean man who'd met her at Southampton docks, the one who'd taken her so eagerly in his arms and kissed her—and not on the cheek, but on the mouth. Even now, if she allowed herself to think about that welcome home, it made her feel strangely giddy.

Howard had told Mabel after Christmas and then again before she left that he intended to win her back. "Back from where?" she had asked.

"Wherever you have been these past six years," he'd replied.

While away, she had sent him only the occasional postcard. She wanted him to experience her absence fully, the emptiness of that place without her there; to rattle about rooms, to sit alone each evening with only the sounds of the owls in the trees outside for company. She wanted him to know how all of this felt. She wanted him to have time to reflect on the past twenty-five years.

"He hasn't been to London much at all," Daisy said now, "or not that I'm aware of."

"No, so I hear."

Daisy moved over to her mother. "Mummy," she said, wrapping her arms round Mabel, "we've all missed you . . . and you know, we all fall apart a little when you're not here."

Daisy had gone to her mother's room that night hoping to avoid

Ben. She wanted to tell her mother; wanted to say that the man had asked if he could come to her; that the hour was approaching and she didn't know what to do. Sitting in Mabel's bedroom, she knew the minutes were ticking by and imagined Ben already stalking the silent passageway beyond the closed door, reeking of brilliantine and cheap cologne. But Daisy said nothing, and when Mabel said she thought Daisy looked "a little overtired," she had done as she was told—and gone to her room.

It was shortly after midnight when the knock came.

"Yoo-hoo," Ben said, poking his head round the door and smiling, "it's only me." He looked completely out of place and looked as though he felt that way, too.

"Golly," he said. "Not exactly the room I was expecting."

"What were you expecting?" she asked.

"Something a little bigger, grander."

"Look here, Ben," she began, not altogether sure what she was about to say, but standing up from the chair at her desk, where she had been waiting.

"I am," he said. "I am here, I am looking, and I see a rather well-dressed Daisy . . . Isn't it time good little girls were in their nightgowns and in bed?"

He had dispensed with his jacket and tie, removed the collar from his shirt, which was unbuttoned, revealing the pale, mottled skin and wiry red hairs on his chest. He moved over to her, placed his arms round her waist. Predictably, his hair was wet and shiny; predictably, he reeked of cheap cologne—almost but not quite masking the smell of alcohol on his breath. His lips were stained blue-red from the claret and port he had been drinking that evening, and his speech was slightly slurred.

"A little nervous, are we? It's only to be expected . . . with a man in your room. Am I the first? Am I the very first man to come here?" he asked.

Daisy nodded; he was, apart from Howard.

"Well, here I am, your Valentino." He ran the back of his hand over her cheek and pushed back her hair. "Sweet little Daisy," he whispered as he lowered his mouth to her neck. "So innocent . . . ," he murmured.

"Ben . . . please, I don't want—"

Then, all at once, his mouth was over hers, his tongue forcing open her lips, a hand on her bottom, another on her breast.

"Stop!" she yelled, turning her head, pushing at his chest with her hands. "Please . . . please stop," she said, stepping away from him, stumbling over her chair.

"What? I thought you said I could come here tonight."

"Yes, but not to maul me . . . not to maul me like some pervert."

"Pervert? Oh, for God's sake! You're wearing more clothes than your grandmother does on the coldest winter's day. What the hell do you think I was coming here for? To read you a bedtime story and then kiss you good night?" He wiped his mouth with the back of his hand. "I know you're a virgin, and I wouldn't be marrying you if you weren't, but to carry on like this with the man you are going to marry . . . well, it's a bit much if you ask me."

"I didn't."

"Eh?"

"I didn't ask you."

"Ha, very clever," he replied. He walked over to the bed and sat down on it. "Look, I know this is all new to you, all a bit queer and strange to have a man in your room . . . but it's me, Ben, and we're engaged . . . and have I ever tried anything on with you? Have I ever been disrespectful or compromised you in any way?"

He hadn't.

"Come over here," he said, patting the bed. "Come along . . . don't be silly. You're not a child."

She wasn't.

She moved over to him, stood in front of him. "I need to tell you something, Ben," she said quietly.

He lifted her dress, ran his hands up her legs, over the tops of her stockings and onto her thighs. "That's it," he said, breathing deeply as he squeezed her flesh.

"I need to tell you something," she said again.

He looked up at her. "Now, take off your dress, darling . . . and let me look at you. That's all I want, you know, just to look at you . . . to look at my Daisy."

She stepped away from him again. "I'm very sorry, but I don't want to do this . . . and I don't want to marry you."

He stared up at her, smiling, and then he laughed. "You don't want to marry me? Oh dear, you really *are* frightened. I hadn't realized—hadn't thought . . ." He paused. "You don't like to be touched?"

"No, it's not that."

"Yes, it is. I can tell. And I'm sorry I shouted, and I'm sorry I didn't wait for you at the station today, but you should know I've had a very difficult time lately. You more than anyone should understand . . ."

"I do, I do understand, but it's not about that, Ben. And it's not that I don't like to be touched, don't want to be touched . . . it's just that it doesn't feel right . . . with you."

"Oh, I see, with *me*. Now I understand . . . ," he said, nodding, continuing to smile, his mouth taut. "Doesn't feel right with me . . . ," he said again. "Do you know what the word *frigid* means? If not, look it up in that dictionary of yours over there, because you need to know . . . You're just like your mother, but at least Howard makes up for you both, scattering his seed about London." He leaned forward, glancing about the room, scanning the carpet with incandescent eyes. "So who do you want to be touched by, then? Is it that half-wit servant—is he the one you fancy, hmm? Is he the one, Daisy? Because I saw the way you were with him today, staring at each other with your own little private memories . . . Is that where you've set your sights?"

Daisy said nothing.

"So I'm expected to take this . . . suffer this humiliation, and all because you fancy some servant . . . What a bloody joke." He glanced up at her. "Have you nothing else to say? Is that it?"

"This has nothing to do with Stephen."

"*Stephen* . . . nothing to do with Stephen," he mimicked. "You know, I did wonder . . ." He laughed, shook his head. "Such a coincidence, I thought, him being on that train, you not being there to meet me. And then, when you disappeared off from dinner tonight . . . I thought, well, I'll just take a look, just see where she's got to, that little Daisy of mine . . . and I saw you, saw you come back from the woods with him. Romantic rendezvous, was it? Did you like him touching you then? Yes, I bet you did . . . Bit of a cliché, if you ask me."

It was quick, over in a second. But she'd always remember the sting of his hand on her cheek.

Her Valentino.

Chapter Twenty-seven

When Mabel walked into Howard's study, he quickly removed his feet from the leather-topped desk and began to shuffle papers.

"A glorious day," he said, smiling over at his wife. "What you've been hoping for . . ."

Mabel closed the door. "I need to talk to you. About the Gifford Situation." She sat down opposite him. "Daisy tells me the man's invested money in the business . . ."

"That's right. When I promoted him last year he was keen to have a stake in Forbes and Sons. I told him that he'd be eligible to buy shares at a very reasonable price."

"And . . . after he'd done this, after he'd invested his money, you gave your permission for Daisy to become engaged to him?"

Howard's eyes flashed back at her. "What are you inferring? Do you really think I'd take money from a man—*any* man—in . . . in some sort of payment for Daisy? My God, Mabel, what do you take me for?"

"No, I don't think you've done anything of the sort," she said quickly, "but I do wonder if the man thought he could buy Daisy and buy his way into this family."

Howard glanced away, frowning. "I intend to pay him back on his investment, and give him a good return, too."

"I thought the business was in trouble, especially since the fire."

Howard turned to her. "It is, and has been for some time, but that's where I *have* been clever," he said.

He went on to say that he knew his family business had no future and that he'd decided some time ago that there was no point throwing good money after bad, no point pouring private money—money from other investments and property—into Forbes and Sons. The business had had its day, he said.

He would inform Ben Gifford of the situation in the coming days, and he intended to write to all of the company's employees, to explain and give them as long a period of notice as he was able. But he felt guilty, he said; some of the men had worked there since his father's day. But what his father—and grandfather before—could never have foreseen, never have imagined, and what he had for some time refused to accept, was the decline of the empire. England may have once ruled the waves, but without any empire, and with the predicted expansion in air travel, the British shipbuilding industry's days were numbered.

"But is there nothing that can be done to . . . to save it?" Mabel asked.

Howard shook his head. "Even if I were to rebuild the factory, we'll be watching the business go bust within the next year or two."

Mabel closed her eyes for a moment. "I hadn't realized . . . You never said."

"I knew at Christmas. And I intended to talk to you about it, but then . . . well, I didn't want to burden you or spoil your trip."

"Oh, Howard . . . I'm so sorry."

"I'm afraid it's the way of the world," he said, and then he opened a drawer, pulled out a folder.

"I've reorganized our finances . . . and set up a trust. It ensures Eden Hall is protected and that, after I die, you and each of the girls will have an income and that you'll be able to continue living here."

But Mabel had no wish to look at the documents in front of her, and no wish to think of a time after Howard.

She sighed and rose to her feet. "Not now," she said. "Let's discuss all of this another time, not today . . ." Then, placing her hands on the desk and leaning over it toward him, she said, "I'm so sorry about the business, Howard. I know how much it means to you, and how heartbreaking it must have been for you to make these decisions."

"It's a business. Not a wife, not a family . . . and not nearly as heartbreaking as it would be for me to lose either of those."

Mabel smiled. "You still haven't explained to me, haven't told me why you gave your permission for Daisy to become engaged."

Howard stared back at her. "Because I let her down . . . Because I wanted her to have the opportunity to make her own decisions . . . and perhaps make her own mistakes and learn from them. And because if I'd said no, she'd have hated me even more . . . and been all the more determined. But it won't last. She doesn't love him."

Locked for a moment in his gaze, Mabel felt the years slip away, and she saw the man she'd fallen in love with twenty-five years ago. Then she blinked, straightened herself and said, "I must get on, but please don't forget about Dosia . . . Please make sure you're at the station on time to meet her."

Mrs. Jessop and Nancy were having their midmornings at the kitchen table when Daisy walked in, in search of a cup of tea. Stephen had gone to the station to collect his auntie Nellie, Mrs. Jessop said. "Nellie'll be exhausted by the time she gets here. Will have been up since the crack of dawn. She doesn't like to be late," Mrs. Jessop added.

"Unlike some of us," said Daisy. "I overslept."

"Well, there's nothing like a good long lie-in to perk you up," Mrs. Jessop said, smiling at Daisy as she placed the kettle back on top of the range. "London takes it all out of a person."

Daisy sat down at the table.

"I hear congratulations are in order, miss. My Stephen tells me you're engaged," said Mrs. Jessop.

"No, I'm not, actually," said Daisy.

"Oh, he got that wrong, then . . . Just like a man," Mrs. Jessop said. "You do wonder what goes on in their heads sometimes, don't you? Different species, I suppose, and will ever be thus," she went on. "Yes, it is what it is and will never change—no matter what they say about equality . . . I imagine you hear a lot about all that up there?"

"Sorry?"

"Equality? What the feminists call *the cause?* Though it seems to be dying out now, doesn't it?"

"Oh yes," said Daisy absently, "yes, we're all for that."

"All for that?

"The cause . . . equality."

"Really? You surprise me, miss. I didn't have you down as one of them."

"I'm not one of anything much, really, but I think it's important for women to have a voice, for all women to have a voice and the chance to vote on things. It's a basic human right, after all . . . and only fair."

"Well, I've never voted in my life and I'm not sure I want to start on any of that now. What about you, Nancy?"

"I quite like Mr. Baldwin," Nancy said dreamily.

The kettle began to whistle. Mrs. Jessop filled the teapot with hot water, then went into the scullery and took the jug of milk from the refrigerator. "Yes, he's a very nice-looking man," she said, returning to the kitchen

"Who's that, Mrs. Jessop?" Daisy asked.

"Mr. Baldwin," Mrs. Jessop replied, moving over to the table, clutching the large tin teapot. "Yes, a nice-looking man and with such kindly eyes and a nice smile. But I don't much care for that other one, that Scotch man. Do you, Nancy? Mr. Lang the butcher says he's a communist and we don't want them in. He should go back up there if he wants to be one of that lot," she said, sitting down.

How she'd missed this, Daisy thought, the kitchen banter and Mrs. Jessop's unique view of the world, where politics, humanity and the future of civilization boiled down to a nice smile and nothing changing. Seasons would turn, years would pass and all Mrs. Jessop wished for was for things to remain as they were, or had been. Change, Daisy thought, not listening but watching Mrs. Jessop and nodding, would pass her by, and perhaps Nancy, too. Nancy, who had been one of those women left short of a husband. One of those women who had had to accept that there weren't enough men to go round. Starved of opportunity, starved of a future, taking nourishment from another family, hers.

"Is it funny being up in London?" Mrs. Jessop asked, wrinkling her nose, folding her arms and leaning them on the table.

"It's different from here; that's for sure . . . I like it, for the moment, but I'm not sure it's where I want to spend my life."

"Ah, a country girl at heart, eh? So am I . . . and so is Nancy, aren't you, Nancy?"

"I like the coast," said Nancy, her kind face devoid of any expectation.

"I'd love to see Brighton," said Mrs. Jessop. "If I could go anywhere in the world, it'd be Brighton."

"Anywhere in the world?" Daisy repeated. "But what about . . . Paris, Rome, Venice . . . Africa or even New Zealand?"

Mrs. Jessop's eyes widened; she sat back in her chair. "Don't mention New Zealand to me. That's where my Stephen thought he was headed a while back."

"Last Christmas," said Nancy.

"Last Christmas," echoed Mrs. Jessop, arms refolded and tucking in her chin.

"But he didn't go . . . and he isn't going, is he?" said Daisy.

"No!" the two yelled out in unison, and then looked at each other and laughed.

"I say, what are we like?" said Mrs. Jessop, gasping and turning to Nancy, and they both continued to laugh, their hysteria building and building until it seemed as though they could barely breathe, and they rocked and tears rolled down their cheeks. Daisy wasn't sure what was so funny about Stephen and New Zealand, but she smiled, tried to laugh too, and pretended that she understood the joke. It would be the precursor to the day, she thought.

"You have," Reg said again, twirling the end of his mustache in a way that had come to irritate her. "You've changed, Mabel."

Mabel shook her head, pretending.

They were standing together in the middle of the marquee, which, Mabel had to admit, really did look splendid. The gilt balloon-back chairs, the tables shrouded in starched white linen, the tall candelabras, table arrangements and hanging baskets— overflowing with purple lobelia and pink geraniums, the magnificent chandelier and polished wood dance floor: It was everything she could have imagined and hoped for.

She said, "You've been such an enormous help, Reg. I don't know how we'd have done it all without you."

"Think nothing of it. It's the least I can do after everything you've done for me."

As they turned and walked out of the marquee, she felt his hand on the small of her back and moved away from him.

"Well, all our prayers have been answered, Reg. There's not a cloud in the sky and the weather forecast in the newspapers this morning is good; more fine weather promised and, more importantly, no rain." They stopped on the terrace where the French doors to her boudoir stood open. "I don't think there's anything else to do," she said, "other than for us all to be here and ready for a party at seven thirty . . ."

He was twirling his mustache again, one hand in his pocket. He said, "Are you sure? I can stay, you know."

"No, really. You've done more than enough, Reg. Too much!" She laughed and immediately realized that it sounded as forced as it felt.

"You do seem a little . . . well, tense, if you don't mind me saying."

She did. But she smiled. "I plan to put my feet up for a short while—until Dosia and the others arrive—and then later, I shall take a long bath, get myself ready and look forward to seeing you here."

"Well, if you're absolutely certain, Mabel . . . if there's nothing at all I can do for you . . ."

"Quite certain, Reg, thank you."

It was quite ridiculous how hard it had become to get rid of the man. He had the sensitivity of an ox.

"Of course, you can always telephone me if you think of something. I'm only minutes away and entirely at your disposal."

Minutes later, standing behind the curtains, inside the French doors, Mabel watched Reg's car amble down the driveway, then immediately returned to the marquee with her seating plan and name cards. She certainly did not need or want his interference in this particular task. He'd insist that he should sit next to her, and Howard would be livid. And as for that comment about her being "tense," had it never struck him that it might be *him*, his presence— fussing on and around her, about the seating arrangements, timings, the number of waiters—that made her so?

It had been in Monte Carlo, she thought, that she'd got Reg's measure *and* had her fill of him. After so many months of it just being she and Dosia—their relaxed days spent wandering aimlessly through shaded streets, venturing into a church or museum or gallery, or sitting under a café parasol with their books as the world passed by—not only had Reg proved that three really was a crowd; he had proved himself an almighty bore. Obsessed with itineraries and schedules, unable to relax for a single moment, he had asked each morning at breakfast what was to "happen" that day, when all she and Dosia wanted—what they had become accustomed to doing—was to take the day as it came, without too much forethought or planning; idling, Dosia called it.

But there was no *idling* about Reg. The army had knocked that out of him, if he'd ever had it. Instead, there was a nervous energy, which made him fret and fidget and shuffle, and constantly drum his fingers or tap his feet through what he called *idle time*: that time

Mabel and Dosia liked best of all. This, Mabel could have tolerated, perhaps, but what she couldn't tolerate, she had discovered, was his knowledge: a knowledge of *everything*, which had almost rendered her and Dosia's views and wishes redundant, had Dosia not stood up to him.

The falling-out, a rather unseemly squabble between him and Dosia on the steps of the Hôtel de Paris early one evening, had begun as a mild dispute about some restaurant or other but had resulted in Dosia calling him "a controlling bully." Reg had called her "a loony feminist with no grasp on reality." Dosia then told him that she would rather be a loony feminist with no grasp on reality than a stifling bore. The sting, Mabel thought, had been when Dosia added, "You really don't have a clue about women, do you, Major?" Reg, unusually red faced, had swiftly turned and gone back inside the hotel, and Mabel and Dosia had dined à deux.

After that, they had seen very little of Reg. He returned home days later, leaving the women to enjoy their last two weeks major free.

Thank God for Dosia, Mabel thought now, placing the card "Major Reginald Ellison" next to "Mrs. Margot Vincent."

Daisy was avoiding Ben. She had seen him earlier from her bedroom window, stalking about the grounds, presumably looking for her. Sitting at the top of the stairs in a warm shaft of sunlight, she wondered how she could manage an entire day with him in her midst, and how she would cope with the party that evening. When she heard the door from the outer lobby to the hallway swing open, she jolted and sat forward. Then she heard Dosia's voice: "Hell-oh-oh!" followed quickly by her father: "Aha, you're early!"

Daisy sat back, peering through the banister spindles, watching and listening, and loving.

"You weren't supposed to be arriving for another half hour."

"No, Howard, I was always arriving on the 12:26. I telegrammed Mabel to tell her so."

Howard banged at his head with the palm of his hand. "Damn and blast it, and you know—she told me," he said, opening his arms wide and then kissing his sister on both cheeks.

"Don't worry; I shan't split on you, not unless you become very irksome or upset me. We shall pretend you were there to meet me and that I didn't have to pay for a taxi driven by an incoherent lunatic with a death wish."

"Oh, darling, I am sorry. Here, let me take your bag. I'm afraid I've no idea where anyone is . . . story of my life."

"I must say, Howard, you're looking rather streamlined . . . and your wife, I know, is looking quite delicious after our sojourn on the continent."

Howard placed the bag at the foot of the stairs, pressed his finger to the bell on the wall. "Yes, quite delicious," he said.

"Did she tell you about the American oil tycoon in Paris who wanted to marry her? Or about Giancarlo—her young count in Rome? He sent twelve dozen red roses to the hotel! *Twelve dozen*, Howard. I counted them myself—oh, my word, what a wonderfully unexpected pun." She laughed. "Count, counted?"

Howard smiled and nodded.

"They didn't have enough vases . . . I had to cut them down and put them in teacups and glasses about her room. It was like a florist's shop, but oh, it smelled heavenly. We really did have the most marvelous time, you know. I've brought all of my photographs . . ." She began rummaging in her large ancient leather handbag. Mabel might have changed but Aunt Dosia certainly hadn't, Daisy thought. "Oh," Dosia said, glancing up at her brother, "they must be in my other bag. Shall I get them out now?"

"Let's leave them for later, shall we? You look rather hot, dear, and I'm sure you're ready for some refreshment," he said. "I think Nancy's put out some lemonade under the parasol on the terrace."

"Sounds divine! Let me just find my sunglasses," said Dosia, rummaging again. "I got them in Rome . . . Just wait till you see them . . . I've never had a pair before, you know . . ."

Today, like any other day—no matter the country, no matter the season—Dosia wore her usual uniform of tweed skirt, fine woolen sweater, string of pearls, and laced leather brogues. But when she finally produced the sunglasses and put them on for her brother to see, Daisy had to put her hand over her mouth.

"What do you think?"

"You look the double of Mary Pickford," he said, deadly serious.

"*Really?*"

"Absolutely . . . a million dollars." He said this in an attempt at an American accent.

Dosia giggled. "Oh, Howard . . . I'm quite sure I don't really look like *her*."

"And I'm telling you, you do," he said, continuing with his American persona and a quick shuffle, which, Daisy presumed, was his interpretation of some sort of modern jazz dance.

Dosia giggled again. And looking down, watching the two of them, Daisy was struck by her father's tenderness and that sense of fun she'd so missed. There was something sweet and simple and bound up in love, she thought, in Howard still playing elder brother to his middle-aged younger sister and trying to make her laugh. And for a moment she saw them as children: Dosia, a little girl in her mother's oversize clothes and those ridiculous sunglasses, and Howard, no more than a boy, swiveling about in his stockinged feet and doing silly voices.

"Dosey!" cried Mabel, emerging into the hallway. She kissed Dosia and then turned to Howard: "I've just seen one of the station taxis on the driveway, but I can't think who it can be . . ."

"No one, it was a mistake. Wrong house."

"Yes, wrong house," echoed Dosia, removing her sunglasses and blinking.

"Oh well, at least you're safely here, my dear," Mabel said. "Your brother's been rather dazed and distracted of late, and to be honest I was rather worried he'd forget to collect you."

Howard and Dosia both laughed.

"Reg, of course, did offer . . . but I know how you feel about *him*," Mabel added.

"Lord, I'd forgotten about the major. Is the wretched man here?" asked Dosia.

"No, not at the moment," said Mabel. Then, with a heavy sigh, she added, "But he'll be here tonight."

"Well, please make sure that I'm sitting nowhere near him," said Dosia. She turned to Howard: "I simply can't stand the man. I'm sure Mabel told you about our dreadful fallout in Monte Carlo."

Howard, already smiling, raised his eyebrows. "No, she did not. But let's have a glass of lemonade in the garden and *you* can tell me all about it."

And as Howard and Dosia walked off arm in arm down the passageway, Mabel glanced up at Daisy. "What on earth are you doing sitting there?" she asked.

"Just taking it all in. Home . . ."

Mabel smiled, blew a kiss up to her; then she, too, disappeared down the passageway toward the door onto the terrace.

Daisy sat for a while longer, listening to the sound of her parents' and aunt's voices and laughter. When she saw Ben's polished black shoes on the carpet next to her, she immediately stood up.

"Please, don't rush off," he said, taking hold of her arm. "I want to apologize to you . . . about last night. I'm sorry. I'm afraid it was the wine, and the port . . . That's no excuse, of course, none whatsoever, and I can promise you it'll never happen again. Never."

Daisy said nothing. She didn't want him there, didn't want to look at him.

"Please speak to me," he said.

"It's over, Ben. Let's just try to get through tonight. And who knows? Maybe one day we can be friends again."

It was the most she could offer him.

Chapter Twenty-eight

Mabel smiled and then looked away when Howard appeared in the drawing room—for once after her and still fiddling with his cuffs. The sight of him was still new to her, and this night, the surprise of him, quickened her heart.

Tall, lean, with silvering hair and dark eyes, he remained a handsome man, and in his white tie and tails, as dashing as she had ever known him. But there was something else, something altered about him. Or was it her? she wondered; her perception of him? Had it changed—or had they both changed? One thing was certain, Mabel thought: Absence *had* made the heart grow fonder.

She had loved him, hated him and experienced every shade of each emotion in between: from adoration to disgust, acute frustration to mild appreciation, but never indifference, she thought, never that. And yet, a new understanding of them both and their marriage, a process begun overseas, had released Mabel from something that at first seemed to have no name. A feeling she had carried with her for so many years, one she had swallowed, stifled, held within her breast and then finally exhaled into the soft Italian air. And it was only after acknowledging it, letting go of it, that she realized it had a name, *anger*: a long-denied and festering anger that had turned to a putrid resentment.

Her escape, her journey across the continent, had pulled Mabel from a precipice and led her to forgiveness and the remembrance of a purer love. Now, with Howard standing next to her—still next to her after twenty-five years—Mabel felt a surge of happiness flow through her veins. She might never again go away on her own, but she would, she thought, take her husband with her.

"Shall we?" she said, offering Howard her arm.

Conversation hummed over the garden; over women in diaphanous pale gowns with diamond-crusted headbands and plumes; over men in starched wing collars and white bow ties, and those in uniform, their medals glinting in the early evening sun.

Older guests, those military men with stiff legs and walking sticks, red faced and bleary-eyed, and those ladies paying homage to more sedate bygone days, kept to the gritted terrace and allowed the young to spill out onto the lawn. Holding glasses of champagne, they tried to recall who was who: "Isn't that one of the Forbes girls?" When they had last seen each other: "It was at the Knights' victory party, I tell you." Caught up on who had died: "Last winter. And quite sudden, I believe." And from time to time they fell into silence as they stared out at those with unlined faces and unbent spines, standing in huddles about the lawn; filled with nostalgia, remembering a time when they too had cut a dash.

When the gong sounded, the young men and women waited as the older ones slowly made their way along the red carpet, laid out across the striped lawn and leading into the tent, where the noise, now contained by canvas, was suddenly louder; and where the older men, holding a hand to their ears, shouted, "What's that you say?" There, the men waited for the ladies to be seated, and the ladies waited for Mabel, and everyone smiled and nodded at one another with nervous goodwill.

The large red flower was easy enough to see. Daisy had followed its path as it wobbled through the tent and then came to a stop at Iris's table. The dark suit, directly in Daisy's line of vision, had its back to her and was facing Iris, who looked quite devastating in a Chanel gown of cream chiffon stripes. She had been to Marcel and had had her bobbed hair dyed jet black, straightened with irons and a heavy fringe cut, so that it hung down like curtains about her face, large green eyes and red-painted lips—which she now puckered to blow a kiss back at Daisy. Then Valentine, seated next to Iris, said something to her and pulled her attention away.

All of them—Daisy and her family—were scattered about, so that almost each table had a Forbes family member seated at it. Only Mabel and Howard sat together—and side by side, Daisy noticed. And now she could see Reg and Margot: Reg leaning in toward Margot, one arm draped over the back of her chair, the other extended, gesticulating, making some point or other. Ben, she saw, had been placed some distance away from the family, toward the back of the tent and on a table with older people and a few uniformed men. Lily and Miles were seated right in the middle of the marquee—under the chandelier. And she could hear Dosia somewhere in the distance, and arguing already: "Fair pay . . . fair pay! It has to be about fair pay."

Daisy smiled back at Aurelia, sitting opposite her, between two of Howard's friends. She had been standing with Aurelia outside on the lawn when Stephen appeared with his parents and the flowery Tabitha on his arm. She had introduced Aurelia to Mr. and Mrs. Jessop and to Stephen, and then stumbled: "And this is Stephen's . . . friend, Tabitha."

With that big red flower on the top of her head and her matching red dress, Tabitha Farley reminded Stephen of one of his father's prize begonias. Though to be fair, there were a few women in similar hats, including his mother and Auntie Nellie. They looked as though they were going to church, or to a wedding, Stephen thought, not that he knew anything much about women's fashions or what was right to wear to this sort of function. And there were certainly a variety of outfits, and all ages, and a surprising number of men in uniform. It was easy for him: He had only the one suit.

He scanned the tent once more. He could see his mother and father and Auntie Nellie at a table with the Singhs and some other neighbors, and Mrs. Forbes's mother; Nancy and Mr. Blundell down toward the back with Howard's cousins and some people he didn't recognize; Benedict Gifford . . . surrounded by silver heads and uniforms; and the major and Mrs. Vincent, deep in conversation. But where was she? Where was Daisy?

He felt a hand on his thigh and turned. Tabitha smiled and winked at him.

"It'll be up to us to start the dancing," Iris was saying, lighting another cigarette. "And there can't be any shilly-shallying, not from *this* table. We need to show them how it's done . . . You look like a dancer, Tabitha. Am I right?"

"Ooh yes! I love a turn on the floor. Not that there are many dances down here, mind you." She laughed. "But the ones they have in the Jubilee Hall aren't that bad, are they, Stephen?"

"Aha! Stephen," interrupted Iris, leaning forward over the table, "do you know the black bottom? Don't worry, Valentine and I will show you . . . We'll show you both how it's done, and you, too, Hilda. We'll have everyone doing it before the night is over."

"I can't wait," said Tabitha, squeezing Stephen's thigh.

It was going to be a long night, Stephen thought, watching Tabitha as she drained another glass of champagne.

After dinner, as pudding bowls were cleared away and bottles of port placed upon each of the tables, the orchestra struck up Irving Berlin's "Always." Howard rose to his feet and led Mabel onto the dance floor. A ripple of applause passed through the long marquee. Heads turned. No one else got up to dance, not yet, and all eyes remained fixed on Mr. and Mrs. Forbes as they moved across the candlelit floor in a gentle waltz.

Howard and Mabel Forbes were, to many there, the embodiment

of a good marriage, and this night—even this dance—seemed only to confirm that to them. Howard in his tails and white tie, Mabel in her shimmering gown of palest silver: They made a handsome couple, everyone said. When the music ceased there was more applause; Howard bowed and kissed Mabel's hand. Then the orchestra began again and a beaming Howard beckoned to his guests to join him and Mabel on the dance floor. Iris and Valentine were first up, then the major and Margot, and there were a few unlikely pairings: Aurelia and Mr. Blundell, Dosia and Old Jessop, Nancy and Mr. Brown, and Mrs. Wintrip and Mrs. Jessop. By the end of the second dance, the floor was crowded, and Lily and Miles, too, had joined the swirling throng.

The only Forbes family member not on the dance floor was Daisy, who remained seated at her table surrounded by a few contemporaries of Howard's, reminiscing about the war, the trenches, lost friends and lost limbs. Ben had quickly found his way over to her and asked her to dance. She declined. The old boys sitting next to her also asked. To each one of them she said, "Thank you, perhaps a little later . . ."

Daisy had no desire to dance with or be anywhere near Ben Gifford, not then or later. And she had been distracted, riveted by the goings-on only a few tables away: watching Tabitha as she tried to drag Stephen to his feet, as he shook his head, as he helped her up when she fell forward onto the table, as she draped her arms around his neck and tried to sit on his lap. Ben had interrupted Daisy's vigil about then, but minutes later, after declining his invitation to dance, Ben had suddenly appeared in her line of vision—at that table. Daisy saw him exchange a few words with Stephen, saw Tabitha rise unsteadily to her feet. Then Ben led Tabitha off through the scattered chairs and onto the dance floor. Daisy watched the red flower move hither and thither, drifting through the sultry air as though it had a life of its own, appearing and then disappearing back into the crowd. The dark suit remained; the intermittent glow of a cigarette like the beam of a distant lighthouse, guiding her in.

"What sort of music do you like, my dear?" one of the old gents asked.

"Oh, all sorts of things, really . . ."

"And do you dance much up in London?"

"Oh yes, sometimes. But I'm not terribly good at it . . . not like Iris," she said, turning her head back to the dance floor.

"Ah yes, she's quite a goer, isn't she?"

"Yes, she is."

"Your mother and father look very happy . . ."

"Don't they?"

"And what about you? Got yourself a young man yet?" the man asked, moving closer. "Someone in particular?"

Daisy shook her head. "No. No, not yet."

"Hmm, but plenty willing, I bet. Pretty young thing like you, eh? Shouldn't be a wallflower, what!"

Eventually, she said, "Do excuse me."

Finally, Stephen saw her. Turned to see her rise from her chair, watched her weave her way through the scattered tables and chairs and leave the tent.

Outside, dusk had descended, stars had begun to emerge. The moon peeped nervously from behind a tall chimney, and along the terrace colored lanterns burned upon tables where people sat smoking in rattan chairs. Waiters and waitresses moved back and forth across the graying carpet from the house to the tent, carrying trays and bottles and glasses, while men stood in huddles, leaning on sticks, murmuring and puffing on cigars.

He found her. Standing in the shadows with her back against the canvas, ethereal in white, barely there. She shook her head and waved him away. When he caught her wrist, a large tear fell onto his hand.

"What's this?" he asked. "Why are you out here, all alone and sad?"

She shook her head again, didn't speak. He released her wrist, stood alongside her, his back pressed up against the canvas now too, his eyes searching desperately for the same stars.

The air was warm, scented with rose and lavender and jasmine. The music inside the tent altered tempo. "That'll be Iris and the black bottom," he said, pulling his cigarettes from his pocket. "You can tell me, if you want to," he added. "You know that. You must know that by now."

"Do you have a handkerchief?" she asked.

He reached to the breast pocket of his jacket and handed one to her. She dabbed her cheeks, then handed it back to him. "I don't want to talk about it," she said. "And I don't want to be sad . . . not tonight."

He lit a cigarette, handed it to her and then lit another.

"But I want to tell you something," she said, turning to him, leaning her shoulder against the taut canvas, the cigarette in her hand.

He couldn't bear to look at her right at that moment, couldn't bear to look back into her tear-filled eyes and not be able to wrap his arms around her and hold her.

"I've called off my engagement . . . But that's not why I'm sad," she quickly added.

"Your *unofficial* engagement," he said, smiling, finally glancing up at her.

"Yes, my unofficial engagement . . . destined never to be official." She closed her eyes for a few seconds. "Oh, Stephen, what a fool I've been . . . Anyway, it's over, finished."

"Am I allowed to ask why?"

She shrugged her shoulders: "I simply came to my senses. Realized, A, I don't love him, B, I never could . . . and, C . . ."

"C?"

She took a moment. "C . . . I don't even really like him," she said, staring back at Stephen, sounding newly dismayed.

Stephen shook his head and then laughed. He stared up at the sky and closed his eyes: *Thank you, God.*

"God only knows!" Howard bellowed.

The music was far too loud. Mabel grimaced, shook her head. He bent down, held his hand to her ear: "No sign of either of them."

It was always the same two, Mabel thought, only vaguely

irritated: her mother and Daisy. Maybe it was genetic, this pen-
chant for wandering. Howard sat down. He moved his chair nearer
to Mabel's. "I wanted to dance with *her*," he mouthed.

"*Noonie?*"

"No! *Daisy.*"

Howard and Mabel had danced the first few dances together,
then taken turns across the floor with various partners. Mabel
glanced back at the dance floor: Iris was leaping all over the place
now, wiggling her bottom about in the most unladylike way . . .
And there was that girl again, the one with the large flower hanging over her forehead—and not wiggling her bottom but *on* her
bottom. Mabel glanced to Howard, who rolled his eyes and laughed.

"Who is she?" Mabel mouthed.

Howard shook his head: "*No idea.*"

Mabel watched Gifford pull the poor creature back up and onto
her feet. She watched the two exchange a few words and then disappear through an opening at the back of the tent, and she looked
to see if Howard had seen, too. He had. She turned her attention
back to the dance floor to look for Reggie and Margot . . .

And there they were, trying to keep up with the young: Margot
following Iris's every move and sticking out her bottom; Reg jiggling
his limbs like an imbecile. It was most unseemly, and though she
knew that he had, she rather wished Howard hadn't seen, hadn't
seen Reg make an ass of himself in that way, and with Margot.

When the music paused, Howard leaned over to her. "I have
something for you . . . something I want to give you, but not here."

"Oh, but, Howard, I told you . . . no more jewelry, no gifts."

He smiled, rose to his feet, took her hand and led her out from the marquee.

Music drifted over the garden. A lantern with stained-glass panels flickered on the table where they sat. Noonie had been taking a breath of air when she'd come across them, standing outside the tent. She was looking for a chair, somewhere cool to sit down, she'd said. "Far too warm in there, and so terribly loud." Stephen had suggested the terrace and had then gone back inside the tent to get the women a glass of champagne. As soon as he'd disappeared, Noonie had turned to Daisy and said, "Is he the one, then? Do you think he's the one for you?"

"Who—*Stephen?*"

"Yes. He's the one you always turn to, isn't he?"

Daisy laughed. The notion wasn't so much ridiculous as her grandmother's suggestion of it, and she was embarrassed, and unsure at first what to say. "Stephen's like a brother, an older brother, that's all," she said.

But Noonie went on—and in something of a rush. "Where love is concerned one must always follow one's heart, not one's head. The brain is useful in making certain decisions, but not where love's concerned. No. It's not needed for that. And you," she said, focusing her gaze on Daisy, "are a child with a strong and true heart. You always have been . . . but of course you're still young and life's a muddle when you're young. I remember that . . . and so easy to make mistakes, so easy to *not* know and walk away . . . thinking it will remain and still be there for you when you unravel the muddle."

The only muddle to Daisy was what Noonie was speaking about. Then she said: "You see, I was once in love, terribly in love, but I didn't realize—had nothing to compare it to."

"Grandpa?"

Noonie shook her head. "No, not *him*."

"Who, then?"

"Oh, well, that's a long story. One best kept for another day. But I can tell you that he was—remains—the love of my life."

"You've never mentioned him—any of this—before."

Noonie raised a finger to her lips. "I couldn't—can't. And it's a long time ago . . . a lifetime ago. But I still think of him . . . Samuel," she said, her voice filled with nostalgia and longing. "He married, eventually, and had a family. His daughter wrote to me last year, after he passed away. He had talked to her about me, you see. At the end, he'd talked about me." She looked at Daisy. "Love never leaves us. It stays right here," she said, placing a hand to her chest. "And then, one day, the mist rises, everything falls into place, and it's so easy to see, to understand, and one wishes one could run back through the years, back to that love."

Stephen reappeared, clutching two glasses. He handed one to Noonie, the other to Daisy. Noonie looked up at him, her eyes twinkling. "Have you ever been in love, Stephen?" she asked.

Howard and Mabel stood by the lily pond where the stars glistened on the flat water and two stone lanterns burned

"As you know, I've never been very good at expressing myself, not about emotions, and . . . not when it matters," Howard said. Then he reached into his inside pocket and handed Mabel a small leather-bound book.

Mabel stared at it for a second or two, then she moved nearer to one of the lanterns. She opened the book, slowly turned a few of its pages, and looked back at her husband. "But it's filled with your writing . . . you've written all of this," she said, confused.

"Yes, I wrote it while you were gone . . . I wanted to record everything—everything about you, and me and our lives . . . and how I felt, how I feel. I suppose, it was—is—some sort of confessional diatribe, but it was cathartic and helped me a great deal. And I wanted you to know—want you to know that . . ." He faltered. "That I've never stopped loving you, and that you are everything— everything to me."

Mabel wasn't sure what to say. It was such a strange present, and not at all what she had been expecting.

"So no jewels?"

"No. No jewels."

"And no speech?"

Howard shook his head. "Just some words from my heart."

Mabel turned another page. She saw the name—a title at the top of the page—and she smiled. It was the first time she could recall having seen it in Howard's hand, but she knew now that her time away had allowed her husband not only time to reflect, but also time to grieve. The day after her return home, she had gone to the churchyard to find Theo's grave blanketed in white blooms, and the air suffused in the same heavenly fragrance as the rose garden.

"He planted all of them himself," Noonie had told Mabel. "And he went there every single evening to water them . . . Yes, he's spent quite a lot of time in that churchyard."

Mabel closed the book. "Thank you," she said. "And thank you for Theo's roses."

"In love?" Stephen repeated, looking away and laughing.

"Yes, do you not have a sweetheart, someone special . . . perhaps here tonight?" Noonie persevered, still twinkling, excited.

Stephen glanced at Daisy, and she had to intervene, she thought. It was unfair of Noonie to put him on the spot like that. "Stephen brought Tabitha with him tonight," she said to her grandmother.

"Oh, I see," said Noonie, her smile falling away. "And where is she?"

"I've no idea," said Stephen. "But perhaps I should go and find her," he added, rising to his feet.

"You shouldn't be so forthright," said Noonie as soon as Stephen had gone.

"Forthright?"

"Yes. Putting words into his mouth. *Names*," Noonie added, shaking her head. "Silly girl," she said, "silly, silly girl."

When Stephen saw Ben Gifford and Tabitha, their arms draped around each other, staggering off down the driveway, he half thought of running after them, of taking Gifford by the collar and dragging him back. What a total cad the man was, he thought, watching the two figures disappear into the darkness.

Finding Daisy crying outside the tent had made him feel wretched enough. And she could only have been crying about her engagement, about Gifford, he thought. But hopefully she *had* ended it, ended it properly and for good. And yet young women seemed to like a bit of drama, and engaged young women had a tendency to call things off and then call them back on. The idea of her being tempted to do this made him contemplate telling her just what sort of man Gifford was, and *where* he was, but he couldn't. How could he? He would rather take a bullet than cause Daisy any distress or pain.

The fireworks at one o'clock signaled an ending to some, the beginning of an ending to others, and simply a beginning to a few others still. As the orchestra played on, everyone poured out of the marquee to watch rockets explode and light up the sky over Eden Hall. Afterward, Howard and Mabel had one last dance together, waltzing to Schubert's "Serenade"; then they stood on the lawn for almost an hour saying good-byes and good nights as a procession of chauffeur-driven cars and taxis moved up and down the driveway, before finally retiring—and disappearing inside the house.

It was after three o'clock by the time the orchestra finished packing up and Valentine and Miles brought out the Victrola from the house and set it up inside the tent. People lingered on, sitting in silence at deserted tables, and a few continued to dance. Others dawdled about the gardens or slumped in the rattan chairs along the terrace. And Daisy sat with Aurelia at the back of the marquee.

"Iris said they disappeared off together ages ago," said Aurelia. "She saw them—and so did Val."

"I couldn't care less."

"So you did it—you ended it?"

"Sort of, but I'll do it properly first thing in the morning."

"Mine doesn't exactly look heartbroken, does he?" said Aurelia, watching Val—still dancing with Iris at the other end of the tent.

"It's all a mockery," said Daisy, leaning forward, resting her chin in her hands and wondering once more where Stephen was. There was no sign of him in the tent, and she hadn't seen him in a while, hours perhaps, though she couldn't be sure because time had slipped away quickly.

"Poor Stephen . . ."

"Why poor Stephen?" asked Aurelia.

"Because it's humiliating for him to bring someone as his guest and then have her . . . walk off with another man. He deserves so much better."

"You really do love him, don't you?"

Daisy sat up and pretended to take a sip of her champagne—now flat. "Yes, but not like *that* . . . not anymore."

"Really? Look at me and say that again."

Daisy turned to Aurelia: *"Not like that."*

"I'm afraid I'm not convinced . . . not at all convinced."

"Not at all convinced about what?" asked Val, suddenly next to them.

"Nothing," said Daisy.

"Aurelia, I thought we should have one more dance together . . . for old time's sake," he said.

Daisy watched them walk off hand in hand. They *would* be friends, she thought; they had called off their life together amicably. It would be a very different scenario for her and Ben.

When Daisy stepped out from the marquee, night had fallen away and colors had begun to emerge. The doors to the house stood wide-open and a couple she did not recognize clung to each other, lost in a moment, swaying to an invisible silent orchestra. Ruby and Boy wandered about the lawn, looking for a pat, a kind word, sniffing at scattered glasses and plates. Then Boy barked at something— or someone—and ran off toward the Japanese garden. And Daisy, adrift and still wondering, followed the dog and found Stephen.

The sun was about to rise—and Stephen wanted to see it, he said, wanted to watch it from there. He did not look at Daisy as he spoke, but she watched him stroke Boy's head, stoop and rub his nose against the dog's nose.

"Well, Aurelia has done the deed," she said.

"What deed's that?"

"Called off her engagement."

"Ah, there's a fashion for it, then."

"Did you find Tabitha?" she asked, shivering, wrapping her shawl about her shoulders.

"Was I meant to be looking for her?"

"Someone said she fell over . . ."

"That sounds about right."

"Don't you care?" she asked, sitting down next to him on the bench.

"I think Tabitha's more than capable of looking after herself."

Daisy didn't want to tell him, didn't want to repeat what Aurelia had told her: that Tabitha and Ben had not only disappeared from the marquee *together*, but had been seen canoodling by the shrubbery, where a large red taffeta flower was later found. She couldn't give a hoot about Ben, who had—as she'd told Aurelia—proved himself an utter cad and a bounder in the space of twenty-four hours, but she was furious with Tabitha.

"Shall we dance?" Stephen asked.

Daisy laughed. "What—here . . . now?"

"Why not?"

And so they did.

He held her in his arms as they slowly circled the pond, again and again, round and round, moving their feet carefully over the flagstones—without any music, without any words, until the first birds began to sing and the pale morning light hung over them.

"Stephen," she said sleepily, her cheek pressed against the white cotton of his shirt, "let's never lose touch with each other again. Let's never lose our friendship." She lifted her head to look up at him. "You see, you're like a brother to me . . . more than a brother."

He said nothing, and she rested her head back against his chest as they rocked back and forth, back and forth, without lifting their feet, lost in a lullaby motion.

"Let's spend some time together tomorrow . . . later today. We could try to find my globe . . . take a picnic down to the stream like we used to," she said, her eyes closed.

And as he tightened his grip around her, she knew that this moment was all she'd ever remember of this night.

She obviously had no idea, and Stephen was pleased. He certainly wasn't going to mention what he had seen, or what Val had later confirmed when he'd told Stephen that he'd seen Gifford with Tabitha in the bushes. She deserved so much better, even from an *ex*-fiancé.

He held her in his arms as they slowly circled the pond, again and again, round and round, moving their feet carefully over the flagstones, until the first birds began to sing and the sky lightened.

When she told him he was like a brother, it stung. Weak with longing, he closed his eyes, lowered his face to her hair, breathed her in. Daisy. Her head resting on his chest, her words—misguided, innocent and weary—were all he'd remember of this night: all he'd ever wish to remember of this night.

Chapter Twenty-nine

The sky was like a washed-out sheet, bleached of color, with a pale yellow sun behind it. Men in aprons and flat caps marched back and forth across the lawn carrying rolls of carpet and furniture to a wagon parked up on the driveway. The rattan tables and chairs on the terrace beneath her window had already gone.

When Daisy saw him—crossing over the grass, head down and moving fast—she was reminded of the previous evening, his absence. By the time he reached the top of the stairs, she was there, waiting. "I suggest you pack your bag and leave as soon as possible."

"Daisy . . ."

She backed away. He reeked of alcohol and stale sweat, and she felt nothing for him, other than contempt.

"You can walk to the station or catch a bus. There's a bus stop at the crossroads. If you're not out of this house in"—she glanced at her wrist—"ten minutes, I'll find my father and tell him where you've been, and what you did—that you came to my room . . . and that you hit me."

"Look here," Ben began, "I'm not sure what you think, but you have it all wrong . . . all wrong."

"No. I have it all *right*. I have nothing else to say to you, Benedict Gifford. You're not worth my words—or a single minute more of my time."

She turned toward her room. "Nine minutes left," she called back to him.

He was punctual, at least, she thought, as she watched him walk down the driveway with his bag—almost exactly nine minutes later. Now she needed to find her father, to tell him that there was no engagement and that she hoped never to see Benedict Gifford again. She would not tell him anything more than that, though she imagined he'd hear soon enough about the events of the previous evening.

The door to her father's room was ajar, his bed made . . . but with his evening suit laid out on it—in a heap. Strange, she thought, that Hilda had already been up there, making beds, and stranger still that the maid had then left her father's clothes like that.

The house was silent as Daisy descended the stairs and headed for Howard's study. He wasn't there. She walked back down the passageway and glanced into the drawing room: no one. She crossed back over the hallway and went into the dining room. The table was set for breakfast, but so far undisturbed.

Daisy lifted a silver lid on the salamander, helped herself to a sliver of bacon. Then the baize door swung open and Hilda appeared.

"Morning, miss. Tea . . . toast?"

"You're a busy bee this morning . . . making beds *and* serving breakfast."

Hilda laughed. "The beds will have to wait, I reckon. It'll be afternoon by the time I get any of those done."

"But you've already done my father's room."

Hilda shook her head. "No, miss . . . we're all a bit under the cosh this morn, what with the men turning up early and all the guests to look after."

"Yes . . . of course," said Daisy. "Have you seen my father?"

"I don't think he's been down yet, miss. Can I get you some tea?" Hilda asked again.

"No, thank you."

Daisy returned to the hallway, climbed the stairs and then stood on the landing, pondering. She didn't wish to disturb her mother, but she needed to tell one of her parents about Ben: that she had called off her engagement and asked him to leave, that he had gone. She moved along the landing toward her parents' suite of rooms, past her father's open bedroom door, toward her mother's closed bedroom door, and then she stopped. Beyond Mabel's door she could hear a male voice . . . then murmuring; then giggling . . . then complete silence. Mabel had a man in her room . . . Reg? Daisy's heart pounded. The door opened.

"Hello, Dodo," said Howard. "Did you sleep well, my darling?"

Daisy felt her face flush. She said, "I need to speak to my mother," and walked past him into the room, where Mabel sat up in bed, holding a cup and saucer. "Hello, darling . . . Wasn't it a wonderful night?"

Howard closed the door; Daisy sat down on the stool by the dressing table. She stared at the bed—the scattered pillows, the sheets. Her parents had slept together. Mabel had taken him back. She said, "Just so you know, I've called off my engagement."

Mabel frowned. "Sad, but very wise, I think."

"Don't pretend you're in the least bit sad, because I know that you're not . . . and neither am I. Anyway, he's gone . . . Ben. I asked him to go when he returned here earlier this morning."

Mabel stared down at her cup and shook her head.

"He proved himself to be just like certain *other* men," said Daisy.

Mabel said nothing. She pursed her lips and glanced about the room.

"Oh, Mummy . . ."

"There'll be another," said Mabel, quickly. "You're still so young . . . there'll be another."

Daisy shook her head. "No, I'm thinking of you. I don't want you to . . . to get hurt."

"Hurt? Who's going to hurt me?"

"The man you married."

"Daisy . . ."

"You don't know. You don't know," said Daisy, turning away, wringing her hands.

"What don't I know?"

Daisy rose to her feet. "You don't know about Stephen," she replied, louder than she'd intended.

"About Stephen," repeated Mabel. "What don't I know about him?"

"Have you never wondered how he came to be here?"

Mabel smiled. "I know exactly how he came to be here," she said calmly, and then took a sip of her tea. "Your father brought him here . . . well, not exactly, but he arranged everything."

So she knew some of it, Daisy thought, and then said it out loud. "Yes, that's some of it . . . but there's more," she said, sitting down again. "You see . . . you see—"

"Are you in love with him?" Mabel asked before Daisy could say any more.

Daisy gasped. "In love with *Stephen?* This isn't about me and Stephen, or about Ben, or Tabitha . . ."

"Tabitha? And who is Tabitha?"

"The one with Ben . . . last night."

"Ah, the one with the red flowery thing?" Mabel asked, making a flower on her head with her hand.

"The same," said Daisy, feeling exasperated; they were going off track.

"Is that why you're angry—because she left with Ben? Or are you angry because she came with Stephen?"

"No! I've told you, this isn't about any of them . . . Well, it's about Stephen, I suppose, but it's mainly about my father—your husband."

"I see," said Mabel, taking another sip of tea.

"But I should've told him, Stephen I mean, about Tabitha," said Daisy, rising to her feet again. "But how could I?" she added, looking back at Mabel as she paced the floor. "I couldn't, could I?"

Mabel shook her head.

"So I didn't. But I should've done—shouldn't I?"

Mabel wasn't sure, was about to say "perhaps," but then Daisy went on.

"It was disloyal of me . . . but I didn't want to humiliate him further, and now he'll hear from someone else." She turned to Mabel. "Is it better to be loyal and honest, to tell the truth—even though you know you might cause that person pain?" she asked, her hands now on her head as she paced in circles at the foot of Mabel's bed.

Mabel was about to say that it depended on the circumstances but didn't have time because Daisy continued: "And it could all have been avoided. If I'd asked Ben to leave yesterday, after he . . . when I knew, when I'd decided. If I'd done that, none of this would have happened, and Stephen would never have had to endure this humiliation. And yet . . . and yet," she said, her eyes narrowing, a new idea dawning, "he didn't seem to be too upset at the lily pond."

"The lily pond?"

"Yes, when we were dancing . . ."

"You were dancing by the lily pond—and when was this?"

"Sunrise," she said, one side of her mouth curving upward and staring past Mabel at a patch of wall. "Sunrise," she said again, lowering her hands.

Suddenly she seemed calmer, Mabel thought. She had lost her daughter to a sunrise, to a slow dance with Stephen Jessop. But a picture was emerging, pieces slowly falling into place. Daisy had never been good at jigsaw puzzles, and now, once again, she was forcing pieces that didn't fit in order to make her picture, Mabel thought. She had all the parts; she simply didn't know—couldn't see—how to match them up, where to place them.

And she had every right to be angry: angry with her father and angry with Ben Gifford. Like Howard, Mabel thought, watching their daughter as she stared into nowhere, she had the heart of a lion, but she had inherited from Mabel her highly reactive nature, which threw everything into disarray and confusion. It was—had always been, might always be—her Achilles' heel.

"It sounds heavenly," said Mabel.

"Yes . . . yes, it was."

"Your father also wanted to dance with you. He looked for you . . . had a particular piece of music in mind."

The dream snapped. Daisy stared back at her mother. "I wouldn't have danced with *him*."

"You must learn to forgive, Daisy . . . to forgive and forget, and move on."

"Forget? Like he's forgotten his *sons*? . . . And not just Theo."

Mabel put down her cup and saucer. "You're right. It did seem as though your father had forgotten Theo for a while," she said. "And perhaps he forgot me, also . . . because I had pushed him away, because I was angry. But there's so much of him you don't know, don't understand."

"And you do?"

Mabel nodded. "Yes, I do . . . There are things that are not my place to tell you. But you should perhaps speak to Mrs. Jessop about Stephen and about your father."

"Right. I will," said Daisy. "I will." And then she left the room.

Mabel sat back against her pillows and closed her eyes. Daisy was determined, and it wasn't for her to explain. Her loyalty to Stephen was such . . . Mabel opened her eyes.

Daisy's loyalty to Stephen Jessop placed him at the forefront of Daisy's mind in almost every situation. His well-being and happiness had always been of paramount concern to her, and though Mabel had known this, and had watched them together for years, she had only recently begun to acknowledge the extent and true nature of Daisy's love. And because he needed to know and understand, too, she had told Howard only hours earlier.

"Are you sure?" he'd asked.

"Quite certain."

"And what about him?"

"Oh, I'm even more certain of that."

Mabel smiled at her gown—draped over an armchair by her dressing table, where Howard had carefully placed it the night before. She smiled at the memory of that night. She had known by their last dance that they would spend all of that night together; that there could be no good night and turning in to separate rooms. And the wonderful thing about it was, there had been no question, no awkwardness, no doubt at all. It had felt like the most natural thing in the world for them to retire together, to walk hand in hand into that house, their home, and then climb the stairs and go to that room, together. To talk as they undressed, to laugh and giggle at the things they had seen; for Howard to unzip and help her out of her gown; for her to regale him with snippets of various conversations she had had as she sat at her dressing table brushing her hair, creaming her face, and then climbed into bed next to him; and for him to take her in his arms. And like arriving back at that place called home after a very long journey, there had been a new and exquisite luxury in the sense of its normality.

They had lain in each other's arms for an hour, at least, listening to the sounds and voices outside: the raucous laughter and music from the gramophone drifting over from inside the tent; the queer conversations and debates going on beneath their window. They heard Iris calling out for "more champagne," and Noonie—still going strong—talking about someone called Samuel. At one point, Howard had risen, crossed the room to pull back the curtains and open the window a little more so they could better hear Reg tell Margot how magnificent her figure was, and how young she looked to him. They had placed their hands over each other's mouths to stifle the sound of their laughter.

"I love you, Mabel Forbes," he'd said.

The door to the servants' hall was closed. Daisy could hear the murmurings of Mrs. Jessop and Mrs. Wintrip on the other side, but this was not the time to listen at doors and hope for answers; this was the time to be bold.

"Stephen's not here, dear," Mrs. Jessop said, looking up with a mouthful of biscuit from her usual chair. "I'm not rightly sure where he is."

"It's not Stephen I was looking for. It's you, Mrs. Jessop . . . I wondered if I might have a word."

Nellie Wintrip slid Daisy a look as she rose to her feet; then she picked up her cup and saucer and left the room, closing the door behind her.

Shafts of pale morning light shone in through the open window onto the faded William Morris upholstery and ladder-back chairs, onto the brickwork fireplace and picture above it of King George. It wasn't a small room, but it was a cozy room, and, like the kitchen, it seemed to belong to Mrs. Jessop more than to anyone else.

Daisy sat down.

"Well?" said Mrs. Jessop.

Daisy wasn't sure where or how to begin, but now there seemed no other way than to ask the woman outright. "Mrs. Jessop, I need to know something . . . about Stephen . . ."

"Yes?" the woman replied, sucking on her teeth.

"Is Stephen . . . is Stephen my father's child?"

"Your *father's*?" Mrs. Jessop repeated, wrinkling up her nose and pulling a face as though whatever was left in her mouth tasted deeply unpleasant. "But how on earth . . . How could he be your father's son?"

"Because," Daisy said and then paused. "Well, you see, I happen to know that Stephen was born at Clanricarde Gardens . . . and I'm not sure how much you know but . . . it was my father who arranged for him to come here."

"Yes," said Mrs. Jessop, nodding, "but how does that make him your father's son?"

"I think it's fairly obvious . . . My father doesn't exactly have the best track—" Daisy stopped. "You know . . . You know he was born there?"

"Yes. I know he was born there."

"And do you know who is parents are—were?"

"I certainly do."

"His father?"

Mrs. Jessop nodded.

"And he's not my father's son?" Daisy asked, her heart beating so loudly she thought the woman might hear it.

"Really, dear . . . I'm not sure how all this has come about, and for the life of me I don't know how you thought Stephen was—"

"I just need someone to tell me the *truth*," Daisy interrupted. "I need to know if Stephen's my brother," Daisy said, louder, her eyes burning. Then, in a whisper, she added, "Please, if you know, please tell me . . ."

Mrs. Jessop closed her eyes, and in a new, softer, younger-sounding voice, she said, "Michael . . . Stephen's father was Michael Hughes."

Daisy repeated the name. It meant nothing to her. She said, "Are you sure? Are you absolutely certain?"

"Oh yes, that's one thing I am certain about," the woman said, opening her eyes.

Daisy heard herself whimper.

"Oh, come now, don't go getting yourself upset . . . He might not be your brother, but he's always been like one to you, hasn't he? And that won't change. No, that won't change."

Daisy shook her head. "But I still don't understand . . . how did Stephen come to be born at Clanricarde Gardens? Was he . . . is he Mrs. Wintrip's son?"

"*No*," said Mrs. Jessop, stretching out the short word. "He's not Nellie's."

"But how do you know? And how do you know about Stephen's father? Did Mrs. Wintrip tell you about him? Did she tell you about Michael Hughes?"

Mrs. Jessop glanced away, frowning, as though trying to remember something.

"And Mrs. Wintrip must know who his mother was," Daisy went on, "because she was there, Mrs. Jessop . . . She delivered Stephen into the world, she told me."

"Yes, she was there. She'd never delivered a baby before—nor had one of her own—but she knew exactly what to do."

"*You* were there? You were there, too?"

Mrs. Jessop nodded. "It's a night I'll never forget."

"But who was Stephen's mother?"

And as soon as Daisy asked the question, she knew.

"I am," Mrs. Jessop said, staring back at Daisy. "I'm Stephen's mother."

Over the next half hour or so, Mrs. Jessop told Daisy all about Stephen's father, Michael. He had been her sweetheart, she said, her childhood sweetheart. They'd grown up together in a village in Berkshire.

"I was no spring chicken, but I *was* ignorant . . . We all were, back then. I had no idea how to stop a baby being made. But we were engaged, and I had put him off for long enough and we would be married anyway in a matter of weeks, I thought." She shook her head vaguely. "Stephen's so like him, not just in his looks, but that same kind, quiet manner . . . so like Michael." She paused. "I didn't have a clue, no idea at all that I was expecting when it happened."

"*What* happened?" asked Daisy.

"Michael . . . He'd been to visit his mother out near Slough, where we grew up, and was on his way back to Windsor, where he was working at the time. He was a carpenter, and ever so good, could turn his hand to anything, a proper craftsman. It was him that did all the shelves and cabinets in your father's study at

Clanricarde," she said. "Oh yes, he used to work in a lot of the big houses."

"But what happened?" Daisy asked again.

Mrs. Jessop stared down at her hands in her lap. "It was June . . . and I didn't know I was expecting, not until the August after my birthday, and the very month we'd intended on getting married." She closed her eyes. "It was an express train . . . it ran through two sets of signals and collided head-on with Michael's train. They said he'd have died instantly, not known anything about it. And that was some small shred of comfort to me," she added, glancing up at Daisy, "because he'd been my world, you see, my whole life, and my future."

"I'm so sorry."

"When I learned I was expecting, it was as though God had given me back something of Michael . . . I was bereft and happy and terrified all at the same time. And that's when your father stepped in. I'd worked for him before, you see, been the one to recommend Nellie, and had only given up my position so I could be nearer to Michael," she quickly added. "So, when your father heard about my circumstances, and knowing the family I worked for would turn me out, he insisted I go back to Clanricarde Gardens."

Daisy smiled. *Of course . . . of course he did*, she thought.

"Your father sent the carriage to collect me," Mrs. Jessop went on, almost laughing now. "Oh my, if you could've seen the other servants' faces . . . And right from the start your father understood, he knew I couldn't give up my baby . . . but neither could I keep it. No one would employ an unmarried woman with an illegitimate baby. And I couldn't stay on at Clanricarde forever because there would've been talk . . . A maid with a baby living under the same roof as a married gentleman—with a wife tucked away in the country?" She glanced over at Daisy and shuddered. "So we agreed—your father, Nellie and me—that after my baby was born, after a month or two, Nellie would take him and care for him until such time as my own circumstances changed—and your father would kindly provide for his upkeep. Nellie was married and it all made sense."

"You were with Stephen for some months then?"

Mrs. Jessop smiled. "You know how your father loves babies . . . In the end, Stephen was almost six months old when Nellie took him, weaned and on solids and everything. Oh yes, we muddled along happily together for six months at Clanricarde, me, Nellie, your father and Stephen."

"He has no idea . . ."

"No, well, he was just a baby . . . and such a beautiful baby," she said, suddenly full of maternal pride.

"And my mother? My mother knew all of this?"

"Well, of course. She came up to town a few times. She was the one who told me about feeding, establishing a routine and all that. Because she had experience; she had had your sisters by then."

"And then you came here," said Daisy, piecing it all together.

"Yes, and that's when I met Isaac—Old Jessop—and after we were married, just as your father had promised, Nellie brought Stephen down to me."

"There was no need for any adoption . . ."

Mrs. Jessop smiled and shook her head.

"But why have you never told Stephen any of this?" Daisy asked.

Mrs. Jessop lowered her eyes. "I've never told anyone. Only your parents and Nellie know . . . No, I didn't tell anyone, certainly not Isaac, because . . . well, I was so ashamed, you see. And I'm not sure he or anyone else would've married me—and I desperately wanted to be married so I could have my Stephen back with me." She paused for a moment, then continued: "My husband had so little memory left when he came back from the war, he thought Stephen was *his*. Thinks he's his," she corrected. "But I'd always planned to tell Stephen when he reached twenty-one . . ." She raised her eyes to Daisy. "Better late than never, I suppose."

Mabel lay in Howard's arms, her head on his chest as his hand moved over her hair. She had spent the entire morning in bed. Howard had told her to stay there, said that he would see to everything. And so she had. After Daisy had gone in search of Mrs. Jessop, Mabel had stretched out on her bed reading Howard's book, devouring words she had so long yearned for, beautiful words that from time to time made her gasp, or tremble, or close her eyes.

When Howard returned to the room, he'd climbed onto the bed and lain alongside her, staring up at the sunlit ceiling as she read, until she closed the book, put it down and kissed him.

"But why did you turn to *her*?" she asked now. "Why did you not come to me—talk to me?"

"I told you. I turned to her as an old friend, to ask her advice—about you, about us, about what I should do . . . You didn't want to talk to me . . . and I thought you'd stopped loving me."

Amidst his words about Theo, words about so many things, Howard had also written about the time he had been banished from Mabel's bed; how he had learned—first heard—that his wife wanted him nowhere near her; that she wanted no more babies, and that she could not bear to be touched by him. Mabel recalled that time, too: the one and only time she had confided in her then maid. That her private words of anguish had been repeated, that Nancy had taken it upon herself to tell Howard was almost unforgiveable; and a greater act of betrayal had the sentiments not been true.

Perhaps she had uttered those words, Mabel conceded. Perhaps she had uttered those words the night Nancy found her on the bathroom floor, lonely, in pain and sobbing. But whatever she had said had come from the very depths of despair, after she had suffered yet another miscarriage and had only Nancy to comfort her.

"I thought you didn't want me here, anywhere near you. I thought you didn't want *me*," said Howard.

"And Margot did . . ."

Howard said nothing. He had been unfaithful, and nothing could alter that fact. Just as nothing could alter the fact that Mabel loved him.

"What about Giancarlo?" Howard eventually asked.

Mabel took her time. An affair with Giancarlo would have been an easy revenge. Yet when the moment had come, when she had had the opportunity to pay Howard back in kind, it had seemed *too* easy. But it was perhaps just, she thought now, for Howard to experience doubt and her to know certainty. And so she allowed the question of her fidelity to hang over her husband for a few minutes longer before she said, "There's only ever been you."

And just as though he'd been holding his breath for every one of those minutes, as though they had, for him, been as long as her six years, Howard exhaled in a long sigh.

"You know, I did wonder where my perfume had gone," she said after a while, smiling.

She knew from the book that Howard had taken to sleeping in her bed in her absence, spraying the pillows with her perfume or onto one of her handkerchiefs—to carry about in his pocket. She knew he had taken comfort from each trace of her. He had written that being there, in that bed, in that room, without her but surrounded by everything to do with her, had been one of the most intimate experiences of his life. He had had many lonely nights and lonely days, wandering about the house from room to room, or about the gardens, working back and forth through forgotten days, the bright and dim seasons of years. And yet, throughout it all, throughout that journey backward, he'd felt himself somehow moving forward, and nearing Mabel. It was, he had written one day in early spring, sitting in his wife's beloved Japanese garden, "almost a spiritual thing."

Unlike his father, Howard wasn't a particularly religious man, but Mabel knew that something had happened to him during her long absence. Howard had called it "a reawakening": a powerful recognition of love, accompanied by a feeling of immense gratitude. It was something he'd felt often as a young man, he'd said, but had lost.

"Do you remember when my hair was so long and you used to help me plait it each night?" Mabel asked now, her head on his chest, his hand upon it.

"I remember."

"Do you wish I was still like that, young and beautiful, and with long, long hair to plait each night?"

"I loved you then, and I love you even more now . . . the way you are now."

Mabel lifted her head and glanced up at him. "Well, you said the right thing, but I'm not sure I believe you."

"It's the truth. I don't see your age; I see you. You've always been beautiful to me, and perhaps more so now than ever."

"Daisy has no idea of her beauty. None whatsoever."

"A good thing, too."

"She's never been concerned about how she looks, how anyone looks . . . so different from Iris. Peculiar, really," Mabel added. They lay in silence for a minute or two; then she said, "And she's finally got all of her pieces . . . got them all lined up and ready to place."

"What do you mean?"

"You . . . Clara, Nellie . . . and Stephen."

"Ah yes, Stephen," he said, laying his head back down.

"Are you still worried about her?"

"A little, but I'm also rather proud of her."

"She was always going to be the one to find any skeletons."

Howard smiled. "Is that what they are?"

"No, she'll find only angels in your closet," said Mabel, glancing up at him again, stroking his cheek with her finger.

The gurgling of a wood pigeon drifted in through the open window. The sounds of activity and people, and murmurings of conversation, although mere yards away, felt like another world to Mabel. A world she had no desire to be part of at that moment.

"She's not too upset about Gifford, is she?" Howard asked.

"No, rather relieved, I think . . . like the rest of us."

"I hope so. I can't stand the thought of her suffering over it."

"Her heart is very much intact and remains devoted. I don't suppose anything's going to alter how she feels, not now."

"And you're sure . . . sure she loves him?"

"Oh, I'm quite certain," said Mabel. "She loves him—just as I love you . . . I'm just not sure *she's* realized it yet."

Mabel got up from the bed and walked over to the window. The tent was down. Like a deflated air balloon, the white canvas lay in an exhausted long heap on the lawn. Below, Hilda stood on the gritted pathway holding a tray of lemonade, laughing and flirting with one of the men. In the distance, Mrs. Wintrip paused in her stroll to bend over a rosebush, then jumped and waved an arm about her head. And Mabel laughed. Then she saw Daisy. She watched her daughter stride out onto the grass, stop, stand perfectly still for a minute, as though reconsidering something, kiss her hands and raise them up to the sky. And then she watched her daughter turn, march back across the lawn toward the house.

"Where's she off to now? I wonder. She looks very purposeful . . ."

"No doubt on another one of her missions," said Howard as he joined her by the window. "You think you did the right thing in sending her to speak with Mrs. J?"

"Yes . . . It's not our story to tell."

They stood in silence for a while; then Howard said, "You know, I sometimes feel guilty, wish I'd done more . . . I can't help but feel sad that Stephen and his mother were ever parted."

"*Guilty?*" Mabel turned to him. "Oh, darling, you have nothing to feel guilty about."

"Hmm. I don't know . . ."

"No, Daddy, you did the right thing."

Howard and Mabel turned.

Daisy walked over to where they stood. "You did the right thing," she said again, standing in front of them, staring at her father. "It was the only way . . . You knew Mrs. Jessop couldn't tell anyone, you knew she hadn't told her husband about the baby. And she trusted you. She knew she could trust you never to tell, and she knew she could trust you to bring Stephen back to her."

"I didn't bring him back to her; Nellie Wintrip did."

Daisy shook her head. "No, you arranged it all. Everything. Without your help Stephen would have been placed in a home, then adopted, perhaps . . . but he would never have grown up with his mother, he would never have come here, and I would never have known him."

She paused for a moment, then continued: "I thought you knew nothing," she said, addressing her mother. "When I found out about Margot Vincent last Christmas, I couldn't believe that you knew . . . that you knew and accepted her. And I was so angry with *you*," she said, turning to her father again. "I hated you. I hated you for deceiving my mother, and me, for lying to us all . . . And I couldn't for the life of me fathom why Nellie Wintrip and Mrs. Jessop were so protective of you, why they had so much respect for you, but now I understand. And I understand why my mother loves you, and why she forgives you . . . because I do."

Chapter Thirty

Daisy had been back and forth to the kitchen all afternoon to ask Mrs. Jessop if Stephen had returned to the house yet. She had asked Hilda, Mrs. Wintrip, Iris—and anyone else she could find—if they had seen him. No one had. She'd wandered about the grounds, the lawn—scarred from the party of the previous night—and sat on the bench in the Japanese garden, remembering that sunrise, that dance. And as the day wore on she became more desperate.

It wasn't a matter of life and death, and yet it felt like that. There was the revelation of his mother, but that was not why she wished to see him, nor was it for her to explain. There was Benedict Gifford and Tabitha: But it was most definitely not that. It was quite simply everything else. Every flickering thought that occurred and needed to be shared; every single thing he needed to know about how she felt now. And *now* was agony: a torturous wretched state between each passing moment and his presence.

It was early evening by the time Daisy walked down through the woods into the valley—calling out the name and listening to it bouncing off trees and echoing back to her. She stood on the ridge, scanning the vast wilderness below, searching for his shape. Then she retraced her steps through nettles and ferns, through the still open gate and back to the courtyard. She banged on the door with her fist.

Old Jessop shook his head. "Gone . . . gone back to London," he said with lugubrious slowness.

"But when—just recently?"

The man nodded.

Daisy turned and ran back to the house.

"Can you take me to the station?" she asked, skidding on the wooden floor and into Howard's study at the same moment the dressing bell rang out.

"But you're not going back to London yet, are you?"

"No, but Stephen has . . . he's gone for the train."

Daisy wasn't sure where her father had learned to drive like that, or if it was legal, and for most of the journey she sat with her hands clasped over her eyes. When Howard slammed on the brakes outside the station, Daisy jumped from the car and raced through the archway. She saw old Peabody, the stationmaster, watering a tub at the other end of the deserted platform and ran toward him.

"Has it gone . . . has the train for London gone?" she asked, breathless.

"Well, hello there, young miss," he said, straightening himself and all ready for a chat.

"Has it gone?" she asked again, her voice shrill.

"Yes, but don't fret now, there'll be another in . . ." He reached to his breast and pulled out his pocket watch.

"No . . . ," said Daisy. "I'm not going anywhere. I needed to catch someone; that was all."

"And who might that be?"

"Stephen . . . Stephen Jessop."

"Ah yes, young Jessop." He pushed back his cap and scratched his head. "Well now, I'm not rightly sure, but I think he might have been on that last train."

"Too late?" Howard asked as she walked back toward him.

Daisy nodded.

"I suppose we could drive up to London . . . do you know where he lives? Have you any address?"

Daisy shook her head.

Howard reached out and pulled her to him. He wrapped his arms around her, and the feel of her father—so missed, so long absent from her life—was enough. She sobbed onto his chest, soaking his shirt and silk tie in her tears. She heard him exchange a few words with Peabody, asking after the man's extensive family and grandchildren, never releasing his hold. Then, finally, she stopped crying and raised her head.

"Important, was it?" Peabody asked, bending his head, smiling kindly at Daisy.

"Yes," Howard replied. "It was rather important." Then he took

Daisy's hand and led her from the platform, out of the station and back toward the car.

They drove slowly, and Howard took an unusual route, for they seemed to take in far more villages than those between the station and Eden Hall. Daisy sat in silence, staring out the window at hedgerows and fields. She felt spent of words, as though they were like pennies and she simply had none left. The last forty-eight hours had been emotionally and physically draining, and the past eight months—too much.

The car made another turn, down a narrow sun-dappled lane, and minutes later drew to a halt outside an old inn.

Daisy turned to her father. "What are we doing here?"

"I thought we'd have a drink," he said, turning off the engine.

Inside, Howard ordered himself a whiskey and soda and Daisy a lemonade. Then he changed his mind and called over to the barman: "Make that two."

"I'm not sure I like whiskey," said Daisy, as the two of them sat down on a bench outside with their drinks.

Howard watched Daisy take a sip and raised his eyebrows in a question.

"Mm . . . all right, I suppose. Might be nicer with lemonade."

"I've missed you," he said.

He lifted his hand to her face, traced her cheek with his finger. "I can't bear to see you unhappy . . ."

They sat in silence for some time, side by side, staring ahead, listening to the bleating of sheep in the sloping field beyond.

Eventually, he said, "Do you love him?"

"Yes," she replied.

∽

Mrs. Jessop had let Hilda finish early. The poor thing had been dead on her feet all day and no use to man after dinner. It was also Nancy's day off, so Mrs. Jessop had done the washing up alone, quietly humming to herself as she stared out of the kitchen window, smiling, remembering the glamour of the previous evening. As her cousin Nellie had so eloquently put it, never again would they see "a function of such magnitude." She had just picked up a linen tea towel and was about to start drying when Mr. Forbes appeared, carrying two glasses.

He asked her to sit down, then handed her a glass and said, "I know you like a sherry at Christmas, and though it's not Christmas I thought you might . . . well, I thought you might appreciate one tonight."

He was ever so kind like that, Mrs. Jessop thought. Thoughtful. Always had been. And it was quite a large glass as well. He said, "Isn't life a funny old game, Clara?" He hadn't called her by her first name for years, not since before she was married, before she was made cook. "Anyway, good health," he said. They chinked their glasses and took a sip of their drinks. "I do hope everything was all right with Stephen . . . before he left."

"Before he left?"

"Before he went back to London."

Clara shook her head. "He's not gone to London. He's been down the valley all day . . . and only just come back. But no time to talk to me," she said, fluttering her eyelids, feigning a little umbrage. "Said he has something important to do," she added.

Howard stared at her. "He's still *here*? But Old Jessop—Isaac—he told Daisy Stephen had gone back to London."

Clara looked heavenward. "He's getting worse, that man, and for the—"

"Where's Stephen now?"

"Well, at the cottage I expect . . ."

But Howard was already on his feet. "Back in a jiffy," he called over his shoulder as he disappeared down the passageway. Clara took another sip of her drink. She wasn't sure what it was that was so urgent, but she hoped he wasn't going to drag Stephen over to the house, to sit with them there. She wanted to tell Stephen on her own. Minutes later, she heard the back door slam shut and Howard Forbes's unmistakable stride on the tiled floor. "Won't be a minute," he said as he sailed past her through the kitchen and out the other door. And as Clara took another sip of her drink, she thought she could hear him calling up the stairs for Daisy.

A few minutes more elapsed before he reappeared—clutching the sherry decanter—and sat back down at the table. He smiled over at her, his dark eyes shining. He was ever such a handsome man: You could understand why women wanted to throw themselves at him, she thought. He refilled their glasses and toasted their health again. He said, "Everything is going to be tickety-boo, Clara. I don't want you to worry about a thing . . . And if you need me, wish me to talk to Stephen about Michael, you know I'm more than happy to."

"No," she said, "it's better I talk to him, explain . . . at first, anyway. But maybe later; yes, maybe later it would be nice for him to hear about his father from another. And you knew him, you knew Michael."

"I did indeed, and I remember him well."

"Stephen's just like him, isn't he?"

"Uncannily so."

"Do you remember that day at Clanricarde, when there was all that work being done to your study and you said him, you said to Michael, 'Never mind about my cabinets, what about my Clara? When are you going to make an honest woman of her?' And he asked me to marry him later that same day?"

"Yes, and I think I made a toast . . ."

"You did! You brought up a bottle of *real* champagne from the cellar. Oh my, how it popped, and then—do you remember—the cork shot up and hit the chandelier? And you said, 'To Michael and Clara, long life and happiness . . .'"

"Well, we shan't tempt fate, Clara, but I think I might be popping a cork and making a toast again soon . . . I think we might be enjoying some fine champagne again *very* soon."

Clara wasn't sure what he meant by that and didn't like to ask—what with fate having been mentioned, and her already feeling emotional. Remembering that time and Stephen's first months had made her wobbly all day.

But it had been a funny few months; a funny year, she thought later, after Mr. Forbes had left the kitchen. And she still couldn't get over Nancy's announcement about her and Mr. Brown, the butler from Beacon House, and they'd be stretched this Christmas without her, even with Hilda's younger sister helping out. Though why Nancy wanted to go on a ship—a pleasure cruise—was beyond her. The *Titanic* had put Clara off ships for life, not that she'd ever been on one, and she certainly wouldn't want to now. No. The idea of being stuck on a boat out at sea with a bunch of strangers . . . She shook her head. She couldn't rightly remember now where Nancy had said she was going on her cruise, but it was somewhere warm, and with islands.

But Clara had to give Mr. Brown his due: He'd been very attentive of Nancy. The romance, if that's what it was, had first blossomed around Easter, when Mr. Brown began to call and take Nancy out for an early evening walk. Nancy had said that he wasn't at all how he first seemed, for he had a very good sense of humor, and the manners of a true gentleman, she said. The latter, Clara knew, was most important to Nancy.

Earlier that evening, she'd bumped into Nancy, returned from another one of her walks and looking just as though she'd been rolling about in the heather, with bits of earth and leaves stuck to her dress and in her hair. She'd been sheepish with Clara, guilty-looking and quite flushed.

"You look like you've been through a hedge backward," Clara had said when Nancy appeared in the servants' hall.

"Oh," Nancy said, her face turning pinker as she brushed off her dress and then fiddled with her hair. "I slipped."

Clara had smiled and turned away. She knew all about courting couples slipping in the heather, or in the long grass.

When Nancy had first told her that she was thinking about going on a pleasure cruise with Ralph—as he'd become by then—Clara had been concerned, but only because she didn't want Nancy to be let down by life again. To have her hopes raised and then

crushed. But Nancy insisted that they were friends above and beyond all else, and that the change would be good for her.

Yes, a change was as good as a rest, and the cruise would surely
do Nancy good . . . as long as she didn't get seasick, or sick of Ralph
Brown, Clara thought, trying for a moment to picture her colleague
on a ship. But try as she might, she could only ever picture the *Titanic*, sinking.

Clara moved over to the chair by the range. She settled back
into it, took a sip of the warm liquid in her glass. She didn't need to
close her eyes. She could see the field, see him, still there, waiting
for her to join him . . .

The sun is high in the sky and the grass is long and filled with
buttercups and poppies. She can hear the stream, the sound of bees,
nothing more. Nothing more. He says, "This is perfect." He says,
"You're perfect." He says, "Remember this always."

She would never forget.

Stephen had cleaned the glass, polished it so that it looked almost
as good as new. It had taken him some time to find, almost the
entire day, but he'd been determined. Feeling with his feet, pulling
back heather and bracken and gorse, he'd walked back and forth,
searching the area Daisy had pointed out to him when she'd said,
"It landed there." The last person he'd expected to meet was Nancy,
out walking—hand in hand—with the chap from Beacon House.
And lost for words, for a reason why he was there, rummaging
among the heather, he had told her: "I'm looking for Daisy's snow
globe. She threw it from up there last Christmas," he'd said, nod-

ding to the ridge, "and she told me it landed somewhere about here."

"Oh yes, last Christmas," Nancy had said, just as though she knew and understood how someone could do such a thing *then*.

Nancy had insisted that she would help him look, and Stephen saw her peck her companion on the cheek, heard her tell him that she'd see him later. And Stephen learned more about Nancy in the hour that came afterward than in all the previous eighteen years at Eden Hall. Searching through the bracken and heather with him, she told Stephen all about her fiancé, John Bradley, killed at the Battle of the Somme: about his farm and their plans, his love of that part of the country, and his love of her.

"We both wanted a large family," she said, staring into the distance and smiling. "Yes . . . seven, we used to say . . . because seven is a lucky number. Four boys and three girls, I thought. But only because John would need the boys to help him on the farm, you see."

When, eventually, Stephen found the globe in a tangle of wild rose and honeysuckle, garlanded with bryony, its glass intact and glinting in the early-evening sun, he'd felt how he imagined Howard Carter must've felt discovering Tutankhamen's tomb. He'd picked it up and kissed it. And holding it to his breast, closing his eyes for a moment, he could have sworn he felt a faint vibration and couldn't help but think of Daisy's heart. And then Nancy came forward and kissed him on the cheek.

She said, "I hope that girl knows what she has in you, Stephen Jessop . . . what she could have."

Clutching the globe to his chest, Stephen had watched Nancy walk back up the hillside and disappear under the trees that bordered the grounds of Eden Hall, and he'd made a wish that she'd know another love in this lifetime. She'd never have her lucky seven with the man she'd loved, not now. But she deserved some happiness, deserved to be loved again.

Later, when Mr. Forbes had appeared in the kitchen of the cottage, Stephen had been surprised. Not so much by the man's appearance as the manner of it: for he hadn't even knocked on the door, but had burst in—as though a baby had just been born.

"Stephen," he'd said, extending his hand, smiling, "I don't think I've ever been happier to see anyone in my entire life."

When Stephen took hold of the hand, the man had pulled him to himself, hugging him tightly. It had been rather embarrassing. It wasn't as though he'd returned from any war; he'd only been down in the valley.

"I need to ask you something," Mr. Forbes said, stepping back, and with unusually intense and glistening eyes. "I need to ask you if you love Daisy . . . and I need you to tell me the truth."

The truth. It wasn't something Howard Forbes had been too extravagant with of late. But it was a question Stephen was able to answer unequivocally and without any hesitation.

"Yes, sir," said Stephen, looking the man in the eye, "I do. I love her."

Howard Forbes nodded. He rubbed his hands together. "Life is very short," he said. "Too short for some . . ." He glanced up. "Could you do me a favor, Stephen? Could you come over to the house in . . ." He shook his head. "No, no—not the house. Could you meet me by the pond in . . . in, say, half an hour?"

Stephen shrugged. "I suppose so," he said. "Though I was hoping to catch up with—"

But he'd gone.

Then he was back: "Oh, and Stephen, no more *sir*, or Mr. *Forbes*, please. I think we've known each other long enough to dispense with formalities, don't you? My name is Howard."

Stephen lifted his jacket from the hook on the back of the door, slipped the globe inside his pocket and headed out of the cottage. He hoped Mr. Forbes—he couldn't possibly start calling the man Howard, he thought—wouldn't keep him too long and he'd be able to find Daisy.

Mabel and Howard stood together at Daisy's bedroom window, watching their daughter as she waited beneath a luminous flickering sky.

Mabel gripped Howard's hand tighter. "I do wish he'd hurry up," she said.

"He'll be there."

But Mabel was anxious. Doubt made her so. An unreliable father had made her so. The only person she'd ever been sure of was Howard, and, bizarrely, even through what they now referred to as the Wilderness Years.

Mabel's mouth twitched and then curved up at one side. They had come through it. They had come through their crisis, somehow held on and weathered their estrangement. They had made it to the other side of twenty-five years.

Together, they had witnessed the dawn of a new century, the death of a queen and empress, and war; and cars and airplanes and telephones; the gramophone and the wireless. It was hard to imagine what else might be invented, or change. But the business, Forbes and Sons, a family business that had been there and grown over two centuries, was finished, or would be soon enough.

Times had changed, fortunes had been made and lost, and would be made and lost again. It was, as her husband had said, the way of the world, and would continue to be so long after they were gone. Where their daughters' lives would take them, how they and any future grandchildren might live, Mabel had no idea. The only thing she was certain of was that her heart belonged to the man at her side. He had been her love—her first love, her only love—and she knew now that he would be for the remainder of her days.

Daisy knew. There was nothing she could do about it. Her life was bound to him, every perfect memory wrapped around him, each shining minute spent with him. And a future without him at its center was not a future she wished to contemplate.

She wasn't sure how her father knew Stephen was back, or how he knew Stephen would be at the lily pond at that time, but neither did she care. The only thing that mattered was that he *was* back. But did he still love her? So many months had passed since she'd read his words—as fresh and breathtaking to her now as the clear evening air: *I love all of you . . . everything about you . . .* But what had happened to that note? Had his precious words been destroyed, torn up and thrown onto a fire or into a wastebasket? Were they and the passion behind them lost—lost forever? It made her heart shrivel to think such a thing. And then she realized: They could never be lost, because they had been read, read and devoured and forever remembered by her: the person to whom they had been addressed.

Sitting on the bench by the pond, Daisy smiled and stared upward, and with her gaze locked heavenward she contemplated the extraordinary and inexplicable nature of love and loves, so infinite, so varied, over millennia and centuries. What strange alchemy, she wondered, made two people know and understand they belonged with each other; that their lives could only ever be whole and complete together? Who or what had arranged such magnificent chemistry?

Then an owl—singular, tremulous, connecting and clear— called out to her. The evergreens took on an ethereal glow and the infinitesimal stars began to appear. Diamonds in the sky, she thought. The universe never had been black-and-white. And like a revelation, a profound momentary connection during which she and the earth and the moon and the stars—and everything she had been and would be—fused and became one, she finally understood the smallness of her body and the greatness of her love.

Sensing his nearness, she rose to her feet; hearing his footsteps, she turned. And desperate, trembling, weak with longing, and uttering only one word—his name—she stepped toward him and buried her face in his warmth. She held on to him tightly as they swayed, gently swayed, just as they had at sunrise.

"Never let go of me."

"I have to," he said. "But only for a moment, because I have something for you."

And with his eyes fixed on hers, he reached into his pocket, lifted her hand and placed the globe in her palm.

"You found it . . ." She looked up at him again. "You found it and you're here, and I thought you'd gone."

He said nothing. He took her head in his hands, lowered his face to hers and kissed her. And kissed her. And kissed her.

Daisy would never be able to recall quite how long that first kiss between them lasted, though Stephen would always claim it had gone on until every one of Eden Hall's lights had been extinguished. He would tell their children, and later, their grandchildren, how he'd had to wait eleven years—his age again—to kiss the girl he'd fallen in love with at eleven; that he'd danced with her as the sun rose and finally kissed her as it set. And each and every Christmas, when the globe came out, he'd tell the story again: about the late summer's day he'd found a snow globe, and a mother, *and* got his girl.

Acknowledgments

Firstly, special thanks to Ellen Edwards, my editor, for her patience and good advice, and to all of the team at NAL/Penguin Random House; special thanks also to my agent, Deborah Schneider at Gelfman Schneider in New York, and to Sam Copeland at Rogers, Coleridge and White in London.

Thank you to the lovely Jo Rees and Doug Kean, and to my friends and first readers—Harriett Jagger, Rivinia Ahearne, Dixie Jenks and Sophie Durlacher. Thanks also to Tim O'Kelly and my favorite bookshop: One Tree Books at Petersfield, Hampshire. Huge and heartfelt thanks to all of my readers, and to my friends and followers on Twitter and Facebook. And, as ever, I send my unending love to Bella, to Max and to Jeremy.

Finally, I am forever indebted to my late agent and friend, Ali

Gunn, who passed away in Switzerland as I was writing *The Snow Globe*. Her extraordinary passion for life and faith in me continue to be a source of inspiration and strength.

JK

HAMPSHIRE, ENGLAND

SEPTEMBER 2014

The
SNOW
GLOBE

JUDITH KINGHORN

A CONVERSATION WITH
JUDITH KINGHORN

Q. The Snow Globe *is your lightest novel to date, a sparkling dual love story and comedy of manners set a number of years after the Great War, when time had softened its immediate impact. What inspired you to go in this direction?*

A. My previous two novels are both set around the Great War and I wanted to move on from that time, and the 1920s very much appealed. I've always been drawn to that era and think the interwar years are a particularly fascinating time in history. It was a period of rapid progress and advancement for women, the beginning of the modern world, a time we're able to recognize and relate to, and yet there also remained these rigidly old-fashioned rules and customs. And I suppose it's that clash that's so appealing to write about: the struggle between the "old guard," those of a certain age who clung onto the traditions and fading glories of the past, and were appalled by what they perceived as a new morality; and a younger generation whose energy was reflected in the new freedoms, music and dancing and fashions. The desperation and defiance of those bright young things of the Roaring Twenties—who were determined to be seen *and* heard, to live life to the fullest—contrasts vividly with the years immediately before and during the Great War, so there's a great deal for a writer to draw on.

Q. You begin The Snow Globe *with Agatha Christie's famous disappearance. Can you tell us more about that incident in her life? Why did you decide to start there?*

A. I'd already decided to begin the novel after the general strike and in the weeks leading up to Christmas 1926 when I realized it coincided with Agatha Christie's extraordinary eleven-day disappearance. When I made this connection and read about Christie's husband's infidelity, it seemed to offer the perfect opening for the novel, the themes of which are also infidelity and betrayal.

The mystery of Agatha Christie's disappearance began on the evening of Friday, December 3, 1926, at Styles, her Berkshire home. At around nine forty-five p.m., without any warning, and having first gone upstairs to kiss her sleeping daughter, Rosalind, Mrs. Christie drove away from the house. Her abandoned Morris Cowley motorcar was later found down a slope at Newlands Corner near Guildford in Surrey, but there was no sign of Mrs. Christie, nor any clues to what had happened to her.

The story was international news, made the front page of the *New York Times*, and for eleven days conjecture buzzed. Some believed Mrs. Christie had drowned herself, others suggested the incident was a publicity stunt, and others still whispered of the possibility of murder and pointed fingers in the direction of her unfaithful husband, a former First World War fighter pilot. Such was the speculation that the home secretary of the time, William Joynson-Hicks, put pressure on the police to make faster progress, and the celebrated crime writers Sir Arthur Conan Doyle and Dorothy L. Sayers were drawn into the puzzle. Conan Doyle, who was interested in the occult, took a discarded glove of Christie's to a medium, while Sayers visited the scene of the disappearance (later using it in her novel *Unnatural Death*).

Christie was eventually discovered, safe and well. Alone, and using an assumed name, that of her husband's mistress, she had been staying at a spa hotel in Harrogate, Yorkshire, since the day after her disappearance, oblivious, it seemed, to the news and national furor.

The two most popular theories offered for Christie's strange disappearance are that she was in the grip of a rare mental condition known as a fugue state, a period of out-of-body amnesia induced by stress, *or* that she had planned the whole thing to thwart her husband's plans to spend a weekend with his mistress at a house close to where she abandoned her car. I tend to believe the latter.

Q. In this novel, romantic love seems almost idealized. Despite miscommunications that keep the lovers apart, their feelings for each other are pure, certain, and uncomplicated—free from the confusion and doubt one tends to find in fiction with a contemporary setting. What made you want to depict love in this context?

A. In *The Snow Globe* I wanted to place older love alongside young, untested love. The young love is ideal and pure, without doubt or cynicism, whereas the married love is about compromise, forgiveness, and understanding. I think we all start out with that pure, idealized notion of love, that it will conquer all and prevail, and through the course of life we learn that in order for it to survive we have to be prepared to make sacrifices and compromises.

In the novel, Daisy learns about love, its differing shades, and what it is and is not. She has grown up believing her parents' marriage to be perfect and longs to be *in love*. From the moment she discovers the truth about her parents' marriage, disillusionment and a cynicism she associates more with her sister Iris nudge at her. She believes—and for a while wants to believe—that she loves Stephen as a brother, but then, finally, has to acknowledge that her love for him is different. And it is the purity of that love—and her acknowledgment of it—that allows her to see clearly, begin to gain some self-knowledge and forgive. At the same time, Mabel has to forgive her husband for his infidelity in order to save her marriage and remember her love for him. And this is Mabel's liberation also, because it frees her from anger and resentment.

Q. Each of your novels has been set around an English country estate. What draws you to such places, and why do you think they are so appealing to readers?

A. In part it's due to a love of history and architecture, but it's also to do with my love of literature. Many of my favorite novels are set in vividly depicted and often grand houses . . . Think of *Rebecca*, *Jane Eyre*, *Wuthering Heights*, and every Jane Austen novel. Some inspiration, too, comes from my childhood, when I was taken to visit such places. Many of them remained unchanged from Victorian times, and I particularly remember going to a country house sale where there was a huge rusting sleigh in a coach house, and old-fashioned clothes and shoes and tiny sailor suits laid out in a nursery, all to go under the hammer. I think those country house sales—now, like the houses themselves, a thing of the past—had a profound impact on me and my imagination.

I'm a member of the National Trust and English Heritage, and I still love to visit these places whenever I have the time. Each one has its own character, and they've all witnessed so much and have so many stories. Sometimes, I think their walls must exude a sort of whispering narrative, because whenever I come back from having been to visit one, I feel inspired and want to know more about *who* lived there. But my desire to know more isn't confined to grand country houses: I'm the same with any old house, large or small. Buildings fascinate me because of the human stories they hold. For readers, I think films like *Gosford Park* and television dramas like *Downton Abbey* have undoubtedly increased the appeal of the country house as a setting.

Q. You describe the tumult caused by the loss of empire and new technologies. Can you tell us more about how these changes led to the demise of the English country house and a way of life, and about the financial pressures felt by the moneyed class during this period?

A. At the dawn of the twentieth century, country house life was still in its heyday. Securely landed families remained confident in the permanence of primogeniture, England ruled the waves, and one-third of the globe was shaded the pretty pink of empire. Even in the early summer of 1914 no one could imagine that those young men who sipped lemonade on lawns bathed in sunshine would be mowed down on the fields of Flanders.

The First World War changed life for everyone, particularly the upper classes, and the impact of that war on the British country house was substantial. Those houses and estates that were requisitioned were badly treated, but, more important, many of them were left without any heir to hand on to. In 1916, *Vanity Fair* declared the British aristocracy altered forever. "The whole social fabric of Great Britain has been changed . . . When the boy dukes and earls grow up they will find their formerly important rank regarded as a quaint and curious survival of an ancient and outworn custom."

Not only were the heirs to these places lost, but the ranks of young men required to fulfill the roles of gardeners, gamekeepers, and outdoor servants were also lost. As a result, vast numbers of these houses and their once well-tended grounds fell into neglect and ruin, and, added to this, there was also what was generally known as "the servant problem."

Ironically, the war that robbed women of husbands, fathers, sons, and brothers had also been the catalyst in providing them with the opportunity to work in new types of employment and better-paid positions. The growth in retail and new department stores offered shop work, and new business and technologies offered factory and office work, with better pay and conditions and shorter hours. Understandably, fewer and fewer chose to go into domestic service.

By the mid-1920s, the age of the country house sale had well and truly begun. Stripped of their contents, these houses were no longer homes but expensive monuments to a faded past, and in order to avoid punitive taxes and death duties, hundreds of them were destroyed. (The total loss over the course of the twentieth century is more than one thousand.) Month after month, during the twenties and thirties, demolitions and what were then known as "smash-ups" destroyed hundreds of country houses in what Roy Strong called "black decades in our architectural history" in his book *The Destruction of the Country House: 1875–1975.*

Like many people after the war, those houses that survived had to reinvent themselves—as schools, hospitals, health spas, offices, or homes for the elderly. Some were handed over to the National Trust and opened to the public, but a way of life had ended, and with it an old order and class system crumbled. The Second World War and demise of the British Empire hammered the final nails in the coffin.

Q. The First World War ended one hundred years ago, and we're seeing in the media many retrospectives and new analyses of the war's origins and impact. The war has played a role in each of your novels. Has your thinking about it evolved?

A. Though *The Snow Globe* is lighter and more humorous than my other novels, it's set only eight years after the end of the war. Consequently, the effects of war are ever present. Every character in the novel is affected by it in some way.

Writing the book made me realize how short a decade it was when preceded by something of such magnitude—because a generation was wiped out, and because it took *generations* to recover from that loss. Watching the television coverage of the centenary of the outbreak of the First World War was deeply moving. In fact, I'm more moved by it now than ever, because I realize its effects are still with us, one hundred years on.

Q. You grew up in the north of England, where the landscape was a strong influence, and you've written previously about how you were able to find your voice as a writer only after you returned to living in a rural village. Aside from the obvious peace and quiet, what is it about the country, do you think, that fosters your creativity?

A. I think one is far more aware of the passing of time in the country, the seasons and changing light and colors. It's that sense of time—and being in the moment—that seems to allow me to tap into my creativity; it allows me to *see* and picture. From my desk, I look out onto my garden and often see deer and foxes and sometimes badgers. Depending on the season and time of day, I hear owls, wood pigeons, and woodpeckers. In the woodland beyond the garden there's a mix of long-established deciduous and evergreen trees, whose shapes and colors are ever changing. All of this inspires me.

The older I get, the more I appreciate that connection with nature. It was something I had as a child and then lost for a while, and it's something we're all in danger of forgetting. In a turbulent, troubled world, I think nature can offer peace and clarity and reconnect us with *who* we are. And I absolutely believe that that connection is healing—to the mind and to the body.

Q. Can you share any books you've especially enjoyed that are set in England during the 1920s and interwar years?

A. I've only recently reread *To the Lighthouse* by Virginia Woolf and consider it brilliant—definitely one of my all-time favorite novels. Other favorites set around that period include *The Pur-*

suit of Love by Nancy Mitford, *The Return of the Soldier* by Rebecca West, *Invitation to the Waltz* by Rosamond Lehmann and *Voyage in the Dark* by Jean Rhys; and *The Diary of a Provincial Lady* by E.M. Delafield and *Cheerful Weather for the Wedding* by Julia Strachey are both amusing and beautifully written. And I have to add *The Cazelet Chronicles* by Elizabeth Jane Howard.

QUESTIONS
FOR DISCUSSION

1. What did you most enjoy about *The Snow Globe*? What do you think you will remember about it many months from now?

2. Who is your favorite character, and why?

3. The author has called the novel a comedy of manners. Did you find it funny? Discuss the various places that made you smile, or even laugh.

4. Did Eden Hall fulfill your expectations of what an English country estate should be? What do you think accounts for its appeal?

5. Discuss the various ways in which a failure to communicate causes conflict in the relationships. How much of this can you attribute to the way people were expected to behave in England

in the 1920s? How might people today handle the situation differently?

6. How does the men's behavior contrast with the women's when it comes to sex and love? Who is faithful? Who is unfaithful? Talk about the double standard for men and women. Does some remnant of such attitudes persist today?

7. One might argue that the rift between Mabel and Howard has its origins in the beginning of their marriage. Discuss those origins. Have you ever experienced a conflict in a relationship that you realized originated in choices or expectations that were established long ago?

8. Discuss the novel's depiction of unwed pregnancy and adoption. Why do you think Mrs. Jessop delays telling Stephen who his real mother is?

9. What did you think of Mabel's going off to Europe, leaving her family behind? Were you surprised by what happens when she returns?

10. The novel takes place several years after the end of World War I. Talk about the many ways in which its impact is still felt by the characters.

11. What does the snow globe mean to Daisy? Do you have a similar treasure?

Read on for an excerpt from Judith Kinghorn's
"enchanting story of love and war"*
set at the end of the Belle Époque, in which
the upstairs-downstairs romance between
a woman living in a large English country estate
and the housekeeper's son will be tested as
World War I looms over Europe . . .

The Last Summer

Now available in print and e-book from
New American Library.

*Penny Vincenzi

I was almost seventeen when the spell of my childhood was broken. There was no sudden jolt, no immediate awakening and no alteration, as far as I'm aware, in the earth's axis that day. But the vibration of change was upon us, and I sensed a shift: a realignment of my trajectory. It was the beginning of summer and, unbeknown to any of us then, the end of a *belle époque*.

If I close my eyes I can still smell the day: the roses beyond the open casement doors, the lavender in the parterre as I ran through; and grass, lambent green, newly mown. I can feel the rain on my face; hear my voice as it once was.

I can't recall exactly who was there, but there were others: my three brothers, some of their friends from Cambridge, a few local people, I think. Our adolescent conversation was still devoid of any faltering uncertainty, and we didn't stand on the brink, we ran along it, unperturbed by tremulous skies, sure of our footing and certain of sunshine, hungry for the next chapter in our own unwritten stories. For lifetimes—lifetimes we had only just begun to imagine—stretched out before us, crisscrossing and fading into a distant horizon. There was still time, you see. And the future, all of our futures, lay ahead, glistening with promise, eternal with possibility.

I can hear us now; hear us laughing.

That morning, as clouds gathered overhead, the earthbound colors of my world seemed to me more vibrant than ever. The gardens at Deyning were always at their best during June and early July. It was then, during those few precious weeks of midsummer, that the place came into its own. And though Mama had often looked anxious, complaining about the incessant battering of her roses, every well-tended bloom and leafy branch appeared to me luminous and fresh. From the flagstone terrace the lawns spread out in an undulating soft carpet, and on the mossy steps that led down to the grass wild strawberries grew in abundance.

I can taste their sweetness, even now.

Mama had predicted a storm. She'd informed us that our croquet tournament might have to be postponed, but not before people had arrived. So we'd all stood in the ballroom, which my brothers and I simply referred to as "the big-room," looking out upon the gardens through the open casement doors, debating whether to go ahead with our game or play cards instead. Henry, the eldest of my three older brothers, took charge as usual and voted that we go ahead in our already established teams. But no sooner had we arranged ourselves with mallets upon the lawn than the heavens opened with a reverberating boom, and we all ran back to the house, shrieking, soaking wet.

"Henry wishes tea to be served in the big-room, Mrs. Cuthbert. We're all back inside now," I said, standing by the green baize door, wringing out my hair.

Mrs. Cuthbert had been our housekeeper for only a few weeks at that time. Years before she'd been employed by Earl Deyning himself, not only at Deyning Park—now our home—but also at his estate in Northamptonshire. It had been lucky for us that Mrs. Cuthbert had agreed to come back to Deyning after the old Earl died, and my mother was delighted to have a housekeeper who knew the place so well. "Such pedigree," Mama had said, and I'd immediately imagined a little dog in an apron and mobcap.

"And how many of you are there, miss?" Mrs. Cuthbert asked, glancing over at me, smiling.

"Oh . . . fourteen, I think. Shall I go and count again?"

"No, that's quite all right, dear. I'll come through myself and see." She wiped her hands on her apron. "You've got my Tom with you today," she said.

"Tom? *Your* Tom?"

"Yes, he came home yesterday, and your mother kindly invited him to join today's little game. Have you not been introduced?"

"No. Well, I'm not sure. I don't think so . . ."

I followed Mrs. Cuthbert along the back passageway, toward the big-room, and I remember looking down at the red and black quarry-tiled floor, trying—as I'd done since childhood—not to step on the black ones. But now it was impossible. My feet were too big.

"He's not like your brothers, miss," she said, turning to look at me. "He's a gentle soul."

In the big-room, everyone had already seated themselves around the four card tables pushed up together. And suddenly I was aware of a new face, dark eyed and solemn, staring directly at me. As Mrs. Cuthbert introduced me to her son, I smiled, but he didn't smile back, and I thought then how rude. "Hello," I said, and he stood up, still not smiling, and said, "Pleased to meet you," then looked away.

There was no thunderbolt, no quickening of the heart, but there was a sense of recognition. A familiarity about his face: the nose, the eyes; his stature.

I opted out of whist. All three of my brothers were playing and I knew I stood no chance. Instead, I wandered to the other end of the room and sat down on the Persian rug in front of the fireplace. As I played with Caesar, Mama's Pekinese dog, I caught Tom Cuthbert looking at me. I didn't smile, but he knew I'd seen him. And, when I rose to my feet and walked back across the room, I was aware of him watching me. I sat down in an armchair, closer to the card tables, picked up a magazine and began to flick through its pages. I glanced over at him, caught his eye once more, and this time he smiled. And I knew it to be a special gesture, meant only for me. I didn't realize what it was like for him then, of course; had no idea of his discomfort as his mother served us all tea.

My upbringing had prepared me for a certain life, a life where I'd never question my role or the cast of players sharing my stage. It was a thoroughly modern idea, then, to educate a daughter, and, in my father's opinion, a pointless expense. So I'd studied at home, with Mademoiselle: a tiny bird of a woman, whose dislike of fresh air and susceptibility to drafts had rendered her pale and brittle. Her lessons in life had depended as much upon the temperature of her heart as the weather outside. Men, she had often told me— usually during arithmetic, and with a rug over her knees—were brutes; they had simply not evolved from animals, she said. However, Keats and Wordsworth appeared to bring out an entirely different side of Mademoiselle's compact and complex character, for then she would sometimes throw back the rug, rise to her feet and tell me that life was *"nuzzeen"* at all if one had never loved. But by that summer Mademoiselle had left my life for good, for by then it was assumed I knew enough to be able to converse in polite society without appearing completely vacuous.

Like my mother's orchids, I had been nurtured in a controlled environment, an atmosphere maintained at a consistent temperature, protected from cold snaps, clumsy fingers and bitter frosts. My three brothers, on the other hand, had been allowed—even encouraged—to develop unruly tendrils, to thrive beyond the confines of any hothouse, to spread their roots, unrestrained, through that English earth they belonged to. It was different for a girl.

Marriage and children, a tidy home and a manicured garden were a foregone conclusion. And a husband with money was always a prerequisite. For how else could that life be achieved? I was a Home Counties girl, happy to be part of a family who enjoyed a sensible, uninterrupted existence, no matter the weather, the visitors or the events beyond the white gate: the boundary between my understanding and the rest of the universe. When I was young I'd sometimes nudged that boundary: I'd walked down the long avenue of beech trees to the gate, and perched myself there, on top of it.

There was little traffic on the road that bordered our land then, but occasionally an omnibus or new motorcar would pass by and I would raise my hand to the unknown faces staring back at me. They were gone in an instant, but I always remembered those fleeting connections: new friends, all at once there, then gone again. Where did they go? What happened to them? Did they remember that moment too? Did they ever wonder what had become of me, the girl on the gate?

That evening, over dinner, I wanted to ask my mother about Tom Cuthbert, but she appeared abstracted. She gazed about the room with an unreadable expression on her face, and I wondered if she was thinking about the servants, again. She'd returned from London the day before, festooned with packages, and with a new hairdo, but noticeably agitated. "It's simply *impossible*," she'd announced in the hallway, and in a voice much louder than usual, "to find any decent domestic staff these days. And when one does, one inevitably finds oneself replacing those months later." I couldn't blame her for her exasperation. She had traveled to London only the previous week to interview a prospective parlormaid, a butler and a new chauffeur, and had stayed overnight—as she quite often did—in the comfort of her Piccadilly club. It was no wonder to me she knew the train timetable to the second and off by heart, but so much to-ing and fro-ing had, she said, left her feeling *quite frazzled.*

"I met Mrs. Cuthbert's son today, Mama. He's called Tom, and he's been away . . . though I'm not sure where."

"He attends university, dear," she replied, without looking at me.

"But where?" I asked.

"Ha! Don't become too intrigued by Cuthbert, sis," Henry broke in. "Mama expects you to have your sights set *slightly* higher, I think," he added, and then laughed.

"I wondered about him, that's all. He's seems rather shy and . . . well, he has only his mother."

Henry looked across the table at me. "Shy, eh? I reckon Cuthbert's probably quite a rogue—underneath that aloof exterior."

"A rogue?" I repeated. "I don't think so. I think he probably prefers his own company to . . . to the likes of us."

"Aha! And she leaps to his defense! First sign, sister dear, first sign," Henry said, and George and William both sniggered.

"Enough teasing, thank you, Henry," said Mama, glancing to my father for reinforcement. My father cleared his throat, as though about to speak, but then said nothing.

"You're simply jealous," I said, looking back at Henry and forcing a smile. It was one of my stock replies to him when I didn't quite know what else to say.

"And why on earth would I be jealous? He's a servant, for God's sake."

"No, he's not. Mama's just informed us—he's at the university."

"Oh yes, learning to polish silver, no doubt," Henry replied.

"You're jealous because he's so much more handsome than you and isn't inclined to boastfulness," I said, staring down at my plate, and then added, "Mademoiselle says gentlemen who feel the need to boast almost always have unusually small *cerveaux*."

"Ha! Mademoiselle . . . hmm, well, she would know of course. And yes, that's right, I'm jealous of our housekeeper's son, for I shall never have what he has and I can never be the bastard son of—"

"Henry! That's enough," my father intervened. "I don't expect language like that from you or anyone else at this table. And I think you should leave your tittle-tattle and gossip at Cambridge. Do you understand?"

"Yes, sir," my brother answered.

And that was that.

I had no doubt that my eldest brother, Henry, knew a great deal of *tittle-tattle*. And more than that: I imagined there'd be idle gossip and tittle-tattle about him, too, somewhere. For of late he seemed to have acquired new friends, and spent more time in London than at home or Cambridge. Everyone knew Henry, and he, it appeared, knew everything about everyone. But his coterie had never been confined to Cambridge. Two of his closest friends from school had gone up to Oxford, another few straight into the army. He was the most outgoing of my three brothers, confident, popular and extremely well connected. He liked to say he had his *ear to the ground* and I often imagined him lying prostrate upon some bustling city street.

Later that same evening I quizzed my brother, asked him what he'd meant by his remark, but he'd heeded my father's warning. "I was being flippant, dear. It meant nothing," he said to me. But I knew there was more, and something specific: something my father did not wish to have repeated, particularly not in front of me. There was no point in my pursuing it with Henry; he'd never go against Papa, no matter how full of bravado he appeared, and I was very much aware that to him I was still a child. But as I lay in my bed that night I pondered on it all again. I wondered who paid for Tom Cuthbert's education; and then I wondered if I'd heard Henry correctly. Had he actually used the word *bastard?*

Photo by Jeremy Kinghorn

Judith Kinghorn was born in Northumberland, educated in the Lake District and is a graduate in English and history of art. She lives in Hampshire with her husband and two children.

CONNECT ONLINE

judithkinghornwriter.com
facebook.com/writerjudithkinghorn
twitter.com/judithkinghorn